Collision Course

S.C. Stephens

Edited by Debra L. Stang
Cover photo © iStockphoto.com/Adrian Hillman
Cover Design by Kelly Iveson

ISBN-13: 978-1467943208
ISBN-10: 1467943207

For my mom…I miss you.

Prologue

I don't remember the accident. That is the line that I give every person who asks…and everybody asks. You would think that people would stop asking after a while, but they haven't. You would think that people would try to avoid talking about such a horrendous crash, but they don't. You would think people would have enough respect for someone's private, personal hell to not bring it up around them, but they do bring it up. When people have the nerve to actually talk to me, it's usually one of the first things they ask.

Because I'm the one that survived.

Yes, I tell everyone who asks that I remember nothing…but the truth is, I remember everything. The squeal of the tires as I lost control of the car, the blistering screech of metal on metal as we hit the guardrail on that too sharp corner, the screams that ripped out of my girlfriend's throat as we went over the embankment. I remember everything…

It was nearly summer when the crash happened. We'd been going through a dry spell in Oregon when a sudden downpour hit the county hard. Within seconds, an inch of water was on the roadway. But my friends and I didn't care about that, we didn't even think about it. We were seventeen, we were invincible. Death happened to people much older than us. Nothing could hurt us…nothing could even touch us.

My best friend, Darren, was in the backseat with his girlfriend, Samantha, or Sammy as we all called her. They'd been dating since our freshman year of school. They were head over heels in love with each other, which resulted in endless ribbing from me. "You're so whipped!" I'd always tell him, when he'd ditch me, yet again, to go hang out with her.

"Lucas, one day you'll get it," he'd always respond.

And in a way, I did. Sammy was perfect for him: smart, funny, adventurous, and most importantly—patient. Tall and athletic, she was the captain of the women's volleyball team, so Darren and I had gone to a lot of games. That suited me fine; those shorts they wore were pretty tight. That was also how I met my girlfriend, Lillian. She was new to the school last year, and Sammy had brought her into our little group after she'd tried out and made the team. She was blonde and blue-eyed, petite and trim, and sculpted perfectly in all the right areas; practically a Barbie doll, as I'd often teased her. She was outgoing and vivacious and a total flirt. It hadn't taken her long to wrap her arms around me, throw her hands into my wavy, brown hair, and with a light kiss on the lips, proclaim me as hers.

It had taken even less time for me to actually be hers. And I was. I'd fallen for that girl in a way that made me suddenly understand why Darren ditched me all the time. I'd do it to him too: blowing him off for a game of basketball in his driveway, canceling on him when we had plans to ride dirt bikes with his brother, and ditching him after school when he wanted to go drinking by the river…all to hang out with her.

Darren wasn't intimidated by the competition though; we'd been friends since kindergarten. Whenever I'd blow him off, he'd laugh and tell me, "See…you get it now, right?"

And I was starting to. I loved Lil, and had been dying to tell her that when she'd slipped into the front seat of the car beside me that night. In fact, I'd been running over ways to say it as I'd driven the four of us away from the party we'd been to, forty minutes outside of our home in Willamette Valley.

The answer to the second question that everyone always eventually asks me, and that you're probably wondering right now, is no…I was not drinking that night. Darren, Sammy and Lil had all been living it up at the party, however. Lil even offered me a few, but it wasn't really my thing and I'd stuck to soda for the night.

When Darren had tried to throw a punch at some community college, frat boy wannabe for grabbing Sammy's ass, I'd decided he'd had enough for the evening and swiped his car keys. He'd fought me for all of two seconds before he'd realized that fighting was pointless. For one, he was shorter and scrawnier than me, barely coming up to my chin and coming nowhere near my muscular frame. In wrestling matches that we'd had before—over all too important subjects like who got the comfortable chair while we watched the pay-per-view fight—I'd always won. And secondly, he couldn't stand straight anymore, and he'd leaned to the side while trying to cuss me out. We'd both busted up laughing.

Eventually though, I think it was Sammy ramming her tongue down his throat and describing all of the things that they could do in the backseat while I drove them home that finally convinced him that it was a great idea. She'd winked at me after she said that, her auburn hair beautiful and shining with life in the firelight, much like herself. Sammy could always find a way to pacify hot-headed Darren.

So, no, I wasn't drinking and I wasn't on drugs. There was nothing physically or mentally wrong with me that night, regardless of what the people in our small town believed. The fact was, I was driving a car that I wasn't entirely used to driving—even worse, it was a stick shift, which wasn't one of my strong points—and I was driving a road that I didn't know very well, since Darren had driven us out to the party. And I was driving much too fast.

Even with all of that though, I would have been fine.

I'd been doing fine before the crash, joking around with my friends while the three of them passed around a forty ounce and laughed over Darren's feeble attempt to defend Sammy's honor. I was fine right up until the point when I wasn't. The night was pitch-black when the sudden downpour hit and obscured my vision even more. I was even fine with that, until I hit an inch of freestanding water a few yards from the corner. The car had started hydroplaning immediately and my gut instinct was to stop the car. I'd slammed on the brakes and the car had fishtailed, starting to spin. I had no control over the car when we entered the bend in the road, and we slammed right into the railing, hitting a weak spot and plummeting over the side.

That was where I forcefully stopped my memory. Even still, it was always with me. The trees whipping past the car. Glass breaking. People screaming. The beer can spilling between Lil and I. A rough hit from a tree branch angling the car to the side. The wind being knocked out of me. Lil's door slamming into a boulder at the bottom of the steep hill. Lil's head slamming into the window, shattering it, and her skull. Her screams stopping. Darren flying over Sammy as their unbuckled bodies broke through the inferior metal of Darren's cheap "starter" car and disappeared into the dark. My body jerking painfully against my restraints. My head whiplashing back to smack the window. Everything going quiet…everything going black.

Yes, I told every person I talked to the same response: I don't remember the accident. But I did. I remembered every single detail, even though I prayed I would forget. It haunted me during daylight hours, but that was nothing compared to the hell I went through at night, when I relived the event in my dreams. My screams often woke me, and my mom's arms were often already around me, as I struggled to remember that I'd survived and I was safe in my bed.

How I wish the same could be said for my best friend, the love of his life…and the love of mine.

Chapter 1 – The First Day of the Rest of My Life

Three months after that fateful night, when September came 'round, my external wounds had healed but I was still a mess on the inside. My mom repeatedly told me that I could enroll in another school, that I didn't have to go back to the memories and gossip awaiting me at my old school.

The town we lived in was a small one, and the crash and the subsequent deaths had been "page one" news every day since it happened. Speculation on my mental state as I was driving away from that party was the number one thing discussed. The freakish rainstorm that had momentarily drowned the county that night was irrelevant to the townies. They'd almost instantly proclaimed me a "drunk," claiming I'd all but murdered my friends myself, by near-purposely plunging the car over the cliff.

Even though no physical evidence supported the theory that I'd done it intentionally, and even though I'd been tested at the hospital and cleared of any mind-altering substances, there were few in the town who actually believed I was innocent. Luckily for me, I guess, my mother was a part of that tiny crowd. I suppose she was predisposed to believe the best of me, though.

As the threat of school loomed closer, and I was struck with thoughts of leaving the safety of my home, where I'd been recovering in body, if not in soul, I started having panic attacks that doubled me over and left me unable to fully breathe. That was when my mom offered to drive me fifteen minutes away to the next closest high school, just so I wouldn't have to tolerate the scrutiny.

I almost took her up on it, especially when I ran into Darren's younger brother one day, on one of the rare occasions when I left my house. Darren's brother Josh was one year younger than us, just starting his junior year. He and Darren had been close and he'd idolized his big brother. He'd hung out with us often, and had almost gone with us that tragic night. In fact, he would have been in the back seat with Darren and Sammy if he hadn't been grounded for sneaking out of the house the night before.

He hadn't said much to me when I'd run into him on the sidewalk outside of the only movie theater in town. He'd been exiting from a show with his girlfriend when his dark eyes had locked onto mine. They'd immediately narrowed in anger and since hot-headedness ran in that family, he'd walked right up to me and slugged me. I could have taken him. He was even shorter and scrawnier than his brother, but I had no desire to fight him. I sort of agreed with his anger. I sort of hated me too.

His girlfriend had dragged him away from me when he looked like he wanted to start whaling on me. Reluctantly, he let her pull him away, screaming as he went, "You fucking bastard! You should have died! You fucking drunk! I hate you! I fucking hate you!" He went on and on with stuff like that until he was finally out of earshot.

Like I said, that was almost enough to convince me that a change of stomping grounds was in order. But I couldn't. I couldn't do that to my mom. She already worked two jobs to make sure she and I had enough to eat and a place to stay. I couldn't burden her further by making her go thirty minutes out of her way, twice a day, every day, to drop me off and pick me up from school. And driving myself wasn't an option. I didn't drive anymore…ever.

It was just the two of us after my dad left her when I was three. I have no idea where he went or if he even thought about us. Truly, I didn't think much about him and Mom never really talked about him. It was only when father and son events popped up that I was even reminded that children were supposed to have a mother *and* a father. Mom and I did just fine, and that felt one hundred percent normal to me.

So with a heavy heart, I told her no, told her that I'd endure the ridicule and curious stares and go back to Sheridan High for my senior year of school. One more year and then I could leave this town to start college somewhere far away from the flood of memories. One more year. I could give my mom that.

"Luc, the bus will be here in a couple of minutes." My mom turned to face me in the kitchen, her green-brown eyes narrowed in concern for her only child. "Are you sure you don't want me to drive you, honey?"

My mom had been a beautiful woman in her youth, but her life had been a hard one, and she was a little run down from it. Her face was always a little haggard looking, her eyes always a little tired, her cheeks always a little sunken, her pale skin always a little ashen, and her 'too early for only being forty-five' gray-streaked, light brown hair, always looked a little lifeless in the hasty ponytail she wore. And this morning, she looked even more worn.

The catastrophe hadn't been easy for her either. She'd adored all of them: Darren was a second son, Sammy an adopted daughter, and Lil—I think mom was already picturing picking out baby clothes for the grandchild Lil would most certainly give her. But none of those aches compared to the ache of almost losing her own child, of being *that* close. That scare had left permanent worry lines deep in her features.

I kissed a streak of gray on her scalp. "Yes, Mom. I'm sure. This will be bad enough without my mommy dropping me off."

She sighed sadly and clasped my large hand in her small ones. The gaze in her eyes held a look that I'd seen all too often in the past few weeks. She was drinking me in, absorbing me, in case she didn't ever see me again. I always let her do this. No matter how long she needed to do it.

Her eyes started on my hair, brown and wavy, and longer on the top than she approved of, then she skipped down to my jaw line, smooth for the first time in weeks, since I'd actually shaved this morning. She glossed over my other features and settled on my eyes, an exact duplicate of her hazel shade.

She smoothed out my black t-shirt and reached behind her to hand me my letterman's jacket. Her eyes drifted over the large letters of our last name—West—the only thing my father had given me really. She nodded as she watched me slip the jacket on. Her sad eyes traveled back up to mine, and a sad smile to match it played on her lips. "Have a good day, Luc."

I swallowed and nodded back at her, attempting a smile of reassurance but failing miserably. "Thanks, Mom." I kissed her head again and headed out the front door.

My mother watched me as I stood outside in the light drizzle of the morning rain. I saw her hand pulling back the flimsy lace curtain in the kitchen and saw the shadow of her face as she watched over me, protecting me with her vision and multiple silent prayers. I turned back to watch the road.

As the rain picked up strength, my eyes lingered on one spot of the pavement where a small puddle was starting to form in a dip in the sidewalk. I watched that puddle, mesmerized. Heavy drops plunged into the small circle of water, splashing the edges out further with each steady drip. Within moments there was a half-inch of depth in the puddle. In my mind, the puddle suddenly became a huge lake on the surface of the now vast sidewalk. In my mind, cars flew over that lake, none of them having an issue with the depth of the water as their tires broke waves into the surface. Then, suddenly, I was driving Darren's Geo across that lake, and almost the instant the tires hit the water, I started losing control. I also started having trouble breathing.

A horn blared at me. Still lost in my vision, I imagined my hand on the wheel, holding down the horn as I attempted to right the floundering car. Someone was yelling…or were they screaming? Always so much screaming. I felt myself hunch over, my breath even weaker.

A touch on my shoulder startled me. I looked over to my mother's worried face, droplets of rain running down her cheeks, like tears. Still confused, I wondered what she was doing crying in Darren's car.

"Are you okay, Lucas?" she asked as she touched my face.

"Is he getting in or not?" A harsh voice snapped me completely back to reality. I looked up at a surly bus driver staring at me grumpily and I realized he'd been laying on the horn and yelling at me while I'd been…confused. I glanced over the windows of the bus and noticed more than a few students laughing at me. Great.

"I'm fine, Mom," I muttered as I gave her a quick hug and slunk into the bus.

Everyone was staring at me as the doors closed and the bus started pulling away. The spectacle on the sidewalk wasn't the only reason, either. It wasn't just that an upperclassman was on the bus and not driving himself to school. It wasn't just that I took the first empty seat and didn't acknowledge any of them. It was because they all knew who I was, even the freshman. I was famous…for the worst possible reason.

Sheridan was a small town in Oregon and Sheridan High was even smaller. The entire high school consisted of about three hundred people, and that was a high estimate. A lot of the people had known and liked my friends. Everyone on the bus knew my story. Everyone on the bus had an opinion on my story. Some were quiet about it…others, not so much.

From behind where I sat in the front row, I clearly heard, "Yeah, I heard he pounded a dozen beers and could barely see straight, let alone drive."

I clenched my jaw as the crystal-clear words hit me; they weren't even trying to hide the fact that they were talking about me. In an equally loud voice, someone beside the first person answered with, "Oh yeah? I heard Darren tried to take the keys away, but he threatened to knock him out cold if he did."

I fisted my hands and closed my eyes as tears started to fill them. They were so wrong…they all had everything so wrong. But nothing I said was going to change their opinion, of me or of the night in question. I gritted my teeth and pictured Darren in the seat beside me, turning around and blowing up at them in my defense, like I knew he would have. I pictured Sammy sitting beside him, putting a hand on his shoulder to try to calm him down, and even though a part of me didn't want to, even though it hurt like hell, I pictured Lillian placing her warm hand in mine, squeezing it tight and whispering how much she adored me, urging my fist to relax.

The babbling behind me didn't stop, however, and those tears in my eyes were threatening to spill down my cheeks. I pushed away the painful image of my friends and the vicious words behind me. To block out everything, I started humming in my head. I could do this. I could give my mom one year and then I'd leave this nightmare…physically at least.

I managed to ignore the humdrum that way for the rest of the bus ride. It couldn't have been more than a ten minute ride, but it felt like hours. When the bus pulled in front of the school, and I glanced over at the two girls sitting in the front seat across from me, I realized my mental humming had switched to actual humming and they were regarding me like I was even more of a mental case. I sighed and shut up.

The hydraulics of the bus screeched as it lurked to a stop and the door immediately squeaked open. I flew out of my seat and out the door, wanting to be away from the bad-mouthers behind me before I did something really stupid. A few feet away from the bus, I stopped and stared.

Sheridan High. Not exactly an impressive Ivy League school, but it was intimidating the hell out of me anyway. As we lived in what would be considered by most a "rural" area, the school wasn't overly large or overly fancy. It mainly consisted of a boring, two-story rectangular building that someone in the architectural world had tried to fancy up with a façade of brick outlining the double doors of the entryway and underscoring every window.

It wasn't the most put-together work though and on occasion those bricks would chip apart or even come loose and pop off all together. In fact, the third brick from the left, on the bottom fourth window, was frequently used as a spot to store your stash, since that brick was completely removable but still seemed perfectly intact unless you touched it. The brick underneath it had eroded into a concave shape creating a perfect little hole. Darren had nabbed a few bags of pot out of there once, probably from some upperclassman who had needed a quick hiding place. It was a pretty discreet spot; I had no idea how he'd found out about it.

Aside from that oddity, the rest of the building was horribly plain. The building next to it was equally austere. It was a squatty square with faded gray paint and windows that were large enough for three people to crawl out of at the same time, if they had the desire to do so. I had a feeling I would frequently have that desire this year. It was the room we were all shepherded into to eat the food the school district considered a nutritious lunch. It was also the room where Lil and I had kissed for the first time. I mean really kissed, not the playful, momentary lip on lip action that she loved to give me sporadically throughout the day, even before we were a couple. No, the let's-get-down-to-business-and-connect-on-a-molecular-level kiss. A kiss that had left me breathless and wanting more, and had probably started the whole process of falling for her.

I was jostled from behind by students meandering through the campus on their way to another year of dreary school life, and I snapped out of my painful memories. The rain had stopped on the short ride over, but a dampness clung to the air and I shivered in my jacket. I started walking with the herd, keeping my head down, watching the grass poking up through cracks in the pavement. Adjusting my backpack on my shoulder, I thrust my hands in my jeans pockets. For a moment I felt invisible in the school that I was sure wasn't excited to see me. That thought was confirmed when from behind me I heard:

"Hey, douchebag!"

I don't know why, but I instinctively turned to look. I probably shouldn't have, but then again, what happened was probably going to happen whether I looked or not. A rock the size of my thumb whizzed through the air and smacked me right in the temple. Focusing so hard on not focusing on anything, I hadn't been fast enough to avoid it, and man, it stung. I brought a hand to my head and felt the blood next to my eye. Great.

"Learn some reflexes, alchy," Josh sneered at me, standing a few feet away with an assortment of laughing friends around his age. He was wearing a slightly-too-big letterman's jacket that matched mine, and I briefly wondered if he'd finally made the varsity football team this year; Darren had been helping him practice for his tryout before the wreck so we could all be on the team together.

Pulling my eyes from his clothes, I moved up to his face. His dark eyes danced as he waited for me to get angry and attack him. He'd probably love it if I did. I knew he blamed me for his brother. I knew he hated me because he assumed, like everyone else, that I'd been wasted. I turned and walked away. As I was turning, I watched his lean body start to quiver with anger. He was itching for it…bad.

"Coward!" he yelled behind me, and I shut my eyes, ignoring him. *One more year.*

I ducked into the main building and immediately turned right. Weaving my way through the loitering crowds that had noticed the incident outside and had definitely noticed me now, I tried my best to ignore the hiss of whispers as I walked past the people who I had gone to school with for years. Even still, I caught pieces as I hurried along.

"Did you hear…chugging beers…Lillian tried to stop…puking as he got in…never should have…always drunk…loser…"

I made myself ignore the stares and the buzzing current of talk that followed me up the hall, and forcefully shoved the door into the restroom open. Feeling my breath start to weaken, I hunched over the sink and rested my head against the cool surface of the mirror. I worked on calming the breath that I could feel getting fainter and fainter.

It was like these people I'd grown up with suddenly didn't know me at all. I was never the one who got wasted and threw up everywhere. Anyone who'd ever partied with me, at least before that night, would have confirmed that to you in a heartbeat. I was the one that held back, that "reluctantly" drank and usually stopped at two. It just wasn't my thing. It was Darren's. He was the one that loved getting buzzed, and he usually tried to pull me along for his ride. I generally didn't follow him, though. In fact, I'd only been "drunk" once in my life…and it had been a bad enough experience that I'd never felt the need to duplicate it.

But these people… You'd think I was the poster child for substance abuse.

I looked up when my lungs felt clearer. The face looking back at me in the mirror was almost unrecognizable. And not because of the small cut right at the edge of my eyebrow that was leaving a trail of blood down to my cheek. No, the face was foreign because it looked…older, like a summer of grief, guilt, anger, and everything else had aged me at least a decade.

I splashed some cold water on my face, cringing as it entered my torn skin, and gently wiped away the blood and the trace amount of dirt on me. Looking back up at my dripping face, I ran a hand down it and choked back the sudden, overwhelming feeling of absolute despair that had snuck up on me.

"Are you gonna cry?"

A soft voice made me spin around and there sitting on the floor at the far end of the room next to the stalls was…a girl. She must have been new, since I'd never seen her before, and in a school this size, you ran into everyone at least once. She had jet-black hair pulled into almost childlike pigtails and was calmly picking at a thread of fabric in her ripped jeans. Her eyes, an oddly light gray that didn't match her super-dark hair, regarded mine with a look that was somewhere between amused and concerned. She jerked her thumb towards the door, a silver ring on it flashing in the lights. "I could leave if you want?"

Surprise at seeing a girl in the men's room, one who had obviously been there for a while, lightened my mood. I twisted my lips like I'd been nowhere near breaking down, even though I had been. "No, I'm not going to…cry. *Guys* don't do that." I emphasized "guys" just in case she wasn't aware that she was lurking in the men's room, although she really couldn't have missed the urinals.

She raised one edge of her lip. "Right…" Cocking her head, she pointed to where I'd been injured. The rock had left a slight welt. "What happened, West?"

I opened my mouth to tell her "nothing" when what she'd called me registered in my brain. I cocked my head right back at her. "How did you know my name?"

She started laughing and the sound echoed around the tiled room, filling it with a certain merry music. She didn't answer me, only shook her head, like I was the cutest, most oblivious thing she'd ever seen.

That's when it hit me, and I'm sure I must have turned bright red as stupidity flowed right through me. Yeah, my name wasn't exactly hard to decipher when it was sprawled in four inch high letters across my back. Thanks to this damn jacket that every member of the football team wore as a symbol of unity or something, everyone within a block of me knew my name. I decided right then that I wasn't ever wearing it again.

"Right…the jacket."

She laughed a little more as she gazed at me. I noticed that her smile was a pleasant one; it seemed to brighten her face under the blackness of that hair. "So…" she tried again, "the war wound?" She pointed again at my face.

I looked away and muttered, "Nothing."

I glanced at her still on the floor and thought she looked about to challenge my answer; pretty bold of her since I didn't know her from Adam. A slight smile came to my lips and I relaxed my stance, only then realizing I was even tense. Her objection died as she noticed me relax as well. Here was one person in the school who wasn't looking at me critically, who wasn't judging me, who didn't hate me. Here was one person…who didn't know. I frowned. At least, not yet.

She frowned when she saw my expression change and looked about to question me again, but I beat her to it. "Why are you in here?" My hand swung around to indicate the room.

She shrugged and slid up the wall to stand. Her ripped jeans were paired with a long-sleeved shirt and she absentmindedly played with the too-long sleeves, like she'd stretched out the fabric from her unconscious habit. She shivered a bit, and I noticed she didn't have a jacket. "Seemed as good a place as any to hide out."

I looked around the room with my eyes. "Interesting choice," I muttered as I took in the graffiti on the stalls, the water marks on the ceiling, and the telltale signs along the edge of the floor around the urinals that clearly indicated "men pee here."

She laughed again at my look. "It *was* quiet here. No girls at least." A look crossed her features that I couldn't quite place. It quickly left her as her peaceful expression returned. "My name is Sawyer…if you were ever going to ask."

"Oh…right, hi." I fumbled around for words while the oddity of her name struck me. I wanted to ask, but didn't want to be rude.

She sighed, interpreting my odd look, and I realized that everyone must ask her. "Yes, as is Tom and Huck. My parents are big Twain fans. I suppose it could have been worse." She shook her head, annoyance clear in her features. The look made her even cuter, and I had to smile at her reaction to her own name.

She sighed again and reached down to grab a faded, olive-colored book bag that didn't look to be holding much of anything. "Well, nice chatting with you, West. See ya around this…whopper of a school."

She opened the door into the much quieter hallway, and before she completely disappeared, I called out, "It's Lucas…"

She vanished so fast I had no idea if she heard me or not.

I sighed forlornly. The next time I saw her…she would know. Someone in this school would feel it was their duty to warn the new girl about the psychopath roaming the halls. A bitter note rang through me unexpectedly. As if they were all perfect, as if none of them had ever gotten behind the wheel when they shouldn't have. And that wasn't even what had happened to me. Hypocrites. I sighed again. It had been nice to have someone look me in the eye when they spoke to me, and that laugh...I hadn't heard a genuine one in ages. Probably since that night.

I wiped the remaining water droplets off my face and then, with a long, steadying breath, I opened the door—right as the bell rang. Damn, now on top of everything else…I was late.

Chapter 2 – An Act of Kindness

I hurried down the hall and up the flight of stairs to the second floor. Passing three closed doors, I found the one that would be home to my first period class—English. I placed my fingers on the handle and closed my eyes for a second, taking a big breath. With a sharp exhale, I opened the door and was greeted with absolute silence.

I scanned the room, not really meaning to, but as a leftover habit from walking into a classroom and looking for my friends. I was immediately sorry that I did. Every person was staring at me. Most faces held tight eyes and tighter lips, some just looked curious, but every head was turned in my direction.

As my eyes flicked over the back of the silent room, I noticed that I was wrong, not *everyone* was looking. One head was still down, the owner of it doodling on a notebook in front of her. A slight curve lifted my lip as I recognized bathroom girl in the back row. She was just doing her own thing, oblivious to the sudden tension in the room. Watching her was soothing, and my eyes lingered for a few more seconds before returning to the front of class where the teacher was awkwardly clearing her throat.

"Lucas, um…go ahead and…take a seat."

Ms. Reynolds, our English teacher, was giving me nervous glances, obviously not sure how to deal with me. I wondered for a moment if she expected me to break down and start blubbering right in front of her. Her pale eyes glanced over my features, never settling on one, as she adjusted and readjusted a stack of papers in her hands.

"I'll…um…let the tardiness slide…just for today. I'm sure…I'm sure you're…having…"

She let her thoughts die out and I was momentarily amused by the irony of an English teacher struggling to put her words together. Was I having…what? A hard time? A horrid morning? Well, sure, of course I was. What else was today going to be for me but a nightmare? It's not like any of the "Ghosts of High School Past" that were going to pop up as I walked throughout the school today were going to be pleasant for me. It wasn't like the student body was being warm and welcoming. No, today was just going to suck.

I didn't say any of that to her, though. I adjusted my backpack and started walking to the only available seat, in the very back row. I wouldn't make Ms. Reynolds look bad in front of her class, that wasn't my style. Besides, I liked her. Every guy in the school "liked" her. She had started working here right after college, and as a result, she looked (and was) not much older than the students. She kept her light brown hair cut in a stylishly short pixie that Lil used to rave about, and her clothes were always the newest, latest trends, which Sammy used to ooh and aah over. As for Darren and me…well, let's just say she filled out those "trends" nicely.

Forcing thoughts of my friends to the back of my mind, I walked past a member of my football team. Will McKinney. He and I'd had a friendly competition for the past two years over who was going to be the quarterback. I'd beat him out both years, but he'd been jovial about the loss, jokingly saying that he'd just break my leg one day and move up from second string. Today was apparently that day.

His foot came out right as I walked by and, like a moron, my toe caught the edge of it. I tripped over him and as if that wasn't bad enough, he raised his foot once he'd jostled me so that I couldn't balance myself. I went right down to the floor, smacking a desk along the way with my hand and banging my knee painfully on the hard ground. Great.

Ms. Reynolds scolded Will up and down and started hustling down the aisle to help me stand. The entire class sniggered as I stood on my own before she could get to me. A teacher helping me to my feet really wasn't what I needed. I shrugged it off, looked behind me at her concerned eyes, and told her I was fine. With a glance at a smirking Will out of the corner of my eye, I finished walking the two seats to the open desk in the back row. Will bumped fists with the other member of the team in the room, Randy Harlow. They both laughed while students around them congratulated them on making me look incredibly stupid.

Sitting down, I cast a quick glance at the person beside me. Bathroom girl. What was her name again? That's right…Twain fans…Sawyer. She'd finally looked up when she'd heard the snickers in the room and was eyeing me curiously. I turned my head and stared at my desk again. She wouldn't have to be curious for too much longer…someone would tell her.

I could feel her gray eyes staring at me and I had the feeling she was going to ask me if I was all right, but at that moment, Ms. Reynolds resumed class.

"Okay, guys, like I was saying, there is a grief counselor on staff full time this year, so if any of you need to talk about…" I looked up at her as what she was saying sank into my brain, and she looked at me at the same time, "well, anything, someone will be there for you." She said that solely to me and I felt my breath quicken in a way that I was getting used to. God, I didn't want to lose it here.

I broke eye contact with her, staring back down at the fake wood grain laminated onto my hard metal desk. I focused on breathing in and out like a regular person, not letting this panic attack take me over. Ms. Reynolds continued describing the counselor's duties and how we'd all gone through something tragic a few months ago and the school wasn't going to overlook it. I wished they would. I wished everyone would overlook it, so I could get through a few seconds in peace. But I wasn't the only one hurting…and some people actually did want to talk about it. I heard a few sniffles around the room and felt hot stares lighting up my body.

I wanted to run.

Clearing her throat and sounding like she was on the verge of tears herself, Ms. Reynolds went on to the next order of business. I hoped it would be something mundane, like a change in the dress code or something. It wasn't. Today was just not my day.

"In light of the recent tragedy, the school has decided to implement a much tougher policy on illegal substances. No drugs, no alcohol, no weapons…on or off campus. Any offense will result in immediate suspension. A second offense will lead to immediate expulsion."

A buzz went around the room and I raised my head to stare at her, disbelieving. It was understandable that the school would be tough on that stuff on school grounds, but the school was going to try to stop high schoolers from partying off campus? Because of me? A few harsh words were muttered and more than a few harsh looks were sent my way.

She raised her hand and the buzzing quieted, but didn't stop. "Now, this isn't to punish, this is to discourage. We want you all to be safe." She extended her slim hands to the side, like we were all in this together. I heard a few people mutter my name and swear. "There will also be a Safe and Sound Club starting, to further promote…a more cautious lifestyle."

Her eyes flicked to mine again and I could tell then that she believed it too. She thought I'd been drunk. By her look and tone, she didn't seem to be condemning me for it—mistakes do happen after all—but she believed it, and she was hoping I'd join this little "purity" club.

My jaw clenched. They were all so wrong. Breathe…in…out. Calm down. I glanced over at the new girl, Sawyer. She met my eye and her brow furrowed, like she didn't get why I was repeatedly being targeted. I sighed softly; she would soon enough.

Ms. Reynolds let out a shaky breath and shook her head, a large smile brightening up her almost gloomy face. I noticed a few girls in the room were wiping tears off their cheeks, and a few guys were still muttering about the no-substances stance the school was taking. No one looked at me again, but I felt the heat of every non-existent stare. Ms. Reynolds's next words did absolutely nothing to dispel that feeling.

"Okay, for your first real assignment, I'm going to go easy on you. Just write a two page essay on what you did this summer. Simple right?"

My jaw dropped as I gaped at her. What I did this summer? I mourned the loss of three of my best friends. I yelled. I cursed God. I cried, no, I sobbed, for countless hours. I went to funerals where kids and adults alike shunned me. I was alone…in my grief and in my overwhelming guilt. I still was. And she wanted me to…write about that?

Her eyes flicked over my face as she scanned the groaning room. They passed over mine again as she looked at all of the students, then her head whipped back around to stare at me. "Oh…Lucas." Her face paled and her mouth dropped open as what she'd just asked me to do sank in. Her eyes watered and she shook her head. "You don't have to…you can write whatever you want."

Every head in the room turned to stare at me; most held bitterness, some outright anger, some just curiosity. My breathing got shallow again and I could feel my stomach start to rise. God, I was going to get sick right here in front of everyone. I grabbed my bag and bolted out of my chair. I couldn't do it. I couldn't calmly sit there anymore. Coming today was a bad idea.

As our seats had a bar holding up the writing table, you had to get in and out of them the same way, so I had to pass Will again. Seeing as how he had the maturity level of a five-year-old, he stuck his foot out again. And since today was really not my day, and I was concentrating more on not throwing up, hyperventilating, or some odd mixture of the two, I tripped over his damn foot again.

I fell hard, both hands and knees hitting the ground this time. The entire room laughed and my head started to swim. I wanted it to be over with. All I did was make a mistake. All I did was drive poorly and lose control of the car. Why did no one believe that?

Soft hands helped me up and a voice cooed in my ear. "It's all right, Lucas. Everything will be all right."

My heart stopped. It was Lillian's voice that I'd heard in my ear. Her sweet, musical tone that had driven my heart straight to near imploding with love back when she was alive, and I was hearing it again, hearing it clearly. My head shot up as my legs straightened underneath me. I snapped my head around behind me, fully expecting to see Lillian, see her delicate arms under my elbows, helping to steady me. But it wasn't Lil's pale hair that filled my vision. No, it was black hair.

My brows scrunched as I looked back into Sawyer's gray eyes. She had sounded so much like Lil. I reached out and grabbed a lock of her hair, ignoring the sound of the class still laughing and Ms. Reynolds trying, without much luck, to subdue them. Her hair was soft but undeniably black. I didn't understand. My eyes watered and obscured vision was added to my breathing and stomach problems.

"Lil?" I asked quietly, wondering if I'd gone completely mad.

"Come on," Sawyer's soft voice responded, not much sounding like Lillian at all anymore.

She reached behind her to grab her bag off the floor and then shuffled me forward. For a moment, I couldn't understand why. When we got to the front, she hastily told Ms. Reynolds that she was taking me to see the counselor. I wanted to roll my eyes and tell her I was fine. I wanted to go sit back down and yell at everyone that I was fine. I couldn't though. I couldn't speak and my eyes were really starting to tear up. I'd just clearly heard my dead girlfriend's voice. I wasn't fine.

Ms. Reynolds nodded and swooshed her arms toward the door, almost looking relieved that I was about to walk through it. A crumpled up piece of paper hit the back of my head as Sawyer opened the door, but I ignored it. I ignored it all and focused on putting one foot in front of the other while keeping my breaths deep and my stomach down. That was enough to think about.

The door shut behind me and I slumped down, putting my hands on my knees and bending over, praying that I didn't get sick in front of her. She rubbed a hand on my back while I took embarrassingly big breaths.

"Are you…all right?" she asked hesitantly.

I forcefully shook my head. All right? No, I hadn't been that in a while.

"Do you want me to take you to that counselor person?" She adjusted her book bag on her shoulder up over her head so the strap rested across her chest.

Again I shook my head. No, I did not want to speak with some high school grief counselor. What did they know about being responsible for ending the lives of three people you loved? What advice could they possibly give me? One day at a time. Things will get better. Time heals all wounds. It was all crap and I didn't want to hear it.

"No…I just want…quiet," I finally got out between big breaths.

She nodded and started pulling me away. Confused, I looked around. "What are you…where are we going?"

She half grinned at me, her pigtails swishing around her shoulders. "Somewhere quiet."

She pulled me down to the first floor and for a moment I thought she was going to pull us back into "our" bathroom. She may have actually been about to do that, but when we reached the last step on the stairs, we noticed Coach Taylor going in there. We both flattened against the wall so he wouldn't see us.

Coach had been my mentor in football since I had played Junior Varsity freshman year. While he was an exceptionally hard and stern man, he'd always been there for me, supporting me and encouraging me in his drill sergeant sort of way. Darren and me both. He'd been the one to see real potential in me and had worked tirelessly to stoke it. I wasn't sure what he believed about the crash…but I was sure I didn't want to find out just yet.

Sawyer didn't seem to want a run-in with a teacher either, so once the bathroom door closed, she pulled my hand in the opposite direction. She pulled us towards the janitor's closet and I felt my body tense up. Kids made out in there, just like they did in every high school across America. That wasn't what was making my already-on-the-edge stomach twist into painful knots though. No, I wasn't afraid of being in a dark, enclosed space with a pretty girl. I was afraid of the ghosts that awaited me in that room.

Lil and I had been nearly naked in that room before. I know…not romantic, but we'd been in love and desperate to connect and just…feel each other. That room held the echoes of light moans and memories of soft skin and heated kisses. Even without walking into the closet, flashes of the encounter filled my head: Lil's shirt dropping to the floor, her bra following, my shirt last to the pile, her sitting me down in a folding chair, her straddling my lap, our bare chests pressed together, my lips on her fragrant skin…fruity, like peaches, her hands snaking between us to unbutton my jeans…

I pulled away from Sawyer just as her hand reached the knob. She looked back at me surprised, and maybe a little hurt too, but I couldn't worry too much about offending her, because I was about to lose whatever trace amount of food was in my stomach. And doing it all over her would most definitely offend her.

I bolted out the front door and down the few steps leading to the building. I had just made it to the edge of the stairs when my stomach decided it had had enough. Falling to my knees at the beauty bark surrounding a few decorative bushes under the windows…I threw up. Great.

It was just once, and very quick, but it was enough to make me feel like a jackass when I sensed Sawyer watching from behind me. I silently thanked fate that I was a few feet from the window and hadn't just done that in front of a room filled with unsuspecting students. With a shaking hand, I wiped off my mouth and sat back on my heels.

After a few calming, deep breaths in the stillness of the cool morning, I turned my head to look at Sawyer. I had no idea what she'd think of that, what she thought of anything about me. If she had pieced together any of the conversations that she'd most likely heard around school this morning, then she probably thought I was hung-over and heaving my alcohol soaked guts.

Looking over at her dark head tilted to the side, brows bunched together, all I could read from her was concern. Still not saying anything, she extended a hand to me. I looked down at the hand, the silver ring on her thumb that shone even in the faded gray light of this overcast day, and finally reached out to grasp it with my own.

Her hand was cool, since we were outside, and I noticed then that she still didn't have a jacket and that she was lightly shaking. As we stared at each other for a moment, I dropped her hand, shrugged off my jacket and flung it around her shoulders. She started to protest and shrug it back off, although her face seemed reluctant to do so, but I immediately broke off her objections.

"I don't want it," was all I said. And I didn't want it. I didn't want the reminder of the popular, outgoing, happy-go-lucky guy I used to be. I wasn't him anymore and I didn't want to pretend that I was. I never wanted to wear that damn jacket again.

She only nodded as she took in the expression on my face and the dead evenness of my tone. She ran her arms through the sleeves and hugged the fabric to her chest, like she hadn't worn a coat in so long she'd forgotten how nice it felt to be warm and cocooned.

I shivered a bit in the chill now, but I welcomed it. It woke up my senses and cleared my head. My lungs indulged in the crisp, damp air as I took long, even breaths. Sawyer studied me in silence for a moment more before quietly saying, "Do you want me to take you home?"

I looked down as I thought about it. Did I want to go home? Had I punished myself enough for one day? I tried to imagine walking back into that building, walking past scores of people who I'd once been friendly with, people who would now barely look at me, walking past multiple reminders of the friends I'd lost…both the living ones and the dead ones.

My eyes swelled with more of those dreadful tears, and looking back up at her I could only say, "Yes."

She nodded as her eyes flicked between mine. I still didn't know what she thought of me, but she was the only one showing me an ounce of friendship and compassion, and greedily, I was going to take all I could from her before she was swept away from me too.

Wanting to take her hand again, but not wanting to disrupt her warmth from where she was snuggling in my jacket, I picked up my bag from where it had slipped off my shoulder when I'd embarrassingly heaved. I slung it over me and shoved my hands in my pockets. Simultaneously, we both started walking towards the student parking lot. Everyone was inside, filling their heads with vital pieces of information that they would surely need to make it out there in the "real" world, so we didn't run into anyone. Sawyer was quiet on the way there, which I appreciated. She seemed to have taken my earlier request for silence quite literally.

We approached an older looking Camaro SS and she slowed and unclipped her bag, removing it from across her chest, underneath my jacket. I smiled at the vintage car while she rummaged inside the bag for the keys. The car was black with white racing stripes and had definitely seen better days, but it was still pretty cool. Darren had loved muscle cars. He'd always joked about pimping out his Geo to look like a Trans Am, with a flaming eagle on the front and a t-top in the roof. I closed my eyes as that remembered conversation flooded through me. He'd never get his Trans Am now.

A light hand on my shoulder woke me, and I looked over to see Sawyer, keys in hand, silently comforting me. God, how often had she done that this morning? I tried to smile, and walked over to the other side of the car, shaking my head. *She must think I'm a nut job.* Well, maybe I was.

She unlocked her side and got in while I waited. This old car didn't have electric locks, so she reached across the seat and unlocked my side. I got in and stretched out my six-two frame in the black leather, bucket seat. For being rundown on the outside, it was well-kept on the inside, clean and shiny and lightly smelling of lemon. I smiled at a tiny disco ball hanging from the rearview mirror as she started the car, the growl from the engine the unmistakable purr of a muscle car.

Sawyer pulled out of the lot and I directed her to the general vicinity of my home. We lived off the main artery that led right to the school. All she had to do was keep going straight and just as town started to fall away, she'd hit our house, the last house before the small trace of city civilization stopped. Quite literally "where the sidewalk ends."

On the drive over, she bit her lip and looked to be barely containing her curiosity. It didn't seem like she was going to cave, but she was fidgeting in her seat. I imagined that if I were her, I'd have a bazillion questions for this odd boy beside me.

"Go ahead," I said quietly, finally breaking our silence.

Her words spilled out in a rush, like once I'd given her permission, she couldn't hold them back. "The accident everyone keeps mentioning, you were involved in that?" She looked over at me, her gray eyes suddenly very sorry that she couldn't contain her questions.

Keeping as calm a face as I could, I simply said, "Yes." In my head I prepared my answer for the question that everyone asks…

"Oh…I'm so sorry. I heard that people died…" Her eyes went back to the road while I tensed, both at her words and where I knew the conversation was heading. Do I remember? Was I drunk?

She looked over at me with only her eyes and I felt the question coming. She bit her lip and I opened my mouth to give the answer. "Do you…are you okay with this?" Her hand flashed out to indicate her driving.

Not expecting her to ask that, my answer for the question I thought she would ask spilled from my lips before I could stop it. "No."

She fully looked at me, alarmed and unsure what to do. The car slowed and she started to turn the wheel, like she was going to pull over. I shook my head and started sputtering on my words. "No, no, that's not… I'm fine. God, I'm sorry." Her face looked hopelessly confused now. It was sort of adorable. "I'm an idiot…this is fine. I'm fine."

She narrowed her eyes. "Why did you say no?" Turning back to the road, her speed increased to normal.

I exhaled, the weight of the world in my breath. *Because I'm a moron.* "I didn't think… I wasn't expecting you to ask that. People always ask…something else."

"Oh," she said quietly. "What did you think I was going to ask?"

I sighed and looked out the window. The houses were getting farther apart; we were reaching the end of town and the end of this weird car ride. "If I remember it." I whispered my words into the glass of the window beside me.

"Oh," was her quiet response. After a few moments of silence she said, "I wouldn't ask that." I looked back at her, surprised; most people were dying to know what I knew. Since I never talked about it, there was only speculation about the wreck, and most of that was wrong.

She shrugged her shoulders as she looked at my face and then back out the window. "You either don't…which is fine, or you do…which must be horrible." She looked over at me again. "Either way…why would I want you to think about that awful moment again?" She scrunched her brow like she was angry. "I'm the idiot. I shouldn't have even brought it up." Her eyes turned back to the road. "Sorry."

I nearly laughed. She was sorry…for asking me about what everyone was surely whispering about today? I was fodder for the town gossip. I was so used to everyone trying to pry their nose into my business and my personal life that it was nearly astounding to me that one person on this earth, not only didn't want to know, but felt guilty for even bringing the topic up. I could have kissed her. A genuine smile crossed my lips as I relaxed back into my seat.

"Don't worry about it. I did say you could ask." A tiny laugh did escape me then and she looked over at me with an odd expression. I really must seem like a mental case to her.

We drove the rest of the way in a comfortable silence, and I pointed at my house when we approached it. The house was nothing spectacular, a basic one-story, three bedroom rambler with fading blue paint and a mailbox that wouldn't ever stay completely closed.

She pulled into the empty driveway and stopped the car but didn't turn it off. I looked over at her as I put my hand on the door. Her presence was so calming to me; I was reluctant to give it up. Being alone right now, while better than being at school, wasn't exactly going to be an easy thing—I had too many ghosts in my head today.

"Do you…" I pointed again to the house, indicating the white door with three tiny windows inlaid at the top of it. "Do you want to come in?"

Sawyer looked me over with a tiny smile on her lips, her hands never coming off the steering wheel. She seemed about to fully smile and I thought for sure she'd say yes and move to shut the car off, but instead her curved lips twisted down into a frown and she shook her head, her pigtails swishing adorably. "No, I can't."

I frowned then, too, and noticing my expression she quickly added, "Don't get me wrong, I wish I could, but my parents…" she rolled her eyes and sighed. "They're sort of on a rampage, and they'd have my ass if I skipped school today." She gave me a wry look. "I'm on probation."

"Oh." I was curious why, but one thing that I'd learned over the past few months was not to pry. If she wanted to say more, she would. I didn't need to force her to. She bit her lip as she watched me, almost like she was worried that I would ask. She visibly relaxed when I shrugged and said, "Well, thank you for the ride." I looked down and shook my head. "And for not giving me too much crap over flipping out."

I looked back up at her when I felt her hand on my shoulder. It was small, but warm, and that warmth seeped into my skin through my light t-shirt. "It's all right. You seemed to be having quite a morning." Her fingers drifted down my arm to touch my hand, the warmth following it. "People don't seem to like you too much…" She was quiet when she said that, and it seemed more a casual observance than an outright question. She'd been so nice to me today that I felt the need to answer it though.

"They don't…they blame me." I looked out the window and my hand tightened on the door handle. "They think I got behind the wheel with my friends while I was out of my mind drunk and then drove recklessly, killing them all. They think I forced them into the car, forced them to ride with me. They practically think I'm a monster."

My voice had turned hard and rough in my sudden anger. No one understood what had happened. None of them at that school believed me when I said I was sober. None of them.

Sawyer gasped beside me. I turned to look at her and clearly saw the pain in her features. I was confused for a moment, until her other hand came up and forcibly relaxed the grip I had on her fingers. I flinched and pulled away. Somewhere in my heated speech, I must have grabbed her hand and clenched it…hard. I'd hurt her.

"Sorry," I muttered.

She laughed a little and rubbed out her palm. "It's all right."

Her laughter loosened my sudden anger and I added, "That's not what happened. I did lose control…but that's not what happened." This was the closest I'd come to admitting to anyone that I remembered. Sure, I'd told everyone that I hadn't been drinking at the party, but the actual wreck? I'd glossed over that with feigned amnesia.

Sawyer stopped laughing and cocked her head while she regarded me. The silence in the car seemed to thicken and swirl around us, but it wasn't oppressive or clingy. Like her hand, it was warm and comforting. I still held my breath though. I could see the debate in her eyes; she was judging my character based on all she'd seen and heard, and she was deciding, at this very moment, if I was guilty of the crime the others had already convicted me of.

Finally she opened her mouth to speak and my body tensed in preparation for her condemnation. It had been so nice to have someone who looked at me differently. I dropped my head as her speech finally made it past her lips. "I believe you."

I slumped my shoulders until her words hit me, then my head shot up and my surprised face looked over at her serene one. "You believe me…why?" No one else did, people who had known me for years, grown up with me. Why would this complete stranger believe me, when they didn't?

That faint smile lit her face again. "I've gotten to be a pretty good judge of character and…" she shrugged, "I think you've got a pretty good one. If you say it didn't happen the way people gossip about, then I believe you. I believe it was just an accident."

I stared back at her, speechless. I felt my eyes watering and worked on controlling the stubborn tears. Just an accident. It sounded so simple that way. Yes, I suppose in the very simplest of terms, it was just an accident, an accident that could have happened to anyone that night. Accidents do happen…did happen. But it happened to me and that changed things. It had happened to me and my friends were dead because of it. That was all that mattered. While it would be nice if the town believed me, and while it was exceptionally nice that Sawyer believed me…truly, it was irrelevant. Drunk or not, sober or not, none of that really mattered…they were still dead. That was my truth.

I didn't say any of that to her though, I only nodded and finally opened the door. She leaned over the seat and called out after me as I stepped out of the vehicle. "Lucas?" I bent down and popped my head back inside; the lemon scent of her car battled with the putrid smell of the garbage can on the sidewalk. She started to wriggle out of my jacket. "Here…you can take this back."

I shook my head. "No. I don't want it." I repeated my earlier phrase, and she stopped mid-wriggle to look at me. "Keep it."

She looked confused and a tad relieved, like she hadn't really wanted to give up her warmth. I nodded at her and quickly shut the door before she could protest further.

Walking up to the front step, I prepared myself for an afternoon of pitying, and most likely, crying. When I heard her car start to pull away, I turned at the door. I watched her wave from the window as she backed into the street and then drove away towards school.

See you around, bathroom girl.

Well, my first day hadn't been great, but I suppose it could have been worse. I could have thrown up *on* Sawyer. There's that.

Chapter 3 – Me, My Friends and I

It was late when my mom came back home, well after midnight. I'd already sulked for hours, watched the rain when it picked back up and re-dampened the pavement outside, and made myself a dinner of pepperoni Hot Pockets. Such a productive day. I was lying on the couch, watching late night TV, when I heard the front door crack open. A flash of guilt washed through me as I looked over at my tiny mother in her waitress uniform.

She looked exhausted, her ponytail barely holding back her hair that had frizzed out a little in the rainstorm. A long piece had fallen free and she tucked it behind her ear as she turned to face me with a small frown on her lips. Ignoring the look that clearly said, 'shouldn't you be asleep?' I glanced down at the large coffee stain on the front of her skirt.

"Have a good night?" I asked, before she could launch into an 'it's a school night' speech.

She sighed and plopped her heavy purse on the kitchen counter before trudging into the living room to sit on the couch beside me. I put my arm around her shoulders and she leaned her head into mine. "It was…all right."

I knew she was lying. I could tell by her voice, her face and the overall look of her that the night hadn't gone well at all. Mom worked nights at a diner on the edge of town. The small eatery was a favorite place for a lot of the locals, but it was also frequented by gamblers from the casino just outside of town and visitors to the federal prison nearby. The mixture of the three groups wasn't always a peaceful one. By the look of her uniform and the haggardness of her sigh, someone hadn't been too pleased with the service tonight. I wanted to ask her about it, but knew my mom well enough to know that she'd never confide her troubles in me. To me, her life would always be…all right.

"How was your first day?" Her head lifted off my shoulder and her gaze narrowed as true concern filled her. The ups and downs in her life might be acceptable to her, but my life was a completely different story. Sometimes I wondered why my life was always so much higher on her list of priorities than her own.

I threw on a tired smile. "It was…all right."

Mom frowned and pulled away from my arm to study me better. I wasn't sure what she saw, but I could imagine it well enough—eyes slightly red from tiredness and an embarrassing bout of crying earlier, face worn and hair rumpled, clothes disarrayed from restless pacing. I was probably pulling off "all right" about as well as she was. Unfortunately for me, she was a mom, and wasn't about to let me get away with an outright lie like the one I'd just let her get away with. Life could be unfair that way.

"What happened, Lucas?"

I sighed and looked away from her. How do I tell her? How do I add to the woman's worries? She had enough of them as it was. I couldn't tell her about the stares. I couldn't tell her about the whispers. I definitely couldn't tell her about the conversation the jerks on the bus were having about me. I couldn't tell her about Josh itching for a fight. I couldn't tell her about Will repeatedly tripping me in English. I couldn't tell her I'd thrown up in the bushes. There was so much I couldn't tell her…just like I couldn't tell her about *that* night. It would do her no good to know. In fact, it would only hurt her if she did. There wasn't a whole lot of ways that I, as a seventeen-year-old boy, could help her…except this one. I'd omit.

I looked back to her concerned eyes and very quietly said, "I skipped a few classes. I'll need a pass."

She opened her mouth to question me more, and then she shut it. Searching my eyes, she must have noticed something in the hazel depths, something that made her realize I wasn't going to go into detail for her. It was my way of protecting her. A tiny smile lit the very edges of her lips and she sighed again. "I'll call the school in the morning." She tenderly kissed my forehead. "Get some sleep, Lucas. You do have school tomorrow."

She stood, rubbing out a spot in her back as she turned to walk down the hallway to her bedroom. "Goodnight, Mom," I called out softly after her, and she called back goodnight in return. I looked down at my hands and wished I could tell her everything. Everything about that night, everything that had happened today, even what had happened this morning on the sidewalk. But I couldn't, and I didn't. The burden was mine to bear, not hers.

I rubbed my eyes and went back to watching an infomercial that seemed to be playing on a never-ending loop. It seemed like just a few seconds later when the cushion on the other side of me compressed, and I looked over to see a very alive and beautiful Lillian smiling brilliantly at me.

"Hey, Lucas! What riveting show are we watching?" Her full lips turned to a soft pout as she turned her head to look at the TV. "Oh, God, that fishing thing again?" She turned back to me, still pouting. "You're not seriously thinking of buying that thing, are you? You don't even fish."

Nothing about her being there seemed odd to me. Lillian had often stopped by at weird hours of the night, just to spend time with me. She'd sneak out of her home and sneak into mine, just to snuggle on the couch and watch television for a few hours before sneaking back. It was always a pleasant surprise when she popped in.

I smiled and brought my arm around her, and she giggled, leaning into my side.

"Maybe I want to start fishing."

She kissed me softly. "Fishing takes forever, Luc. What am I supposed to do while you're out playing with trout?"

I cupped her pale cheek, lightly highlighted with a rosy blush, and kissed her tenderly, savoring the feel of her lips against mine. "You could come with me? We could do this while we wait."

She giggled against my lips and ran her hand down my chest while our mouths moved in perfect sync. Something about the conversation triggered a memory in me. Like déjà vu, I felt like I'd seen and done all of this with her before. I pulled away from her mouth, the familiar scent of cherry lip balm almost overpowering me. "I'm dreaming…aren't I?"

She sighed and her pale eyes saddened as she looked over my face. "Yeah, I'm sorry."

Despite the sudden ache in my chest, I smiled. "Don't be. As far as dreams go…" I shook my head, "…this one's not so bad."

Her hand on my chest rested on my heart and my other hand snaked around her waist to pull her into me. My realization that this wasn't real didn't alter the fact that it felt real. Her hands on me were warm and alive. Her breath against my face was soft, and held a lingering smell of her favorite candy, mint Mentos. Her body was curvy and enticing—perfect—as she pressed against me.

She kissed me and then a sad sigh escaped her. "Why don't you talk to anyone, Luc? Why are you letting them all…?" Her eyes narrowed in fury. It was such an adorable look on her that I grinned. "I'm gonna kill Josh for that rock!"

I laughed and she scowled at me. "That's an amusing thought. My dead girlfriend is going to defend me." I kissed her nose and she crooked a smile when I pulled away. "Even deceased, you're adorable."

Lillian shook her head and kissed my cheek. Then she nestled into the crook of my neck and let out a content sigh. I closed my eyes and held her tight, suddenly scared that any minute I'd wake up and she'd be gone.

"You should talk to someone, Lucas. You shouldn't go through this alone."

"I can talk to you," I whispered.

She pulled back to look at me, seriousness marking her features. "You know why that's ridiculous, right?" I looked away and shrugged and her hand came up to my cheek, bringing my gaze back to her. "Tell someone you remember. Tell them what happened…with the water, the road. They'd stop this nonsense about you being drunk, Luc. They'd understand."

I was already shaking my head though and tears were already starting to form. "I can't, Lil. I can't talk about what happened, about what I did. I can't talk about killing you." A tear slid down my cheek and her fingers brushed it off. Her eyes watered, watching mine fall. "It doesn't matter how or why it happened. I still killed you, all of you."

"No, it was an accident, Luc. Talk to someone." She looked down for a moment and her voice was oddly subdued when she spoke again. "Maybe…maybe that new girl."

I blinked and confusion rang through me before I understood her strange expression. My hand reached up and grabbed her chin, making her sad eyes look at me. "Nothing is going on with me and her, Lil. I'm not interested in her…only you."

Lillian smiled such a sad smile that her eyes suddenly looked happy in comparison. "Don't you realize how awful that is?"

"Awful? That I want to be with you?"

She leaned over and kissed me. The sweetness of her lips stole my breath and for a moment this was the most real experience I'd had in months. She pulled back from our intimate touch slowly, her lips reluctant to leave mine. I hungered for more.

"Yes, Lucas…I'm dead," she whispered.

I wanted to argue. I wanted to scream at her that she was more real than anything I'd felt in so long, I was beginning to believe being awake was the dream. I wanted to tell her that with her in my arms, I could finally breathe again. I wanted to keep her in my arms and breathe steadily that way, forever. I wanted to finally tell her that I loved her.

But at that moment…I woke up.

My head lifted off the couch with a start and, looking around, I noticed the TV was still on, playing some early morning news show with hosts that were entirely too happy for the inhuman hour. A hazy pre-dawn light filtered in through the eastward facing windows. I also had a crick in my neck the size of Texas. Great. I'd slept on the couch…again.

I closed my eyes as the memories of my dream flooded me. In some ways, it was better than the nightmare I often had of the crash. In some ways, it was worse. Her memory was fresh again. I could feel her arms, her lips…her body. I could hear her laughter. God, I could even smell her again. Tears welled up under my closed lids, waiting to fall the moment I opened them. I drew in a stuttered breath that exhaled into a racking sob. My hands came up to cover my face as the insistent tears didn't wait for my permission to fall. I sobbed as quietly as I could, so I didn't wake and worry my mom.

God, I miss you, Lil.

After a while, I showered and got dressed for the day. I wasn't even going to bother with trying to get back to sleep. I didn't want to dream about her again…and I desperately *did* want to dream about her again. But school was in a couple of hours anyway. Any dream I had would've been a short one, and if I was going to see her that way again, I wanted as much time as possible. God, what a messed up thought: To sleep, perchance to dream…but only if you've got the time to commit to it.

Sighing, I made a pot of coffee. Mom frowned on me drinking the stuff, but, like a lot of things in my life lately, she let it slide. It was almost as if I had a permanent "get out of jail free" card. She let me get away with doing things that I'd never have gotten away with before. Cutting school for instance. If I'd done that last year, she'd have had my head. Of course, if it were last year, I'd be cutting to go get into trouble with Darren. A lot can change in a year.

I thought about my friend as I grabbed the pot of thick, black and incredibly strong coffee—once I'd decided to start drinking it, I hadn't messed around; I went right for the hard stuff.

Darren's joking face popped into my head easier than it had in a while; maybe seeing Lil had sharpened Darren's memory in me as well. I could clearly see his quick-to-light-with-mischief brown eyes and unruly, dark brown hair that was always sticking up somewhere, even though Sammy was continually trying to press it flat. It usually made him grunt in mock exasperation and playfully push her mothering hands away.

I pictured him leaning back in my kitchen, arms crossed over his chest, frowning at me and shaking his head. "Come on, Lucas, blow off class with me today."

I smiled at the remembered conversation we'd had months ago. "I can't, Darren. I have a math test first period."

He rolled his eyes and shook his head again. "So…M80s, Luc! Freakin' M80s! Let's go blow some shit up!" His eyes lit up at the prospect. Even though he was two months older than me, sometimes he seemed about three years younger. He and Josh had scored the fireworks…somewhere. They were always finding questionable entertainment.

I smiled wider. "We will. I'll meet you after school."

His normally happy face darkened a bit and he twisted his lips in clear displeasure about something. "I can't after school. Josh wants to come, too, and he's still grounded. He has to go right home after school, and Mom would have my head if I didn't take him."

I'd never asked what Josh had done (he was constantly getting grounded for something), so I had no idea now why that had been an issue. But apparently, Josh missing class wouldn't bring wrath down on Darren, so he'd been all for that plan. Of course, with those two, forging notes had become almost a form of art.

"I'll meet up with you guys at lunch, okay? We'll blow some shit up then."

I almost felt like laughing when I remembered what we'd ended up blowing up. Darren had swiped a garden gnome from his neighbor's house and the poor concrete bastard had met its maker down by the river. Darren's neighbor had asked his parents for weeks if they'd seen that thing. Luckily for Darren, they'd never found out…although, I suppose it didn't matter now.

"Luc?"

The vision of Darren, nodding at my suggestion and growing animatedly excited over what we could do, suddenly vanished from my sight at the sound of my mother's voice. I turned my head; my hand was still clenched around the full coffee pot, ready to pour it into my cup. I realized that, to her, I'd just been standing still at the counter holding a pot of coffee, doing nothing for…God knows how long.

"Are you okay?"

I nodded as she walked into our small kitchen. The room consisted of a stove next to a dishwasher next to a small sink next to a fridge. Somewhere in that cramped space, the builders had thrown in a little counter room, just enough for the coffee pot. The other wall of the room had a narrow rectangle of a table underneath a large window that overlooked our driveway. There were only two chairs, one for Mom and one for me. After giving me a quick hug and a look-over, Mom sat down in her traditional chair.

I automatically poured a mug for her. As usual, she didn't delve any further into my thoughts, giving me my space. By what even I knew was a solemn look on my face, she had to have known, anyway. There were really only three things I ever thought much about: Sammy, Darren and Lillian. Either of the three would cause her, and me, a handful of pain, so I didn't go into any details.

I poured a mug for myself and joined her at the table. Neither of us ate anything; we'd never much had the stomach for food before ten in the morning. We weren't what you'd call "breakfast people."

Mom was dressed and ready for her first job of the day, her hair in an orderly ponytail that I knew would be falling apart by lunchtime. She was dressed in jeans and a uniformed polo shirt with 'Andy's Hardware' in the upper left corner. She worked there until five and then she switched clothes, sometimes in her station wagon, and headed out to the diner. She had taken a job at a hardware store, not just to make sure we got by, but also to ensure that she'd be knowledgeable about home repair and maintenance. She'd completely depended on a man once in her life, and she didn't ever want to have to do that again. She taught me everything she had learned over the years; I'd learned a lot from my mom.

Feeling her eyes drinking me in again, I brought up a topic that I thought might bring her a small amount of cheer. It had certainly been the only bright spot in my day yesterday. My lips curled into a tight, contained smile. "I met a girl yesterday."

Her eyes widened before returning to normal. She wore an expression of weariness and happiness. I liked seeing the latter, if not the former. Mom knew that when I said, "I met a girl," I meant it in only the most literal way it could be taken. There were no potential love interests for me. Not right now. Not when my heart was lying in a cold, dark...

Mom interrupted my swirling thoughts. "Oh, did you?" She sighed softly as she looked over my face again.

I coughed and made myself cheer up for her. "Yeah, in the bathroom." I leaned in conspiratorially. "The *men's* bathroom."

Mom laughed. Her laugh was short and seemed a little rusty from being unused for so long, but it had been genuine and the smile on my face was suddenly as real as that laugh had been. "Sounds like an interesting girl."

I thought over the encounter and nodded as I took a long draw from my potent coffee. "That she is." My smile again was genuine and my mom noticed it and cocked an eyebrow before letting her face relax into neutrality. She didn't want to get her hopes up that I'd moved on. Either that or she was struggling with me moving on as well. She'd loved Lil, too.

"Does this bathroom girl have a name?"

I let out a soft laugh at my mom using the same nickname I'd used; my laugh was a little rusty too. "Sawyer." Mom raised her eyebrows and I nodded. "Yeah, like Tom Sawyer." I shook my head. "Her parents are fans." Mom laughed again and I delighted in the rare sound, happy that I had given her a reason to produce it. In a thoughtful voice, I added, "She's new this year and she was really...kind to me yesterday."

Mom's laughter ended as she took in my tone of voice and the look on my face. Mom heard the gossip, too and could probably guess how my day had actually gone. Someone showing me an ounce of warmth would have been held in high regard in her eyes. They started to water now as she, for the seemingly hundredth time this morning, looked me over.

"I'm glad, Lucas," she whispered.

I nodded and we both went back to quietly sipping our caffeine. After long, silent moments, when my mug was finally empty, I stood, gave her a kiss on the head, and left to grab my backpack. I also grabbed a plain, gray jacket buried in the back of the coat closet. Mom stood and watched me from the kitchen entryway. Her eyes took in my missing letterman's jacket, but she didn't ask where it went. Its absence, along with mine, must have filled in a lot of the blanks for her on what really went down at school. She sighed and offered me a ride again, which I declined, again. Wishing me luck, she told me she loved me and I returned both sentiments to her. Then she hugged me and we parted ways for the day.

I headed outside to walk the couple miles to school. It was early and I had the time today. It was also still overcast, but the morning was dry, and it seemed like it was going to stay that way. But really, even if it were pouring, I'd rather walk a few miles in a downpour than hop on that damn bus again.

The walk to school was long and a touch monotonous. I found my mind blanking out as I counted the cracks in the pavement. It did stay dry, and at the three thousandth, four hundredth and fifty-second crack, I finally arrived back at Sheridan High. It was early, and only a couple of bodies were milling around the school. I didn't look up to see if they noticed me. Instead, I immediately made my way to the main building and up the stairs to my English class.

The room was empty as I went to take my seat at the desk I had sat in yesterday. I glanced around at the twenty or so other desks, all empty and awaiting their occupants, those students still on their way to school or eating breakfast, or possibly even still sleeping.

For a second, I remembered that Sammy was supposed to be in this class with me. The four of us had worked out our schedules so that one or all of us would have classes together. It had ended up with just Sammy and me in this first period. Lillian had been really excited that her best friend would be in a class with me again. Her "plant" as she put it, to subtly remind me of birthdays, holidays, and our anniversary. What it would have ended up being though, was what last year's Geometry class had ended up being—Sammy digging secrets about Darren out of me.

I pictured Sammy in the seat in front of me, twisting around to grin at me, her auburn hair dangling over her shoulder. "So, Luc…seriously, what did Darren say about…our night?"

I blushed and rolled my eyes as I remembered her asking me about a very private conversation I'd had with Darren after their "first" time. "Sammy…I'm not talking about that with you."

She leaned over her chair, smiling even wider. "Come on, you have to tell me, Luc. I know he talked to you about it. He talks to you about everything.

So…what did he say?" A tiny frown drew down the corners of her mouth. "Was it bad? Did he not…like it?"

I gave her my best 'are you kidding?' face. "He's a guy…of course he liked it."

Her corresponding grin was brilliant, and her eyes sparkled with merriment. "Ha! I knew he talked to you."

I sighed over getting trapped by her questioning, while she laughed and begged for details. I looked around the room with my eyes and then leaned forward; she leaned towards me as well. "You can't tell him I said anything. He'd kill me." She made a quick pledge with her fingers and I sighed again, wondering how I'd gotten sucked into girl gossip. "He said it was amazing…like, the best thing he'd ever experienced." Her eyes misted up as she bit her lip. I shrugged, getting a little uncomfortable. "He said he loved you even more." I cringed a bit as she looked about ready to squeal with girl delight. "Is that enough? Can we not talk about this again…ever?"

She grinned and nodded, then leaned all the way forward and kissed my forehead. "Thanks, Luc! God, you're the best!"

I shook my head at her and smiled warmly at the beautiful girl who had captured my friend's heart. Her auburn hair framed the cutest, heart-shaped face and her brown eyes were so light they were almost gold. Those eyes were always so full of love and laughter. She rarely had a down day. She was so darn happy, she was almost bubbly, but never in an obnoxious way. Just in a way that made you want to be around her. Her zest for life made you want to have that zest too. I missed that…

"Good morning, Lucas."

I blinked out of my memory and looked up at the teacher's desk where Ms. Reynolds was setting down a stack of papers. "Good morning, Ms. Reynolds."

She sat on the edge of her desk and crossed her arms over her chest. On a normal day, I'd have noticed that her legs were long and lean under that tight skirt she wore, but I hadn't noticed stuff like that in a while. She gave me a soft, repentant smile. "I'm sorry about yesterday. That was…" She paused, rethinking her comment. "This is going to be an adjustment period for everyone, Lucas. Things will get better."

I nodded but said nothing. I supposed things would get better. I mean, how could they possibly get worse? She bit her lip and cocked her head as she looked me over. I wondered what I looked like to her. Did she see the out-of-control, troubled teen that the students made me out to be, or did she only see a teen that had made a horrible mistake? Either way, I knew she saw me as guilty, and that closed up my throat and I could only watch her watching me.

Finally, she spoke. "Did the counselor help?"

I paused, debating whether I should be truthful. That almost made me chuckle. Being truthful in this town didn't seem to matter much. Not wanting to go into any details with her, I only nodded again. She sighed and looked like she desperately wanted to get me talking to her but had no idea how to do it. I didn't either and remained silent.

An awkward silence built up in the room as we watched each other. It was finally ended by the arrival of a few more students. Ms. Reynolds straightened as they entered the classroom. Her face relaxed into a pleasant smile as she greeted each of them by name. She did seem to really love her job. I just made her uncomfortable. Understandable, I suppose.

The students ignored me as they settled into their seats. Well, most of them ignored me. A couple of them openly stared and a few glared, but I ignored them, and they eventually ignored me in return.

I stared down at my desk as Randy and Will arrived together. I heard their deep laughter and felt their heavy steps as the linebacker and now-quarterback walked to their seats. I heard my name, followed by more laughter, and felt my cheeks heat. I was sure they were laughing about my repeated falls yesterday. Oh, and fleeing the room. I definitely hadn't earned any cool points. Oh well, today would be better. At least I wouldn't be fleeing…hopefully.

They collapsed into their chairs, the metal scraping against the floor as their bulks shifted the desks. I glanced up and watched them bump fists in a show of camaraderie and friendship. Last year, I would have been included in that ritual while they jokingly asked when I'd break up with Lillian so Will could date her. He'd had a huge crush on her from nearly day one. I figured that only added to the reasons why he didn't like me.

I stared back down at my desk and reveled in the silence of everyone ignoring me. It was better than questions, better than accusations, and much better than being bullied. I was still staring at my desk when I felt a body sit in the chair next to mine. I glanced over at Sawyer sitting beside me. Her long, black hair was straight down her back today and covered the large letters of my name on the letterman's jacket she was still wearing. I was a little surprised that she was still wearing it. Maybe she didn't have another jacket? She did appear to be wearing the same ripped and faded jeans. With all the alienation tied to me at this school, I'd think she'd want to avoid associating herself with me. Good thing her hair covered my name on her back, I guess.

I looked back down to my desk, but looked over again at hearing her soft voice. "Hi, Lucas."

A trace of a smile lifted my lips as I watched her gray eyes flick over my face, judging my mood today, perhaps wondering if I'd be making another run for the border. "Hey, Sawyer."

She glanced up at the jocks a few seats in front of us and then back to me. "How…are you?"

I looked down as I checked my emotional temperature. How was I? How was I ever these days? Barely holding on by a thread… Waiting for the next catastrophe to strike… Haunted by images of my friends and girlfriend…

"I'm fine," I whispered.

From the corner of my eye, I watched her hand start to raise and come towards me. My nerves shot right up to my chest at the thought of her placing a comforting palm on my shoulder. I had enjoyed her caretaking yesterday, and a part of me wanted that again today. Another part of me wanted to get through this on my own and, for the moment, I listened to that part. I twisted in my chair to face her and she hastily brought the hand reaching out for me up to her hair, tucking a piece behind her ear. I mentally cringed at the absence of her touch, but threw on a tiny smile for her benefit.

"How was the rest of your first day yesterday?"

She didn't look to buy my fake smile, but she didn't press me on it either. Instead, she sighed and rolled her eyes. "Boring. Standard high school stuff...cliques and clichés." She said the last part quietly.

I frowned as I looked over her face. Her eyes suddenly focused on her desk, and her teeth worried her lip. Something had happened to her yesterday after I left. It hoped it had nothing to do with the fact that she'd left with me. Maybe she'd been associated with me already, and she'd been ostracized for it.

In some ways, this microcosm of a world could be exceedingly cruel to newcomers. It hadn't been that way for Lil last year, but she'd fallen in with our crowd almost instantly and, even though it sounds horribly conceited, Darren, Sammy and I…well, we were kind of at the focal point of the popular crowd. We were the ruling class at the school, and when Lil had joined our ranks, especially when she and I had started dating, the school had practically worshipped her. But it could also go the exact opposite of that, and from the expression on Sawyer's face, I was starting to think that that's how her day had gone.

"Hey, do you--?"

I started to ask her about it, when the bell suddenly rang. The students loitering around their friends' desks found their seats and a few more trickled in from the hallway. There was a restrained shifting in chairs as people prepared themselves for another day of fascinating learning. I watched Sawyer for a few more seconds as she studied her desk. Suddenly her eyes came up to meet mine and I saw something in that visual contact—an almost unshakable feeling that we were connected, that she and I were the same. I smiled and nodded at her, no longer feeling the need to ask her about how her day had gone. It wasn't necessary. I understood that her day had gone badly, just as she understood that mine had gone badly, and I wouldn't press her, anymore than she'd press me.

I wanted to reach out and hold her hand, to be physically connected to her while we were visually connected. I didn't, though. We were too far apart for that to be a hidden maneuver and the last thing I wanted to bring her was more gossip. We stared at each other for a few moments longer and then pulled our gazes away as Ms. Reynolds started class.

Aside from a few pointed looks thrown my way, the class went by with no horrific moments. Everyone turned in their papers on their summer and I handed in the paper that I had managed to write in one of my calmer moments the night before. I'd written it on "The Plight of the Single Mother." It was as far away from my own personal hell as I could get, but close enough to home to mean something to me. It seemed the right thing to do.

After class, I hesitated at my desk until the majority of people in the room filed out. I felt better about the day, since I'd made it a full hour, and I didn't want that feeling ruined by Will and his childish form of torment. As I thought back to him stuffing freshmen in lockers and dunking unpopular kids in garbage cans last year, I started to wonder why he and I had even been friends. Was it an inevitability to become friends with the people in your social circle, even if those people were sort of…dicks? Something to analyze later, I guess. Maybe in my third period Philosophy class.

But for now, I had to get to History. I slung my backpack over my shoulder and smiled at Sawyer, who was waiting for the class to file out with me, or maybe as well as me. She smiled back. "Congratulations, West, you made it through an entire class."

I laughed and marveled that that was the second time today I'd done that, and both times had been because of her. "Yes, thank you…" I frowned. "What is your last name?" I crooked a grin as a thought struck me. "Is it Finn? Because that would just be awesome."

She scowled and I laughed again at the cute look on her face. "No." She finally laughed as well and rolled her eyes. "It's Smith."

My laughter died out as new students started arriving in the classroom. "Well, thank you, Smith." I indicated the door. "Shall we?"

She grinned at my gallantry and then headed down her aisle and out of the room. Once in the hallway, I asked her what her next class was.

"Science…Chemistry." She frowned, not looking very excited by the prospect. I frowned too, wishing she'd said History. Chemistry would put her in the long rectangular building behind the main building that housed the Science and Astronomy classes. My History class was on the first floor. Just as I was wondering if I should walk her to class anyway, she looked up at me. "What's your next class?"

I sighed dramatically. "History…blah."

She chuckled at my expression. "Don't knock history. It's very important." Suddenly her face got overly serious for a teenage girl. "You know what they say about it."

I sort of knew what they said about it…something about learning from it, or you're destined to repeat it. I opened my mouth to ask her what the quote was, but she started looking around and muttered, "I gotta go." She indicated the first floor doors that led to the Science building; I hadn't realized, walking with her, that we'd made it back to the first floor already.

"Okay, maybe we'll have another class together today." She gave me a knowing glance, like she already knew the answer to that, and I suppose she already did, since she'd sat through a day of attendance already, and would have heard my name spouted repeatedly at my absence if we did have any more classes. By her look, I was guessing we did. I wondered which ones?

I was debating over Sawyer's odd look as I entered the classroom. Thinking about her expression when she'd made that comment about history had stopped me from thinking about my own situation. As I was greeted by a roomful of silent stares, I suddenly remembered it. Sweeping the room, I noticed that at least none of my football team was here…perhaps I wouldn't get tripped today. I shook my head as I made my way to a seat. I really shouldn't think of it as *my* team anymore. I hadn't gone to tryouts over the summer, for obvious reasons, and the team was already well established for the year, a couple months into practices already. I had expected Coach to call me about joining the team, but he hadn't, and it wouldn't matter if he had. That life wasn't important to me anymore. I didn't want it.

I took a seat in the back of the classroom and ignored the stares around me. As the bell rang and the teacher stirred from being nearly asleep at his desk, I felt eyes on the right side of me. A couple of girls were staring at me relentlessly—and not just the curious or baleful stares I was used to getting. No, these two held…determined stares, and I mentally sighed. Here we go again.

"Lucas," one whispered. I looked over at the strawberry blonde and recognized her as Eliza Wood. Darren had had a crush on her in the fifth grade. She'd dated him for a day and then left him for a sixth grader; he'd been crushed.

I smiled inside at the memory but didn't show it on my face. I only glanced over at her while the teacher went about prepping class. He wrote something in large letters on the white board, and the smell of dry erase markers suddenly filled the small room.

Eliza looked up at the teacher and then back to her friend. I recognized the short Latina girl too—Gabriela Hernandez. Sammy had once nearly socked the girl for spreading rumors about Darren sleeping with her. It was the only time I'd ever seen Sammy really mad. Darren had found the whole thing, well, his words were "effing hot."

Eliza leaned towards me and I suppressed the urge to lean away. "So…Luc, tell us…what do you remember?" She raised her eyebrows expectantly, like I was suddenly going to lean into her and confess all of my innermost secrets. I resisted every urge in my body to scowl and tell her to fuck off.

I exhaled slowly and looked back down to my desk. I didn't talk about this to anyone. I'd never said anything to my mom. I'd never said anything at the hospital. I'd never even said anything to the cops. I had nothing to say to anyone, except, what I was about to say to the nosey girl beside me.

"Nothing, Eliza. I remember nothing."

She sighed in exasperation. "Oh come on, Luc, no one believes that. I mean, how do you forget something like that?"

Gabriela popped up beside her. "Right, that should be like, seared in your brain or something." I clenched my jaw as her tone got thoughtful. "Unless…you were just too wasted to remember? That makes sense." I glared up at them as they nodded to each other knowingly.

"I was not drinking!" My tone was heated…and a little louder than was necessary. Every head in the room swung around to me and I felt my cheeks flush. Great.

"Lucas West." The teacher, Mr. Davis, a graying man with thick glasses and a wide stomach, looked down at me from the front of class. Crossing his arms over his chest he glared at me while Eliza and Gabriela giggled. "So glad you could join us today. How about keeping it down while you're here?"

He raised an eyebrow at me and I quickly looked back to my desk, blocking out the amused voices in the room. "Yes, sir." I usually didn't say "sir" to teachers, but it was an easy way to slip back into their good graces and I really just wanted to sit there and quietly disappear.

The girls snickered beside me but didn't ask any more questions. It wouldn't have mattered if they did; I was done answering them. My answers never mattered anyway. I glanced at the chair to my left. In English, Sawyer had been in that seat and I suddenly wished I was back in that class, even with Will and Randy there. Her presence was just so calming.

Currently, a pale, blond guy named Simon was sitting there, ignoring me. That seat was supposed to have been Darren's. This was our class together this year—just us guys. We would have used this class to catch up and plan "outings," without the constant interruptions from our beautiful, but chatty girlfriends.

Darren was great at finding things to do in this small town, and this would have been the class we'd tune out to discuss it. I pictured him over there, an annoyed look on his face at hearing the drivel the teacher was spouting about the civil war, and in a hushed voice going over his plan to abduct his neighbor's cat and see if the mewing creature could find its way home from a mile away. I had quickly talked him out of that plan last year.

The rest of class went by quietly. No one else was brave enough to ask me anything. I'm pretty sure they'd all heard my answer, anyway. Again, I let most of the people in the room filter out before I left—fewer awkward moments that way. I headed back upstairs to the second floor to my Philosophy class. It was the last door in the hallway, and I slowly trudged towards it. There were stares and whispers in the hall. I vaguely heard my outburst in class repeated back to me and, of course, by the time I made it through the dwindling crowd of people, the story had been changed so that I had shouted, "I *was* drinking."

I sighed and pushed it from my mind. I couldn't stop the gossip train, and I couldn't alter its course. These people needed a villain and my survival had ensured them one. We all have to play our parts, right?

I paused with my hand on the door to my third period class, suddenly nervous. Not for the stares that I was getting more and more used to. No, my nerves were for the fact that Lillian and I had planned on taking this class together. I'd signed up for it because the class looked good on college applications. Lil had signed up with me because she loved the subject. She'd even had lofty goals of becoming a counselor someday. I wasn't sure what demons were going to haunt me when I opened this door. I turned the knob with last night's dream in my head. Maybe it wouldn't be so bad picturing her again. I had sort of enjoyed seeing glimpses of Sammy and Darren today, maybe seeing Lil like this would be pleasant.

I quickly opened the door and stepped through. I'd made good time and the class was only half full. I halfway expected a specter of Lil to hover in the middle of the room, but she didn't. The room was empty; a generic high school classroom with mass-produced posters of Socrates and Freud on the walls.

I hurried to take a seat in the back while they were still open. Luckily, our school had a first come, first serve policy on seating. Students started piling in, and, as I could have predicted, none of my former teammates walked through the door, choosing to get easier A's elsewhere. But a pleasant surprise did enter as the bell rang.

Sawyer hopped through the door right as the obnoxious thing sounded, and she quickly sprinted to a seat. She looked a little winded as she plopped down in her now traditional spot on my left. Her gray eyes turned to sparkle at mine as a playful smile curved her lips. She'd known I'd be here. She'd known we'd have this class together.

I smiled as I watched her work on calming her breath. It was a long way from the Science building to the main building's second floor. I leaned in close to her. "You didn't plan your schedule very well."

She frowned as she took a couple of deep breaths. "I planned it just fine."

I smirked at her. "You just went from the second floor, to the farthest building away, and then right back to the second floor. How is that good planning?"

Her lips twisted as she thought of a response. "I didn't sign up for gym this year." Her head indicated the path she'd taken. "That just made up for it." I shook my head at her and she sighed, admitting defeat. "I registered late. They gave me what was still open."

The smirk left my face as I realized that she was taking spots that had been vacated…by my friends. I turned back to the front of the room, suddenly seeing that vision of Lillian—right over the top of Sawyer. It was too much, too hard. I felt the tears forming and the overwhelming desire to run. I closed my eyes and took long, deep breaths. I felt Sawyer's hand on my arm and felt that peaceful heat that she seemed to generate all the way through my jacket. Not caring who was watching at the moment, I reached up and grabbed her hand with my own. I squeezed it, and for long minutes we sat in the back row, our hands clasped together in the aisle way between us.

I finally felt normal enough to open my eyes. The teacher had already begun class and was taking attendance; my name was last, as usual. While I waited, still clutching Sawyer's hand, I felt the stares around me. I felt them and ignored them. I heard the whispers too and I heard Sawyer's name repeated in those whispers. I felt bad that my attempt to keep her out of the gossip circle this morning, by not doing exactly what I was doing now, had failed horribly. If I hadn't already managed it yesterday, I'd finally dragged her into my misery.

Feeling guilty, I dropped her hand. I glanced over at her and thought she looked hurt for a moment. The look faded as she met my eye though, so I couldn't be sure. She only gave me a small, reassuring smile…and it did reassure me. The peace in her gaze washed over me, and I felt myself returning to normal, my painful moment pushed back. I couldn't think about Lil here just yet, not like I could the others. My dream had brought every detail of her right back to the surface. She was crystal clear in my head, and memories of us right now would tear me to pieces. It was too hard. With her, it was just too hard.

I missed hearing my name being called the first time and the teacher had to repeat it. I looked back and Mr. Varner was staring right at me; he obviously knew I was here, but was waiting for a response. "Here," I muttered, and he smirked at me.

Mr. Varner was the male equivalent of Ms. Reynolds: young, stylish, and as Sammy had informed me once—"hot as hell." There were rumors around the school that he was sort of a playboy, and from the thick, dark hair, piercing blue eyes and overall movie star good looks, I could see it. Darren had told me once that he'd heard that Mr. Varner "dated" students sometimes. I didn't think it was true, and certainly no one had ever caught him or accused him of anything, but the girls in the class were all staring at him like he might try to sweep them off their feet at any moment. While the gossip floating around this teacher was more socially acceptable than my gossip, I thought maybe, of all the teachers in the school, he would understand my situation and be all the more compassionate for it.

I was wrong.

He berated me for a good five minutes on ditching class the first day of school, and then loaded the entire class down with a paper due by Friday, which he highly indicated was my fault. The girls in the classroom never lost their adoring look for him, only hardened their glances at me, like *I* had actually given them the assignment. I decided that no amount of studying philosophy would ever help me understand the female gender—they were just incomprehensible.

After class, Sawyer walked around her desk to come over and stand by me. As most of the bodies shuffled out of the room, she indicated the door with her head, her long, dark hair flowing over her shoulder at the movement. My eyes rested on her jacket—*my* jacket—and I hoped my name was still covered on her back, for her sake.

"Come on." She put her hand on my elbow and gently pulled, and I had the sudden feeling that she really wanted to grab my hand again. I debated grabbing hers. It had felt so nice during class, but I loathed the idea of creating more problems for her. Besides, only a handful of students had seen our intimate contact. The two of us walking down the hall hand in hand, even if it was just a friendly gesture, would be a neon announcement in this school. I didn't want her being scrutinized, so I scooted away from her touch and started walking towards the door. She frowned, but followed me.

"Where are you off to next?" I asked, as we started walking side by side down the hall.

She crooked a grin. "I need to make a pit stop at my locker and then we have fourth together."

I matched her grin as I looked over at her. One benefit of a small school, I suppose, is that you run into a lot of the same students class after class. There was a fifteen minute break between third and fourth period, so we had time to leisurely make our way down to the first floor, where the upperclassman lockers were. I thought over the upcoming class and swallowed a lump that was suddenly in my throat. Math Analysis. We were all going to take that class together. We were going to make our own study group and help each other get through tests. Okay, Lil, Sammy and I were going to study and help each other get through tests. Darren's plan was to copy off of Sammy.

I pictured her in the hallway, just as we approached the lockers. She'd harshly smacked Darren on the arm after he'd told her that and informed him that he absolutely could *not* cheat off her. Darren and I had given each other small smiles—of course she'd let him cheat. There wasn't a whole lot that Sammy wouldn't let Darren do.

I walked to my assigned locker and paused before it, taking in the lockers right and left of mine. Darren had bribed someone in the office last year to get all of our lockers together. Lillian had joked at the time that it was almost like we all lived together while we were at school. I ran my fingers over the locker beside mine, the one that would have been hers. My breath started getting fainter.

Fingers brushed mine and I started, almost expecting to see Lillian again. I looked over and saw Sawyer watching me curiously, her fingers over mine on the locker. She was currently twisting the combination lock with her other hand. It finally hit me then, that she was opening Lil's locker. Shock knocked my breath back.

"This is yours?"

Her face was inquisitive as she looked over my paling complexion. "Yes…is that one yours?"

She indicated the one beside hers, and I absentmindedly nodded. "They gave you Lil's," I muttered under my breath.

"Lil?" Her hand closed around mine, and she stopped trying to open her locker. "Who is Lil? I've heard the name in whispers, but no one will really talk about her…and yesterday…" She looked down as my eyes watered. I wasn't even sure if I could tell her about Lillian.

"Yesterday?" I asked quietly, trying to prolong my agony.

She glanced up and down the hallway, where I assumed a cluster of people were watching us stand beside each other with her hand over mine. I resisted the urge to pull away from her, to spare her the rumors. She stepped closer to me when she looked back up to my face, our bodies nearly touching now, and I again resisted the urge to get some space between us. She shouldn't be so close to me. I wasn't good for her.

"You called me Lil yesterday in English…you looked really confused."

I dropped my head and closed my eyes. I'd nearly forgotten that I'd heard Lil's voice and gotten confused, thinking for a moment that Sawyer was her. I'd been such an emotional wreck that day…I suppose I still was. I felt a tear bubble up under my eyelid and tried to will it back into my body, but it escaped with my words. "Lillian was my girlfriend…she died in the crash."

The beginning of a sob started to come out and I bit my lip hard and rested my head against my locker, not wanting to break down in the middle of school. Sawyer's other hand came up to my back where she rubbed me consolingly over my jacket. She stepped even closer, so we were pseudo-hugging, the movement shielding me from the public's view and creating a tiny bubble of privacy as we stood close together, next to my dead girlfriend's locker.

"I'm sorry, Luc. I didn't know."

I nodded against the cool metal and concentrated on long inhales through the nose, and exhales through the mouth. I would not break down in the hallway. Not around these people. Sawyer put her head against her locker and looked up at me. I looked down at her as another tear rolled down my cheek, and I instantly felt the connection again, like here was someone who knew my pain. Our eyes held for long seconds, and then she released her hold on my hand and brushed aside the tear from my face.

Just when I was feeling better, a hand shoved my back, hard, and pushed me into the lockers. I automatically turned my head and stepped in front of Sawyer. Josh stood in front of me. His face twisted into a scowl and his dark eyes flicked between mine and Sawyer's. I could almost see the accusation in those eyes—*How dare you move on! Did Lillian, Sammy and my brother mean nothing to you?*

I swallowed my angry retort to the unasked question and tried to remember that, not too long ago, Josh had been a good friend…and he was all I had left of Darren. "Josh, can we talk about--?"

The minute my soothing tone hit him, his face twisted in rage. He didn't want to hear it. He didn't want to think of me as anything but an evil, soulless creature that had devastated his family. It was almost like he had died in that car as well, as unattainable to me as he was now. He brought his hands up and shoved me again, pushing me and Sawyer back into the lockers. She squeaked away at the last minute and tried to pull Josh off while he yelled obscenities at me.

"Hey, break it up!" Coach Taylor strode up to where a circle of encouraging students had gathered, students encouraging Josh. He pulled Josh off of me while those students started groaning at the fight being broken up. "You! To the principal's office—now!"

He grabbed Josh's shirt by the collar and started dragging him away. While he walked with him, Coach turned back to where I was still leaning against the lockers. "I want to talk to you later, West." He raised his eyebrows and gave me the look that had most freshmen scurrying to do his bidding. It didn't intimidate me, though. I didn't really want to hear what he had to say.

The crowd started dispersing after Josh's disappearance, a lot of them throwing me sulking glances, like it was my fault that Coach had stopped Josh from kicking my ass. I shook my head and watched them leave. Sawyer opened and closed her locker next to mine and shook her head as well. "Never a dull moment around you, is it?"

I looked over to her, wanting to explain and also not wanting to explain. Finally, I decided a little information was called for. "My best friend Darren was in the crash, as well as his girlfriend Sammy. They were both killed." I nodded my head in the direction Josh had gone. "That's Darren's little brother."

Sawyer turned to look after him before swinging her dark hair around to look at me again. Her gray eyes narrowed in anger and I interpreted her look. "Yeah, he blames me for killing Darren." I looked up at the ceiling and closed my eyes. "We used to all be friends and now he hates me…spreads lies about me." I was positive that more than a few of the rumors around the town were continually circulated because of Josh, and after he'd witnessed my tender moment with Sawyer, I was positive that rumors would now be flying about her as well. It wouldn't surprise me if, by the end of the day, I'd knocked Sawyer up. Pretty funny, considering I was still a virgin.

Sawyer's tone matched the heat I'd seen in her eyes. "No offense to your hometown, Lucas, but I'm starting to hate these people."

I cracked my eyes open and looked down at her cutely angry face. I smiled a little watching her, thinking that her irritation looked sort of like the female version of Darren's. "Yeah…sometimes I do too." I straightened and pushed myself away from the lockers, deciding right at that moment to not use them. I'd rather lug around a heavy bag. "One more year…that's all I have to give this place."

She finally smiled at me and together we made our way to Math class.

Chapter 4 – Feels Like Home to Me

Math was taught by Mrs. Chambers. She was short and wide with frizzy, brown hair and an exuberance for mathematics that I'd never understand. She bounced around the front of the room, clearly excited to teach our absorbing minds all the intricate facets of advanced equations. As Sawyer and I took seats in our preferred section in the very back row, I hoped that she allowed calculators.

As usual, several students stared at me as they entered the room. Several stared at Sawyer now, too. I ignored the stares; Sawyer calmly returned them. I cringed when three members of the football team entered. They sat around the smartest girl in our class. With the adoring looks she gave each of them, I was pretty sure they'd each get "tutored" and would have no problems passing. They each gave me a hard stare before settling into their seats, luckily, near the front of the room. None of them bothered me physically, though. Maybe Will had proclaimed me *his* whipping boy and no one else was allowed to mess with me. Or maybe their plan was just to ignore me. I shoved back the memories of each of them clapping me on the back after a tough win the year before. It was hard to believe that at one time I'd considered the team near-family.

Mrs. Chambers energetically started taking attendance. She stuttered on my name and looked up at me with a surprised face, like she'd only just realized who I was, and that I was in her class. Apparently things outside of addition and subtraction took a while to filter though her brain. I uttered, "Here," and stared down at my desk, not wanting to see yet another teacher giving me either condemning or sympathetic looks.

The class went by with the numbing boringness of an uninteresting subject being shoved down your throat. Math wasn't a high point for me on a good day…and today wasn't exactly a good day. It was better than yesterday, but still, not a great day.

I spaced out halfway through the lecture and visions of Sammy sighing and leaning her chin in her hand in front of me filled my head. I imagined Darren beside her smiling indecently and whispering dirty words. She'd giggle quietly and whisper back at him to shut up, which only made him use even dirtier words. I'd watched them play this game before. By the end of class, she'd be faintly blushing, either embarrassed…or possibly turned on. I tried not to think about it either way.

I felt a remembered vision of Lillian by my side, but I didn't turn to look. In my vision, I heard her laugh softly at Darren and Sammy. I closed my eyes at hearing that laugh in my head. It had been the most beautiful sound in the world. I slowly opened my eyes and considered turning my head to let the vision completely take me over…but I resisted. I remembered my dream and the ache I'd felt when that dream had ended. As much as I'd like to dwell in memories of her, if I did it now, I'd probably start bawling.

Instead, I clenched my fists and dug my fingers into my palms, banishing the image of Darren and Sammy's flirting, forcing my mind to return to the present. I struggled to absorb the lesson being taught but felt eyes on me, and finally turned my head. Sawyer was watching me with a slightly concerned look. She'd seen my twisting emotions, and after our moment by the lockers, probably thought I was going to either completely break down or bolt. I forced my body to relax and smiled at her, letting her completely memory-free face bring me back to calmness. If I was going to make it through a year of this, I really needed to shut my mind off better.

Sawyer smiled back at me, her fingers twirling around a dark strand of hair. She looked up at the boisterous teacher and then back at me. Cocking her head, she mouthed, "Are you okay?"

I forced a wider smile and nodded, returning my gaze back to the teacher. Yeah, I definitely needed to relax.

After Math was lunch. I sat at my desk and pretended to flip through the math book, like I was horribly interested in the subject. I wasn't. I just wanted the entire room to clear out before I bailed. I wasn't planning on heading to the cafeteria with the rest of them. I wasn't sure where I was going to go, but doing a perp walk through the cafeteria wasn't something I wanted to partake in.

Unfortunately, my feigned interest in mathematics led to Mrs. Chambers approaching me and chatting my ear off about it. She seemed oblivious to the whispers and rumors around me as the other students left the classroom, the jocks giving me a final glare before they left with their real teacher, the straight 'A' student who clearly worshipped them.

With her energetic personality, it was hard to gauge what Mrs. Chambers thought about me and the wreck. That didn't have anything to do with math, so she didn't discuss it. But she did go into an exceedingly long lecture on the infinitely surprising ways trigonometry could be applied to everyday life.

I think she would have chatted with me for the entire lunch period. Fortunately, Sawyer smoothly interjected herself and politely excused the both of us. Mrs. Chambers seemed reluctant to let her potential protégé go (I probably feigned my interest a little too well, what with the nodding and agreeing with her at every possible opportunity), but eventually the peppy woman backed off and Sawyer and I left the empty classroom.

"Thanks," I muttered as we walked down the empty hall.

She grinned over at me. "Not a problem. I didn't realize you were such a nerd."

I matched her wide grin as I looked over her pale gray eyes and shockingly dark hair. "That's me…total dork."

I adjusted my heavy backpack and shoved my hands into my jeans pockets. Sawyer slung her arm through the hole along my side that I'd created by pushing my fingers in my denims, and walked close by me. It was sort of an intimate move, and instantly, memories of walking down these very halls with Lil that way assaulted me.

I remembered her pale, blue eyes looking up to my hazel ones as she'd leaned her head on my shoulder. "What do you want to do for lunch? We could eat with Darren and Sammy…or…" she bit her peach stained lip and raised her eyebrows suggestively, "we could try making out in the closet again?" She laughed and squeezed me tight. "Maybe we won't get interrupted by another couple this time?"

I shut my eyes and stopped walking. I jerked my body away from Sawyer, knowing I was being rude, but needing the memory of Lillian to leave me. Not yet…it hurt too much. I felt my eyes well up and my breath quicken. God, calm down. I should be able to think of her. Can't I at least think of her?

"Luc?"

For a moment the vision was still so strong, that I heard Lil's voice again and not Sawyer's. I pushed that feeling back, along with those stubborn tears, and forced my eyes open. Sawyer was watery in my vision and I knew that for the second time today, I was about to let out some tears in front of her. She had such a hurt and compassionate look on her face that I felt my body relaxing and my breath returning. I concentrated on the things about Sawyer that were nothing like Lil, nothing like anyone who could stoke a memory in me—the slope of her nose, the angle of her chin, the slight almond shaping of her eyes that hinted at Asian heritage somewhere deep in her blood.

Focusing on her uniqueness shut my mind off, and I gave her a slight smile as her lips turned to a slight frown. "Sorry," I muttered as I resumed walking.

She waited a couple of steps and then she met up with me, her head down, her hands now in my letterman's jacket that she was wearing. I wondered for a moment if she'd read too much into me giving her that jacket yesterday. Maybe she thought we were a couple now? If so, my rejection just now had probably hurt her feelings. I supposed I did owe her an explanation. I looked over at where she was studying the ground while we walked.

"It's not you, Sawyer." I nodded my head back to where I'd had my latest freak-out. "Lil and I used to…" my voice choked up and I had to clear it to keep talking, "…we used to be like that and for a moment, I remembered how it was with her and I just can't…"

I closed my eyes and swallowed the knot in my throat. I felt Sawyer's hand on my arm and paused to look over at her. "I'm sorry if I have to push you away sometimes. I'm just not ready to…be that close to someone…right now."

God, I hoped she wasn't offended by that.

She didn't appear to be. Her cheeks flushed as understanding flooded through her. She glanced down the hallway and then back to me. "I'm sorry, Lucas. I wasn't trying to…" She shrugged and looked a little embarrassed. "I'm not trying to… I'm just really comfortable with you. But I know you're going through something awful and probably don't feel the same way about me…"

I smirked and cocked my head. "You have no idea, Sawyer…none. I don't think I'd have lasted twenty minutes today if it weren't for you." I shook my head. "If you only knew how much…peace I find with you."

She flashed me a smile, but then her face stilled to seriousness. "I'm not trying to replace her, Luc. I just want to be your friend."

I stared at her for long seconds while a comfortable silence built between us. Finally, I whispered, "You *are* my friend…you're the only one I've got." I may have only known her a day, but the truth of that sentence rang through every part of me.

Her eyes watered and she stepped towards me uncertainly, like she wanted to hug me but wasn't sure if that was okay. I closed the distance for her, bringing my arms around her as platonically as I could. We both sighed at the comfort the hug brought us. After a long moment, we pulled apart and continued our walk out of the building to…somewhere.

We ended up eating our lunch in her Camaro in the parking lot. It was perfect. She'd parked on the edge of the lot and the very few people we saw didn't come out that far to bother us. She flipped the switch on her car and turned the radio on to a sixties rock station. I relaxed back in the seat and grabbed my food out of my backpack; sometime in my haze last night, I'd made a lunch. When Sawyer didn't appear to have anything but an apple in her bag, I gave her half my sandwich and a bag of pretzels. She smiled apologetically, but didn't refuse my offer, and we finished out the lunch period in the confined comfort of her vehicle.

When the clock on her dash showed that our free time was up, we headed back out to the campus to finish up our day. Sawyer made her way to her fifth period computer class, where she planned on killing time on the Internet whenever she could. I grinned at her as we parted ways. I had Astronomy, in the squat, rectangular building that housed all the science classes. As I walked along the sidewalk under the overhang, I remembered that this was supposed to have been my class with Sammy and Lil. They would have sat side by side in front of me, gossiping about the latest celebrity foible or fashion faux-pas. I smiled as I pictured Sammy's reddish hair brushing against Lil's pale hair. I pictured Lil turning in her seat to wink at me, and I felt my heart seize. Swallowing, I banished the vision I wasn't ready to have yet and walked up to the outside door that led to my class.

I immediately spotted Josh when I opened the heavy door. His eyes locked onto mine and narrowed in anger, a state he seemed to permanently reside in. He was sitting next to some cheerleaders and Randy from the football team. He looked back at Randy and whispered something and Randy glanced up at me entering the room and scowled. Great.

Keeping my head down, I made my way to an empty seat in the back, on the other end of the small room from them. Unfortunately, Josh had other ideas. He walked across the room to stand right in front of me. I counted to three as he stood there, fists clenched at his sides. The teacher was at the front of the room, writing something on the board as kids filtered through the door, so I figured Josh wasn't going to try to slug me. Taking a deep breath, I looked up at him.

"What, Josh?" I said quietly.

His jaw clenched before it relaxed. "I got detention because of you, dickwad." I wondered how him slamming *me* against a locker was my fault, but didn't say anything. He leaned in close at my silence. "I finally made varsity this year. If you get me kicked off the team, I'll…I'll…" He searched my face as he searched for words.

"You'll what, Josh? Kill me?" My lip curled in a tired smile.

His face went red all over as he stared at me in a sudden rage. I turned my head to stare straight ahead of me as I felt eyes in the room watching our every move. I was sure more than a few of those eyes were willing Josh to finally hit me. In a weird way, I *wanted* Josh to hit me again. Maybe it would get it out of his system this time, if he did it in front of so many people, and maybe then our relationship could be…well, at least not so antagonistic. The teacher cleared his throat as the bell rang, and out of the corner of my eye I saw Josh flinch a little at the unexpected sound.

Josh glanced around at the students sitting. He turned back to me and looked me up and down. "This isn't over, Lucas."

I sighed as he walked back to his seat. "I didn't think it was, Josh."

He shot me a glare once he sat back down with Randy, and I wondered if he'd heard me. I shook my head and thought that Darren would get a kick out of his brother so worked up over me. Darren and I got along pretty well, for the most part, but we'd certainly had our disagreements before. He'd actually slugged me once, when he'd thought I'd hit on Sammy.

Someone in school had started the rumor that Sammy and I had kissed in the library, and Darren had immediately punched me as soon as he saw me.

That had thrown me, especially since I hadn't heard the rumor yet. I'd been walking with Sammy at the time and she'd whaled on Darren after he'd swung at me. She'd started laughing once he confessed why he'd done it, and then they'd spent five minutes sucking face while I rubbed my sore jaw. Darren had apologized for slugging me and I'd accepted his apology…by slugging him right back. Eye for an eye, right?

As class began, I smiled over the memory of Darren's shocked face. His surprise had quickly turned into amusement, and we'd pretended to fight for fifteen minutes while Sammy laughed at the both of us. I'm pretty sure the words, "You guys are morons," crossed her lips at some point. I never did find out who'd started that little rumor. I'm sure whoever it was, was probably having a field day with me now.

The class went by quickly. I actually found the subject fascinating and paid attention to the teacher instead of daydreaming about my long-gone friends, like I had done so often today. All too soon, the bell rang, and our teacher, a shriveled older man named Mr. Thomson, whose balding hair and thick rimmed glasses made him the epitome of a science nerd, gestured some sort of goodbye with his hand and turned back to the board, erasing his drawings. I waited for Josh to leave before I stood. He gave me a glare that I was getting used to seeing from him, and then he ducked out the door with Randy and one of the blonde cheerleaders.

I stood and picked up my bag before making my way to the exit. Josh wasn't outside waiting for me, as I'd sort of expected him to be, and aside from a few stares, I made my way to my last class in peace—art. All four of us were supposed to be in that class, too. It was going to be our goof-off class before Darren and I went to football practice and the girls went to volleyball practice.

Art was in a building that almost looked like a shack, opposite the back door to the gym. I ducked into the class and discovered that people were already starting to draw or doodle on paper and weren't paying any attention to me whatsoever. Enjoying the invisibility, I found a seat.

I sat at an easel and waited for the teacher, Mrs. Solheim, a post-dated flower child with wavy, waist-length hair and a look of self-medicated peace on her face, to walk over to me. Her smile was bright when she approached, and the warmth in it shocked me for a moment…until she called me Tom. I shook my head and said, "No, I'm Lucas." Then she frowned and nodded slowly, like she suddenly remembered who I was…and what I'd done.

She glanced at a couple of the empty seats in the room, and I had the feeling that she was seeing my friends, too. I followed her gaze and momentarily saw Darren making a 'she's loopy' signal with his fingers, making my vision of Sammy laugh into her hand. Before I could stop it, I thought of Lil giving Darren an admonishing look, her full lips puckered in displeasure. I remembered my dream of kissing those lips last night and felt my eyes get heavy as her beautiful, shiny hair danced around her shoulders when she shook her head at Darren. My breath seized as her face turned towards me and I watched in awe as the lips curled into an easy smile and she opened her mouth to speak.

"Lucas?"

I blinked at the unfamiliar voice coming from her lips and glanced up at Mrs. Solheim, who was trying to explain the assignment that I'd missed the introduction to yesterday. I'd been completely wrapped in my memories and I'd tuned her out. I had no idea what she'd been talking about. I swallowed the ache in my throat at seeing Lil so clearly again and forced myself to concentrate on the teacher.

"I'm sorry…what?"

She sighed, rolled her eyes, and explained the assignment to me again. Her looking at me like I was the space case and not her was sort of funny, but I couldn't find it in myself to laugh. That vision of my girlfriend had been a sudden one. I hadn't been prepared for it, not that I ever was. As the teacher walked away, I felt the ache in my chest start to turn towards despair. I flicked my eyes around the room, wishing Sawyer had this class with me, too, but she didn't. She wasn't there. I'd have to get through this on my own.

I closed my eyes and pictured Sawyer's face—her black-as-night hair and stormy gray eyes. It was an odd combination, but an appealing one, too. The vision of her face held no added recollections of my friends, only a peace that I could almost feel washing over my body. My pain momentarily left me. I opened my eyes and picked up a pencil on the easel. Our assignment was to draw something that felt like home. At that moment, and as odd as the thought was, only one thing felt like home to me. Very carefully, and in as much detail as I could do in an hour, I began to draw *her* face…Sawyer's face.

After class, I was a bit startled to see her actual face again. I'd been walking out of the shack building and debating walking home, when I'd nearly run right into her. She'd just come out of one of the rooms attached to the back of the gym. One of the rooms was used for the band, the other for the choir. I wondered which one she belonged to, but didn't ask her because she looked like she'd been crying. She started as she bumped against me and looked up into my face. My jacket was in her hands and her bag was haphazardly slung over her shoulder, crammed papers visible in the top of it, like she'd fled the room in a hurry.

"Sawyer, are you all right?"

She swiped a hand under her eyelids and put on a stiff smile. "Yeah, I'm fine." She flicked a glance over her shoulder, and my eyes followed. She was looking at a tall, honey-haired girl coming out of the choir room. I frowned when I recognized her—Brittany Faulkner. The Faulkner family was the oldest in our small town. Their ancestors were the founding fathers of the town, actually. That's right—our town had actual freaking Founding Fathers. The town was still big on heritage and all of the Faulkners had a holier-than-thou attitude. They also had a good sum of money to go along with that prestige and kind of ruled the town. And Brittany…ruled the school.

She'd been a part of the social circle with Darren, Sammy, Lil and me. She was again one of those people who I wasn't sure why we were friends with her. She was in no way nice. But she was attractive, very attractive, and she'd had her eye on me since the ninth grade. She was actually the first girl who had let me feel her up. It had happened after practice my freshman year, and I'd always known that it wouldn't have necessarily had to stop at my hands up her shirt. I'd always known that I could have gone much farther with her…I just hadn't wanted to.

Sawyer quickly averted her gaze from Brittany's glare as Brittany's brown eyes swept over us. I continued to look at her, wondering just what she'd done or said to Sawyer. An odd look crossed her face; her eyes narrowed at me in contempt, much like Josh's, actually, but her lips curled into a small, inviting smile, like I could still do more than just feel her up…she would just hate me at the same time.

Brittany smirked and then stalked off. She had been in a huff around me ever since I'd started dating Lil, maybe even before that, but definitely after Lil and I'd hooked up. I suspected she was jealous, but she had never really acted like she was. It was just an odd sort of feeling I used to get while hanging around her. A sudden light went off in my head as I wondered if she was the one who used to circulate cheating rumors around about me.

After she walked away, I focused my attention back to where Sawyer was putting my jacket back on. "Is she bugging you?" I asked her.

She shook her head. "Don't worry about it, Luc. I can handle bitches."

I frowned and started to reply when she met and held my gaze. Her eyes were back to their crystal clear peacefulness and her voice dropped to that oddly serious tone. "I've dealt with much worse. I can deal with her." She shook her head as I wondered what she meant. "It's nothing."

I shrugged, figuring she'd tell me when and if she was ready. An idea struck me as I realized that I'd made it through an entire school day and I was now free. I smiled genuinely for the first time today. "We're done, Sawyer…we're free." I smiled wider as she gave me a crooked grin. "Want to come over to my house?" I leaned in and raised an eyebrow. "We have Hot Pockets."

She laughed and started to nod, but then she closed her eyes and her happy look fell into a disgruntled one. "Ugh, I can't." I started to ask why as my face fell as well, but she answered before I could. "I had to sign up for that Safe and Sound Club." She sighed and kicked a rock on the ground. "Part of my probation," she muttered sullenly.

"Oh. You're joining the purity club…really?"

She looked back up at me and grimaced. "Not by choice. It was the only way my parents would give me the tiniest bit of slack." Her shoulders slumped as she spoke.

I cocked an eyebrow at her as I looked over her crestfallen expression. "Did you burn down your old school or something?"

Amusement lit up her face as she laughed. "I wish." As her laughter faded, her eyes turned guarded. "No, it was…something else." She looked away, obviously not wanting to talk about it, and I let the conversation drop. Again, she'd tell me when she was ready. I wasn't about to push.

"All right then…let's go."

She looked back to me with a satisfyingly startled face. "What? You're coming?"

I shrugged. "I've got nothing else to do…and I could use a ride home."

Beaming, she hugged me tight. I savored the warmth of her embrace and delighted that I had actually made someone in this school happy…by staying. I laughed and hugged her back. She abruptly pulled away from me and looked a touch embarrassed for her sudden attack. I laughed again at the look on her face as we started walking back towards the main building.

We walked past groups of people heading out to the parking lot, and watched other groups of kids head out to the numerous parked buses waiting for them. Several students eyed us walking together, but we both ignored them. We were getting good at this, although I still felt a little bad that just my presence was causing a small gossip storm to swirl around her. I hoped Brittany wasn't attacking her over me…maybe for her wearing my jacket, or something stupid like that.

"Don't you have practice?" she asked as we walked, her fingers picking at the sleeves of my jacket, her habit of playing with them still in full effect.

I smiled sadly as I looked down on her. "No. Not this year. Not anymore." I thought about Josh, Randy, Will and all the others on my old team meeting with Coach on the field right about now. While I was glad that I wouldn't be running into any of them anymore today, a part of me missed my old routine. But that had changed, along with everything else.

Sawyer looked up at me with curious eyes. "It just doesn't seem so important anymore," I answered her unasked question quietly. Her pale eyes regarded me with a deep understanding and she nodded, like she knew exactly what I meant. I smiled and felt that deep connection again as we walked the rest of the way in silence.

The purity club met on the first floor in the main building. As we approached the classroom door we saw the handmade sign taped over the window—*Safe and Sound Club: Because We Care About You.* I rolled my eyes. God, I really didn't want to be here, but I didn't want to part ways with Sawyer yet, either. I was still hoping she'd come over later. It would make the night go by a lot faster, if I could share a chunk of it with her.

Sawyer put her hand on the knob and turned to look at me. She rolled her eyes, too, and sighed. "Ready?" she muttered.

"Sure," I answered, as she swung the door open.

The room wasn't very full, not too surprising, I suppose. There were maybe eight people there and the supervising teacher, Ms. Reynolds. She brightened as Sawyer entered the room; I thought she'd start glowing when she noticed me.

"Sawyer, Lucas. I'm so glad you decided to join us." She came over and put a hand on my shoulder and again, I felt like her statement was just for my benefit. We gave her halfhearted grins and she directed us to some open seats.

A wave of whispers followed us as we made our way to the back of the room. We sat on a couple of desks, pushing them close together and dangling our feet off the edge. We waited silently as a couple more students trickled in. Sawyer looked down and started playing with the hem of my jacket sleeve around her wrist while I scanned the room. I caught more than a couple of people giving me questioning glances. A couple of people smiled sardonically and one even smiled encouragingly, but the majority frowned slightly, sure I was only here to mock their stupid club probably. Well, I wasn't. I wasn't here to mock or engage. I was here to spend time with Sawyer. As the stares kept up, I started wondering if I should have just parted ways with her. Oh well.

Eventually Ms. Reynolds started the meeting and thanked us all for coming. She assured everyone that together we could help steer the student body to a clean and sober life. I bit back an amused smile. One tiny club was going to stop high schoolers from rebelling with secret parties and illegally obtained alcohol? I didn't think so. Sawyer snickered softly beside me, and then skillfully switched it to a cough in her hand when a couple of people glanced back and glared at her. I bumped her shoulder with mine and whispered for her to take this seriously. She looked up at my half grin and laughed.

After the introductions, we were subjected to an hour of choosing club positions. The speeches for the potential President went on for fifteen minutes. By the actual vote, I was ready to make for the hills, but I stuck it out and enjoyed Sawyer's presence on the desk beside me as we whispered more interesting speeches for the candidates during the entire meeting. Sawyer brought me near to laughing out loud several times with her dry sense of humor. In some ways, she really reminded me of Darren, and I had the sudden feeling that he would have liked her.

Luckily, neither Sawyer nor I were nominated for any positions, and eventually the elections ended with Sally Hoffen winning the coveted Presidential position. I picked up my stuff to get out of there, and just when I was going to ask Sawyer if she still wanted to come over, Ms. Reynolds walked up to our side.

"Lucas…could I speak to you for a moment?" Her young face looked greatly concerned, and I cringed at whatever she wanted. I didn't have it in me to deny a direct request made by a teacher, though.

"Um…sure," I said slowly.

Beside me, Sawyer slung her bag over her shoulder and gave me a sympathetic look. "Sorry, Luc, I can't hang around. My parents are expecting me home right after the meeting." My face fell as I looked at her. Damn, I'd so been hoping that we could hang out longer, but she had to go. Damn, I was going to have to walk home now too. She put a hand on my arm and muttered, "Have a good night. See ya tomorrow."

I nodded and watched her comforting presence leave the room. With a sigh, I turned to face Ms. Reynolds, who was watching Sawyer leave as well. Finally, she turned to face me and her lips compressed to a thin line. "You didn't take that very seriously." I replayed the meeting in my mind, trying to understand what she was talking about. I was here. I participated. Heck, I even voted. Seeing my confusion, she filled in the blanks. "The meeting, the entire time you were either spacing out or talking to Sawyer." She lowered her voice and leaned into me, bringing her hand back up to my arm. "You, of all people, Lucas, should take this seriously. We're here to help you." Her voice conveyed her true concern for what she clearly saw as a severely troubled teen, and I immediately bristled at the implication.

I jerked away from her. "I came here for Sawyer." I shook my head, suddenly feeling very angry. "I'm not interested in your little club." The sneer in my voice was unmistakable, and Ms. Reynolds straightened and backed up a step.

She set her jaw at my tone and her eyes flashed with something that almost looked like anger, too. "Well, for your future…I hope you reconsider." Her face softened as her sudden anger left her. "We're always here for you, Lucas."

Shaking my head, I turned away from her and left the room. Her implication was all too clear—you have a problem and you need to join our little group so we can get you sober. God, since when did being drunk once in my life constitute a drinking problem? Just goes to show you how easy it can be for people to believe the lie…and how resistant people can be to believe the truth.

In a huff, I made my way to the parking lot that let out to the street that took me home. I didn't like being angry at Ms. Reynolds. I did like her, and she *was* only concerned for my well-being, one of the few individuals in this town who actually cared about me. I was just tired of being looked at like some after school special.

Halfway through the parking lot, a horn beeping snapped me out of my reverie. In a daze, I looked over at what car was making the noise. I stopped walking and cocked my head when I noticed Sawyer's Camaro driving towards me. My lips automatically curled into a smile as she pulled up beside me. I bent down as she rolled down her window.

"What are you still doing here?" I asked her.

She smiled and shrugged, her hand resting over the steering wheel. "I just remembered that you probably needed a ride." She shook her dark head. "My parents can wait a few minutes."

I smiled and walked around the front of her car to get in the passenger's side. Settling into the familiar bucket seat, I laid my head back and inhaled the clean scent of lemons. I was extremely grateful that I didn't have to walk home, but I didn't want Sawyer to suffer for my comfort. "You don't have to do this. I don't want you to get in trouble because of me."

She laughed and looked over at me. "I'm already in a constant state of trouble. Really, this is nothing." Her smile turned into concern as she turned back to face the road. "What did Ms. Reynolds want?"

I sighed and ran a hand though my hair. "Oh, just your basic, 'You've got a problem, let us help you' speech." Grunting in irritation, I stared out the window at the small town streaking by. "You'd think I was Lindsey Lohan by the way they all look at me."

Sawyer snorted. "I don't think they're looking at you like you're a whacked out, washed up starlet." She looked over at me and grinned and I couldn't help but grin back.

"You know what I mean," I muttered.

She laughed for a minute more while she turned back to the road. Then her expression got more serious. "Did you…did you drink a lot, Lucas?" She peeked at me from the corner of her eye and I tried to keep the scowl from my face. Apparently I hadn't done a very good job, because she quickly added, "I just…I don't know, Lucas. I've only just met you. I don't know what you were like before…." She shrugged. "I do still believe that you weren't *that* night, but I was just wondering why they are all so quick to believe the stories."

I relaxed and looked back to the sidewalk blurring by. I shouldn't get snippy at her; it was a fair question. She really didn't know me, and I'm sure she'd been getting an earful of unpleasant information on me. She must wonder if my being sober *that* night was the rarity. Softly, I sighed into the window.

"No…I've never been a really big drinker. I just don't care for it, for being out of control like that." Weariness took me over as I looked back at her. "I've been drunk exactly once in my life…and it was sort of a disaster." I stared out the windshield as I remembered that one night of drunken debauchery, and my reluctance to ever repeat it. "They all know that about me, too. My…resistance…was sort of an inside joke with my friends. 'Oh, let's get Lucas drunk—cue the Mission Impossible music.'" I sighed again and felt her hand snake over to clench mine. I laced our fingers together and relaxed even further into her touch.

"Why do they all believe it then?"

"I don't know," I whispered.

She squeezed my hand and we let the conversation fade. A warm silence fell upon the car and I closed my eyes and concentrated on the feeling of her tiny hand in mine. It was nice to hold someone's hand again. I stroked my thumb along the side of hers and felt her hand stiffen before relaxing. Her skin was soft and silky and I smiled at the feeling of it sliding under mine. I was sure my hand felt rough in comparison, but Sawyer never complained or pulled her hand away, just continued to let me hold hers and stroke it with mine.

I pushed back the memories of doing this with Lil as Sawyer's car sped to my house. Lil and I had held hands a lot, but usually only walking between classes in the more traditional 'cup' hold. If we were alone in a quiet car…well, we were generally doing more than holding hands. I pushed those memories back as well. Trying to distract my mind from wandering down an alley I wasn't ready for yet, I focused on the dips and curves of Sawyer's hand as my thumb stretched out to feel more of it. I swept my thumb over the back of her hand, sliding over the long, elegant bones and the smooth knuckles. I adjusted my hand so I could sweep my thumb up to her palm, feeling the hill-like edges that led down to the valley in the exact center. Then my thumb traveled straight down that valley, heading towards her petite wrist.

She abruptly jerked her hand away from mine and startled, I opened my eyes. I blushed a bit, thinking I'd gone beyond the terms of our friendship with my little "body exploration." I was about to sputter an apology, when I noticed she was turning the steering wheel to pull into the drive of my home. I studied her face as she did, but I didn't see any irritation or embarrassment. Actually, she looked kind of blank as she straightened the wheel and put the car in park.

The apology was still on the tip of my tongue, but she beat me to it. "We're here…" She looked at me a little sheepishly and ran the hand I'd darn near been caressing back through her hair, tucking some dark strands behind her ear.

I glanced at my house and then back to her. "Oh…thanks for the ride." She nodded and gave me a small smile. I couldn't shake the feeling that I'd messed up, so that apology finally did seep out of me. "I'm sorry about…" I pointed to her hand that was picking at her jacket sleeve. "I just…I wasn't thinking. I'm sorry if that made you uncomfortable."

She looked down and I thought I saw a light coloring flush her cheeks, but her hair had fallen down around her face and I couldn't be sure. I resisted the urge to sweep that hair back so I could see her better. "It's fine, Lucas. I liked it…" I felt a lingering "but" in the air, but she didn't say anything else. That non-explanation filled the car with a strange tension and I opened my door to break it. She finally looked back up at me when I did.

I put one foot out the door and paused, looking back at her. "I know you have to go, but…do you want to come in?" I grinned at her. "After all, you're already in trouble."

She smiled a little and then looked down at her hand…*the* hand. "No, I better not push it." She looked back up at me. "I'll see you tomorrow, Lucas."

I had the sudden feeling that she would have said yes if that awkward moment in the car hadn't happened, and a strange guilt washed through me. I looked down at my foot on the pavement before swinging my head back around to her waiting gray eyes. "Okay. See you, Sawyer." I started to stand and then stopped, settling my weight back down in the car seat. "Thank you…for today. I don't think I'd have made it without you." I smiled warmly on the end and she returned it, her eyes searching my face.

I wondered what she was looking for, when she finally replied. "You're welcome, Luc…any time." She sighed, and then her roaming eyes settled on mine. I smiled, nodded and started to exit the car. I was halfway standing when she spoke.

"Luc?" I turned in the door. "Do you want me to pick you up in the morning? So you don't have to walk," she quickly added.

I perked up at the thought of spending more time with her *and* not having to walk all the way to school again tomorrow. Plus the added bonus of not hopping on another bus, should the weather take a turn for the worse. "I'd love that…thank you."

Her bright smile matched my own and I jauntily exited the car and shut it. I was grinning and waving goodbye like an idiot when she pulled out of the drive and sped away, back towards town. I wondered where she lived for a moment and then, shoving my hands in my pockets, turned and made my way inside my small house for an exciting night of doing homework, watching bland television shows, and maybe for dinner, just for something different…ham and cheese Hot Pockets.

Chapter 5 – And Things Had Started Out So Well…

I stirred in my bed and sighed as the rustle of the sheets brought me to consciousness. I knew it was dark, still in the middle of the night, and didn't bother with opening my eyes. As I moved my legs under the covers, I collided with another pair of legs. Confused, I reached out with my hand and indeed felt another pair of long, bare, shapely legs. Even more confused, I followed those legs up to a very firm backside. My hand slipped over what could only be my favorite pair of silky bikini panties.

I smiled at the remembered cut of them, the way they'd looked against ivory flesh, the light pink color with one giant, red heart in the back and the word 'love' in red script across the front. My fingers ran around to the front and I felt where the different fabric of the word stood out against the silk. A soft feminine sigh met my searching hand and I adjusted my body to feel more of the person lying next to me. My hands ran up a bare stomach and my body responded instantly. I felt the quick inhales and exhales as my hand ran up her naked skin. I felt the light breath on my face and heard a soft moan in my ear. I bit my lip and continued on up, hoping to find what I knew was typically paired with that sexy underwear. My fingers ran over the fabric covering a breast. I traced two letters on one side of the bra 'L' and 'O', then my hand moved over to feel the other silky cup. Sure enough—'V' and 'E'.

I pressed my incredibly ready body right up against the figure beside me. I was rewarded with lean legs tangling over mine and a warm hand on my lower back pulling me in tight. I groaned as our lower halves connected. My hands continued on up from that amazingly sexy bra to a slender neck; I could feel the heartbeat raging in her veins as I brought my lips to them. The familiar scent of perfume mixed with peach body wash filled me. My hands went up even farther to tangle in long, silky hair and a low, passionate exhale escaped soft lips as my tongue found a sensitive spot in the crook of her neck, a spot I knew very well.

Small hands came up my back, under my t-shirt, and clutched at my bare skin as our bodies shifted and moved together, teasing each other, satisfying each other. My lips moved up her fragrant neck and, not able to take it anymore, I hungrily found her eager mouth in the darkness. I pressed against the length of the nearly naked body beside me as my tongue felt for and found its match. My midnight companion returned both of my actions readily and let a loud moan escape into the still air.

"Quiet, Lil, you'll wake my mom," I muttered between our lips.

"Sorry, Luc…that just feels amazing," she breathily muttered back.

I smiled and rolled her onto her back, pressing my hard body firmly into hers. I knew exactly what felt amazing to her; this was something we'd done several times. In fact, we'd done this very thing a couple of nights before the accident, when I'd been awoken from a deep sleep to find Lillian undressed and in bed with me.

Oh, wait…we'd done this exact thing, even right down to the underwear. I pulled back from her lips.

"I'm dreaming again…aren't I?" I finally opened my eyes and looked at the vision of a blonde goddess, biting her lip and writhing beneath me as our bodies pressed together.

Her hands reached up to tangle in my hair as she pulled me in for a kiss that left me aching. "Yes…God, yes," she muttered. I had no idea if she was answering my question or being…satisfied. And with the look on her face, I really didn't care. My dream of her weeks ago paled in comparison with this one, and even though I knew waking from this would kill me, I eagerly returned her deep kiss and decided the pain would be worth it if I got to feel *this* again.

Her hands reached down to pull off my shirt and I let her. There was an eagerness in our desire to be as naked as we could with each other and I found the lounge pants I'd slept in quickly discarded beside the bed with my shirt. Our bodies hungered for each other as small gasps and moans filled the air. She shushed me and on occasion, more than a few actually, I shushed her.

We'd done all of this before. Lil had a habit of sneaking out of her bed and into mine. It was a habit I greatly enjoyed. She'd appeared in next to nothing a few times and had driven me nearly to madness, but we'd never gone all the way. While we'd both said we weren't ready, during moments like these, I think it was only the fact that my mom was down the hall and we were afraid we'd wake her that had stopped those intimate sessions from being our first time together, our first time ever.

Not that we hadn't experimented. Not that we hadn't brought each other to release. We'd just never technically had sex. As our bodies frantically rubbed together, and I realized none of this was even real, I began to wonder why we couldn't now. We wouldn't wake my mom up in a dream…and it felt so real…

My hands slid down her smooth skin to her underwear, and I started slipping them off. Her hands quickly found mine and stopped me. "No," she breathed. "I'm not ready for that." Her legs wrapped more firmly around mine and she pulled our hips together. "Like this, just like this. I'll be quiet…promise."

I groaned softly as I realized that I was pretty close to finishing already. "I want more, Lil. I want all of you."

She kissed me and sped up her hips, maybe hoping to speed up the finale so I couldn't convince her otherwise. "Not yet, Luc…soon, but not yet."

My mind shifted back to a similar conversation that I'd had with the real Lillian. "Why not? We're so close, Lil. I'm so ready for you. I want to please you like that. Don't you want to?"

Her back arched and her head fell back. "Oh, yes…God, yes." As she let out a moan, I moved to pull down her underwear…but I was too late. With a muffled cry into my shoulder she hit her peak. Seeing that, hearing it, knowing that I'd done that to her…well, damn if I didn't hit mine too. I gave up on her underwear and slumped over her body, shuddering as I rode out the sensation with her.

Breathless, I pulled back to look at her. I stroked her hair back from her face and softly kissed her. "God, Lil, that was…but…we could have…"

She bit her lip and shook her head. "I'm not ready, Lucas."

"But this is my dream. You're still not ready, even in my dream?"

"I know, Luc, I'm sorry. At least I can give you this." She slung her hands around my neck as I rolled off to her side. She frowned as she looked me over. "You shouldn't be dreaming of me, Luc, especially like this. This won't help you move past me."

I blinked at her. "Why would I want to move past you?" I kissed her nose. "I like being with you. This is better than anything that's happening to me in the real world. If I could never wake up…I'd be so happy."

She immediately pulled away from me. "Don't say that." She pushed me away from her and confused, I attempted to pull her back towards me. Nimbly, she slipped away and stood up at the side of the bed. "Don't ever say that again." She put her hands on her hips in a way that was supposed to be threatening, but really, was just endearing. "Or I won't come back." She raised her chin defiantly and a soft chuckle escaped me.

Lillian narrowed her eyes at me until I conceded. "Fine. I hope I wake up soon and join the ranks of brooding teenagers worldwide."

She smiled and then immediately frowned. "Oh…sorry. Goodbye, Lucas."

"Goodbye? What do you--?"

A sharp, high-pitched buzzing in my ear woke me from my dream and shattered my conversation with Lillian. I slammed a hand down on the stupid alarm clock and looked over to where Lil had been standing with her hands on her hips. Instead of the pitch black of night, a pale morning light lit my room…that was completely empty.

I hadn't expected to have a dream like that about her. Grief welled up in me but after a long moment, I managed to push it back. No, that had been nice, more than nice, and I wasn't going to grieve over a nice memory. Besides, it had felt so real…maybe I'd found a way to be with her again. God, that sounded insane. But still, it felt so real. I'd felt her body again. I'd heard her moans again. I'd watched her glorious release. I'd… Oh, damn it.

I carefully felt around myself and, sure enough, some things that happen in dreams also happen in real life. I sighed irritably and got up to take a shower. Oh well, it was still a pleasant dream, and I wasn't about to cry over it, though I did let loose a couple tears in the shower.

After cleaning and dressing, I shuffled out to the kitchen for a cup of coffee with Mom. As per our usual routine, she asked me general questions about how things were going. I gave her general responses that things were going fine.

School had been in session for a few weeks now and while the student body hadn't exactly warmed up to me, I had become less of an object of interest and more of a forgotten relic in the back row. That suited me fine. If they were ignoring me, they wouldn't talk to me. And if they weren't talking to me, they wouldn't ask me painful questions that I didn't want to answer, questions that I'd endured too often in that first week of school, when more of the kids like Eliza and Gabriela had become braver and flat-out asked me if I (A) remembered anything and (B) was drunk. I always said no to both and hoped they dropped it.

Eventually I faded into the back of their consciousness. Everyone's except Josh and Will's that is. They still picked on me relentlessly. Will took every opportunity to make me look like an idiot, questioning the class loudly about my actions or even trying to cause me physical harm with more "accidents." It was annoying, but I did my best to ignore it, hoping he would eventually get bored with his game and give up.

Josh…he was still determined to kick my ass, but never seemed to have a free moment to do it. Being new to the football team probably helped with keeping him occupied. It also helped that his girlfriend caught him with his hands all over some cheerleader's ass after practice one day. I'd heard that the fight was a blowout and would have made any fight between us seem civil in comparison. While I had nothing against Josh's girlfriend (she ignored me for the most part when she wasn't pulling Josh away from me), I was glad for Josh's meandering hands. Better him groping some cheerleader's backside, than permanently damaging our friendship—if it wasn't already permanently damaged.

Mom and I sipped our coffees in silence, facing each other at the tiny table in our tiny kitchen. Her work hadn't let up any and she still looked tired and haggard. I suppose a good chunk of that was her still worrying about me, about how I was reintegrating into society. I wanted to assure her that everything was fine, so I tried to slap on a genuine smile around her. She didn't seem to buy it, but at the same time, she didn't argue with it, giving me my space to grieve.

And I *was* still grieving.

My visions of my friends were still with me. I remembered conversations I had with them around every corner of school. I remembered tackling Darren on the front lawn, having a rousing snowball fight with Sammy, when a soft spattering on the ground had greeted us as we exited a class last year, and…I remembered Lil. I sighed into my coffee cup as I set it down on the table. Eventually, I'd started adding her memories into the mix. Hers hurt the most, of course, and they'd been the most insistent to pop up. Giving in, I'd swallowed the painful lump and let her memories wash over me. Tears had stung my eyes the first few times it happened and Sawyer's calming hand on my arm would snap me out of whatever vision I'd been lost in.

But over time, the memories didn't cause me as much pain, and visions of us together filtered through my day: leaning against the wall with her in my arms while we watched kids go by in the hall, chucking gummy bears at each other as we studied in the library, her teasing me with those tiny, tight shorts when I'd come watch her finish up practice. I remembered her breath, her smell, her laugh, her eyes, her love…a love never spoken out loud, but evident in every move she made around me.

But the most intense memories were in dream form and this morning was definitely the most intense of them all. It was in dreams when she seemed alive again. If I was having a good dream, we'd spend it talking, laughing…and kissing. Last night was a very good one. As strange as it sounds, I was starting to live for those moments when I was asleep.

Deep in thought, I turned my coffee cup in my hands. A short honk broke the silence. I started and looked out the window. Sawyer's Camaro was idling in the drive, just like it was every morning when she came to pick me up. I stood up, grabbed my bag, and gave my mom a kiss on the head. She stood as well and walked with me to the door.

"Have a good day, Lucas." Her eyes drifted over my features, studying me.

I paused, letting her soak me in, and a momentary sadness filled me that she still needed to do that every time we parted ways. "You too, Mom." I gave her a brief hug and opened the door to meet Sawyer.

"She could come in sometime," my mom said as I walked out the door. She peered outside and waved at Sawyer's form in the car. Sawyer waved back. "I don't bite," she finished.

I laughed and looked back at her. "I know, Mom. We're just…running late. Another time, okay?"

She nodded and leaned in to kiss my cheek. I let her and then walked over to Sawyer's car and climbed inside. Sawyer's jet black hair was pulled back into a neat ponytail and my name across her back stood out clearly. I tried not to worry about that. The school had definitely associated her with me now, since we were rarely apart, and if they picked on her for it, well, she never let me see more than the occasional frown and a quick swipe of an eye.

Her pale eyes looked past me, to my mom still watching from the door. She put the car in reverse and quietly said, "Your mom seems really nice."

I leaned back and looked over at her. "She is. You should meet her sometime."

She backed into the road and shifted her car into drive. "Umm…sure. Maybe...sometime." She bit her lip. "Parents…make me nervous." She glanced at the smirk on my face and giggled, her ponytail bouncing with her laugh.

I shook my head and smiled at her. She'd resisted coming over to my house after school, even though I asked her practically every day. She always said her parents wanted her home right after our "purity club" meetings, but I often wondered if she just didn't *want* to come over, and was using that as her excuse. When she picked me up in the morning, she always honked for me but never came in. My mom wondered about that, too, and I tried to give her plausible explanations…which were almost always, "We're running late." I'm sure my mom knew we had plenty of time for the relatively short drive, but she didn't question my answer. She rarely did.

I turned my head to watch the town go by while Sawyer turned the music up. I wasn't sure what Sawyer was so reluctant about, but I didn't press her on it. If she really wanted to come over, she would. And aside from the weekends, when I became one with my couch, we did spend a lot of time together, at school and after.

We'd both stuck with the club; her, because her parents demanded it, for some reason, and me, because I liked spending time with her. There were meetings three times a week that usually turned into "troubled teen" group therapy sessions. Sawyer and I usually tuned them out as we whispered away in the corner of the room, much to Ms. Reynolds's annoyance. Outside of those meetings, the club met twice a week at "events." These were usually practices for one of the many sports teams, from where the teachers seemed to think the problems stemmed. Unfortunately, these events brought me in close proximity with people who didn't much care for me; Josh, Randy, Will and the rest of the football team. I hid on the back row of the bleachers with Sawyer while the rest of the club members walked up and down the field, trying in vain to recruit more members.

I shook my head at the memory of Josh glaring at me during the last event. He'd stared at me the entire time, like I'd amassed this group of people personally, just to bug him. If Coach hadn't been there, eyeing me with almost as much interest as Josh, since he still hadn't managed to corner me into that "talk" he'd wanted, I'm sure Josh would have tried to start something.

Sawyer noticed me shaking my head in the car. "You all right?" She seemed to ask me some form of this question nearly every day.

I smiled and looked back over at her. "Yeah, I'm good."

The only reason I put up with all of it was to hang out more with her. Our little purity club gave me an extra hour and a half with her and that was one more hour and a half that I didn't have to spend alone. She brought me so much comfort. I only wished I could return the favor.

"Are you sure? Did you have a bad dream again?" She said that last part quietly and I cringed in my head.

She had picked me up once when I'd awoken late from a particularly bad dream. No, nightmare was a more appropriate description. I'd still been a crying, blubbery mess when I'd shuffled out to her car. Mom had wanted to pull me that day, but I'd wanted to be with Sawyer, so I sucked it up and went to school. I'd only been able to tell her that I'd had a bad dream. Sawyer hadn't asked for any more details. She knew that any dream I had that brought me to my knees could only be about one thing—and she didn't need an explanation of that.

I shook my head at her question. "No, I had a pretty good dream." I flushed as I said that, remembering my steamy fantasy. Sawyer gave me a curious look but thankfully didn't ask for any explanations on that, either.

"Good. I'd rather your dreams were nice. You should get a release somewhere."

I bit my lip and looked out the window as my blush deepened. Luckily, Sawyer was looking back out the windshield and didn't notice.

God, nice choice of words. I sighed softly, running through this morning again in my mind. That had been one realistic dream. If separating from the dream hadn't been painful, even though I'd tried not to make it be that way, I'd damn near say that dream had been…amazing. I closed my eyes and leaned my head back on the seat, reliving that moment…reliving Lil.

"Luc?"

Sawyer's voice startled me, and I lifted my head to look around the school parking lot. I looked over to her pale eyes studying me; her head was slightly cocked, like she was wondering if I'd left my body for a while. I wondered how long we'd been sitting here while I'd been reminiscing about being with Lillian again. My body had felt warm and safe in that dream. I shuddered a bit as the chill of the quiet car hit me, and I wished I could crawl right back into that warm dream.

"Sorry…spacing out." She looked about ready to ask if I was okay again and I interrupted her by cracking open my door and saying, "Ready?"

She nodded and cracked open her door as well. We both exited and made our way across campus to the main building for first period English. We still attracted stares as people watched us, but no one said anything or did anything to bother us. We were noticed with distaste and then disregarded. I was relieved for that, but as I looked down on Sawyer, I wondered if things would be better for her if she distanced herself from me, too. Maybe she'd have more of a social life here if she wasn't always hanging around the pariah.

She looked back up at me and smiled warmly, not caring in the least about the student body's reaction, not if she got to walk with me. That's what I liked to think that she thought anyway. Forgetting that I shouldn't, for her sake, I slung my arm over her shoulder and pulled her tight to me. This morning had started pretty wonderfully, and maybe I could relax today and let the rest of it be…well…not sucky would be an improvement. Sawyer stiffened under my almost intimate move, but then relaxed and slung her arm around my waist. Warmth seeped into me, strangely reminding me of my dream. Before I could analyze it further, though, I noticed Josh and Will. I couldn't help but notice them…they were blocking our path.

I stopped and took a step in front of Sawyer, breaking our contact. Whatever these guys wanted, it had nothing to do with her, and I wouldn't let them hurt her. I had no desire to fight them, but I would if it meant protecting Sawyer. Josh looked over my shoulder at Sawyer and made a disgusted face. I bristled at the look and struggled to keep my anger in check. I didn't need to be the one starting something. I needed to get through this year in peace, with nothing too damaging on my record.

"What do you want, Josh?" My eyes flicked over to Will, wondering what role he'd play in all of this. He crossed his arms over his chest and smirked at me, but said nothing.

A small circle of students started to form around us, feeling the tension building in the air. I cursed silently. If Josh hadn't planned on fighting me before, he might do it now that he had an audience. On the other hand, he wouldn't want to get kicked off the football team, and Coach had a strict policy on fighting. If he punched first…he was out. I straightened from where I'd unknowingly been crouching in anticipation. He wasn't going to attack me, not like this anyway. He couldn't afford to.

He sniffed and frowned as he seemed to realize this too. Then a devilish smile lit his face with a dark glow. I swallowed under that look, wondering what it meant. "Have a good day at school, Lucas." His brows rose meaningfully as his voice darkened to match his eyes. "You deserve it."

Then he turned and brushed past, bumping my shoulder and jostling me back a step into Sawyer. I risked a quick glance at her and she looked about ready to go off on Josh. I didn't want her getting into trouble for me and quickly shook my head at her when our eyes met. She understood and bit her lip to remain quiet, her arms crossed defiantly over her chest.

I looked back to see Will uncrossing his arms and straightening his stance. He stood there with a crooked grin as he watched me. He didn't make any threatening moves towards Sawyer or me. He just continued to stand there. Feeling uneasy but wanting to leave, I carefully walked around him.

I should have expected it, I really should have. I did know he had the maturity level of a kindergartner, but I'd truthfully been more concerned about the dark expression on Josh's face—that had definitely meant something—and I didn't notice Will's foot. I didn't catch it rapidly snaking out to catch mine and he did have fast feet. That made him a good replacement for me on the football field. Unfortunately, it was also my downfall this morning…literally.

I caught the edge of his toes with mine and stumbled. He raised his foot higher and I felt myself lose balance. Before I lost it completely, a shoulder went under mine and a hand steadied my chest. I fumbled a bit, but managed to not fall. My face heated anyway as the small circle still loitering, hoping for a fight, found my near trip-up hilarious.

Sawyer did not. After completely steadying me, she dropped her bag at my feet and shoved both hands into a laughing Will's chest. "Grow up, you son of a bitch!"

He started at the unexpected outburst and then his face clouded in anger. He stepped into her attack and leered down at her. "Oh, the juvy whore has a voice." He looked like he wanted to shove her back, but didn't go so far as to start something with a girl. Instead, he held her wrists down and looked over her wildly thrashing body to me, standing dazed behind her. "Getting your slut to fight your battles for you, Luc?" He rocked his hips towards her suggestively. "Maybe I should tap this too. She's kind of hot, in a fiery, bitchy sort of way." He looked back at her with a leer while the students around laughed even harder. Seriously, where was a teacher when you needed one?

My face heated more, but in anger this time. I took a step towards Will, already bringing my arm back for the strike I was committed to. I'd get in trouble to protect her. Sawyer didn't need me to though. She managed to wrench an arm free and flat out decked him. No girly slap across the face—she clenched her hand into a tight fist and socked him right in the jaw.

He released her, stepping back in shock and bringing a hand up to rub his injury. His eyes held pure fury now. Sawyer took a step away from him, massaging her hand. I took advantage of the space between them and stepped up to Will, shoving him farther back from Sawyer with both of my hands against his chest.

"Gonna hit a girl now, Will? Is that where you're going? Coach would love that…wonder how long you'll *stay* quarterback." Will paled as my words sank in, and he suddenly realized that fighting Sawyer, or me, was not in his best interest. He spat at my feet and turned, trudging towards the main building.

I sighed as I watched him leave. We'd be seeing him again in a few minutes;

one of the major drawbacks of attending a small school. So much for my not-sucky day. Well, maybe the worst was over with. Sawyer came up behind me and put a hand on my arm. The crowd began to disperse as people started to realize that no one, meaning me, was going to get knocked to the ground.

I looked over at Sawyer and her hand that had to be aching. I pointed at it. "Are you okay? Want to stop by the nurse's station?"

"No, I'm fine." She smiled impishly. "It's not my first time hitting an asshole."

I raised an eyebrow at that and she laughed a little at my look. She nodded towards the front doors. With another sigh, I nodded and reached down to grab her bag for her. Then we both continued on to first period English. We got some looks as we headed down the hall but we ignored them; we were used to looks. True, the kids were slightly more interested in us now than they had been of late, thanks to Josh and Will's testosterone display outside, but if Sawyer and I were getting good at anything, it was tuning the world out.

Trudging up the stairs, I noticed she was still rubbing her hand. "Are you sure you're all right?" I asked, as I reached over and grabbed her hand, taking over the massage.

She looked up at me and then down at our hands for a long moment before she answered. "Sure, it feels better already." She grinned. "Totally worth it."

I grinned back, gave her a brief hug around the shoulders, and released her hand. "Well, thank you for your valiant attempt to defend my honor." I smirked when I said that, momentarily remembering a dream version of Lil threatening to beat up Josh. Lil would probably love Sawyer for clocking Will.

Coming to the top of the steps, Sawyer stopped and looked over my face. Perhaps misinterpreting my expression, she frowned. "I just cost you cool points, didn't I?"

I laughed. "You think I still have cool points? I'm pretty sure I lost all of those when I kill…" I closed my mouth and bit my lip. *When I killed all my friends. When I killed all their friends.*

Sawyer's eyes widened as what I hadn't finished saying registered with her. She started shaking her head and had an expression of "Don't talk like that," clearly written on her face.

Before the after school special could begin, I grabbed her hand and led her to English. She didn't like it when I said stuff like that…truth was hard, but, I didn't need a lecture this morning. I'd be getting enough of those by the teachers.

Not resisting my pull to class, but still having an "I want to talk to you" look on her face, Sawyer and I entered the room together, hand in hand.

Several sets of eyes tracked the intimate movement, a gesture generally reserved for boyfriend/girlfriend behavior. But we weren't; it was different with us. I didn't want to care what the students here thought. Hell, I was pretty sure they all thought we were sleeping together, anyway, but I did care about Sawyer getting picked on, so I dropped her hand and made a beeline to my seat, carefully avoiding a stormy-looking Will.

I looked over at Sawyer as she sat in the back row with me; she studiously ignored me, studying her desk. I wasn't sure what that meant. Was she still thinking about things to say to me? I hoped not. I didn't need a lesson on cheeriness. She usually didn't try to offer me any, either. She just seemed to instinctively know when to press and when to back off, when to ask me questions and when to walk away. But right now, she looked like something was troubling her.

Ms. Reynolds started class by giving us details on a pep rally today after last period. All classes were going to be fifteen minutes shorter so we could all gather together in the gym to celebrate the "can't miss" football game of the season against our school rivals—meaning they happened to be the closest school next to us and had thus been deemed "the enemy".

I tried to ignore Ms. Reynolds's speech about how great the game would be and how school spirit can make you feel like a part of something bigger. I had been a part of something bigger, and a part of me still missed that. I missed the games and the camaraderie of the team. I missed Darren sitting beside me on the bench, waiting for our turn on the field so he could score the winning touchdown. Well, that's how he always thought the game was going to end.

Returning my focus to the present, I twisted in my seat to face Sawyer. She heard my movement and looked over. "What's up?" I mouthed to her. She shook her head and I frowned.

She looked down real quick and then back up at me. "Nothing," she mouthed back. I frowned harder and crossed my arms. She sighed and held out her palm. I glanced at it and back to her, confused. She sighed again while Ms. Reynolds prattled on about school pride and the joy of experiencing it "substance free".

"You dropped it," she mouthed, as she pointed to her hand.

I was hopelessly confused until I realized what she meant. I'd dropped her hand as the students had been staring at us. I suppose that could have looked like rejection to her…especially if she thought we were more than just close friends. Damn, I really didn't want to have that awkward conversation, but I really couldn't let her go on thinking there was anything between us; nothing more than a close, almost familial, bond that I couldn't bear to have taken from me. I loved her…just not like *that.* My heart was still Lil's.

I started to speak, breaking our silent speech so I could break her heart, if she *had* fallen for me.

She beat me to it however. "Are you…mad at me?" she whispered. "Did I do something wrong?"

I'd hurt her feelings, made her think I was angry? I immediately shook my head once I realized where her head was at. "No." I indicated the room with my eyes. "Everyone was staring at us, at you. I didn't want them looking at you like that and whispering about you, about us."

She laughed quietly and her face relaxed as she realized I had no bad feelings toward her. "Luc, they already talk about us." She shrugged her shoulders like it didn't matter. "I've already been pregnant, had a miscarriage and begged you to marry me." She leaned in while my eyes widened; I'd assumed we'd been linked sexually, but I hadn't actually heard the rumors. Only the ones about my lack of sobriety seemed to make it to me. Maybe I was just starting to tune out ones that didn't revolve solely around me. Wow, how narcissistic.

Sawyer continued when I leaned over to her, "From what I hear, Mr. Varner caught us full-on having sex in the first floor men's room after school one afternoon." She giggled a little while my mouth dropped; the rumors were much more sordid than I'd imagined they'd be. "Of course, then the rumors say he joined us."

I laughed out loud to that and got a firm reprimand from Ms. Reynolds while Sawyer chuckled softly beside me. Muttering an apology to the teacher, I glanced over at where Sawyer was still laughing. She met my eyes and the genuine happiness in her pale, gray ones lifted my spirits back up. This morning didn't matter, because here was one human being that looked at me, not only like I was worthwhile, but like I was the most worthwhile person in the school.

As we went about our English class, I thought over the rumors circulating about us and wondered what I could do about them. It didn't seem to bother Sawyer in the slightest, but I really didn't want her to suffer because of me. And the nature of the rumors… I caught Sawyer glancing up at me a few times during class and thought her expression was close to one Lil used to give me, almost dreamy. Maybe we'd have to have that awkward conversation after all.

As we parted ways for the next class, I wondered how to bring it up to her. Maybe I should talk to my mom first. She'd been a looker in her youth, and had probably swatted away more than one suitor. Not that I was a looker…although, before Lillian, I'd had my share of girls with crushes. There was this one girl who used to hang out by my locker every day. It used to make Darren laugh really hard, and he'd always teased me to kiss her. He seemed to think that would make her faint and he'd really wanted to see that. Sammy had smacked him when she'd heard his comment. Then she'd calmly walked up to the girl and said a few sentences to her. The girl had nodded and walked off, never to haunt my locker again. I still have no idea what Sammy said to her. I could use a little of Sammy's magic now.

But Sawyer didn't strike me as one of those types, one to crush on a boy simply because he was attractive. Maybe I was wrong about the occasional feeling I got from her. I'd never been friends with a girl before. I mean, Sammy and I were friends, but I'd been friends with Darren first and her and my friendship had been born out of their attraction to each other, and the fact that Darren had hardly gone anywhere without her. Not liking Sammy had just never been an option, not if I wanted to stay friends with Darren. But I *had* genuinely liked her, everyone did. She was my only real experience with female friendships. Maybe I was just reading too much into it. Maybe I was letting the rumors warp the way I imagined Sawyer felt about me. Wow, there was that narcissism again. I'd have to work on that.

By the time I met up with Sawyer again, I'd gotten over myself, and any weirdness between us was completely gone. We were just the normal, friends-only couple that we always were. And I was happy. My happiness stayed with me all the way through Mr. Varner's class, even surviving a blushing incident when I caught a couple of girls staring at the teacher and then back at Sawyer and me. Now that I knew what their smirks meant, my cheeks flamed red hot and I studied my desk for a good twenty minutes, probably confirming their suspicions. Sawyer, catching the whole exchange, chuckled beside me.

My good feelings stayed with me all through Philosophy, Math, and lunch in Sawyer's car. They stayed with me right up until the point where I had a class with Josh. Then they sort of faded from me. Well, faded is too relaxed of a word. They were crashed out of me by Josh forcefully slamming into me.

When I'd walked into Astronomy, the teacher, Mr. Thomson, had been absent, running late to class or off on some quick errand. Either way, he'd left us alone. I should have immediately noticed that something was wrong by the multiple sets of eyes watching me through the windows as I walked up to the door. That should have been a red flag, but I was so used to people eyeing me, that it didn't even faze me.

What happened next did.

I opened the door like normal, and it shut behind me like normal. That was when normalcy stopped. I'd walked a few feet into the room when a "hut-hut" was sounded down one of the aisles. I turned my head to see Randy making the sound, a wicked grin on his face. I wasn't sure why until I was hit full force in the chest, landing heavily on the cold tile of the floor. The wind was knocked out of me and my head slammed back with a crack that surely even the kids in the last row must have heard. My hazy vision picked out the form of Josh on my chest sneering at me. He pressed down with all his weight so I still couldn't inhale. I couldn't breathe and my sight was shifting from hazy to gray to black around the edges. I was going to pass out.

With a pained grunt, I shoved at Josh as hard as I could. I was weak and hurting from the sudden attack, but Josh was smaller than me and I was starting to panic from lack of air. I pushed him off of me and sweet oxygen seared my lungs. My vision returned slowly…along with my hearing. Instead of the sound of blood whooshing through my ears and throbbing in my head, I heard laughter, what sounded like the entire room laughing.

Josh was standing in front of me, bent over he was laughing so hard. Carefully, I looked around. I noticed most, but not all, were laughing along with him. I rubbed my head and sat up, trying to steady my breath. Panicked voices started from the back and filtered up to me. People started shifting and sitting in the seats, still struggling with giggles. I started to stand when Josh walked over and shoved me back down before heading to his seat. My dazed body couldn't respond fast enough to stop him, and I sat back down with a thud.

"Fuck you, Josh," I snapped…right as the teacher entered the room.

"Lucas West! Watch your language or you'll go straight to detention! And get off the floor." Mr. Thomson looked annoyed, for quite possibly the first time I'd ever seen. As hastily as I could, I stood up and grabbed my bag from where it had fallen from my shoulder and crashed to the ground, some of its contents spilling out onto the floor.

I gingerly made my way to my seat, wondering what part of my body hurt worse, my head or my hip. My ego wasn't a problem anymore; it remained firmly attached to the cold, tile floor. Not that I'd had much left to begin with, but still, the entire class laughing at me, and me looking, once again, like a moron…well, it sucked. I kept my eyes glued on my textbook all throughout the lecture, while the occasional bout of giggling popped up around the classroom. Great. How had I ever thought today was even a semi-happy day?

I waited in my seat until all of class shuffled out afterwards. Josh and Randy snickered as they left, Josh throwing me a devilish smile. I hoped whatever he'd felt I'd "deserved" had been accomplished, and he'd leave me alone for a while. The teacher gave me a last reproachful look as I left his room, muttering an apology for my earlier outburst. With no one staying behind to further torment me, I made my way to art class in peace.

We'd finished our "feels like home" projects a while ago and I'd turned in a nice portrait of Sawyer that had actually earned me an A. Last year, I'd planned on art being an easy, goofing off class for Darren, Sammy, Lil and me, but I found that I actually had a knack for it. Mrs. Solheim praised whatever piece I turned in, offering a few suggestions and helpful comments, although she still, more often than not, called me Tom. I even found myself responding to the name on more than a few occasions.

Currently, we were working on abstract art, and I was working in varying shades of gray that highly complemented Sawyer's eyes. I usually painted or drew something that reminded me of her; it made the class more enjoyable for me than trying to channel my artistic feelings toward my dead friends. Sawyer was peace. Sawyer was comfort. And I hoped against all hope that when I saw Sawyer after class, she'd have something to help with the splitting headache that Josh had given me when he smacked my skull into the floor.

Mrs. Solheim walked around the class while other students diligently worked on their projects, offering tips for emphasizing the style. She passed by me and patted my shoulder, muttering, "Good work, Tom." I smiled and bit back a chuckle as she continued walking through the room.

Halfway through the class, I felt like dying. A tender spot on the back of my head was throbbing, and every pulse of blood made my forehead feel like it was trying to expand outwards…and failing. I was sure something inside of me was broken.

Biting my lip and stopping myself from asking for a pass to see the nurse, I somehow made it through the rest of that class. I shuffled out, rubbing my temples, and came upon Sawyer outside of the building, waiting for me. Her jet black hair was still in a sleek ponytail and she had her hands shoved in my letterman's jacket pockets. She was looking back at the choir room, chewing a piece of gum and watching Brittany leave the class with a handful of fawning girls, most of them in their cheerleader outfits for the pep rally.

I walked up beside her and glumly said, "Hey." She started from whatever she was thinking about and looked over at my cringing face.

"God, you look like shit. What happened?" Her eyes roved over my body, searching for some external injury.

I sighed and squeezed the bridge of my nose, hoping to somehow stop the pounding. "Oh, I just had a run-in…with the floor."

"The floor? Huh?"

I dropped my hand from my nose and adjusted the strap of my backpack on my shoulder. "It was nothing, just Josh proving that he's big man on campus now…and he hates my guts." I shook my head, which caused pain to slice all the way down my shoulders. "Nothing I didn't already know."

Her mouth dropped as she gaped at me. "He attacked you? In *class*?" Her hands came to my head, feeling around for bumps. I sucked in a breath when she found the tender spot on the back.

I gently removed her hands. "It's fine. He just sort of tackled me and I smacked my head. I'm fine, really. It was more embarrassing than anything, him catching me off guard like that."

"That little prick!" Her jaw set in anger, and for a moment I worried that she was going to try and find Josh to get even. Then her face relaxed as she looked over me again. "We should get you to the nurse. You could have a concussion."

I chuckled and she twisted her lips at me. "I don't think he hit me that hard. I could use some Advil or something. I have a raging headache."

Her face brightened. "Oh, I have Aspirin."

She dug through her bag while I reached back in mine and grabbed the half empty water bottle from my lunch. She found a little white container and opening it, dug out a couple of pills. I popped them without looking and swigged my drink. "Thanks," I muttered after polishing off the rest of my water. My body hoped the damn things kicked in soon.

"Sure." She looked me over again, almost looking like my mom for a moment. Then she grabbed my elbow and pulled me toward the gym. I gave her an odd look. She sighed, then explained, "The purity club is promoting safety at the rally. We're all supposed to be there, encouraging kids to join in the 'clean' fun." She looked glum as she pulled me towards the rally.

"And why aren't we just skipping it?" I asked, equally glum.

"Because my parents found out about it and think it's a great idea." She gave me a dry look. "They told Ms. Reynolds to call if I ditched. Apparently, she agreed." She rolled her eyes.

I repeated the gesture, but I followed her. If she had to sit through hell, I'd sit with her. We entered the gym, and I took in the familiarity of it with a pang. I clearly saw a vision of Sammy and Lillian goofing off on one of the bleachers that lined the lacquered floor. Darren, proudly wearing his football jersey, was standing on the floor in front of them, cupping his hands and shouting at the cheerleaders to flip their skirts up. Sammy smacked his ass, laughing at his display. She rolled her eyes at Lillian, who was waving across the gym to where I'd been about to walk over to them in my memory.

"Luc?" I looked over at Sawyer watching me. "Are you okay? Does your head feel better?"

I gave her a small smile and nodded. My headache *was* receding. Actually, I was starting to feel really nice, almost light and airy. I smiled wider and put my hand on her shoulder. She nodded back at me, and we started walking down the line of bleachers to the end. I heard several derogatory shouts at me, coming both from the stands and the floor, where the team was gathering for the event, but I ignored them. I felt nice and I was going to hold on to that feeling for as long as I could.

There were enough teachers and staff around that we made it to the far side of the gym without being accosted. We waved at Ms. Reynolds as we passed her, so she'd know we were here; then we snuck past the other purity club members and ducked into the slim space between the last section of bleachers and the wall. Once there, we slumped against the wall to sit on the floor. I leaned my head back and closed my eyes, waiting for the swelling of school spirit to be over with.

Resting like that, my head started to swim, and I felt a little dizzy as the music of the band piped up and was answered with a resounding roar from the student body. The students on the bleachers directly across from where we were sitting on the floor starting hollering and stomping their feet; the pep rally had begun. I suddenly didn't care that we were here...here was nice. As the sounds of someone on a microphone introducing members of the team filled my ears, I reached over and grabbed Sawyer's hand.

I smiled as my head drifted into a pleasant fog...*here* was very nice.

Chapter 6 – Strike One

Soft. Smooth. Small. Perfect.

My fingers traced lines over Sawyer's hand. Peace washed over my body as my huge smile spread even farther. Over the noise of the loud gym, I heard Sawyer's musical voice asking me if I was feeling better.

Hmmm…I was, so much better. I nodded at her and noticed how disconnected that movement felt from the rest of my body. It was almost like my head wasn't mine. I chuckled at the thought and did it again.

I laughed again and turned my head side to side, enjoying how light and sluggish it felt. It was like my brain was two seconds behind my head. I giggled and looked over in Sawyer's direction. Slowly opening my eyes, I saw Sawyer knitting her eyebrows together. The look wasn't at all like the peace I felt, and wanting her to relax, I brought my hands up and tried to smooth out the worry lines. I cupped her cheeks and stretched my thumbs over her brows and forehead. Her brows knitted further as I tried to flatten them and I laughed again. Her skin was like silk under my fingertips and I gave up on trying to relax her expression and felt that silkiness with all of my suddenly-sensitive digits.

"Wow, you're perfect," I whispered, my voice feeling slow and slightly slurred. I leaned in closer to her, her breath light on my face as she watched me with wide eyes. "Your skin is so soft, like flower petals." My fingers traced her liquid cheeks, forehead, down the line of her nose, across the fullness of her lips. She inhaled a quick breath at that and I tracked the movement of those lips, mesmerized. I leaned in even closer to her and her scent hit me; a sweet, light perfume that made my mouth water. "You even smell like flowers." I leaned in even closer until our noses touched, my hands still caressing her features. The heat of our flesh together burned all the way through my body, scorched me in sensitive places. "I wonder how you'd taste…"

I leaned in even closer, inching my lips to her full ones. Anticipation filled the space between us and her light breath on my skin stopped. Heat rushed through my body and every part of me felt light and airy, carefree…fearless. I giggled at the feeling and then our lips finally brushed together. She sighed into my skin as we met.

Oh, wow.

Her skin was nothing in comparison to that soft flesh. I wanted more. I wanted that softness everywhere on me. I wanted it now. I moved my hand around to her neck and forcefully pulled her into me, shifting our heads so I could part our lips and sneak my tongue inside her. I was harsh in my eagerness and she pulled away from me. Or tried to; I had a firm grasp on her neck and pulled her back in. I pushed my tongue back in her mouth, tasting her again. She was heaven. She was sweet and soft and enticing and arousing, and I wanted so much more.

"Stop it, Luc!"

My world suddenly shifted backward and confused, I blinked and looked around. Sawyer's mouth was no longer on mine. In fact, she was about two feet away from me, scrunched farther back along the wall, breathing heavily, and looking at me like I was a stranger. "What's wrong with you?" she asked between pants.

I stood up and scrambled away from her. There was nothing wrong with me. My body disagreed. The sudden movement of standing made my head go dizzy and then black. I fell to my knees and landed harshly on the wood of the gym. My breath came out in a rush as my hands fell to the floor. I took a deep, steadying breath and felt small hands clutching my shoulders. Sound rushed to my ears—sounds of the noisy gym, sounds of the band, sounds of the cheerleaders' chants, sounds of Sawyer, asking me something over and over again. My head couldn't separate the pieces. I started to panic.

When my vision started to clear, I stood up more slowly. But my vision swam and twisted almost violently. I couldn't focus on one object for long. I saw Sawyer, looking concerned, and then she shifted to bleachers and blues and whites and a sea of multi-colored shirts. It was making me nauseous. I backed away, away from the bleachers. Sawyer tried to grab my shirt, to stop me, but I pushed her hands away and backed up…onto the court.

The light of the full gym hit me and my eyes felt like watering. I looked over at the sea of faces, not recognizing any of them, and clutched my head, trying to stop the spinning. I couldn't. I started breathing heavier and backed further away, until a giant hoop hovered over my head. I thought I heard my name and laughter, but language was mumbling before reaching my ears and I couldn't make sense of anything.

A long, black ponytail filled my vision, but I was suddenly twisted and facing a short, pixie cut of brown hair. "Lucas?" Arms pulled me back towards the bleachers and I stumbled along, my feet suddenly too big for my body. The short hair in front of me turned to the black hair beside me. "What's wrong with him, Sawyer?" Concern filled both faces and as my head stabilized in one position, I made out Ms. Reynolds in front of me, her slim arms over mine, her svelte body close to me, and my hand hanging tantalizingly close to her hip. A surprising fire shot through me at her nearness.

"I don't know. He said he had a headache earlier…?"

I stepped even closer to Ms. Reynolds and brought my arms around her waist. She was slim and curvy and warm. She made me warm. "Hey, Ms. Reynolds. God, you're hot, totally fuckable." I leaned into her, so our heads were touching. My words were still slurred and slow, but she apparently heard me just fine…along with everyone in the bleachers near us. A simultaneous gasp echoed around me and Ms. Reynolds pulled back and went about three shades of red.

Just as my sluggish head was wondering what I'd said that was so wrong, Ms. Reynolds brought her hand up like she was going to slap me. I blinked and tried to focus on her hand and then the hand relaxed and dropped back down to her side. Not saying a word, she extracted herself from my arms and grabbed my wrist, dragging me out of the gym. We passed all of the bleachers again on our way out, but I barely noticed. I could only stare entranced at the lines of the laminate on the ground, while I stumbled and tripped my way after her.

And then suddenly, I was falling. I had no reflexes to speak of, and no way to catch myself, and I landed heavily on the side of my face. Oddly, I didn't feel the impact. I only felt the coolness of the ground beneath me. It actually felt a little nice against my slightly heated skin, so I giggled and stayed where I was on the ground. Other giggling sounds filled my ears and I laughed harder, thinking we all sounded nice together.

Then I felt a pair of arms under me and I was being roughly lifted into the air. The sudden movement made my head swim and my stomach lurch. I tried to vomit, but nothing came out, and I groaned. As I was righted, the upset feeling passed and I breathed out a quick sigh of relief. Then I was shoved forward. Someone behind me said something along the lines of "be gentle" and then firm hands were on my shoulders and I was being guided out of the room.

As the door closed behind me, a mass chorus of laughter broke out. I thought it sounded beautiful, and turned to head back to the sound. I was forcefully re-routed and made to walk down steps and another set of doors, to a chill that made me shiver.

"What's wrong with him?" A black head spoke these words beside me and a warm hand clamped over mine. I held it tight, savoring the heat as the sudden iciness around me made my teeth chatter.

"He's obviously drunk, Miss Smith…are you?" A deep voice behind me said that and I tried to place the voice.

"No, Mr. Varner…and he isn't either. I've been with him most of the day and he hasn't been drinking." I leaned my head into the voice speaking beside me; it was beautiful…like an angel's.

The deep, male voice behind me continued, "Most of the day—not all. He could have sneaked something into his last class." Hands lightly pushed my shoulders and I tripped on my huge feet, almost stumbling to the harsh concrete, before those hands shifted underneath my shoulders, keeping me upright.

The warm hand in mine was joined by its mate and I turned my head to stare at a beautiful set of gray eyes…angel eyes, I was sure. I smiled warmly at her and she frowned. Had I upset my angel? The gray eyes flicked from my face to the voice, behind me. "We'd be able to smell it if he had, and he didn't. I'm telling you, he was fine before the pep rally." Her bottom lip stuck out in a perfect pout and I stopped walking. I wanted to feel that lip again. So soft.

I leaned in to make contact with her and was harshly shoved forward. My feet stumbled, and only the strong arms under me saved me from the cold ground. A long, exasperated sigh sounded from my helper behind me. "Well, he snuck something on the way there. He's obviously not fine now."

The warm hand returned to mine from where it had been jostled free. I clenched it, never wanting that warmth to leave me. The black hair shook side to side while my angel spoke, "No, he didn't. He only had Aspirin…just…just Aspirin."

Another long sigh behind me and a surprisingly feminine sigh on the other side of me. "Right…strong Aspirin then." A hand was taken from supporting me and pointed out between my angel and me, to a distance that seemed so far from me, it could have been a different continent. "Go home, Miss Smith. Ms. Reynolds and I will take care of this." I tried to copy the pointing movement, and automatically fell back into the strong chest behind me. I was shoved forward and the hand returned to my shoulder. The sigh returned as well.

"No, I want to stay with him." My angel's voice was sweet in my ear as she leaned close to me. I turned my head and tried to rest mine on her shoulder, but tripped over a rock instead and nearly plummeted to the ground again.

The voice behind me got stern as hands righted me again. "I wasn't asking…go home!"

"Yes, sir."

Very reluctantly, the warm hand pulled away from me. I panicked. No, my angel couldn't leave me. She made everything okay. My life was okay because of her. If she left me, the darkness would settle in…I knew it. Somehow, it was the only thing my frazzled brain knew for sure—she couldn't leave me.

I pulled away from the strong hands behind me and flung my arms around my angel's waist. "No, no, no, no…please don't send her away. Please don't send my angel away." Hands tried to pull me off and I fought against them with every uncoordinated muscle I had. Tender hands swept my face and a soothing voice cooed that everything would be okay. But everything wouldn't be okay, not if she left. I started to cry. "Please, God…no. Don't take her, too. I need her. Please don't take her away from me, too. You take everyone away."

My arms cinched tight around her and I started to sob into her shoulder. The strong hands stopped trying to separate me from my comfort and soft hands ran up and down my back soothingly. Another set of hands lightly brushed my shoulders. "It's okay, Lucas. She can stay with you…at least until your mom gets here. It's okay."

My sobs stopped as two small hands eased the ache of sudden loneliness in my body. My head relaxed into an even fog of semi-peace and I pulled my head from my angel's damp shoulder to see her face. Her cheeks were as wet as mine felt. I frowned and cupped them in my hands. "No…don't cry. Angels don't cry." We stared at each other for a moment, her gray eyes flicking over my face, looking concerned and scared. I felt happiness surge deep within me and longed to share it with her. Still cupping her face, I leaned in close. "I love you. You mean everything to me…everything." Joy overwhelmed me and I leaned in to feel the softness of her lips again.

Rough hands pulled me back and got me walking toward a boring-looking building. "Jonathan, be careful with him." The other feminine voice sounded displeased at the male one behind me.

"It's getting cold just standing around out here. I'm not just gonna wait while these two make out. I'd like to get home sometime tonight." Hands shoved me forward and I reached out for my solace. She reached back, easily catching up to my shuffling form, and clutching my hand tight. All was right with the world with my angel again by my side.

Time ebbed and flowed around me, none of it making sense and none of it mattering. I had a soft hand in mine, and that was all I focused on. Some part of me was conscious of moving to the nurse's station on the first floor, where something cold and wet was placed in my free hand and a firm voice ordered me to drink it. I laughed at that until a sweeter voice asked me to drink it, and I complied. As the bland beverage hit me, my throat squeezed in sudden thirst and I finished all that was given to me in a matter of seconds. My body was forcefully shoved down onto a hard, flat square and another cold cup was given to me. I drank that one down as well.

A male and female voice shifted away from me and I thought I heard the words "call his mom." I ignored them as the warm hand in mine squeezed me tight and a head lightly rested on my shoulder. I relaxed back onto whatever I'd been placed on, and rested my head on top of the one on my shoulder. I laughed and it felt nice, so I did it again. The head beneath me sighed and shifted to look at me.

"Lucas…what's wrong with you?"

I shrugged, giggled and rested my forehead against hers. "Nothing…I feel great." My words still felt thick in my mouth, and I laughed again and rocked my head against hers.

"What did you take?"

I laughed and tried to think back to some point when I didn't feel like this—light and airy and free. I shrugged again. "I don't know."

A sigh escaped my angel and she looked down. I brought my hand up to her cheek and made her eyes lift to mine, pulling back a little so I could look into them. "Don't be sad…I feel great." I smiled and stroked the soft, silky skin under my thumb.

Her eyes flicked over mine. "Sure, you do now. Call me tomorrow." She sighed again while I obliviously laughed. Then she bit her lip and my eyes focused like laser beams on that soft skin. The lips parted and words escaped them. "I know…I know you're wasted right now…but, did you mean it?"

I nodded. "Yes…mean what?"

She sighed, the air brushing over my face smelling wonderfully of the gum she was still chewing. "When you said you loved me?"

I drew my eyes up to meet hers. "Of course I love you." I shrugged again, loving how wonderful those words sounded out loud. "I love you more than anything. You're my best friend."

She closed her eyes when I said that. "Right…best friend."

I smiled as my eyes focused back down to her soft, soft lips. "I love you, Sawyer." My head inched down to feel those lips again. I brushed against them and sighed, happy. They moved slightly, parting just a little, bringing new surfaces to feel, a new softness to explore and I sighed again, very happy. My hand ran along a slim neck and around behind her to string through her silky ponytail. So nice. I leaned into her more, wanting to feel more of her body, more of her skin, more of her lips. More…just…more. Our lips opened wider, and I flicked a quick feel for her tongue, finding it warm and receptive. So very nice. I groaned and felt for her again.

The head turned sideways, breaking our contact. "No, Lucas…stop."

I moved my lips to her soft neck, hungering for her skin. "Why? It feels nice…so incredibly nice."

A soft moan escaped her, doing unexpected things to my body, but she pushed me back and held my head away from her. "Nice isn't enough." I cocked my head in her hands, confused, and she sighed. "Friends don't do this. *We* can't do this." Her eyes turned sad as she looked over my face. I hated it when she looked sad. "Especially when you're like this…"

I pulled back and looked over her expression, something starting to register with me. "*I'm* making you sad?" She bit her lip and nodded, and I suddenly wanted to cry again. I could even feel my eyes watering. "I only wanted to make you feel nice, like me." I grabbed her face, suddenly scared. "I don't want to hurt you. I never want to hurt you. You mean everything to me."

She removed my hands from her face and nodded. "I know, Luc…and you mean everything to me." She ran a hand down my face. "More than you realize." I smiled, but didn't understand. She shook her head. "Let's just sit here and wait for your mom."

She curled up on my shoulder, a hand on my chest, and we waited…and waited…and waited. Somewhere in all the waiting and water drinking—from the never ending cup that Ms. Reynolds never let go dry for long—my head started clearing and I started remembering. I still felt light and airy, but I could think more with my head and less with…my body.

I closed my eyes and let my head hit the wall behind me. The tender spot from my skull whacking was also returning, and I sucked in a quick breath. Sawyer looked up at me from my shoulder. "Oh God, Sawyer…my mom's gonna kill me." My speech was still slow, like it took a second for my brain to think it and my mouth to create it.

I peered down at her and she grinned up at me. "Yeah, I think she is." She sat up from her slumped position against me and shrugged her shoulders. "If it's any consolation, my parents are gonna kill me too. I'm really late getting home."

I sighed and looked down. Suddenly, I remembered all the things I'd done and said…to her. I looked back up at her, a little scared. "Hey…I'm…I'm really sorry about…"

She blushed and didn't let me finish. "Don't…don't worry about it. You're just…messed up. Happens to the best of us." I blushed and looked away, but looked back when I felt her eyes burning into me. "Do you know what…what you took?"

My still sluggish brain tried to remember what happened to it. All I could remember was having a headache and then not having a headache. I scrunched my brows, trying to think harder. "No, I just remember you handing me…" I looked over at her, a horrid knot forming in my stomach. "What did you give me, Sawyer?"

Her face looked puzzled as she looked back at me. "Aspirin. I told you that. I always carry some for headaches and stuff."

The knot in my stomach grew and my hazy mind tried to think rationally and not emotionally. "No…that wasn't just Aspirin. Aspirin doesn't do that to me. What was it?"

Now she looked angry. "It was just Aspirin." She put her hand on my arm while I brought my hand to the bridge of my nose. My head was still so foggy…things just weren't making sense. "Look, Luc, I know you're still messed up, so I'll try to not get mad here…but I don't do drugs any more than you do, and I definitely didn't 'slip' you anything. Why would I?"

I dropped my hand from my face and sighing, looked back at her. "I don't know." I shrugged. "What's going on with me, Sawyer? I feel like I'm about to start flying." I frowned. "Or falling…really, it could go either way."

She patted my arm and shook her head. "I don't know, Luc. I wish I did." I wanted to ask her more. I wanted to talk to her more. I wanted to apologize for shoving my tongue down her throat, but at that moment…my mom showed up.

Looking frazzled and panicked and wearing her hardware uniform, she flew into the nurse's station and immediately brought her eyes to mine. I found I couldn't meet her identical-to-mine hazel depths and stared at the floor. Sawyer clenched my hand while my whole body tensed, waiting for the parental blowup that I could feel coming.

I felt a body move in front of me and a pair of petite, black shoes filled my vision. I held my breath. Then my mother squatted in front of me, placing her small hands on my knees and moving her head so she was looking up at me. I tentatively met her gaze, praying that my still floating brain didn't say anything stupid.

Her concerned eyes flicked between mine. "Lucas…are you okay?" I waited to hear the anger in her voice, but all I heard was concern. I exhaled and relaxed. Stupidly I nodded, my vision twisting for a bit as I did.

My mother's entire face relaxed and with a heavy sigh she flung her arms around me and clenched me tight. "God, you scared me. When they called, I thought…I thought… You scared me, Luc."

From somewhere in my body, guilt welled up, filling all of me, until it physically manifested as tears in my eyes that ran down my cheeks. I'd hurt this small, warm, loving woman…deeply. "I'm sorry, Mom," I said brokenly, my voice struggling with the words. I felt like sobbing…and then I did.

She rocked me and shushed me as her hands rubbed my back. I felt Sawyer squeeze my hand and then release it and I slung my arms around my mom, pulling her in tight as I sobbed on her shoulder. I couldn't understand why I was losing it…and I couldn't stop it either.

"It's okay, Lucas…breathe…it's okay."

She kept repeating that until eventually I stopped blubbering. My mom pulled back from me and wiped my face with her thumbs. I sniffled and looked over her sad features. I'd done that. I'd made her sad. I only ever made her sad. She looked to Sawyer sitting beside me and smiled slightly at her.

"Mrs. West?"

My mom turned to look at Ms. Reynolds standing behind her. "Can I take him home?" she asked quietly.

Ms. Reynolds nodded at her, flicking a quick glance at me before motioning with her thumb to an adjoining office. "Yes, I just need to speak with you privately for a moment." Her expression grew tired and perhaps a bit sad, and she continued slowly. "I'm sorry, but we have strict policies on substance abuse. There's going to be repercussions from this."

My mom swallowed and looked down. She let out a heavy sigh and nodded before standing and following Ms. Reynolds into a small room, where Ms. Reynolds closed the door behind them. I watched them through the glass and wondered what my fate would be. Tiredness seeped into me and I had the strongest urge to lie down on Sawyer's lap and take a nap. Her warm hand returned to mine and I looked over at her.

She wiped a stray tear away. "Are you okay, Lucas?"

I smiled with one corner of my mouth. "You ask me that a lot."

She smiled in a way that matched mine and laid her head on my shoulder. I laid my head on hers again and closed my eyes, my light and airy feeling changing to heaviness.

"That's because I never believe your answer," she said.

"Oh," I muttered sleepily.

I felt her head shift beneath me and lifted mine up, resting it gently against the wall behind me, my eyes still closed. "What do you think they'll do to you?" she asked, and I pried my eyes open to look at my mom talking to Ms. Reynolds, who was shaking her head, looking apologetic.

"Kick me out." I said quietly.

"No, they wouldn't…would they?"

I slowly swung my head around at hearing the genuine concern in her voice. I shrugged my shoulders. "I'm on campus…fucked up." I shrugged again. "They're gonna toss me." I looked back to the windows where Ms. Reynolds was saying something to my mom, who was now holding a hand over her eyes. "They hate me anyway," I muttered.

Sawyer squeezed my hand, but I didn't look back at her. Guilt filled me again as I watched my mom hopelessly try and fight for me. "They don't, Lucas," Sawyer quietly said beside me.

I finally did look back at her. "What?" My tongue felt solid in my mouth and my eyes wanted to close again.

She sighed and shook her head, her dark hair swishing over my jacket. "They don't hate you…not all of them anyway. Some are just confused. You don't remember the accident…and there are so many rumors about it." She shrugged. "They just don't know what to believe."

Anger shot through me, and I turned my head straight and didn't look at her. "I wasn't drinking…they could believe that."

She sighed and rested her head on my shoulder again. "I know, Luc…I know."

We stayed that way until my mom and Ms. Reynolds returned from the small room; both women looked sad and worn out. Ms. Reynolds clasped her hands in front of her and, clearing her throat, spoke to me in her most professional voice. "Lucas, we don't know what you took, but it's obvious you took something. I've spoken with the principal and you are hereby suspended from school for two weeks. You won't be allowed on or near the campus until your suspension is over, but if Sawyer wishes, she may gather your schoolwork so you don't fall behind. We have no desire to have your good grades suffer, and even though you will now have this on your permanent record…I believe you're a good enough student to not have that affect you too much when you apply for colleges later this year." She smiled warmly, like everything was just fine. My mom sighed softly beside her.

My tired mind tried to process the long stream of words, but I sort of got stuck on the first part. I scrunched my brow, not really understanding. "You're…giving me a vacation?" I heard Sawyer beside me snicker for just a fraction of a second before she shifted it to a cough.

Ms. Reynolds's face hardened. "No…it's a punishment, Lucas. Time for you to think about what you've done…whatever that may be." Her expression relaxed and she added, "It also brings you that much closer to our two strikes out rule. One more infraction like this, Luc…and you'll be gone."

I swallowed as that thought actually *did* sink in. "I didn't do this," I whispered.

Ms. Reynolds gave me a smile that clearly showed she completely didn't believe me. "Don't let it happen again, Luc." She looked down for a moment and with a small sigh looked back up. "We also…" She sighed, shook her head, and started over. "I'm sorry, Luc, but the principal thinks you being in the Safe and Sound Club is setting a bad example. I'm sorry…but you're out."

That actually shocked me more than the vacation I was being given. I stood up. Well, I tried to. It took a couple times before I completely did it. Sawyer stood up with me, supporting me with a hand on my chest. "What? No…" That was my free time with Sawyer, if they took that away from me, I'd be spending that time alone in my house…with thoughts I didn't need to be thinking anymore than I already did. I wanted Sawyer, I wanted her peace. "Please?"

Ms. Reynolds gave me a sympathetic look at the pleading in my voice. I glanced at my mother and she looked surprised. I hadn't told her about the club, and my obvious desire to stay in it was taking her back. I looked over to Ms. Reynolds with eyes that I hoped matched my voice. They couldn't take this from me too…

She bit her lip. "I'll talk to the principal again, Luc. Maybe…" She put a hand on her chin and then her face brightened. "I'll ask her about you seeing the counselor. Maybe if you complete a session with her, she'll consider letting you rejoin our group."

Her face brightened more as my mouth dropped. My addled brain stuck on the word "counselor". I didn't want a counselor…but I did want Sawyer. I looked back at Sawyer and she smiled at me encouragingly. "Yeah, okay." I found myself saying the words without even meaning to say them.

Ms. Reynolds made a pleased noise and even my mom seemed to sigh in relief. Ms. Reynolds walked over to me and put a hand on my arm. "I'm really glad this club has come to mean so much to you, Lucas." Her eyes took on an impassioned glow. "I know we can help you."

Internally, I sighed. Externally, I gave her a hint of a smile and nodded. I wanted to leave. I wanted to forget this day had ever happened. I wanted to finally nap. With a swift goodbye hug from Ms. Reynolds and a great deal of help with my sluggish body from Sawyer, I was finally in my mother's car and waving to Sawyer through the glass while she bit her lip and watched me pull away. After a quick, and thankfully silent, ride home, Mom helped me into bed, and I gratefully fell asleep…letting my nightmare of a day seep off of me.

I'd been asleep for mere seconds when a loud voice across my room woke me up. "So, what the hell was that, Luc? You were wasted at school…*you*?" I cracked my eyes open and saw Darren on the far side of my bedroom twirling one of my footballs in his hand. Instantly, I knew that I wasn't awake, and one of my dead friends had decided to make an appearance in my drug-induced sleep. I wasn't in the mood for it at the moment.

"Go away…my head still hurts." I threw the sheets up over my aching skull and tried to ignore his loud chuckles.

"Go away? I finally got my shot at some screen time." I pulled back my covers to glare at him. He smirked at my not-amused face. "Lil's been hogging it all." His grin turned devilish as he approached the bed. "Of course, she *can* entertain you in ways I can't." Tossing the football in the air, he groaned indecently as he sat on the edge of the bed. "Nice job on that midnight rendezvous by the way…that was awesome."

I blushed and then rolled my eyes. "I know you're just a dream, but quit poking around in my other dreams."

He laughed as he tossed the football a few more times. "But those are the interesting ones." He caught the ball and abruptly threw it at my chest. Luckily, I managed to catch it in time. "Besides," he pointed at his own head, "I'm you…it's not like I can keep you out of your own head." I gave him a blank look as I tried to absorb that, and he laughed again. He lay back on the bed as I sat up. I tossed the football to the ground and ran a hand through my hair. "Anyway, happy endings are the best," he muttered as he looked over at me pointedly. "Right?"

I blushed again. "Are you done?"

Laughing, he sat up. "Yeah…I guess." He frowned as a sudden thought struck him. "Hey…you better not ever invite Sammy to your little sexcapades. I'll kick your ass."

I shook my head at him and then laughed at the absurdity of it all. He eventually laughed with me. "It's good to see you, man. I've missed you."

Darren got a sappy look on his face. "Ah, do we get to hug now?"

I laughed and tossed my pillow at him. He effortlessly caught it. I shook my head again, which suddenly felt fine, and his face turned pensive. "Seriously, what was that, man? At school? What happened?"

My face got speculative as I looked over his darkening eyes. "I don't know."

"You need to figure it out, Luc. You didn't do it, so someone dosed you…and if it happens again…" He shrugged and I sighed and ran a hand down my face.

"I know…I'm screwed."

He laughed and I peeked at him from under my fingers. "God, Lucas…what you said to Ms. Reynolds. Damn, that was hot!" He laughed harder. "I wish I'd had the guts to tell her that."

I groaned and laid my head back on the wall. "Crap…I'd forgotten about that. Everyone heard me say it too." Darren laughed some more and I lifted my head to glare at him. "It's really not that funny."

He cocked his head at me again, still chuckling. "Really? If I was the one that told her she was 'totally fuckable' you wouldn't be laughing your ass off right now?"

I tried to glare, but broke out into laughter instead. He had a point. If anyone but me had said it, I'd be rolling on the floor. As my laughs subsided, I tossed the covers off of me. Looking over my fully dressed self with an amused shake of my head, I placed my feet on the floor and sat on the edge of the bed with Darren. His laughs died down too as he looked over at me, his elbows on his knees.

I stared at the shoes on my feet. "They're gonna make me see a counselor," I muttered sullenly.

"Good," Darren responded immediately. I looked over at him, and he shrugged. "You should talk to someone, Luc, after what you went through." I started to object when he cut me off, "And no, talking to figments of your imagination doesn't count." He rolled his eyes and I looked back at my shoes.

"You guys are the only ones I want to talk to. You're the only ones that matter." My tone was soft, but firm.

He sighed and then chuckled and I looked over at him again. "What about that hot, fiery girl…Sawyer?" I grinned but then stopped and shook my head.

"No, I don't need to bring her into my drama…more than I already do." I exhaled loudly and slumped my head into my hands. "God, I totally kissed her. I'm not sure if she likes me like that but…"

"Did she kiss you back?" Darren said simply.

I peered up at him, my hands still tangled in my hair. "Yeah….from what I can remember."

He crooked a smile at me. "Well, then, yeah…she likes you."

I sighed and looked back at the floor. "Great…now I'm going to have to hurt her. I wish that hadn't happened." I sighed again.

"Why?" Darren stood and walked over to a mirror on the wall. On the inside edge, a picture of the four of us was tucked under the frame and he pulled it out to look at it. "She's pretty and interesting and you guys seem to like each other. Why not go for it?" He looked back over to me, my eyes straying to the photo as his left it.

"Because I'm with Lil," I answered automatically.

"What?"

I looked from the photo to his face. His brown eyes were narrowed at me and his perpetually sticking up hair seemed to emphasize his questioning expression.

"I'm with--" I started to repeat.

He interrupted me, "No, I heard you…I just don't get it." With the picture still in hand he walked over to stand beside me. "You're turning down a living girl who clearly adores you," he pointed to Lil in the photo, her thin arms encircling my neck, "for a dead girl that you only get to be with…in your dreams?"

I swallowed the painful lump in my throat at the happy memory that photo was invoking in me. My mom had taken it on some random Saturday afternoon here at the house. There was nothing special about the day, it was just a Saturday, a Saturday we'd all spent together, a Saturday we'd all thought we'd get hundreds more of. They'd died three weeks after that photo was taken.

"It feels real Darren. *This* feels real."

He tossed the photo at me, sending it flying into my chest before it fluttered to the ground at my feet. I picked it up as he made an annoyed sound. My fingers traced the sharp edge of the picture before trailing down Lil's face. In the picture, Darren was standing behind a brilliantly smiling Sammy, his arms around her trim waist, his head resting against her neck. Lillian and I were standing next to them, my arms around her waist, her head tilted slightly to look up at me. She was so beautiful. For just a moment, I wondered if I could control my dream enough to bring her to me. I wanted to concentrate on it, but Darren snatched the photo from me and my train of thought vanished.

"You're a touch crazy, Luc," he muttered, still shaking his head.

I stood up and, grabbing the picture from him, returned it to its spot on the mirror. Pressing it flat against the cool, reflective surface, I muttered, "Yeah…maybe. Killing your friends will do that to you."

A long sigh answered me and as my gaze shifted behind me in the mirror, I saw Darren's face soften in sympathy. He walked over and placed a hand on my shoulder. He was about to speak, when suddenly, Sammy stepped out from behind him. I smiled as I met eyes with her in the mirror. Hers were a warm, beautiful golden-brown and her smile was soft and friendly as she walked up to Darren and grabbed his free hand.

"Hi, Lucas," she whispered.

I turned to look at her, her auburn hair shining in the dim light of my room. "Hey, Sammy…it's good to see you."

She nodded and bit her lip. She looked over at Darren and he looked back at her. The love that passed between them in that gaze hit me like a wrecking ball in the center of my chest, and for a moment, I wanted to sob for taking that love from this earth. I swallowed back the pain and watched my soul-mated friends.

"It's time to go, Darren," Sammy said softly, her other hand going to his cheek.

He nodded to her and looked back at me. "I'll see you around, Luc…and be careful. Someone has it out for you."

I smirked at him. "Who doesn't, Darren?"

He frowned at me and looked about to argue, when I suddenly woke up.

Chapter 7 – What the Hell Happened to Me?

I woke from my dream with a fogginess in my head. The moments of the dream were slipping from me but I tried to hold on to them. Darren and Sammy. I closed my eyes and committed what details I could to memory—joking around with Darren, him teasing me again, him concerned for me and wondering what had happened to me. What *had* happened to me?

I opened my eyes and looked around my light-filled bedroom. By the looks of things, I'd slept 'til nearly the noon hour. My head felt better…groggy, but better. My limbs felt heavy with sleep, but I stretched them out and attempted to work out the kinks. Memories of the pep rally filled my brain over the memory of my dream. I'd seriously made an idiot of myself.

Sighing, I sat up in my bed, stretching my arms over my head. I was sore and stiff…and so thirsty it hurt to swallow. I stood up and my head swam. I stayed perfectly still until the rushing feeling passed. I had no idea what had been done to me yesterday, but I knew I didn't do it. As I took small, calculated steps to my door, I ran through a list of people who'd love to embarrass me. Unfortunately the list was exceedingly long.

By the time I shuffled my way to the bathroom, I had a list that consisted of a third of the high school. That wasn't helping. Leaning over the sink, I turned on the water and forgoing a cup, held my head under the sink, letting the cool water hit my tongue and nearly sighing at the joy of the hydrating liquid coursing down my throat.

Yes, yesterday had been embarrassing…but there were several other ways to embarrass me. That had been a rather elaborate plan to get me messed up at school, and while I'm sure it had been hilarious for my tormentor, that was just a side effect of his or her true purpose…to get me expelled. Water continued streaming down me, parching my thirst as I thought about that. The school was cracking down on drugs and alcohol. Everyone thought I had a problem anyway, so no one would question me being messed up on school grounds. And now, one more strike and I was gone from that school. Well, at least Josh would love that.

I immediately stood straight and stared at myself in the mirror. Water dripped off my chin and I listened to the surging force of it pouring out of the faucet. Josh. On the list of who not only wanted me embarrassed, but wanted me gone…he was at the very top. But what did he do to me…and how? I tried to think back to when I'd seen him last. It was easy to remember. He'd smacked into me and then sat on my chest until I couldn't even breathe. His words earlier that morning echoed in my head—*'Have a good day at school…you deserve it'.*

That's what he'd meant…he wanted me out.

I turned the water off and stared at the few remaining droplets hanging ferociously to the chrome metal. Water…Aspirin. That's when I'd started feeling…different. If Sawyer really did only give me Aspirin, and I believed that she did—she was the only person in that school that genuinely cared for me, then it had to be my water. He did something to my water. But when?

I thought back to when he'd tackled me. He'd held me down for a long time. I'd been more concerned with trying to breathe than what else was going on.

Maybe he got Randy to go through my bag, dose my water. I closed my eyes and ran a hand down my face as I remembered picking my bag up from the floor…and putting the contents back inside. I'd assumed they'd fallen out from slipping off my shoulder, but a lot had fallen out. It really made more sense that someone was rifling through it. I used to eat lunch with those guys all the time. Randy would have known I always had water with my lunch and I usually saved some for after school. They used to tease me about it—that I couldn't even down water.

I clenched my hand into a fist and slammed it into the wall next to the mirror. I heard the plaster crack and felt the pain jolt up my arm, but I ignored it. Josh must have figured that if he hurt me enough, I might take something with my water. Truly, for him it had been a long shot that his plan would work…that I'd actually drink it at school, but odds were, I'd drink it *somewhere,* and I guess he had hoped I would get busted by someone; the school's new policy was being messed up anywhere…it happening at school, at a pep rally, well, that was just a happy bonus for him. Fucking Josh and his fucking vendetta. Darren would have his ass if he knew what he'd orchestrated against me.

I didn't know what to do about Josh now. A part of me had hoped that somehow, over the course of time, some of our old friendship would return. A part of me hoped beyond anything that he'd stop hating me. I'd wanted to talk to him on several occasions, but his baleful glares or cruel words had always stopped me. He didn't want to talk; he wanted to fight. So now what should I do? I really didn't want to fight with a friend…but then, we really weren't friends anymore. If yesterday showed me anything, it was that I was failing at not letting him engage me. In my current mood, I wasn't sure if I'd be able to not engage him. If he kept this up, I wasn't sure what I'd do, and that thought didn't thrill me.

God, I just needed one more year. Less than that, really. I could be out of this town by summer.

I removed my fist from the wall and guiltily looked at the cracks in it. I'd have to fix them before Mom noticed. I gingerly opened my hand and looked at my raw knuckles. I ran a finger over them, wiping a smidge of blood away. Great. I turned the faucet back on and washed off the blood. Harming inanimate objects wasn't going to help anything. Hastily, I finished up in the bathroom and then shuffled my way out to the kitchen for food. I was starving.

I walked slowly through the living room, looking around for my surely-angry parent. Not seeing her, I cautiously continued on into the kitchen. I peeked around the corner, but didn't see her there, either. Curious at her absence, I headed to the fridge. Plucking a note off the door, my curiosity was instantly squelched.

Had to go into work to cover the hours I missed yesterday. Eat something. I love you, Mom.

I sighed and read the note again. Guilt washed through me that she had to work this afternoon because she'd missed her shift at the diner last night. She didn't get paid time off and we couldn't afford even a few hours without pay, so she went in on what was supposed to be her day off, to make up the hours. Because of me.

I sighed and put the note on the counter. Nothing in it sounded angry. No

"We're talking about this when I get home." No "You are grounded, so no leaving the house." Nothing. Just, I love you, eat something.

Once again, Mom was going to let this slide. Feeling horrible, I went about making myself a sandwich. Mom might let this one slide, but the school would not. I was out of there for two weeks. I had to smile a bit and shake my head that being released from the obligation of school was considered a punishment…but then I frowned. Two weeks without school meant two weeks without Sawyer. She couldn't skip with me, and she might already be in trouble with her super-strict parents for being so late in coming home, waiting around school for so long with me. They may have even grounded her…which meant I really wouldn't see her for quite a long time. I wasn't sure if I could handle that. I may have crossed the line in our friendship, but I'd meant it when I'd said she was my best friend. She was…and I was going to miss her.

I finished making my peanut butter and jelly sandwich and shuffled into the living room to eat it. My head felt marginally normal, if three times too big for my body. I found, if I sat still and didn't move much, it wasn't so bad. I turned on the TV while I ate at a snail's pace, trying not to move or think.

I'd finished my meal and was getting lost in the simplicity of some cheesy tween show, when a soft knock sounded at the door. I looked down at myself, at the lounge pants and ratty t-shirt that Mom had helped me change into the night before when she'd gotten me ready for bed, and sighed. Nothing like a nearly grown man needing help changing. I pushed aside that humiliation and stood up, deciding that I was decent enough to answer the door. It was probably just the mail anyway.

Walking slowly and carefully, each step meticulously plotted before being executed, I finally made it to the door as another soft knock echoed through it. "Hold on," I muttered as I turned the knob. Expecting to see our squat mail lady with a frazzled look on her face and a stack of mail too big for our box, I was beyond surprised at seeing Sawyer standing on my step, rubbing her hands together and nervously shifting her weight.

I smiled and opened the door wider. "Hey…what are you doing here?"

She returned my smile and twirled the ring on her thumb, a habit she sometimes did when she was nervous. I frowned as I wondered if I made her nervous. How badly had I messed things up yesterday?

"I wanted to make sure you were okay." Her pale eyes ran over my face, studying me like my mom sometimes did.

I shifted my weight and noted the heavy feeling throughout my body…and the return of my thirst. "I'm fine, I guess."

She frowned, but nodded. An awkward silence built up as I stood in the door and she fidgeted on the steps. Finally she muttered, "Well, okay. I just wanted to make sure…"

She started to turn away, to go to her car, and I reached out and grabbed her arm to stop her. She looked back at my hand and then up at my face. I couldn't read her expression, but I hoped she was okay with the contact.

"Wait…" I said. "Will you…will you stay with me for a little while?" I prayed she would say yes. It would be so nice to be with her for a little bit before our forced separation.

Finally, she nodded and stepped forward. "I guess, for a little bit. My parents had to run out of town on an errand, so I have a few hours before they send a search patrol out for me." She raised one corner of her lip and I got the feeling she was only half teasing.

I relaxed my grip on her and stepped back from the door so she could enter. "My mom is gone too…so you don't need to be nervous about running into her."

She nodded as she entered my house, and a part of me thrilled that she was finally inside my home. She looked over things as she entered—photos on the wall, knickknacks on the shelves, the mismatched furniture. I followed behind her as she made her way to the living room couch and motioned for her to sit when she looked back at me uncertainly.

She shrugged out of my jacket, slinging it over the side of the couch, before she finally sat down. I carefully sat next to her, my head and body still feeling the effects of yesterday's multiple abuses. Suddenly I remembered my aching thirst and I looked over at her.

"I need some water…do you want anything?" She shook her head and continued looking over my home while I slowly stood back up and got a large glass from the kitchen. When I sat back down, she was picking at the sleeves of her shirt but a soft, genuine smile lit her lips. I smiled in kind at seeing it…and at seeing her on my couch. "I'm glad you came over. I'm glad you finally came inside." I raised an eyebrow, or tried to anyway, and she laughed.

"Yeah, well, yesterday was…" she pulled at her long sleeve and studied the fabric of the couch in the space between us, "…weird." She looked back up at me and I felt my cheeks heat in remembered embarrassment. "I just wanted to make sure you were okay."

As if her words had reminded me of my body's situation, I took a long drink of my water. Her eyes watched my every move as I tilted it back, taking as much as I could. The cool liquid relieving my ache reminded me of my revelation in the bathroom. As I removed the glass from my lips and set it on the coffee table, I sighed softly.

"I know what happened to me."

"What?"

I looked over at her and her long, dark hair flowing over her shoulders. I had a strong desire to tuck a strand behind her ear, but I locked my hands together and leaned over my knees, resisting that urge. I didn't want to mislead her…anymore than I knew I already had.

"Josh," I said simply. When her eyes looked bewildered, I filled in what little detail I could. "He had Randy dose my water bottle with…something, while he was busy tackling me in Astronomy. When I drank it later with your Aspirin, I took whatever drug he slipped me. Acid, ecstasy, speed…something like that."

Her eyes widened as she moved closer to me on the couch. "What? Why would he do that?"

"I think…" I looked over her features before I continued, "I think he wants to get me kicked out of school. If he gets me kicked out…well, my chances of getting out of here would greatly dwindle. He either really wants me to hang around…or he wants to ruin me." I shook my head and stared over at the innocent looking show on TV. "I'm guessing the latter."

Sawyer's hand came up to rest on my knee and I looked down at it and then over to her. Feeling an emptiness starting to overwhelm me, I leaned back on the couch and put my arm around her shoulders, drawing her in for a tight, side-by-side hug. Her arms slung around me, her hands cradling my body, and she softly exhaled. I swallowed back the sudden emotion…and the guilt that I could never keep our relationship on a not-physical level for very long. I couldn't help it. I needed her so much.

I dropped my head into the crook of her neck and exhaled a stuttered breath that sounded on the verge of tears. I hoped that wasn't where my body was going. I really didn't need to cry anymore around Sawyer…she'd seen quite enough of that. She started rubbing my back and whispering soothing words in my ear. I relaxed under her hands and felt that familiar peace wash over me.

I pulled back and turned my head so we were just inches apart. Her lips parted as she softly breathed on me. I recalled my dream with Darren, him wanting me to go forward with Sawyer and leave Lil behind. I glanced down at Sawyer's lips, so close to mine, the sun sparkling off them invitingly. I remembered the soft warmth of them yesterday, the soft sound she'd made when I'd touched her. Her breath stopped as I stared at the form of those shapely lips. Beautiful lips, really.

But different from Lil's…different from what I wanted. I still wanted to be with Lillian, and I couldn't keep playing with Sawyer's head. That wasn't fair.

Those lips started coming towards me and I instinctively pulled back. I glanced up at Sawyer's eyes and saw hurt and rejection there. She started to turn her head away from me and dropped her arms from my body. My hand went to her cheek and turned her back to me.

"You're my *only* friend, Sawyer. I'm so sorry about what happened yesterday." I held her face gently, making sure she kept eye contact with me. "I'm sorry if I hurt you…or misled you." My eyes flicked between hers as hers flicked between mine. "You're my best friend. I don't ever want to lose you…but that's all I can be right now."

Her eyes glassed over, but she nodded and removed my hand from her cheek. She held it in her lap. "I know, Lucas. I understand…about yesterday. I'm not angry…or misled." Since I felt like we'd just almost had another inappropriate moment, I wanted to say more, say something, but she switched topics on me, effectively closing that door, for now. "What are you going to do about Josh?"

I relaxed back into the couch, dropping my head back on the cushion and staring up at the ceiling. She laced our fingers together. I closed my eyes and sighed softly. "I have no idea…" I turned my head and opened my eyes to look at her.

"Suggestions?"

She smiled and brought her legs up underneath her, shifting to face me on the couch. "Kick his ass so hard that he'd be too afraid to try anything else?"

She laughed softly and I joined her. "Yeah, I could always try that…"

She stopped laughing and a seriousness blanketed us. "Luc…you should tell one of the teachers. Ms. Reynolds maybe? Tell her that he drugged you." Her other hand closed over our entwined fingers and she gently squeezed.

I looked at our hands for a moment, and then I shook my head. "Why? You know how they see me. They wouldn't believe me. Even Ms. Reynolds wouldn't believe me. No one believes me." I whispered that last part.

She sighed and shifted her body to rest her head on my shoulder. "I believe you, Luc."

I pressed my lips into her hair. "Thank you," I breathed.

She stayed with me for a while on the couch, holding my hand and watching that mindless show on TV with me. I relaxed back on the cushions, careful not to move too much as my head cleared, and drinking continually from my super large glass of water. Sawyer rested her head against my shoulder and a comfortable silence fell between us.

I watched her from the corner of my eye while we rested together. She'd occasionally adjust her head against me, her dark hair flowing down my arm as she snuggled closer into my side. Her fingers against mine were warm and dry, comfortable. Her other hand played with a frayed patch of denim on her often worn pair of jeans and her toes, just showing from where she'd tucked them under herself, unconsciously drew patterns in the couch. She seemed completely comfortable and relaxed with me, and I relaxed in kind, happy that I hadn't messed things up too much with my impaired mind yesterday.

She noticed me seemingly checking her out and pulled back to look at me. "What?" she asked as she looked over herself quickly.

I smiled at her reaction and shook my head. "Nothing. I was just watching you." She looked back at me with an odd, almost appraising look, and I quickly covered what, once again, could be a misleading statement. "This is nice. Why haven't you wanted to hang out with me here before today?" I cocked my head as I watched her reaction.

She pulled back from my shoulder and bit her lip. "I *have* wanted to…it's just…"

"My mom?" I asked, as I shifted slightly to face her.

She shifted as well and tucked her long hair behind her ears. "No…not really." She looked down and sighed. For a moment, I thought she wasn't going to explain it to me. That would be fine; I still wouldn't press her for details she didn't want to give. Just when I was about to pull her back into my shoulder, so we could keep watching TV, she looked up and answered me. "I did something really stupid with an even stupider guy, and I'm trying…" she looked away from me, "I'm trying to be smarter." She looked back at me and frowned. "Sometimes, I don't feel like I succeed at that."

I frowned, too, my mind suddenly full of questions. "You don't...you didn't want to be here with me, because you thought..." I wasn't sure where to go with that and I let my sentence trail off.

She looked over my confused face and sighed. "I always wanted to come in, Luc, really, I did...I do. I just didn't want to get too fond of you," she looked down and picked at a strand of fabric on her knee, "if this wasn't going to last."

"Hey...Sawyer..." My hand started to reach for her cheek but she looked at it and I paused.

I dropped my hand when she looked up and met my gaze. "I know you're hurting, and you need someone around, Luc." She shrugged. "I just wasn't sure if that would always be me."

I shook my head, not even able to comprehend that. Why wouldn't I want her around? I always wanted her around. "Sawyer, you mean every..." I couldn't finish my emotional thought and let it die between us.

She silently watched me struggle to find something compelling to say to her, then she said, "Besides, my dad really wouldn't let me come over. They wouldn't even like me being here now, on the weekend." She shrugged, like she was just used to how protective they were.

A bit of the tension that had been building in the room faded away, and I let my more emotional thoughts drift off with it. Embracing the semi-playful look on her face I asked, "Why are your parents so strict with you?" I raised an eyebrow mischievously. "Besides hanging out with me, you seem to have good judgment."

She laughed a bit at my statement and leaned into me. "Well, remember the stupid thing I did?"

I frowned as I thought back to her earlier comment. "With the stupid boy?"

She nodded. "Yeah..." Then a deep sadness marked her features. "They moved me out here because of what I did. They both gave up a lot to do that, and we didn't have a whole lot to begin with." She ran a finger over her holey jeans and sighed. "I messed up a lot for them, and I just...I don't push it." She looked up at me and sighed while I frowned. "I deserve their strictness."

Without meaning to, I muttered, "What did you do, Sawyer?"

She bit her lip and shook her head, obviously not wanting to talk about it. "I made a mistake," she finally whispered. She raised her eyebrows at the end of her sentence like I should understand that. And I did. If anyone understood mistakes...it was me.

As her eyes started to water, I dropped the conversation and pulled her tight to me. I felt her silently cry against my shoulder and cradled her head with one of my hands while the other clutched her back, pulling her even closer.

"It's okay, Sawyer...I understand."

I didn't understand the details, but I understood the emotion. Whatever she'd done had uprooted her family and put her under near house arrest. Whatever she'd done had hurt her and continued to hurt her. Whatever she'd done made her feel like an outcast from the rest of our school. And whatever she'd done had probably been the reason why she and I had bonded so quickly. She really did understand my pain and loneliness. She'd felt her own version of it.

I held her a bit longer, until, wiping her eyes, she pulled away from me and said her parents would be home soon and she needed to go. I nodded and walked with her to the door, handing her my letterman's jacket before she opened it. She smiled as she slipped it on, and I smiled watching her. I didn't know all of her story, just like she didn't know all of mine, but we needed each other anyway, and I liked that it was a mutual feeling.

I waved as I watched her drive away. Then I sat back down on the couch and avoided moving or thinking. I sort of managed both.

The rest of my afternoon was dull and unproductive. Well, I suppose I did eventually fix the cracked wall in the bathroom. I didn't get around to it until after my mom came home, but she didn't say anything about it if she saw it. She didn't say much of anything, really. Just that she loved me and if I ever wanted to talk to her about anything, she was here for me.

I took that to heart but decided to keep my demons to myself. Mom didn't need to know the things I knew. She didn't need my memories haunting her, like they haunted me. I remained silent on all of the painful subjects that swirled around in my head as I helped her make a more substantial dinner than my usual Hot Pockets.

She talked about some of her nicer customers while we ate our meal. She only ever mentioned the nice ones to me, both at the diner and the hardware store. She usually held back anything painful, and a split second after I wished she'd open up to me, I realized just how alike we were. I didn't ask her to spill her secrets and let her keep her own demons, just like she usually let me keep mine.

Between a forkful of food, she casually tossed out, "I saw the sheriff today at the diner. He says hello."

I smiled and nodded, resuming my eating while I thought about him. Sheriff Whitney had been the first one to find me that night. I don't know how long I'd lain in that ravine, slipping in and out of consciousness, but his voice calling down to me had been as miraculous to me as the fact that I'd managed to live through that ordeal with only a few scrapes and bruises.

He'd scrambled down to me, immediately prying open my door and checking my pulse. I'd weakly looked over at him, at his silver hair and silver-blue eyes. He'd looked almost unreal to me at first. Of course, my vision had been swimming in and out as icy shock had flooded through me. But I'd still taken in the tan, crisp uniform, splotched with mud, his knees saturated with it, like he'd fallen a few times on the way down to me, and the impressive black belt, holding his cuffs and gun. As I'd stared at the silver cuffs, I'd wondered if he'd use them on me when he shoved me in the back seat of his car; surely, he'd arrest me. Lil's beer had spilled all over the seat, soaking my jeans, and I knew I reeked of it.

But he hadn't. His face softened with sympathy as he checked my vitals.

"Everything will be all right, Lucas. I'll take care of you."

I'd had no idea what that meant at the time, and honestly, I still didn't. Moving away from me, he'd checked on my friends while calling for help again on his radio clipped to his shoulder. I'd closed my eyes so I wasn't tempted to watch him examine Lil. I'd already seen her. I'd already shed tears for her, a lot of tears. I didn't want to do it again.

The shock kept me in a sort of frozen numbness as I waited for the ambulance to get me out of there. With Sheriff Whitney's help, the paramedics managed to get me back up the steep hill in some sort of odd stretcher thing. As they were about to close the doors behind me, I looked back at the sheriff who was watching me with a morbid expression.

"My friends?" I whispered.

He closed his eyes briefly and then shook his head at me. That's when the numbness of my shock-induced state had worn off. That's when I'd started sobbing. I think I sobbed all the way to the hospital.

I sighed as I peeked up at my mom. She had a soft smile on her lips as she ate her dinner. I suppose to her, the sheriff was a happy memory. He did sort of save my life, after all. I picked at the food on my plate while I thought about another memory with him…later at the hospital. I don't know how long I'd been there, but I'd been tested and scanned, poked and prodded. An IV of some fluid was dripping into me, and I could barely keep my eyes open as I'd lain in the sterile bed, while my mom sat in a chair beside me, holding my hand, her eyes red and bloodshot from crying. I'd lethargically looked over at him as he'd entered the room, still looking muddy and disheveled. He'd met eyes with my mom and walked over to gently put a hand on her shoulder. Looking back up at me, he sighed, his eyes overly moist.

"I'm sorry, Lucas. We tried…Miss Tate was already gone." He looked down while I swallowed back more tears. Tate…that was Lillian's last name. He looked back up again and continued in a thick voice. "We found Mr. McCord and Miss Carter not far from the wreck…they were both unconscious, barely alive."

A surge of painful hope went straight through me—Darren and Sammy were alive. My mouth dropped open to ask where they were, how they were, if I could see them, but his face shut off my questions. He had fallen into despondency, and my mother softly sobbed. I shook my head while he gave me news I didn't want to hear. "Miss Carter…died, shortly after we found her. There just wasn't anything we could do for her."

A tear leaked down my cheek…not Sammy. I closed my eyes and prayed that he'd tell me Darren made it, that I wasn't alone, that I hadn't killed them all. Please don't take them all.

A soft exhale met me and my entire body tightened in anticipation. "Mr. McCord…had several internal injuries. We thought he might still…" I opened my eyes, my body shaking with tension. Sheriff Whitney's face looked worn and haggard when he met my gaze. "He died in the ambulance, Lucas. I'm so sorry…they're all gone."

I tried to shut off the memory of breaking down into hysterics after hearing the fate of my friends. Even so, flashes of screaming, crying, yelling and trying to damage anything around me filled my head. I'd been so wild with grief that the sheriff had had to restrain me, pinning my arms down on the bed. I'd had no control over myself…but, how often do you hear that three of the people you love most in the world are gone? Hopefully, not very often.

I looked away from my mom's soft smile and pushed my half eaten plate from me. I couldn't finish it now; my appetite had vanished with that last memory. I excused myself and stood from the table. Mom looked over my face, concerned, and asked if I was all right. I lied and told her I was, that I was just full, and then slipped on my jacket and walked out the back door.

I sat on the back step and stared at a football in the yard. It was the ball from my dream with Darren. In reality, it had been out here. I picked it up and gripped it in my hands, relishing the familiar feel of it. The ridges under my fingertips automatically lined up in the correct spot, and its bumpy texture sent more pleasant memories my way. I flexed my arm and faked a pass, keeping the ball in my hand, but allowing my body to remember the instinct of throwing. It relaxed me and I did it a few more times.

Sheriff Whitney. I wished Mom hadn't brought him up. It wasn't his fault that I associated him with something so horrendous, but I did. He was actually a very nice man and was one of the small handful in this town who believed me. Of course, he was a man of facts, and my blood had tested clean so—boom—innocent. If only everyone else could be so easily convinced.

He'd visited a few times over the summer, mainly talking with my mother in the living room while I was curled up in a fetal position on my bed. But he did stop in and tell me everything would be fine, and eventually everything would get better. He always put a reassuring hand on my shoulder and spoke in that soft voice reserved for those on the verge of an emotional collapse. I suppose I had been. Maybe I still was.

I tossed the ball in the air a few times and nimbly caught it. Sheriff hadn't charged me with anything. Not manslaughter, not reckless driving, not an MIP…not even a speeding ticket. The town and even some of the deceased's families (Josh in particular), had been in an uproar about that. They all felt I was guilty, and had basically gotten away with murder. Most people felt that I wasn't being charged because the town liked my mother, had a soft spot for her, even. People sympathized with her situation and didn't want her to be punished any farther, for her reckless son's, reckless behavior.

I don't know if that was true or not. I didn't know the legal system well enough to know what the sheriff could have charged me with anyway. All I knew for sure was that I wasn't being "legally" punished, and I did feel horribly guilty about it.

Chapter 8 – Isolation

The first week of my forced isolation was the longest in my life. Not that I missed school or the majority of the student body. I didn't. No, I definitely didn't miss the stares or the whispers or the unconcealed glares. And I definitely didn't miss Josh and Will trying their best to make every second of my life a misery.

No, what made my week long, what made loneliness seep into every part of me, was the fact that I missed Sawyer. She was really the only thing that I longed for daily. After we'd parted ways that Saturday afternoon, she'd gone on with her life and I'd gone on with mine. The first part of my punishment went by without even a word from her. That was worse than anything else the school could have dreamed up for me.

I tried to believe that that was because of her overprotective parents and not the couple of awkward moments we'd had recently. I tried to believe it, but I wasn't one hundred percent sure. And I had no real way of keeping in contact with her. She didn't own a cell phone and I wasn't about to get her in trouble by calling her home phone, not if her parents had an issue with me, which, if they'd heard even half of the rumors floating around, they probably did. I had no way of asking her if everything was all right between us, so I ended up sitting and staring at the phone most evenings, waiting for her to call me—just like some lovesick school girl waiting for a boy to call. I knew it was ridiculous, but I couldn't stop doing it. I missed her voice.

And I suppose I wasn't helping my loneliness any. I didn't do anything constructive during my time off. Mainly, I sat around the house and dwelled. Dwelled on subjects I didn't want to think about. Dwelled about my embarrassing moment at the pep rally—all thanks to Josh. Dwelled on just how wrong that relationship had gone. Dwelled on my friends. Dwelled on the night they'd been taken from me. I thought more about the wreck that first week than I had since it happened. With nothing to do and nothing to distract me, I'd gone over it fifty thousand ways in my head. Things my friends could have done differently. Things I could have done differently. Things I could have handled better. Goodbyes I could have said…

Oddly, the only escapes from my troubling thoughts were my dreams. I'd been having pleasant dreams of my friends and, more often than not, I was cognizant in my dreams. The minute I saw one of my should-be-deceased pals, my mind seemed to instantly register that I wasn't in reality anymore. I guess the fact of their deaths was just too great a truth to ignore, even in REM sleep.

But it didn't bother me, them showing up and having conversations with me. Quite the opposite—I enjoyed it, even looked forward to it. I talked with all three of them, Darren, Sammy and Lil, even getting strong enough to bring them to me at will sometimes. I'd also begun to have more control over other aspects of my dreams. I could hold onto them longer and sometimes I could even change the setting, like when Darren came by and wanted to go dirt bike riding. We'd walked from my living room to what should have been the kitchen, but instead was an empty field with awaiting bikes, because that's what I'd wanted to see. It was empowering to have that level of control.

Now, that's not to say I had perfect control. Sometimes there was a blue sky in my bedroom, and sometimes it rained Mentos (which Lil actually quite enjoyed), and sometimes, just sometimes, I dreamed of driving. While I hated those nightmares, the good dreams I had were powerful enough to make sleeping worth the risk.

Sometimes I met with my friends individually, sometimes in groups of two and sometimes we'd all hang out together. But the most intense dreams, the ones I could have lost myself in for days—those were all with Lil; just her and I together, alone in my bedroom, in the dark. Half naked and wanting each other desperately. We still never took it farther than we'd gone in real life, but I was close to being ready, close to *wanting* that memory…more than fearing it.

I grew to relish my time spent dreaming, and dreaded my time spent awake, so much so, that I'd started searching for ways to prolong the slumber. I napped as often as I could throughout the day, and when that stopped working, I'd scrounged through my mother's medicine cabinet until I found her stash of Ambien, the stash she didn't know I was aware of. I'd started popping them like candy, wanting to zone out and be with my friends, even if it was all in my head. I knew it was a bad habit to start, and I was never one to pop prescriptions before, but I wanted to see them, and it actually did help.

I'd just taken two when Sawyer unexpectedly showed up.

From what I could remember of the passing days, it was Thursday afternoon when a light knock filtered through my door. Just starting to feel the sleepy side effects of the drugs I'd taken, I shuffled to the door, not really caring who it was. Still in my lounge pants (that I'd been living in), I squinted a bit as the bright light of day hit me. My starting-to-lull mind startled into semi-awareness at seeing Sawyer and her super dark hair standing before me.

"Hey…hi," I mumbled when her face filled my vision. I leaned against the doorframe and blinked away the sleepiness trying to settle on me.

"Hey," she answered back, as her pale, gray eyes flicked over my face. They narrowed with concern while her lips curved down into an adorable pout. "You look awful. Are you okay?"

I smiled and a sleepy laugh escaped me at the familiar phrase passing her lips. "I'm fine…just resting. Come on in." I stepped back and swung my arm out to indicate the room behind me.

Still frowning at me, she walked past. I ran a hand through my bed-head hair and then down my scraggly face, realizing I hadn't shaved in a while and…actually, I hadn't showered in a while, either, and I probably did look—and smell—a mess. I considered popping in the shower while Sawyer looked around my living room, but discarded the thought when she sat on my couch and looked back at me still in the doorway. I hadn't seen her in so long; I didn't want to miss a minute.

I shook my head to clear the cobwebs and softly closed the front door before joining her on the couch. I wanted to throw my arms around her and squeeze her tight, but I didn't. And not just because I didn't want to be misleading anymore…I also didn't want to offend her with my rank scent.

She put her school bag on the ground before us and opened it. She began rummaging around inside it as that splendid voice that I'd missed so much spoke softly to me. "Sorry I'm so late in getting you your stuff." She sighed in irritation while my slow mind tried to understand what she was talking about. "My parents had issues with me coming over here." She shook her head. "I told them it was just to give you your homework, but they still flipped out."

She grabbed a folder and some papers she'd found and handed them to me. My mind put the pieces together after she said "homework" and I smiled as I took the stack. I'd forgotten that she was going to do that for me. She sighed again and met my eyes, just as I was about to thank her. "Ms. Reynolds eventually had to call them and explain the situation." She rolled her eyes. "She actually had to ask them to let me help you. I think she was going to come over here herself if they refused again. Luckily they didn't, and I have exactly twenty minutes after purity club to get you caught up each day."

My slow smile stretched wider at hearing her story. I'd missed her so much, and she'd been out there fighting for me. She was shaking her head at her parents' over protectiveness when she narrowed her eyes again and searched my blinking ones. "Are you sure you're okay? You seem…out of it."

I rubbed my eyes to try and keep myself awake, to enjoy my twenty minutes, if that was all I got. "Yeah, I just took a couple of my mom's sleeping pills before you got here. They're starting to kick in…sorry."

Silence answered me, and I looked over at Sawyer who was sitting very tall and straight on the couch, her eyes wide. "You *what*?"

I furrowed my brows at her odd expression. "I took a couple pills so I could rest. It's no big deal, Sawyer." I put a hand on her shoulder. "Relax."

She looked at my hand briefly before leaning into me and cupping my face; her eyes searched mine intently. I inhaled a quick breath at her nearness and nervous energy shot through me. "What are you doing, Sawyer?"

Her face and voice took on that too-old-for-seventeen tone that it sometimes could. "How many did you take, Lucas?"

I scoffed and pulled away from her, grasping her hands with mine. "Two…relax."

I held her hands firmly when she tried to lift them to my face again. The irritation on her face matched the irritation on mine. "I thought you didn't do drugs, Lucas."

Feeling ashamed and angered by her question, and her tone, I tossed her hands away and stood up from the couch. "I took two pills to help me sleep, Sawyer. It's no big deal. You're acting like I'm a drug addict!"

She stood as well and stepped in front of me. "It's dangerous, Lucas. It's too easy to…" She closed her mouth and slowly shook her head, her dark hair rippling around the edges of my letterman's jacket that she wore every day. "It's not a good habit to start." She stepped closer to me, ignoring whatever odor I was surely producing, and put a hand on my arm. "Please."

I looked down at her concerned face, her eyes starting to mist over.

Confused, I could only say, "I just want to sleep, Sawyer. I just…I need…" I shrugged and my shoulders suddenly felt like concrete blocks. "I just want to sleep my way through this. Through all of this…"

Her arms encircled me as she held me tight. "You can't, Luc." I felt her exhale in a stuttered breath and I put my arms around her protectively, drawing her in tight. "Please…don't…" She shook her head against my chest. "Find another way to deal with it…"

I leaned over her, resting my head on hers and savoring her warmth. I felt lighter with her near me, safer with her holding me. Feeling like I could do anything with her arms around me, I finally sighed in defeat. "Okay, Sawyer…I won't take them anymore. I promise." I ran a hand down her back, through her hair and we started to sway together. She nodded against my chest and we held each other for a few long moments.

As time pressed in on us, we finally pulled apart. She wiped her wet eyes and looked up at me. I brought a hand to her cheek and frowned. I'd hurt her, and I didn't understand why. I shook my head and whispered, "I'm sorry, if I worried you."

With my hand still on her cheek, my thumb started to brush back and forth across her cheekbone. Her lips parted as we faced each other and that warm, comfortable feeling took hold of me. I could make it through the day if I knew I'd get this moment of peace with her. It wasn't the same as the hours of school that we used to have, but for now, it would have to do.

Without thinking about it, I lowered my head and lightly pressed my lips to hers. I was only aware of doing it after the fact. I pulled apart from her, my eyes wide and fearful. Great. Had I just crossed the lines of our friendship again? How often would she put up with me emotionally jerking her around? "Sorry," I immediately sputtered.

Her eyes were half closed and her breath was coming faster. I dropped my hand from caressing her cheek as her eyes opened fully and met mine. Her cheeks faintly deepened in color and she looked away from me. "We should…we should go over your homework," she muttered, as she stepped away from me and sat down on the couch.

I ran a hand through my hair and cursed under my breath. *God, Lucas…what happened to not being misleading?*

"Right." I carefully sat down beside her, watching her face for any sign of anger or embarrassment. "Thank you for doing this for me."

She nodded as she picked up the stack of papers that had fallen from my hand when I stood up. She started flicking through them, picking out notes she'd written, a lot of notes actually. I watched her carefully while she went over all the assignments she'd gathered for me. I realized I wouldn't be bored anymore while she went over lesson after lesson. I tuned out the work as I watched her. She seemed fine…but she did avoid looking at me directly.

When she was finished, she glanced at a clock on the wall. "Damn, I'm late." She grabbed her bag and stood up, still not looking at me. "I'll come by tomorrow, okay? Maybe I'll skip out of club early and we'll have a little more time together."

She walked past me and started for the door. I stood up and reached out for her, just catching her fingers as she hurried away from me. She looked back at me, her eyes guarded.

"I'm sorry about earlier, Sawyer. Sometimes I just…I don't think." I shook my head, feeling really stupid.

"No…sometimes you don't. You're either pushing me away or pulling me close, Lucas." She shook her head and removed her fingers from mine. "One day you'll have to decide what direction you want to go." She backed away, searching my face, and then turned and opened the door. "I'll see you tomorrow." Her face turned distraught. "Please, don't take any more of those pills."

I nodded and she started to leave. Right after she disappeared, her black head popped back into view. Her lips twisting into a grimace, she added, "And maybe tomorrow…you could shower."

Although it was hard, I did what Sawyer asked and stopped taking the sleeping pills. I wasn't addicted to them or anything, but it was tempting to know that I could be sleeping, could be with Lil, but now I had to wait until my body was ready for sleep, instead of trying to force it there. When it took a few days for the drugs to fully leech out of my system, for my body to stop feeling sluggish during the day, I realized that maybe I *had* been overdoing them, and I was grateful for Sawyer's request. She was right; they weren't a good idea. And I did still get to see my friends. My good dreams kept up, even after I stopped medicating myself.

It was a perfectly warm spring day, and I was walking in a field alongside a stream near my house. The sound of water gently splashing over small boulders met my ears and warmth from the sun hit my face. Light peeked through holes in the cloud cover, and the tall, green grass that tickled my bare feet was highlighted by those bright rays. The field almost looked like a giant chessboard, and there, standing in the space where the queen would rest, was *my* queen. Her hands were clasped behind her and a beatific smile was on her face as she waited for me.

My smile matched hers as I walked through the patches of darkness and light to where she stood, drenched in rays of golden sunshine. Her pale hair nearly outshone that sun and the loose fabric of her light pink dress fluttered in the gentle breeze, lifting a bit at the knee to hint at the shapely thighs underneath.

Joining her in that patch of sunlight, I cupped her soft cheek and exhaled in relief at the contact. Firm but tender skin met my fingertips and once again, holding her was as real to me as anything I'd ever felt while awake. Her chin lifted and her blue eyes caught the light and sparkled with life. She leaned into me and I leaned down; her lips were warm and soft when we connected.

I pulled away from her slowly, one hand snaking around her slim waist to sit at the small of her back, the other sliding from her cheek to finger the thin strap of her dress. "Hey, Barbie, I missed you."

She laughed in kind as her warm hands moved to rest on my chest. "I missed you too, Luc…and don't call me Barbie."

I chuckled at the familiar argument and pulled her body flush to mine. I kissed her before responding. "Why not?"

Her hand ran up and down my chest, feeling the muscles under my thin shirt. I bit my lip as I watched her eyes follow the path of her fingers. "Because, it implies that I'm fake and plastic." Her eyes lifted to meet mine and the corner of her lip rose in a wry smile. "And I'm not."

I leaned down to kiss those smirking lips, lingering on the corner, as the smell of her filled me. She was so real. "I know you're not, Lil…you're real." I pulled back and gave her a wry grin of my own. "And I think you're being a little unfair to Barbie."

Her head tilted back in a laugh and her eyes danced with happiness when they met mine again. I swallowed a bit, at the vision of this beautiful woman before me, and I couldn't quite contain the calmness of my breath. Her body twisted in my arms as she managed to get even closer to me, one of her legs sneaking between mine. "Just how am I being unfair to Barbie?"

I tried to smile, but my breath was definitely coming out faster as blood rushed through my body. She felt real and, as always, I was super aware of every inch of her that was in contact with me: my hand against the firm contour of her back, her leg against my knee, her hips pressed against my thigh, her stomach pressed against mine, her hands running over my chest, her mouth inches from my lips.

"Well," I said breathily, "look at everything she's done with her life: Doctor, Lawyer, Vet, Teacher…"

She laughed again and brought her nose up to mine, rubbing it against me as our mouths got even closer. "Great. So now I'm plastic and flighty."

I closed my eyes and sought her lips, finding them ready and eager. We pressed against each other, needing each other, but she pulled back before I could deepen the kiss. Her breath heavier, her eyes filling with desire, she ran her hands up my chest and slinked them around my neck. "I'm not flighty…I know exactly what I want."

I exhaled heavily at her words, my heart racing. "I want you, Lil."

Her hands reached up to clutch the back of my hair. "I want you too, Lucas."

Without another word, my hand at her shoulder clasped her neck and pulled her mouth to mine. Passion ignited us both and our tender and soft kisses turned into searing and scorching kisses. I leaned back, pulling her with me and let myself fall onto my back. She came with me, our lips breaking for a short laugh as, instead of harshly landing on the grass, we landed on the soft mattress of my bed. I rolled her over, my hand slipping up her thigh and under her dress as a cloud passed across the sun, momentarily darkening the section of the field we were still in.

She sighed and arched her back as my hand slid farther and farther up, sliding effortlessly up her creamy skin. Her hands in my hair tangled, pulling me deeper into her kiss. Her tongue met and stroked mine, tasting, savoring. She tasted like she always did, she smelled like she always did, she felt like she always did. My hand finally reached all the way up her leg to cup her backside and I groaned softly when nothing impeded its progress; she wasn't wearing any underwear.

"Oh, God, Lil," I muttered, as I dropped my head to the crook of her neck. She lightly moaned and moved her hip against my body. Blood surged straight down to my lower half and I hardened almost painfully. I rocked against her hip and let out a ragged breath. "I'm ready, Lil. I'm finally ready."

I pulled back to look at her, passion in her eyes, mouth open and waiting for mine. So perfect, so beautiful and so real. "I don't want to stop this time." She closed her eyes and pulled my hair, roughly bringing my lips back to hers.

As a new intensity seized us, one of her hands let go of my hair and trailed down my chest. She snaked it between us, unzipped my jeans and wrapped her hot fingers around me. I bit my lip at the sensation. "Lil…"

My hand cupping her bottom moved around to the front and lightly stroked her sensitive skin. I gasped and muttered something incoherent. She groaned and bucked against my hand. Almost unintentionally, my finger slid inside her. She moaned and rocked against me. "Luc, don't stop…"

Barely coherent of anything but where our bodies were intimately touching, I miraculously *did* notice something. Everything outside of my outdoor bedroom had stopped. The shadows moving across us had stopped. The sounds of the brook beside us had stopped. The rustle of leaves high in the trees had stopped. The squeaks of the birds calling to their mates had stopped. I'm sure even the sun stopped. It was as if the whole world was holding its breath and nothing existed but Lil and me…and this moment. This was the moment we'd never gotten to have in real life. This was the moment we'd finally get to have here, in my dream world. I was sure it was going to kill me afterwards, but for right now…I was ready.

I removed my hand from her. Lil clutched me close when I did. I gently removed her hand from around me. She looked at me then, her eyes blurry with need. Never breaking eye contact, I slid my jeans down, scrunched her dress up, and moved on top of her. Our clothes vanished at that point and our skin rubbed together; hers was warm and soft as she adjusted herself beneath me. Her hand caressed my cheek and a strange expression, almost sadness, crossed her face. I paused as I watched the emotion pass over her.

"Lil?"

She bit her lip and nodded and I pressed myself against her, feeling her warmth urging me onward. I took a deep breath and Lil did the same, both of us preparing for something bigger than each of us. Leaning in to kiss her, I slowly pressed forward. We both gasped as the tip of me slipped in. It was intense…and only the beginning. I panted against her lips, her breath matching mine, and adjusted myself for that first push.

"Lucas?"

A loud knock on the door and my mom's insistent voice instantly brought me back to reality. My mind at least, my body was still struggling with the emotions I'd just left behind. I cursed silently and gulped down air, trying to steady my breathing. I carefully sat up in bed and noted that, once again, dreams sometimes manifest in real life. I was hard as a rock. Great. *Nice timing, Mom.*

"What?" I said, with what I hoped was a groggy voice.

"Sorry, honey, I need to get going to work…but someone's here to see you." My mom's voice through the door was rushed, like she was running late.

I quickly threw out a, "Thanks!" so she would leave me and my *situation* alone. I wished whoever else was out there would leave too. Then I got nervous that maybe it was Sawyer. I really didn't need her seeing me like this.

I stood up and tried to think about something other than my dream…like who was visiting at this hour. I didn't really think Sawyer would come before school, and I couldn't help but wonder who would. As the remnants of my dream faded from me, sadness swept through me. That dream had been so real…and new. I'd wanted it to keep going and I'd wanted it to end. The opposite emotions cleared the sleep from my system and…evened…my blood flow. By the time I opened my door, I was physically, nearly normal. Emotionally, I was all over the place.

I looked around as I entered the living room, but I didn't see my mom anywhere. It was unusual for her to leave without saying goodbye to me face to face. Even if I was still sleeping, she'd crack open the door to look me over before saying goodbye. Whoever was here must have really frazzled her. I wondered who that could be as nervous knots tightened my stomach.

Cautiously, I walked into the kitchen and froze immediately in the doorway, my breath catching.

A man sat at the table, staring at his hands. "Sheriff Whitney?" I said timidly, as I took a step into the room.

It wasn't that I hadn't seen the sheriff since that night, but like always, upon first seeing him, memories flooded me. Painful memories. A past tense voice filled my head as I took in his imposing form, dressed in the head to toe tan of his uniform, '*I'm sorry, Lucas…they're all gone…*' I shoved back that horrid conversation and focused on the present tense version of the sheriff before me.

He turned to look at me as I entered, his steely eyes shifting over my body before resting on my face. I flushed slightly, hoping that my situation had calmed down enough that he couldn't tell. I didn't think he'd mention it or anything, but it was still embarrassing.

I swallowed back my unease and went over to the table, taking the seat opposite him. Curiosity overtook me and I spoke into the still air. "Why are you here?"

I realized how rude that was right after I said it. I blushed more, but sat quietly, waiting for some response.

He sighed and ran an aged hand through his silver hair. "Your mom. She told me about what happened at school—you being suspended."

My eyes widened. She told *him*? Him, of all people? A lawman who could possibly…well, I didn't know what he could do about it, so long after the fact, but still, what was she thinking?

"I…um…" I sputtered on my words, not having any idea what to say.

His eyes narrowed at me. "I know you've been through a lot, son, more than most your age." He hung his head, our eyes breaking contact, and again his past voice entered my brain—*'they're all gone…'*

I clenched my jaw, holding onto my emotions by a thin thread while he continued. "That night was…horrid…for a lot of people." He looked back up at me and I begged my eyes not to water. "But I hope you are smart enough not to go down this path." The steel gaze in his eyes softened to concern. "I've seen so many lose their way like that, with drugs or alcohol. Don't let yourself be one of them, Luc. You're stronger than that."

My mouth dropped open at his implication. He believed I wasn't drinking *that* night, but now he thought I was a druggy? "I didn't… I'm not..." I took a deep breath to calm myself. "Someone slipped me something. I don't use drugs."

His steel gaze returned. "Yes, your mother said as much." He nodded thoughtfully while I reflected on his comment. My mom had believed me readily when I'd told her someone had dosed me. Of course, she would; she believed everything I told her of late. She'd passed that information on to the sheriff, for some odd reason, and he seemed to believe it as well. I wondered what he'd do with that information. Well, whatever he managed to ferret out about the incident, he wouldn't get the information from me. I wasn't about to give up Josh's name—not to the school, or my mom, and definitely not to Sheriff Whitney. I already had enough trouble being accepted in this town; no need to add "narc" to my list of reasons for people to hate me.

The sheriff adjusted himself in his chair, leaning forward over his hands clasped together in the center of the small table. I involuntarily leaned back, maintaining the space between us. "I just hope you'll think about what I said. Maybe that will shape how you react to this…to all of this." He stood and put a hand on my shoulder. I looked up at him, torn between the desire to yell my innocence, and the desire to burst into tears at the flood of emotions that always resided in me. "It will get better, Luc…you'll see."

He looked as if he wanted to say more, his face wrestling with some emotion before returning to the air of professionalism he generally wore. He patted my shoulder a few times while I ridiculously nodded. Was I agreeing with him? If I was, it wasn't voluntary. He nodded back and then walked from the kitchen, leaving me with my swirling thoughts. A vague remnant of my dream rose up in me, *'I want you too, Lucas,'* followed immediately by the sheriff's haunting words that night, *'they're all gone.'* I closed my eyes and forced out everything, only allowing myself to listen to the sheriff's vehicle as it pulled away.

Seeing the sheriff disturbed the remainder of my day. Sawyer noticed when she came by after school. Although she usually asked if I was all right, and if my "vacation" was going okay, today she hounded me for a more honest answer when I gave her my typical response of, "Fine." Maybe it was the look on my face, or maybe I'd freaked her out enough with the pills that she just wasn't going to let generic answers fly anymore. Whatever the case, she kept up on sussing out my mood until I confessed about the sheriff's visit.

It wasn't as though the visit was bad, or that he'd done or said anything to upset me, not really anyway, but seeing him again, and especially being alone with him, had reopened old wounds and the fresh scars hurt. Instead of going over the day's homework with me, Sawyer sat with me on the couch, holding my hand and telling me that she wasn't going anywhere and she'd help me through everything. She assured me that I only had one more school day and one last weekend, and then we'd be together for most of the day, almost every day.

I clasped her hand gratefully, not sure what I'd do without her. I both looked forward to being at school with her again, and dreaded being at school with her again. I'd left sort of a mess behind with my spectacle in the gym. The students weren't going to easily let me forget about that.

My mother said nothing about the sheriff's surprise visit when she came home late that night, only asking me how I was and how my day went. My answer to both was predictable—fine. She nodded and accepted that and gave me a soft kiss on the head before yawning and walking down the hall to her room. I watched the spot where she'd left my sight for a long while before standing and heading to my room, hopeful that maybe I could bring Lil to me. I wasn't really looking to continue what we'd been about to do this morning; I just needed her to talk to me. I needed her tonight. I needed her comfort.

My head had no sooner hit the pillow than I was suddenly sitting upright…and behind the wheel of a car. Confused, I started panicking. I didn't drive. I didn't ever drive. Not anymore, not since the night of the crash. Why was I behind the wheel? And whose car was it? I didn't even own a car.

My hands tightened on the wheel and my heart surged painfully as thick drops splattered on the windshield. The rubber wiper squealed in protest as it rapidly flicked back and forth across the glass, smearing the rain more than removing it. I could barely make out the yellow slashes in the middle of the asphalt. I couldn't peel my eyes away from the road and my breath started hitching as I lifted my foot off the gas and prepared to slam on the brakes. I wanted to stop.

"Hey, I wouldn't do that."

I snapped my head to the right and let out a heavy exhale when I saw who was seated next to me. "Darren?" He twisted his lips and smiled at me, and I instantly started relaxing. It was just a dream. I should have known that, but usually in dreams you don't. My grip on the wheel, the wheel of Darren's Geo I suddenly realized, loosened. I took in a deep breath and tried to calm myself, looking back to the road and focusing on the yellow lines again.

"What are we doing here? I don't drive, Darren…ever." I tried to lift my foot off the gas again so the car would gradually slow to a stop, but I couldn't raise my foot, and the car actually sped up.

Beside me, Darren chuckled and I glanced at him. "Yeah, I know, Miss Daisy." His amusement softened to seriousness. "That's why I'm here. I'll stay with you, Lucas." He put his hand on my arm. "I'm with you, man."

I swallowed and concentrated on the road again, wishing I could control my dream right now, change the setting, slow the car…stop the car. I thought of slamming the brakes again and my foot successfully lifted from the gas.

Darren coughed beside me, pointed his finger at my foot, and then shook his head side to side while wagging his finger.

Confused and frustrated, I dropped my foot back to the gas.

Darren raised his eyebrows at me. "You can't slam the brakes, Lucas. I know you want to, but you can't. That's how you lost control the first time." He shook his head at me again. "Did you learn nothing from License to Drive?"

I relaxed farther and even laughed a little. "Right. I almost forgot your theory that all of life's lessons can be learned through watching eighties movies."

He chuckled beside me and I turned to watch his happy face, momentarily forgetting my horror at driving again. "That's right." He held his hand up to me and started ticking off fingers. "You've got The Breakfast Club—everyone can learn to get along if they're locked in a room long enough." He ticked off another finger while I laughed next to him, my eyes still glued to his. "Top Gun—face your fear head on and you're sure to conquer it." He splayed his fingers out and sighed contently, closing his dark eyes. "And my personal favorite…Weird Science."

I frowned and cocked my head at him. I'd seen that movie before, and aside from kids turning a Barbie doll into the world's most perfect woman, I didn't see any profound meaning in it. "What is there to learn in Weird Science?"

He opened his eyes, the glint in them matching his devilish grin. "Oh…the things Kelly LeBrock could teach me." I laughed heartily at that and shook my head. Darren twisted his lips at me while I was still laughing at him. "Speaking of women…what's up with you and Lil?"

I took a hand off of the wheel and twisted even more, so my body was nearly facing him. "What do you mean?"

He raised an eyebrow at me. "Um, I think you know. A little meeting in a field, a bed suddenly appearing, clothes suddenly vanishing…you remembering any of this?"

I narrowed my eyes at him. "You were supposed to butt out of those dreams."

His face turned grim. "Luc…you can't do this, man. You can't be with her like that…not anymore."

"Why can't I? It's my dream…my head." My tone was getting a little irritated, but I couldn't help it.

Darren shook his head, holding my gaze. "Because it's stupid. You'll only hurt yourself. All of this is stupid. You should be letting us go, not pulling us tighter."

I leaned into him, my free hand going to my chest. "You know what, my life kind of sucks! And your asshole of a brother isn't making anything easier. If I can get even just a moment of peace and comfort when I'm with *my* girlfriend, then I'm going to take all I can get!"

Darren's face stormed up as he looked at his lap. "I'm gonna kick Josh's ass for drugging you," he muttered. Lifting his head, he brought his intense gaze to mine.

"But that doesn't change the fact that you shouldn't be hiding out with us in your dreams. She's not your girlfriend anymore! You can't keep ignoring real relationships for Lil, for us—we're dead, Luc. Let us be dead!"

Sudden and unexplainable anger shot through me. "I didn't bring you here, Darren. If you don't want to see me, then don't show up!" I instantly regretted saying that, as I loved seeing him. I immediately cooled and wanted to take back my words, but Darren scowled and turned away from me, biting his lip to hold in his quick temper.

Then his mouth fell open and his scowl vanished. He noticeably paled before slowly turning back to face me. With a soft voice he said, "Hey, man, I'm sorry."

My eyebrows drew to a point as I tried to figure out why *he* was sorry for *my* outburst. "What…why? I'm sorry, man, I shouldn't have said that."

He shook his head and pointed out the windshield. I started, remembering that I wasn't really in a nice dream, having a friendly spat with Darren. I was in a nightmare, driving along a wet, dark road—*the* wet, dark road. I twisted back around and I gripped the wheel with both hands, trying to focus on what I was doing. My heart shifted to triple time and my breath came in ragged pulls; I could easily make out a disturbingly familiar curve in the road through the rain-streaked windshield.

Darren's voice echoed hauntingly at my side. "I'm sorry. This is the part you're not going to like."

The car started to skim across the water and I instinctively slammed on the brakes.

Chapter 9 – First Day, Round Two

I woke up screaming and throwing my hands out on the bed, trying to stop myself from going over that cliff again. My heart raced as I screamed over and over, not able to fully disassociate from that horrid nightmare. Warm arms scooped me up and a soft voice repeatedly hushed in my ear. Eventually my mother's calm voice tore me into reality and as I let the dream go, my screams shifted into sobs. God, I hated dreaming about driving. Even with Darren's help…I hated dreaming about driving.

Mom crawled into bed with me and stayed there until she had to work the next morning. I embarrassingly clutched her tight, reluctant to let her leave, scared the nightmare would find a way to return and haunt me, even awake. She softly kissed my forehead and whispered that everything would be all right and she'd be back as soon as she could.

I stayed awake, staring at the cracks of my ceiling and begging my mind to stay blank. It didn't. Flashes of rain and road and blood streaked my vision. Memories of screaming swirled in my brain, some Lil's, some mine. I was still staring at the ceiling when Sawyer appeared in my door. I blinked as I looked over at her, wondering how long I'd been lying in bed, swirling in dark thoughts. She started to explain that she'd been knocking for forever, when she noticed the look on my face and immediately stopped talking.

"Luc? What is it?" She came to the edge of the bed and sat, brushing some hair off my forehead.

"Nothing…I'm fine." Even as I said it, I felt a tear dripping down my cheek. Her thumb brushed it off and she immediately crawled under the covers with me, slinging both arms around my neck.

"It's okay, Lucas. It's okay." Her soft voice cooed in my ear and any strength I had left in me failed. I caved into the despair that my nightmare had filled me with. My arms slung around her body and I sobbed, heart wrenching sobs that I couldn't hold back anymore. It was embarrassing and I hated doing it, but I couldn't stop the overwhelming grief anymore than I could stop the stuttered breaths I was taking.

Sawyer never complained or tried to pull away from my ever tightening embrace. She slipped a hand into my hair and rubbed her other down my back in soothing patterns. Eventually, her voice and her calming touch soothed me to silence. Either that or I'd exhausted every tear in my body. Probably the latter.

With a few ragged breaths, and a quick swipe of my nose on my sleeve, I pulled back to look at her. She smiled warmly at me, her black hair pulled back into the childish pigtails that I'd seen on her that very first day of school. I lay back on my pillow and she propped herself up on an elbow, gazing down at me. I sniffled a couple times and looked away from her, embarrassed. I felt her fingers brush over my forehead again and then down to my cheek, turning me to look at her. With sheepish eyes, I did.

"I have some assignments for you."

I smiled genuinely and relaxed back into the pillows, grateful that she wasn't going to ask about my breakdown, grateful that she wasn't even going to mention it. I laughed lightly and ran a hand across my eyes, hoping to wipe away the remnants of my despondency.

"Oh good…I was getting a little bored."

She gave me a quick smile, her eyes glancing over my face before resting on my eyes again. "I'll just go get my bag." Her face hardened into seriousness. "I'll be right back, Lucas."

I swallowed and nodded while she slipped out of my bed and out of my room. I flung an arm over my eyes and tried to not be too embarrassed over my meltdown. I still was though. Just as I was thinking that I should go out to her, I felt her return to my room and heard her rummage through her bag. I peered out from under my arm when I felt her lift the covers and crawl back into bed with me. She'd taken my letterman's jacket off and draped it over her bag on the floor. She played with the too-long sleeves of her shirt as she balanced a book on her knees under my sheets.

I sat up and leaned back against the wall, smiling at her familiar habit. When I was alert enough to listen to my homework, she started laying everything out for me. I cringed over our math homework and smiled over the easy essay Ms. Reynolds had given us. Before I knew it, Sawyer was glancing at a clock on the wall and cursing, muttering that she was late.

She slipped out of my bed and started putting her stuff back together. I scooted around to the edge and sat up, putting my feet on the ground. I watched her shove stuff in her bag and hurriedly put my jacket back on. This was the last time she'd be coming over to give me my homework assignment. I wasn't sure if her protective parents would even let her visit after this, and her being in my room right now might be the last time this ever happened.

I reached out for her hand once she had everything all ready to go and laced our fingers together. She glanced down at where we were joined and looked up at me with a soft smile.

"Thank you, Sawyer…for everything." I softened my gaze and hoped that she understood that by "everything" I truly did mean *everything*—much more than just bringing me my homework daily. She may not understand, but she'd helped me survive my isolation. I don't think I could have done it without her.

Her eyes watered as she held my gaze. "You're welcome, Lucas." She swallowed and shook her head. "Well, I guess I'll see you Monday then. I'll kind of miss coming over." Her thoughts were running in line with mine; I was going to miss that too. "Maybe my parents would be okay with short visits…" She let the sentence trail off and bit her lip.

I smiled and nodded, trying not to get my hopes up. "I hope so…I'd really like that." Standing up, I encircled her in a warm hug. She paused for a moment and then returned the gesture. I resisted the urge to kiss her head and whisper just how much she meant to me. I resisted the urge to tell her how sorry I was that I was so messed up emotionally, that I couldn't give her what I suspected she wanted from me. And I resisted the urge to pull her in tighter, to never let her go. Instead of all that, I held her for another couple seconds, and then I let go and took a step back. "See ya Monday, Sawyer."

She nodded and adjusted her bag on her shoulder before turning to exit my room. I stopped her at the door. "Sawyer? How bad is school going to be?"

She grimaced and looked down. I didn't take that as a good sign. Sighing, she reluctantly raised her head to look at me. "Most people think you took something, got high or drunk…or something. I heard Brittany saying that she saw you take some pills outside of Art class."

I wasn't too surprised by this; the gossip mill was predictable. Sawyer's expression darkened. "And then, that bitch spends most of choir telling stories about how you get messed up every night and show up on her doorstep, trying to have sex with her." A faint blush filled her cheeks as anger went through her. "She always looks at me when she says that, like you're cheating on me or something." Her face went white. "Not that we're a couple. It's just…they all believe that we…"

I shook my head as she sputtered a few times, trying to explain herself. "I know, Sawyer. I understand." The school had unfortunately linked Sawyer to me from practically day one, even with my failed attempts not to bring unwanted attention to her.

I frowned as I considered Brittany's flat-out lies. Interesting that she'd paint me in that light for the school. Well, I'd always suspected that she was more interested in me than she let on. This was a way for her to live out a fantasy with me and make me look even worse, all at the same time. Win-win for her, I suppose. It wasn't like I was going to call her out on the lie. No one would believe me anyway.

I smiled crookedly, knowing no humor was in my face. "Oh well, I suppose it could be worse." She nodded and looked down. I remembered my suspicions that she was being ridiculed more than she let me see and walked over to her, placing a hand on her arm. "Are you okay, Sawyer? Do they…am I making things worse for you? Would it be better for you, if we weren't friends?" I whispered that last part, hoping she wasn't going to say "yes" and take the opportunity to walk away from me.

Her head snapped up and her wide eyes looked over my face. "No, no, Lucas…don't ever think that." Her hand sneaked up to rest on my chest and she took a step closer to me. "You make my life better, Lucas. If you only knew how much…" She bit her lip and shook her head, her eyes starting to water again. I started to ask a question, but she interrupted me. "Don't worry about what they say to me. I don't care. None of that matters to me—the cliques, the gossip, I don't care." She brought her other hand up to rest it on my chest, her fingers lightly pressing into me as she leaned closer. "This is what matters to me." She swallowed and searched my face. "You…you are what matters to me."

I swallowed and warmth flooded through me. My comfort, the only living person who really brought me true peace, found peace in me as well. I didn't understand how that was possible, how I could in any way bring her joy, but somehow, I seemed to, and that thought made me feel content and full—full of something I didn't even know how to completely express. I shook my head at her, a huge smile lighting my face. "You don't know what that means to me, Sawyer. You couldn't possibly understand how much I love you."

I froze as what I'd just said registered with my head. In all the time I'd had with Lillian, I'd never actually said those words to her. And here, now, I'd known Sawyer for only a few months and the words had slipped out effortlessly. I watched her face pale and her mouth drop open. I vaguely remembered that this wasn't the first time I'd told her I loved her. Some hazy memory of a drug-tainted conversation floated around my head, but embarrassment at my behavior then, and my outburst now, forced it back. Not knowing what else to do, and not really understanding what I meant by telling her I loved her, I quickly added, "As a friend, my best friend."

Her mouth closed and she swallowed; a strange emotion passed over her face before her peaceful smile returned. "I love you too, Lucas…as my best friend."

I smiled at her words, and the fact that I'd gotten myself over that could-be friend altering situation. I pulled her in for a tight hug before pulling back and playfully pushing her away. "You'd better go. You're already late, and you'll never convince them to let you come over, if I'm always getting you home late."

She laughed and nodded. "Yeah, you're right. Have a good weekend, Lucas."

Mentally I frowned at the prospect of more long days without her, but to her, I only nodded. "You too, Sawyer."

Monday morning came without much fanfare, just a light drizzle in the crisp November air. I dressed and got ready for school with a knot in my stomach. I'd been gone for a while now and, while my exile hadn't been pleasant, neither was the thought of roaming through those halls again, feeling all the hot stares and hearing hushed voices as I walked past. I'd gotten pretty good at tuning that out before the incident, but now it felt like I was starting the year over. Well, at least I had Sawyer with me. That helped tremendously.

Finished with getting ready, I smoothed a hand over my white, long-sleeve shirt and studied myself in the mirror of the bathroom. I'd run some product through my wavy hair, trying to tame the mess, and shaved this morning, but even to my eyes I looked freaked out. The hazel irises staring at me in the mirror were just a bit too wide, the breath coming out of my pale lips, just a bit too fast. I splashed some water on my face and closed my eyes, taking long, deep breaths.

I didn't need another bout of panic attacks. After my first horrid day of school, those had actually subsided, and I didn't need them popping up again. Of course, I also attributed that to Sawyer and her calming presence. I opened my eyes and forced a smile to my stressed face. I'd see her soon and most, if not all, of my anxiety would slip away with her perky smile.

I shuffled out to the kitchen and started a pot of coffee for my mother and me. She'd been out late last night, picking up an extra shift at the diner, and I'd woken up before her. I made the pot extra strong, feeling like we'd both need the boost today. Just as I was sitting down at the small table, she appeared in the doorway, yawning and stretching.

She smiled at me and ruffled my hair, ruining whatever semblance of put-togetherness I'd achieved this morning. It didn't really matter to me, so I returned her warm smile. She frowned when she saw it, and I realized I was still using my forced smile. My face wouldn't relax into a genuine one.

"Do you want me to call the school, Lucas? One more day surely wouldn't hurt anything." She ran a hand down my cheek, looking over my features as she worried about me.

I swallowed and attempted to smooth out my rigid smile. "No, one more day won't help anything either. I need to get this over with."

She nodded and stared at me for a few more long moments before pouring herself a mug and sitting at her spot at the table, the same spot the sheriff had been at last week. I thought about that conversation as Mom took her first sip of the steaming beverage. "Did you have a good visit with Sheriff Whitney last week?" she asked quietly.

I looked up at her face, startled that our thoughts were running so parallel with each other. "Um, yeah…I guess." I wanted to ask her what she was doing telling such personal things about our life to such a high-profile person, but I couldn't get the words out to question her. She'd given up enough for me already. If she needed someone to talk to…well, I'd prefer it wasn't him, but that wasn't really up to me.

She nodded and a small smile lit her lips before she took another sip. She grimaced a little bit and I twisted my lips consolingly. "Sorry…it's a little strong, isn't it?"

She chuckled and looked up at me over her cup. "Yes, even for you." She lowered her mug and her voice softened. "But, I suppose you needed the extra help today." Her eyes misted over as she continued staring at me. "I'm sorry, Lucas…for what today is going to be for you."

I nodded and darted my eyes down to my mostly full cup. I busied myself with draining it, shutting my head off at the sight of my mom getting emotional over my well-being. That sight would surely unhinge me today, and I didn't need it right now. Right now, all I needed to do was focus on maintaining my inner peace. The rest would work out just fine.

I was practically inhaling the bottom of my cup when a honk at the door signaled Sawyer's arrival. A true grin spread on my face as I looked over to the window and saw her checking out her appearance in the rear view mirror. I looked over at my mom to say goodbye. She was watching me with a small, crooked smile.

"What?" I asked cautiously.

She shook her head. "Oh, nothing." Her eyes flicked to the window and then back to me. "I'm just glad that there is someone out there who can make your face look like that again." Her eyes got momentarily wistful, and clouded over again with what could easily become tears.

I looked down and shrugged, not wanting to delve into Sawyer's and my relationship. It was too complicated for me to think about on most days, I didn't need her trying to analyze it, too. "I better go, she's waiting."

Mom stood and gave me a swift hug. "Of course, dear." She pulled back to look at me, her eyes slowly sweeping over my face, taking me in. "Have a good day, Lucas."

I gave her a half-hearted grin before picking my bag and jacket off the floor near the front door. "I'll try," I murmured, as I slipped them both on. With one last hug to her, I opened the door and waved to Sawyer with an idiotic grin on my face. It had been a long time since I'd seen her in the morning.

Sawyer waved back at me and then my mom in the doorway as I opened her door to get inside. The all too familiar lemon scent washed over me and I was instantly calm. The familiarity of the fragrance eased my breath and my squeezed heart. I exhaled and sank back into the seat as she pulled out of my driveway. With one final glance at my mom's retreating figure at our front door, I turned my head to face Sawyer.

"Hey," I said pleasantly, with a spring in my voice.

She looked over at me and grinned, her face beaming under that curtain of straight, dark hair. "Hey, yourself. You're in a much better mood than I expected to find you in." She raised an eyebrow and then turned her attention back to the road.

I laughed and turned my attention to the threat of school looming before us. "Not really. I'm just glad to see you."

I felt her turn to look at me and met her gaze. "I'm glad to see you too. I've missed this."

My eyes softened as I looked at her while she turned back to the road. The early morning sun glinted off her freshly applied lip gloss and a strand of dark hair strayed close to her eye, begging to be tucked behind her ear. She really was quite beautiful. "Really?" I whispered, without meaning to say anything.

She turned back to me. Her eyes lingered on my lips and a strange feeling welled up in me before she suddenly broke the contact, and firmly fixed her eyes to the road ahead of us again. "Well, yeah." She shrugged nonchalantly. "I didn't have anyone to complain over my music choices."

She gave me a sly grin before reaching down and turning up the volume on her indie, chick rock. I groaned dramatically and rolled my eyes, grateful that the odd feeling was leaving me and the familiar, comforting peace was returning. We both chuckled as we listened to her man-hater music for the last few minutes before we reached my personal hell—Sheridan High.

She shut the car off, the music suddenly stopping in the middle of an 'I'm better off alone' sentence. I felt a crushing dread close in on me. My chest squeezed as I looked out over the assortment of cars already on the lot. I recognized more than a few—Will's, Randy's, Brittany's, and the battered pickup that Josh had been driving this year. Looking at the cars was like looking at a lineup of the people who would love to see me be run over by them. I tried not to care, but my chest started constricting and my breath started hitching. It was getting harder and harder to keep it even.

A warm hand touched my chin, carefully turning my head. I looked over to

Sawyer's calm face. "I'm here, Lucas. It will be okay." She nodded encouragingly and cupped my cheek.

I swallowed and held eye contact with her, feeling that serenity wash over me. I could do this. Just a few more months, and then I would be gone. I could do this. My breath evened and the ache in my chest loosened. With one last long exhale, I nodded my readiness to her and opened the door.

We made it all the way to the main building doors with barely more than double takes from the student body. I was starting to feel calm and confident that everything would be fine—well, normal anyway, which was usually me being completely ignored, which was fine. I opened the heavy door and gallantly ushered Sawyer inside, her breath a visible puff as she laughed at me in the chilly air. I laughed with her and together we walked through the doors like any pair of normal high school students.

But I wasn't normal. I wasn't really wanted around here. And as the heavy door slammed shut ominously behind me, I was reminded of that fact by a heated set of eyes.

"Oh good...*you're* back. Enjoy your time off?" Josh leaned back against the row of lockers directly in front of the main doors and sneered at me, his arms crossed over his chest.

Anger swelled in me, as I thought back to what this little punk had done to me two weeks ago—the embarrassment, the banishment, but mainly, the forced separation from my best friend. I didn't give him a chance to say much else, as a low noise surprisingly came out of my chest and the words, *"You son of a bitch!"* rested on the tip of my tongue.

But I didn't get a chance to say it, as my hand was suddenly grabbed and yanked away from my body, and I had little choice but to follow it. I started to pull away from the hand, to return to where a smirking Josh was slapping a friend of his across the chest and muttering something that made his small group laugh and point after Sawyer and me.

"Don't, Lucas. He's not worth it."

I turned and found my voice heated when the words finally did come out. "He drugged me, Sawyer. He deserves to get his ass kicked!" For a moment, I pictured Darren blowing his top and slamming his brother back against the lockers. Darren could be fiery when he got going and, while he'd never taken a swing at his brother, I knew he would have if the situation called for it. And this situation definitely called for it.

Sawyer continued tugging my hand, pulling me away from the fight I was all geared up for. "True, he does deserve it," she muttered sullenly. Stopping when we finally reached the stairs, she put a hand on my cheek. "But not in the middle of the hallway around all these people. Not when you have one strike against you already. You don't need the trouble, Luc."

I sniffed and my body started to shake with the desire to do...something, hit...something. It had been a long time since pure anger had coursed through me and for a moment, I let that heat rush through my veins and darken my countenance.

"Maybe I want the trouble," I growled. Josh had gone too far this time. Maybe getting expelled would be worth it.

Sawyer's eyes widened, but she was interrupted by a voice behind her before she could say anything. "Is there a problem here?"

I looked over Sawyer's shoulder to Coach Taylor standing behind her. I instantly straightened my stance at seeing the man who'd been an authority figure to me for a long time. "No, Coach," I automatically replied. The heat left me as I stared at him, and my voice lost its hard edge.

Coach had always been tough, but fair, on Darren and me and we'd grown to respect him. Darren used to always joke that Coach could be my long-gone dad, since he really did look like an older version of me—a crew cut in the same brown as my scruffy head, the same hazel eyes, if a little more intense on him, the same chin, the same nose, the same overall build. I always laughed it off when Darren got into hysterics about it though. I may not have actually known my…biological father, but I knew the coach was *not* him. For one, I've seen pictures of my dad, and he and Coach look nothing alike. Second, I really didn't like to think about Coach getting it on with my mom. Ugh.

Coach sniffed and cocked his head as he looked at me and then down the hallway to where Josh and his friends were still laughing. "Let's talk, West." He crossed his arms over his blue and white polo, the school's colors, and narrowed his eyes at me. The look in them did not invite questioning.

"I have to get to class…" I began lamely and nodded my head in the direction of the stairs. Sawyer, beside me, shifted uncomfortably, looking like she wasn't sure if she should stay by my side or leave me alone with the coach.

He sniffed again and twisted his lips, the look on his hard face displeased. "That wasn't a request."

I looked down and nodded before giving Sawyer a "sorry" face, and telling her I'd meet her in English. She nodded back at me and then quickly glanced over the intimidating man beside me before hurrying up the stairs. I watched her leave, turning the corner and being followed by what seemed like a squadron of kids, and then I sighed and twisted to face the coach.

He immediately started in on the speech he'd probably prepared for me on day one. "I've invested a lot of time in you, West, and this is how you repay me?" His arms crossed on his chest moved to his hips and his face took on a stern look, all sharp angles and hard edges, not looking much like me at all anymore. "You ditch the team your senior year, not even bothering to show up for tryouts this summer, or even telling me you weren't going to." He pointed irritably down the hall where a few students were watching us converse, or rather, watching the coach converse *at* me. "You left me stuck with McKinney as your replacement for God's sake."

"Will's good…" I tried meekly.

His eyes narrowed as his voice got even sterner. "Will's got good feet, but his hands are crap. He's more awkward with the ball than a freshman trying to unhook his first bra. We needed you this year."

I looked away from him. "Things came up…"

He snorted and I looked back. "Yeah, I know all about what *came up*." His hard eyes turned disapproving. "Getting hammered with your friends, getting behind the wheel when you shouldn't have, getting them killed…"

His face softened in a way I'd never seen before, and my throat closed up. God, I did not want to cry in front of this man. He put a hand on my shoulder in a rare show of compassion. "They will be missed…Darren especially." An odd half smile lightened his face and I blinked at seeing it; Coach didn't smile much, even if we *won* the game. "Now, *he* had great hands. I'd have made him quarterback, if he wasn't such a great running back."

As his words died between us, and his momentary softness over the deceased students passed, his eyes and face hardened right back up. I swallowed and tried to focus on what he was saying and not how he was making me feel. Besides the pang of my friends being mentioned, no teacher had yet called me a drunk outright like that, and my stomach was twisting. Coach never was one to mince words though. He removed his palm from my shoulder and stuck both hands on his hips again. "I would've taken you back, even with all that. I would have drug tested the hell out of you, and probably kept you on the bench more than usual, but I'd have taken you back. I'd have gotten you sober and gotten you back out on that field."

I sighed and bit my tongue; he wouldn't believe my innocence, even if I tried proclaiming it. Coach was not easily swayed once he went down a path. And right now he was firmly on the "Lucas has gone to the dark side" path. He tossed one hand up in the air as he shook his head. "But then you go and get high at school, and prance around my pep rally like it's your own personal rave! What the hell was that, Lucas West?"

I swallowed my embarrassment and my pride and bowed my head, not saying anything. Finally, he made a disgruntled noise. "Sports would have been a better outlet for you, West. It still would. It's too late for football, but maybe you'll consider something else. Baseball…or something."

His voice softened, just fractionally, and I glanced up at him. Some of the hard edge was gone from his face and his brows were slightly scrunched, almost like he was concerned. "Anything but drugs and alcohol, Luc." Then he dropped his head and the stern mask of adolescent disciplinarian completely fell off his face. He sniffed a bit and shook his head, while a tender emotion touched his voice. "I'd hate to lose another one."

Without looking at me again, he clapped my shoulder and strode off down the hall, barking at a few loitering students to get to class. The stern disciplinarian snapped right back into place. I found that I couldn't move after he left. My vision swam as my eyes watered and I could just barely make out the shape of Coach leaving the building. There had been a time when his stern words meant everything to me. He could crush me or lift me with one sentence. He apparently still had that effect on me and I swallowed several times to fight back my overwhelming guilt and remorse. He was wrong about me…they all were, and sports didn't matter much anymore. I exhaled for ten long seconds, closing my eyes. A few more months. That's all of this that I had to take.

Sawyer's eyes locked onto mine the second I set foot in the room. I gave her a vague smile and a quick nod. The bell had rung on my way up the steps and Ms. Reynolds was just starting class as I walked inside. Just like my first day, I was disrupting things again. Ms. Reynolds seemed better equipped to deal with me this time, though.

She gave me a warm smile as I approached her. The room was completely silent and I felt the physical heat of all those eyes staring at me. It made me shift uncomfortably as Ms. Reynolds put a friendly hand on my shoulder. A snigger went up around the room at the contact, and I instantly remembered what I'd said to her in front of a good chunk of the student body. The words *totally fuckable* flashed through my head and my cheeks flushed with warmth, probably turning bright red.

The barely contained chuckles got louder, but Ms. Reynolds ignored them. "Oh good, Lucas, you're back. Go ahead and take your seat." As she seemed to be letting my tardiness slide again, I didn't say anything, only nodded and started my way to Sawyer.

"Oh, Luc?" Her hand touched my arm to stop me, and a fresh burst of laughter hit the room. She seemed to notice it this time and scowled at some of the louder people, Will among them. "I just wanted to remind you that your appointment with the counselor starts today." Her eyes lit up at that prospect and her voice was near bubbly when she continued. "The principal is going to let you rejoin the Safe and Sound Club once you complete a six week session. Isn't that great?" She squeezed my arm for emphasis and I resisted the urge to roll my eyes and sigh. *Six weeks…great.*

"Uh…yeah. Thank you."

Full of exuberance, she raised her arm toward the aisle, indicating that I should sit. I met eyes with Sawyer while a soft chorus of laughs followed me down the row. Sawyer grinned and rolled her eyes for me and I chuckled.

As I was about to pass Will, I carefully watched his feet. I didn't need today to be a complete recap of day one.

Apparently it wasn't. Will had other ways to embarrass me. Right as I walked by, he clutched his desk with both hands and thrust his hips up, making the font legs of the desk lift off the floor a couple inches. He laid his head back and softly moaned, "Oh God, Ms. Reynolds. Oh yeah, yeah, fuck…yes, teach me."

I stumbled a bit on my feet as the entire class, with the exception of Sawyer, of course, burst into loud laughing. Ms. Reynolds had been writing something on the board, carefully transcribing it from the textbook, and had apparently missed Will's display. She loudly called for quiet and gave the room a stern stare, but she didn't say anything directly to Will. I was pretty sure she would have if she'd heard that. He'd probably have gotten detention at the very least.

With flaming cheeks, I sat in my chair and laid my head down on my desk. I wanted to crawl up in a tiny hole and never come out. But hadn't I been in a tiny hole for the past two weeks and still been miserable? I sighed and wished I could take a nap through first period—I would have given anything to see Lil right then.

A soft hand on my arm made me look over at Sawyer. I laid my head to the side as quietness enveloped the classroom. She laid her head on her desk and we stared at each other while Ms. Reynolds went over the current lesson plan. Eventually looking at Sawyer brought my emotions back to level, and I smiled at her. She smiled back and mouthed, "Are you okay?"

I closed my eyes and chuckled at her never ending concern for me. Reopening them, I nodded at her and mouthed, "Just embarrassed."

She bit her lip and then grinned devilishly. "You should be," she whispered, "talking to a teacher like that." She raised an eyebrow at me and shook her head. "Dirty boy," she mouthed.

I bit my lip to not laugh out loud and raised my head off my desk. I marveled at Sawyer's odd ability to always make me feel better, whether with silence or a comforting touch, or even a smartass comment. Or maybe it was just her very presence. I stretched out my hand to her across the aisle while Ms. Reynolds went over last week's homework—homework I'd only been able to do thanks to this beautiful godsend beside me. She lightly grabbed my hand and looped our index fingers together.

"Thank you," I whispered.

"Anytime," she whispered back.

Sawyer and I both waited around in the back of the room after class, waiting for most, if not all, of the students to leave. Ms. Reynolds watched us, but said nothing, probably used to how Sawyer and I always seemed to linger in class until we were alone. When Sawyer couldn't wait anymore, her next class being so far away from this one, we headed out to the main doors.

Sawyer asked about what the coach had wanted and with a heavy sigh I told her. She was unsure how to process the conversation. On one hand, he seemed to care about me. On the other hand, he thought I was waist deep in life-altering drugs. Finally she shook her head and again encouraged me to tell a teacher about Josh, about what had really happened. I gave her a faint smile but kept my mouth shut. I wasn't going to narc on Josh, and I didn't much see the point in talking about it, anyway. Just like the coach, people's minds were already decided.

She twisted her lips as we parted ways, seeming to understand where my head was at. I suppose she'd handle all of this differently. Well, maybe not. It's much easier to give advice than follow it.

History went pretty smoothly, with only a handful of stares and whispers, usually followed by light laughter. I kept my head down and did my best to ignore it all. Thanks to Sawyer's diligence in keeping me caught up, I got back into the swing of things smoothly, and if Mr. Davis was startled by my presence in the room after being absent for so long, he didn't show it. In fact, the only comments I got were from Eliza, who asked if my girlfriend was going to stop bugging her for the assignments. I stared at her blankly as I processed that. I never did find out how Sawyer had managed to get all of the work from all of my classes, even the ones we didn't share. I must have mentioned Eliza to her at some point and she'd gone out of her way to talk to the woman. Pretty impressive. I wondered who she'd talked with in Astronomy?

I asked Sawyer about it when we met up for the next period, and she only smiled and shrugged it off, like it was no big deal. She explained that she'd heard Eliza talking about me in computer lab one day and had deduced that we had History together. She had choir with one of the cheerleaders in Astronomy and had talked her into handing over her notes, and she'd met with my art teacher after choir, since the buildings were right next to each other. I shook my head at her and smiled, amazed at the lengths she'd gone to help me, and also a little amazed that she'd found students in this school that would help her, knowing full well they were really helping me.

We were whispering back and forth to each other about it during Philosophy when Mr. Varner came down the aisle and stopped right in front of my desk. A soft giggle went up around the room, and I remembered the gossip that had floated around about the three of us. Staring up at his narrowed eyes, I also remembered him helping my drug-riddled body out of the gym and into the main building, where he'd called my mom, freaking her out with his vague responses. He'd had a close-up view of my high, and he hadn't been too thrilled about it. He looked even less thrilled as he scowled down at me now.

"Something you'd like to share with the class, Lucas?" His voice was low and while not threatening in any way, it wasn't friendly either.

I shook my head. "No, Mr. Varner."

He crossed his arms over his chest and half smiled. I heard a soft sigh from a student beside me and I had to stop myself from rolling my eyes. Yes, he was attractive…but he was also an asshole. I didn't understand why the girls around here could be so quick to overlook that fact. "Are you sure? Wouldn't you like to enlighten us on how you spent your…break?"

The room quieted down, and I heard the rustle of people turning in their seats. I didn't remove my eyes from the teacher, but I imagined that everybody had just shifted to watch this. I shook my head, hoping he'd drop it before I either yelled something at him or burst into tears. The way my morning was going, I could do either.

He leaned over my desk and I involuntarily leaned back. "Next time you want to get high…you do it on someone else's watch." He glanced over at Sawyer before shifting his eyes back to mine. "Now both of you—be quiet." And with that, he stood straight and walked back to the front of the room.

I swallowed and looked around. Sure enough, most people were turned to face me, some with open-mouthed, shocked faces and some with barely contained smirks. One by one they followed Mr. Varner, and turned in their seats. My cheeks felt hot to the touch as his words flashed through me. So, no "your life is better without drugs" speech from Mr. Varner then. Nope, just an "I know you're a messed up kid, who is just going to do it anyway, so go do it far away from me so I don't have to pick up the pieces of your worthless life" comment. Odd point of view for a Philosophy teacher to have. As I stared down at my desk, I started to think that maybe Mr. Varner should have picked a different major in college.

"Well, that was uncalled for," Sawyer muttered, as we huddled around her locker during break.

I looked over at her while she put some books away and got others out, stuffing them in her bag. I adjusted my heavy backpack on my shoulder as I leaned against a cool, metal locker. I never used mine. I wouldn't even have come near these lockers if Sawyer didn't want to use Lil's…hers. I generally avoided looking when she opened it, like somehow, a part of Lil had gotten trapped in there when she'd died, and every time the door was opened, a bit of her light shone, and I couldn't bear to watch. Ridiculous? Yes, I know, but that's the feeling it gave me.

Today though, I stared at the lifeless thing while Sawyer adjusted some stuff inside it, just hoping for a spark of Lil to fill me. I hadn't dreamt of her since our last…encounter. Since that had kind of been an intense dream, and it had been cut off so abruptly…and I was just having a crappy kind of day, I really wanted to see Lil again. I wanted to see if she was okay, if we were okay. God, I really did sound insane. I wanted to dream about my dead girlfriend again, so I could make sure she wasn't freaked out by the almost sex we had…in a dream. All of it was in my head. Still, she felt as real as anything else.

"Lucas?" Sawyer's voice broke me from my bizarre thoughts.

"What? Oh, Mr. Varner, right." I pushed myself away from the lockers and watched some of the kids walking down the hall. Most of them were staring at me. Some whispered, some laughed, and a few even scowled. I turned back to watch Sawyer close her locker. "Yeah, he's just an asshole."

She frowned and then grinned. "Odd that he teaches Philosophy, right?"

I laughed and slung an arm around her shoulders, pulling her tight to me. "What's odd is how alike you and I are sometimes." She frowned at me when she looked up at my face, but then she laughed with me.

I dropped my arm from around her shoulders, still reluctant to be too friendly with her around so many gossiping eyes, even though that was pretty pointless by now, and they would all make up whatever stories they wanted to, anyway. I mean, just this morning, hadn't Eliza called her my girlfriend? I frowned as I realized that I'd never corrected her on that. Quickly slipping my grin back on, I started walking down the hall with Sawyer. And standing close to each other, but never touching, we made our way to our next class.

Math.

It's a tricky subject to try and learn on your own, even if you're pretty good at it. And I…struggle with it. Mentally planning to ditch this class next semester, I spent the whole hour with my head darting from the board to my textbook to my paper, in an odd, haphazard triangle pattern. I practically chewed through my pencil as I tried to grasp what the bloody hell Mrs. Chambers was talking about.

When it came to free study time at the end of class, she came over to her "favorite" student and attempted to help me catch up. I was immensely grateful that she cared more about her beloved subject than the rumor mill running through these walls. I think I could have been lying in a pile of my own alcohol-induced vomit, and she'd still try and help me if I showed just the tiniest bit of interest in mathematics. She had definitely chosen the right major.

While I knew passing the class with a B would be a lofty goal, I felt much better about the situation once the period was over. I felt even better about it as I shared my sandwich with Sawyer in the car. She got a serious case of the giggles as she described my face to me when I'd been trying to grasp algorithms. I tried to sneer at her, but ended up bursting out with laughter, too. Feeling a need for the cathartic release, I brought up Mr. Varner chewing me out, Coach trapping me in the hall and Will's sexual display during class.

With tears of laughter streaming down her face, she lost nearly all control when I re-performed Will's shining moment for her. "Oh, yes, yes…fuck, teach me."

I started laughing uncontrollably and we both settled in for a long, happy release. Eventually, we calmed down and rested back in her bucket seats, looking over at each other. We'd drifted close in our gaiety, and our shoulders touched between the gap created by her center console. Our heads rested on the very edge of the headrests as we faced each other.

Trying to even our breaths, but still smiling, we stared at each other. The familiar comfort washed over me as I lost myself in her gray depths. A similar look passed over her, and I wanted to stay in this car for eternity.

She leaned forward and a dark lock of hair fell over her eye. Without thinking about it, I reached up and tucked it behind her ear. Then I found myself running my fingers back through her hair before bringing my palm up to cup her cool cheek. Then my thumb started stroking that cheek. Even though the car was slightly chilly, I felt warmth spread in me as we touched. I watched her breath catch and her eyes flick over my face. My eyes flicked over hers, settling on her lips. Subconsciously, I found myself leaning forward.

"Luc…we're gonna be late," she whispered, just moments before we brushed together.

Startled back to reality, I dropped my hand from her skin and pulled back. "Right." I looked down and then peeked up at her from under my brow. She was chewing her lip. "Sorry," I muttered.

She gave me a vague smile and turning, opened her car door. I shut my eyes at my stupid lack of self-control, and with a heavy exhale, opened my door. She didn't say anything as she waited for me at the front of her car, just played with the sleeves of my jacket and bit her lip. I felt the need to say something, but didn't know what to say, so I gave her a half smile and nodded my head towards school.

She fell in beside me and was quiet on the way to our next respective classes. Her head was down and her dark hair covered her expression. I wanted to stop her and sweep that hair back from her face so I could see what she was thinking. I wanted to tell her that I was sorry, yet again, for getting near the borderline of our friendship. And an odd, tiny speck of me…wanted to kiss her, wanted to find comfort in those lips, just like I found comfort in her voice and her laugh…and her eyes. I wouldn't do that, though. That would be selfish. Not if she was interested in more. Not when my heart still belonged to Lil…

Lost in those thoughts, I started when Sawyer's hand caught my elbow and stopped me. I looked up and noticed that we were at our crossroads, left for me to get to Astronomy and right for her to get to computer lab. I hadn't even noticed the journey.

I looked over at her and took in the serious expression on her face. I swallowed, thinking she was finally going to tell me she couldn't handle being my friend anymore, not when I constantly pulled her close and pushed her away. My stomach hurt as I waited for her rejection.

"Don't you dare…start something with Josh. Just let it go, Lucas." Her eyes bored into me, demanding and pleading at the same time.

I relaxed when I realized she wasn't going to toss me aside.

Then a slow fire started burning in me. I'd nearly forgotten that I'd have this class with Josh. I'd nearly forgotten that I'd have to endure sitting in a room with him for an hour, not able to do anything about the mix of rage and sadness swirling within me. Sawyer's eyes narrowed even more as she took in my expression.

"I'm serious, Lucas." She shook her head. "He's not worth you getting kicked out of here. Don't give him what he wants."

I blinked and took a step back. The anger started to fade from me as I realized that she was right. If I let my emotions take control and got myself kicked out of here, he'd have exactly what he'd hoped for with his stupid little stunt. He'd win. While I was sure it wasn't really a game to either of us, I wasn't about to give him the satisfaction of running me off. No, if I had to deal with him for the rest of the year, then he'd just have to deal with me too.

"I won't touch him, Sawyer…I promise." Her stance relaxed, along with her face. She searched me for a sign of some lie to my words and I gave her a wry smile. "I *promise*, okay?"

She bit her lip again and nodded.

A small laugh escaped me. "Besides, I think I'll let *you* fight all my battles for me. You hit better than me anyway."

She laughed and gave me a quick hug before darting off to her class. I smiled, watching her leave, and then turned to the path that led me to my next encounter with Darren's little brother. As I walked along that concrete road, I remembered walking this exact path last year with Darren. Back then, our biggest dilemma had been the approaching teenage milestone known as junior prom.

"Three hundred bucks, Luc. That's how much this stupid dance is gonna cost me…three hundred bucks." Darren shook his head at me in my memory and frowned at his money woes.

I grinned over at him. "Yeah, but Sammy will be endlessly grateful to you for showing up in the limo she wants."

He gave me a devilish grin while we walked, pausing a fraction of a second to wave at a group of friends as we strolled by. "Dude, Sammy is 'grateful' to me five times a week…and it doesn't cost me three hundred bucks."

I stopped walking. "Five times a week?"

He grinned and nodded. "At least. Sometimes more if her parents leave for the weekend." He shrugged. "What can I say—my girl's a horny freak."

I grinned at the words I knew Sammy would soundly smack him for if she ever heard them repeated. I started walking beside him again, shaking my head. He looked over at me thoughtfully. "You and Lil still haven't…"

"No, we're…waiting. The moment has just never been right…" I shrugged and let the sentence die. Lil and I had talked about it several times, but somehow, neither one of us felt like it was just the right time. We were waiting for the "perfect" time.

Darren laughed beside me. "Well, don't wait too long or something's gonna come up and snatch that hottie away from you. Besides, it's only sex, Lucas. I think you guys are making it out to be a much bigger deal than it really is."

I scowled as we walked under the overhang of the Science building, Darren nodding a greeting to another group of friends passing by us. I switched my frown to a sly smile as I glanced over at him. "Says the man who waited two years to be with his…freak."

Darren's face clouded up as he glared over at me. I knew he and Sammy had a different situation than Lil and me. I mean, they *were* only fourteen when they got together, but it was fun to tease him about it, especially if he was going to tease me.

Darren was about to respond to my jibe when a set of arms slung over his shoulder and mine. "Who's a freak?"

I looked behind me at Josh hanging off of us, his face glowing with adoration for his big brother. "Your future sister-in-law," I playfully told him.

Darren smacked me in the chest as Josh suddenly gripped both of Darren's shoulders, shaking him. "Really? Like kinky-freaky? Lucky bastard, Shelly will only let me feel her up."

Darren grinned at Josh, rumpling his hair, and slinging an arm over his shoulder. He pointed at me. "Well, you're further than Lucas," he mocked. They'd both laughed heartily at me then, while I'd smacked Darren on the chest and told him where he could shove it.

As I passed under the considerably darker overhang, I clearly remembered Darren and Josh's laughing faces. The way their eyes had sparkled with life and joy, the way they'd had an arm around each other, supporting each other. Best friends in a way Darren and I never would be. It tore me that the jovial face I'd seen on Josh then was all but lost now. Sadness for that faded childhood leeched away my remaining spikes of anger and I felt only melancholy as I opened the door to class.

Chapter 10 – The Game of Life

Josh's eyes were the first thing I noticed as I walked through the door. They were locked right onto me, like he'd been waiting for me to walk through them. I kept my expression blank as I watched his shift into a mean sneer. He was sitting on his desk talking to Randy, who also turned to look at me. Randy gave me a brief look and then averted his eyes to stare at the front of the class. With memories of a happier time playing in my head, I thought again that maybe I'd try to have a civil conversation with Josh.

I took a deep breath and closed my eyes for a second before making the attempt. His entire body stiffened as I approached him, and I watched his sneer twist into anger. He obviously did not want me close to him and probably did not want me talking to him. I slowly let out my deep breath and stopped at the edge of his desk. Randy turned around to watch, his eyes nervous.

The teacher, Mr. Thomson, was staring out the window, waiting for the bell to ring and the rest of the students to filter into class. He was completely oblivious to the drama and tension building up inside the room. The students were not. I felt eyes turning to me and heard chairs squeaking as bodies shifted in them, anxious for a fight.

I wasn't going to give them one. That wasn't my desire anymore. Cautious of Josh's stormy face and excitable temper, I slowly began. "I don't want to start something with you, Josh, I just want to talk."

Josh's eyes narrowed. "I have nothing to say to you."

I sighed. "Come on, stop this already. You made me look stupid, all right? You got me fucked up and almost kicked out of here." I lifted my hands in an exasperated expression. "Isn't that enough?"

He stood by his desk and I felt the tension in the room triple. He was shorter than me, by a lot, but his confidence that he could kick my ass was evident in every move he made. His lips twisted into a small grin. "I don't know what you're talking about, Luc." He eyed me up and down contemptuously. "You made your own bad choices...like always."

I closed my eyes at the clear insinuation of *that* night. "Josh, we used to be friends. Come on, man…"

I opened my eyes as fingertips pushed me back. Josh's face looked even stormier. "I used to be a lot of things, Luc." His voice rose, and he took a step towards me, until we were toe to toe. "A brother…a best friend." His finger jabbed me in the chest and his voice went even higher. "You took all of that away from me! You! So don't give me the 'come on' crap!"

At this point, Mr. Thomson finally noticed that a storm was brewing in his room. He stood up and quickly raced over to Josh and me. I was so twisted with emotion over Josh's words that I hadn't backed away from him and Mr. Thomson had to use his arms to literally wedge us apart. We both looked over at his annoyed face when he spoke. "Enough! Break it off or you'll both get detention!" He pushed me away from where I was still standing in a dazed funk. "Sit down, Lucas!" He turned me and shoved me towards my desk. Stumbling a bit, I finally started moving on my own. I heard him turn around and bark at Josh, "You too!"

The bell rang right as I sat down, and with a quick glance at a glaring Josh, I turned my attention back to Mr. Thomson; his eyes narrowed and flickered between the two of us. "There will be no fighting in my classroom! Understand?"

I reluctantly nodded and looked over at Josh who was doing the same. The tension in the air started to dissolve and a few students around me let out held breaths. A few snickered, and a couple started placing bets on an after school knockout. From what I could make out, the odds were not in my favor. I clenched my jaw and tried to relax my body. I don't know why I even tried that. There was no reasoning with Josh, not with how much he hated me.

Closing my eyes, I listened to Mr. Thomson start class and focused only on relaxing and breathing. I'd tried. I'd tried to let go of my own anger and salvage some of my friendship with Josh. But I'd failed. I'd failed, and now I had to let him go. I wouldn't try talking to him again. I'd just have to ignore any more attempts he made to engage me. In fact, I'd just ignore any detrimental thing that he did to me. Even if he did somehow manage to kick my ass, all he would get from me was silent acceptance.

Because, while I might not agree with Josh's methods, I did sort of understand his anger; I'd be angry too, if I thought Josh had gotten drunk and killed them all. That would tear me up inside, and I'd probably never forgive him, either. And while I don't think I'd ever go to Josh's extremes…I hated myself enough that I could sympathize with Josh wanting to destroy me.

The rest of class went by with the traditional stares and whispers. For the first half of class, there were some odd tension-filled glances among the students in the space between Josh and me. They seemed to believe that we were going to launch at each other right in the middle of Mr. Thomson's speech on the mysteries of black holes. I kept my head straight and focused on listening to the teacher and eventually people started to relax, realizing nothing was going to happen.

I tried to focus on the teacher, but all I heard in my ears was Josh's searing words, *You took all of that away from me!* I knew he was right. I knew that whether I was drunk or not, he was right. I was the one driving that night. I had done it…me, and now Darren was gone because of it. Josh would never see past that and whatever semblance of friendship we once had was gone. I sighed as I thought of how disappointed Darren would be about that. I knew he'd prefer it if Josh and I had bonded over his death, leaning on each other for support and comfort. But this was no Disney movie, and what Josh wanted from me wasn't comfort—he wanted vengeance.

It saddened me to let that friendship go. Josh really was all I had left of Darren, but I couldn't hold onto someone who didn't want me, someone who actively hated me. My letting him go would be the best solution for both of us. It would be hard to let his anger and torments slide away from me without reacting, but even with all he'd done so far, I hadn't hit him yet, and really, I thought him drugging me was the worst he could do. I'd just have to be more careful with my stuff around him…or his helpers.

With a nasty glare at me after class, Josh was forcefully dragged out of the room by Randy, who looked at me with an odd, almost apologetic face. I had no idea why. Surely he'd been more than happy to carry out Josh's orders and spike my water. It's not like he'd been warm towards me at all this year.

By the time I shuffled out the door, both of them were gone, and I sucked in a deep breath, letting the crispness in the air clear my thoughts. I walked with my head down and concentrated on placing one foot in front of the other; that was enough to concentrate on for now. I heard a vague buzzing of whispers as I walked along and felt more than a few eyes, but I did my best to not worry about them. One more class and I'd be able to see Sawyer again. Then this feeling of discord would lift from me.

I walked into art class and immediately smiled as Mrs. Solheim turned at my entrance and exclaimed, "Welcome back, Tom!" I shook my head and made my way to my seat, not feeling the need to correct her. I grinned as I thought that maybe I'd just change my name and be this elusive 'Tom' from now on. A small chuckle escaped me when I realized how my new name would fit in so nicely with Sawyer's. We were connected on so many surprising levels.

A couple of intensely working students looked up at me upon hearing my laughter. They blinked, looked surprised to see my seat occupied, and then went back to whatever they were working on. I smiled and let the sounds of busy activity relax my mood. Light scratches on paper, the faint smell of oil paints, and the gentle murmurings of Mrs. Solheim as she walked throughout the room, checking the students' progress, eased the tension of the last class away from me. Settling in, I prepared to work on my latest version of my saving grace, Sawyer.

Mrs. Solheim never commented on the fact that all of my subjects, in whatever medium she was teaching us, were all dark haired girls with pale gray eyes. I wasn't even sure she had made the connection, as she was more interested in nurturing our techniques than in what we chose to paint. Art was the one class that I hadn't had any real homework in for Sawyer to collect—which was a good thing, since I'd have been really embarrassed handing Sawyer pieces of her own image to turn in for me, and nothing else moved me enough to paint it. The teacher had only told Sawyer that I could work on one project while I was gone, and hand it in when I got back.

I dug through my backpack until I found the charcoal sketched version of her that I had created during my hiatus. I unfolded the paper and stretched it out on my easel to make some finishing touches before I turned it in. It was my favorite piece of her, maybe because of the style, or maybe because I'd had so much time to work on it. During my more lucid moments, I'd spent hours going over the tiny details of her face, details I loved: the delicate bridge of her nose, the tiny freckle right beside her left eye, the one dimple in her cheek that she'd only get when she was giving me a wry half-smile, the look in her eye when I knew she was worrying about me, the way her upper lip formed the perfect, double arch of a heart…

A face leaning down next to me startled me from my work, and I glanced over at the teacher leaning in, inspecting my drawing. "Is this what you did while you were gone, Tom?"

"Yes…and it's Lucas, Mrs. Solheim." I really shouldn't let her call me the wrong name forever, as nice as the alter-ego was.

She glanced at me and frowned a bit as she looked over my features. "Oh, right, of course." She looked over my drawing again and sighed, a smile coming to her lips. "It's a beautiful piece, Lucas. Your strokes are delicate and intricate, quite an accomplishment with charcoal. You really are very talented." She straightened and patted my shoulder. "I can see you put a lot of work into this. It's very good. Nice job, Tom…Lucas."

I grinned from ear to ear as she walked away, happy that my picture had pleased her. I stared at Sawyer's face for long moments, almost sorry to let go of it. Oh well, I'd get it back soon and I did need the grade. I sighed and wrote my name on the back, mentally preparing myself to let yet another thing I cared about go.

I exhaled a happy sigh when school finally let out for the day. I'd done it. I'd survived what was essentially another first day of school. It had been emotional and embarrassing, frustrating and definitely difficult, but now it was over, and none of that mattered. Now I got to see Sawyer, and that was enough to put a spring in my step as I exited the classroom.

I stumbled on my step when I saw Sawyer in a heated conversation with Brittany outside of the choir room. I hastily made my way across the space between the two buildings, hoping I could stop whatever they were arguing about.

Brittany was surrounded by her legion of followers. Most of them were girls I'd known for years and hung out with on several occasions. They noticed me coming and patted Brittany on the shoulder. She broke off on her comment to Sawyer and looked up at me, her brown eyes narrowing. Her shoulders straightened and she swept her almost-blonde hair back over her shoulder. Her face twisted into a cruel sneer, and I wondered how I'd ever found her attractive.

She took a step toward me, casually shoving Sawyer's shoulder back. Sawyer's eyes flicked to mine, her jaw clenched, her fists in tight balls. She looked like she wanted to slug Brittany, although her eyes looked like she wanted to start sobbing. My heart seized at the hurt I saw in her face and I hoped whatever had started this…hadn't been because of me. She had suffered enough because of me.

Brittany took a step up to me, her sneer turning to a knowing smirk. "Back for more, Lucas? I've already told you 'no' a dozen times. You really need to get over me." Her voice dropped seductively and I got the feeling that that really wasn't what she was saying at all. I got the feeling that if I secretly told her to meet me in my bedroom tonight…she would.

My face darkening, I took a step over to Sawyer and pulled her into me. Sawyer tried to step back, but I held her tight. "Are you okay?" I whispered as I looked down at her, momentarily ignoring Brittany and her laughing group of friends. Sawyer bit her lip and nodded that she was, but her eyes still welled with unshed tears.

A hand reached out and pushed my shoulder. My head snapped back to Brittany, right as she stepped up to me, practically in my face. Brittany didn't like being ignored. "I was talking to you, druggy…or are you just too high to notice?"

I resisted the urge to smack the smug look from her face. Knowing Brittany, she'd probably like that. "What did you say to her?" I said through clenched teeth, trying desperately to hold in my ever-shifting emotions.

"What did I say to the white trash?" She shrugged like she really couldn't care less about the argument they'd been having. "We were just going over your extracurricular activities." She glanced at Sawyer and her grin turned cocky. She was loving this.

I closed my eyes, wanting to walk away, wanting to pull Sawyer out of this school and away from these people. "What are you talking about?" I muttered instead.

She leaned in close to me, her lips practically on my ear. I cringed away from her when she spoke in a husky voice. "I only apologized that her boyfriend was a no good man whore." Her eyes flicked down my body seductively *and* contemptuously. "But what can you expect from a drugged out alcoholic?"

Sawyer went bright red and her mouth opened in clear protest. "He is not a--"

Only thinking about getting away from Brittany, and her odd mixed signals, I cut Sawyer off…and said something really, really stupid. "I'm not her boyfriend, Brittany. Leave her alone."

With those words, I grabbed a suddenly-pale Sawyer's hand and dragged her away from the group. From behind me, I heard Brittany exclaim, "Oh God, he's fucking her, but he doesn't even want her!" Then even louder I heard her yell, "Sorry, white trash! I guess I had nothing to apologize for!"

I exhaled slowly and clenched Sawyer's hand in mine. I cursed under my breath at saying something so stupid to Brittany. True, there was nothing false about the statement, but, of all the things Brittany had said, that was the worst one for me to object to. By picking *that* statement to deny, I'd just given Brittany an arsenal of torture to spout at Sawyer. In one sentence, I'd pretty much confirmed everything else she'd said about me *and* downplayed the importance of Sawyer in my life.

God, I'm an idiot.

"I'm sorry," I muttered, as Sawyer hurried beside me to keep up with my fast pace. I glanced over at her and saw that her eyes weren't as watery, but they still seemed sad. The rest of her face had returned to her normal composure and I was sure that no one but me would even notice the faint unhappiness in her eyes. I slowed my pace and she looked over at me. "Sawyer…I'm sorry about what I--"

She shook her head and cut me off. "You didn't say anything that isn't true."

I stopped walking and she stopped with me, searching my eyes, like she was looking for some clue about how I really felt about her. I wished I could explain it, wished I could tell her that she was the one that made me light up in a way that made my mom smile, that she was the one that I painted in every art class, that she was home to me. I couldn't say any of that, though, not without confusing her even more.

"I shouldn't have said it like that…especially to someone like Brittany. It came off like I don't care about you at all and that's not true. I feel like I just made things worse for you."

Her hand came up to brush my cheek and she swallowed. "It's fine, Lucas. They just..." She sighed and looked away, dropping her hand.

"They what, Sawyer?"

She turned back and her eyes stared at my shoes. "She's teased me with the whole 'white trash' thing since the first day, when I ran into her in the parking lot. I was hiding out in the bathroom that day, because she hounded me all the way to the building about my hand-me-down clothes and cheap-ass book bag. She thought it was hilarious that I didn't have a jacket when it was pouring and..." she looked out over the campus to where we'd left Brittany and her wannabes, "when she saw me wearing your jacket later that day...she just...picked up her teasing a touch more."

I opened my mouth, surprised by her revelation and looked back with Sawyer. I had the sudden desire to run back there and tell that bitch Brittany that I'd never cared about her and never would, so she was the one who should just get over it...whatever the hell *it* was to her. Sawyer's words brought me back, though.

"It doesn't matter, Luc. It may bother me sometimes, the teasing and putdowns, but," she sniffed and straightened her shoulders, "I know my family struggles with money and stuff. They do the best they can for me." A wisdom seldom seen in a person her age crept into her voice. "I know what's important...and what's not, and Brittany and her cronies...aren't." Her face hardened into that serious mask that she could sometimes slip into. "I won't let someone like that destroy my life. All of this..." she gestured to the school grounds without taking her eyes from mine "...it's only temporary, Luc. Remember that."

I nodded and then shook my head at her in disbelief. Most kids, myself included, couldn't get past how high school could seem like the be-all and end-all of our young existence. "How old are you?" I muttered.

She giggled, like the schoolgirl she really was, and started walking towards the main building again. "I'm seventeen, Lucas...eighteen in January," she added with a grin.

I threw an arm around her shoulders as I matched her pace. "Wow, I'm hangin' with an older woman." I grinned down at her. "I think I got some of those cool points back."

She let out a genuine laugh and slung an arm around my waist. I felt the tension of our conversation, and the face-off with Brittany, die as her comfort seeped into me. Sawyer looked up at me. "Hey, good job by the way."

"Huh?"

She smiled as we approached the door to the main building, where the Safe and Sound Club met. I pulled open the door for us while she gingerly answered. "Well, you're not bruised or bleeding, so I take it that you did what I asked and left Josh alone." Her face beamed up at me as she stepped through the door.

I frowned as I followed her. "Maybe I just won the fight." I raised an eyebrow at her and she giggled again.

"Well, you weren't carted off the campus, so I'm assuming that you didn't haul off and hit him."

I laughed and then shrugged. "I said I'd stay away…I did." I didn't mention that I'd tried to have an actual conversation with him. It hadn't gone well anyway, so, not much to tell.

She snuggled back into my side as we walked through the empty halls. "I'm glad, Luc." She rested her head against me and I smiled. "I don't want to see you in anymore trouble."

I rested my cheek on her head. "Me either," I muttered.

We came to the classroom door and I pulled it open, preparing to go in with her. She put a hand on my chest. "Don't you have to get to your…thing?"

Confused, I was about to ask her what she was talking about when it suddenly hit me. Oh, damn it…the counselor. With everything that had happened today, I'd completely forgotten about *that* hell waiting for me. I frowned as I realized that we'd be parting ways now.

She brought her hand up to my cheek, stroking it with the back of her knuckle. "Hey, smile. It won't be so bad. Maybe you'll even like it?"

I gave her a "Yeah, right" face and sighed, staring longingly at the purity club door. The thought that I was longing to be at a purity club meeting made me chuckle. With a shake of my head, I said goodbye and gave Sawyer a swift hug before she entered the classroom without me. Staring at the closed door, I waited for ten long seconds before turning around and heading for the office…where my new personal hell was waiting for me.

I knocked softly on the closed, opaque door with the word "counselor" in rub-on, black letters across it. This was technically the guidance counselor's office, where she set up shop to help seniors apply to colleges, juniors put together a senior year with the most free periods, and freshman and sophomores find a way to weasel out of gym and typing. The "grief" counselor that they'd brought in full-time this year, courtesy of me, was sharing the office with her. I supposed this arrangement was quite handy for the custodians, since technically, they didn't have to resign the door.

I waited a couple seconds, hoping she hadn't heard me and I could leave, knowing that I'd tried. No such luck. Just as I was turning to dash away, to wait in the hallway for Sawyer, a soft voice answered me.

"Come on in, Lucas."

I cringed, both because she'd heard me, and because she knew it was me out here. With a heavy sigh, I opened the door and stepped inside. I'm sure it was my imagination, but the temperature seemed to drop a few degrees once I passed through the doorframe. I closed the door behind me and felt the echo vibrate morosely throughout the room. Rolling my eyes at my own dramatics, I took a step into the room and looked around at my "home away from home" for the next six weeks.

I'd been to the counselor's office a few times, but that was when the guidance counselor had it to herself. I internally smiled at the school's attempt to casually split a room into two. Their solution to the problem was an obtrusive line of two six foot tall lateral file cabinets in a straight line down the center of the room. The drawers faced out into the guidance counselor's "area," with her desk shoved haphazardly in the corner. She had a chair for visitors and a sturdy case full of thick, hardbound books, and that was about it. I bet she loved having her personal work space halved like that.

The back of the file cabinets were equally cramped, but an attempt *was* being made to create a soothing work space. The grief counselor's desk was specifically made for corners and fit nicely into the space it was given. Expecting a chaise lounge or couch in front of it, I was a little surprised to see a standard office chair for the "client's" seat. The rest of the room was filled with an almost spa-like ambiance: candles, soothing pictures of waterfalls and rock gardens, light jazz playing softly. A Japanese-like accordion room separator was folded back in on itself against the file cabinet. I suppose when a "session" was taking place, she'd extend it, giving the poor, depressed soul some false illusion of privacy. Like there was any true privacy in this school, or this town for that matter.

"Come on in, Lucas. Have a seat."

I took a final glance at the empty room, well, empty except for the counselor sitting at her desk, tucked in the oasis of her small office, and sighed. Irritated at having to do this, I grumpily walked over to her, tossing my backpack on the floor before unceremoniously dropping into the chair. She watched me sit down, and a small smile lifted the corners of her lips. She reminded me of a leprechaun. Why? I don't know. She wasn't a tiny pixie wearing buckled shoes and a green top hat. No green on her at all, actually. It was probably the hair—bright red with springy curls and a splattering of matching freckles marking her nose and cheeks, all of it highlighting her incredibly blue eyes. If I hadn't heard her speak already, I'd have expected an Irish brogue to pour from her mouth.

I adjusted my body uncomfortably in the seat as we both stared at each other. She sat back in her chair, absentmindedly flipping a pencil in her hands. She had strong looking hands. They matched her sturdy frame and solid bone structure. A delicate and tiny flower she was not. I could easily imagine her grabbing a plow and tilling one of those Irish hillsides.

Getting uneasy with the silence enfolding us, I coughed and looked around her office again. She finally spoke as she watched me assess my environment.

"Looking for an escape, Lucas?"

I shifted my attention back to her, noticing how often she'd already used my name. Maybe that was some "counselor" technique to make us seem like we were old friends already. It might work better if I knew her name too. I shook my head, but didn't answer her verbally.

She smiled and extended her hand. Almost reading my thoughts, she said, "My name is Mrs. Ryans, but you can call me Beth."

Feeling strange, I grabbed her hand. Her grasp was as firm as I'd suspected it to be. I awkwardly shook it for a moment and gratefully pulled my hand back to my lap when she let go. She tilted her head as she assessed me and I couldn't help but wonder what psychosis she'd already assigned to me. "Do you know why you're here, Lucas?"

I sighed and looked at the ceiling, hating this already. "Because I was fuc…" I looked back down at the teacher-like person before me and shifted my coarse language, "…impaired…on school grounds."

Her lips twisted into a wry grin and I was pretty sure she knew exactly what I'd been going to say. "That's what you did to get here. But why are you here, Lucas?"

I scrunched my brow, already lost. Why did therapist people feel the need to talk in circles? Couldn't she just tell me I was a messed up waste of space and let me go? "I don't understand…aren't they the same?"

She smiled and shook her head. "No, not even remotely."

I scowled, still confused, and shook my head too. "Well, you're the one with the diplomas. Aren't you supposed to tell me?"

She lifted a red eyebrow at me. "Do you want me to?"

I sighed and rolled my eyes. "Are you going to do the 'answer every question with a question' thing?"

"Do you want me to do that, Lucas?" When I scowled again, she laughed a little and added, "That was a joke."

Surprise washed through me that she'd both laughed and teased me. I don't know why. I guess I'd just expected all sternness and severity from a counselor. I found myself relaxing just a little bit and felt a small smile lighten my features.

Her face brightened considerably. "Ah, you do know how to smile. I was beginning to wonder." I looked down and shrugged my shoulders, trying to not be amused by her. Softly she added, "You seemed angry when you sat down. Why?"

I looked back up at her, not sure why she couldn't guess that. I'd been caught doing something inappropriate, that wasn't even my fault, and this was my punishment. Why would I be happy about any of that? A shot of true anger seared through me then, as I remembered all that had transpired to get me here, in this office, talking to someone I didn't want to talk to. I didn't want to talk to anyone, anyone alive anyway. I sneered as I answered her. "I'm only here because the Safe and Sound Club kicked me out, and I want back in. It makes me angry that I have to do this."

"Why?"

She cocked her head at me, looking like she was truly fascinated by my answer. I wondered if that was another technique—feigned interest. She was probably prepping a grocery list in her head. That thought incensed my already revved up temper. I *really* did not want to be there. "Because!"

She only stared at my response and I floundered for a more substantive answer. "I mean, God, the club's entire frickin' motto is 'because we care about you.'" I flung my arms out, as I started to get myself really ticked off. "It's supposed to be a club for troubled teens who want to turn their life around…and they kicked me out!" Tears surprisingly came to my eyes as I truly for the first time thought about this. "Me, the one kid in this school that people look at like…like I'm a washed up, messed up, worthless piece of shit! The one most in need of help, the most messed up one here…and they won't help me!" I brought my hands to my chest as I felt actual tears drop to my cheeks. "I want in…and they won't take me. What does that say?" I threw my hands out again, embarrassed at my words and my tears, but also feeling relieved for getting that unknown hurt off my chest.

I expected her to tell me the school was right. I expected her to tell me I didn't belong in that club. I expected her to berate me for my language. I expected her to recommend several different twelve step programs. What I never expected…was for her to say this:

"Well, Lucas…it kind of sounds hypocritical to me."

A rebuttal had been on my lips and it immediately fell off my tongue as my mouth dropped open. I realized then that the tilt of her head was her truly listening to me, that the glint in her eye was her showing true concern for my well-being. I stared at her, suddenly not seeing someone sent by fate to torture me even farther for my mistakes. For the first time ever…I saw a living human being whom I could potentially talk to. I mean, really talk to. It terrified me. I swallowed and pushed the icy terror back. What I said or didn't say was still my choice.

Letting my momentary panic subside, I quietly answered, "Yeah…me too."

We talked about more mundane things for the rest of my time there—my relationship with my mom, my non-existent relationship with my father, what I liked to do, what I used to like to do, my plan for next year. She didn't ask me about the crash. She didn't ask me about the gossip that swirled around me. She didn't ask about my relationship with Sawyer, or any other girl for that matter. She didn't even ask me about the incident that got me in her office in the first place. After my emotional outburst, her questions were tame and easy to answer. As I stood to leave, I was a little surprised by the entire thing and relieved that I'd gotten through it without making too big a jackass out of myself.

Only five weeks and four more days to go. Great.

I waited in the hallway outside of Safe and Sound Club for Sawyer since my session hadn't lasted as long as her meeting. I was deep in thought over my hour with Mrs. Ryans…Beth, when the door opened and kids started pouring out. I barely noticed the whispers and stares as I sat on the floor and waited for Sawyer to see me. Eventually all the kids left. I could see Sawyer still talking to Ms. Reynolds in the classroom. She had her head down and was listening to Ms. Reynolds talk with a solemn expression on her face.

Ms. Reynolds reached down for her hand, but then surprisingly took her wrist instead. Sawyer's head snapped up to look at her and she pulled back reflexively, an almost alarmed expression on her face. I stood up, wondering if Sawyer was about to get into another fight, but this time with a teacher, a generally nice teacher. Sawyer started shaking her head at Ms. Reynolds, her face looking more and more frightened every second.

As I stepped through the door, Ms. Reynolds turned to look at me and dropped Sawyer's arm. Sawyer looked back at me and gave me a wide smile, although her face was almost sickly white. Scrunching my brows, I walked up to her side.

"Everything…okay here?" I asked, feeling odd at having to almost confront a teacher.

Ms. Reynolds gave me her warm, sympathetic teacher face. "Of course, Lucas." Her eyes flicked over to Sawyer's then back to mine. "Sawyer and I were just having…a conversation." Before I could answer, her eyes brightened. "How was your session? I hear Mrs. Ryans is great. Was she? Did everything go okay?"

Her questions came out in rapid succession and I had to focus on them so hard that I momentarily forgot about the incident I'd walked in on. "Uh…it was…fine, I guess."

She put a hand on my shoulder. "Great! I'm so glad, Lucas." She patted me before nodding at Sawyer and then turning to leave the room.

I turned back to Sawyer. "Well, that was weird." Sawyer's face was still a ghostly white shade as her eyes locked on the door Ms. Reynolds had just exited from. "Hey, you okay?"

Sawyer snapped out of her daze and lifted her eyes to mine. Some color returned to her as she looked me over. She gave me that wry smile I loved on her, the one that showed my favorite dimple. "Isn't that my line?"

I laughed and slung my arm around her shoulders. "Apparently, not today."

She leaned into my body as we started walking from the room. "How did your meeting go?" she asked.

Keeping my head straight, I flatly told her, "It was fine."

She pulled back from me, frowning. "Luc…"

I sighed and looked down at my feet shuffling along, crossing over the multiple cracks in the hallway tile. "Really, it was fine. Not great, not horrible…just…fine."

She nestled into my side again. "Okay…well, I'm glad it wasn't horrible."

I leaned my head against hers. "Yeah, me too," I muttered into her black, silky hair. A faint scent of the lemon that filled her car hit my nose and I smiled—content, once again.

Sawyer was quiet on the ride home, and I didn't intrude on whatever she was thinking about. Myself, I chose to stare out the window and reflect on my own day. Aside from Will's teasing in English, really, the encounter with Josh was the worst part of my day. Even my outburst with the counselor hadn't trumped that moment. I sighed and thought again about Darren being disappointed in me, in the fact that I couldn't save my friendship with his brother. Maybe I'd dream about him tonight and we could talk about it?

A hand on my leg snapped me out of my weird thoughts. Blinking, I glanced around my driveway. How long had I been spacing out in Sawyer's car?

Her fingers touched my cheek. "You okay?" she asked, studying me.

I grinned and shook my head at her. "You just had to get one in today, didn't you?"

She grinned and giggled a little. She let just one knuckle stroke my face before pulling her hand away. I watched her slightly almond shaped eyes watch me, neither one of us feeling the need to break the contact. I smiled and then nodded my head at the door. "I don't suppose your parents would let you come in for a little bit?"

She twisted her lips before sighing. "No…I asked, but, they know you're back in school, and they don't think I need…to be here." I nodded and looked down, hating that her parents felt so strongly about me when they'd never even met me.

Her fingers came back to my cheek and I looked up at her again. "It's not you, Lucas." She frowned. "Well, it's mostly not you. Mostly it's me…okay?"

I smiled again and leaned into her fingers, nodding, but not understanding. I still didn't know what she'd done to cause her parents to be so distraught. She just didn't seem that outrageous to me. She seemed well-adjusted and responsible and wise beyond her years. A part of me wished her parents would just get over whatever had happened with that boy and start trusting her again. I briefly wondered if they disliked me simply because I was also a boy. Maybe it had nothing to do with my reputation after all, although, I doubt that helped.

Her fingers still on my cheek, I reached behind her neck and pulled her forehead to mine. Sighing, I rested our heads together for a second before preparing to leave her. At least it was only a few hours today and not a full day. That thought encouraged me and I was smiling as I pulled away from her and opened the door. She had a small, thoughtful grin on her face while she watched me leave. I waved at the door and then shut it and stood there, while she pulled away.

Feeling that the day had ended on an upbeat note, I entered my house for a long night of homework, bad TV and Hot Pockets.

Mom worked late at the diner and was still gone when I dragged my tired body to bed. I changed into my pajamas, laid my head on the pillow and closed my eyes, all with the thought of *please let me see my friends* repeating over and over in my head.

Within moments my eyes felt heavy and sleep lulled me under. I floated in that realm of unconsciousness for what seemed like an eternity—just blackness, darkness, nothingness…peace. Then, I was standing in my living room, fully dressed and staring out the sunny window. A hand on my shoulder startled me and I slowly turned, a grin spreading across my face as I did so. "Lil?"

Auburn hair and gold eyes met my vision and I smiled wider. "Hey, Sammy."

She laughed and engulfed me in a warm hug. "Oh, Luc, it's so good to see you." She pulled back and looked over my face. "Our last visit wasn't nearly long enough." I nodded and smiled as I held her close to me. Our last visit had been a while ago, back when I'd first started my hiatus from school; she'd come in with Lil, and the three of us had met up only briefly before the dream had fallen away from me. That had been ages ago, or so it seemed now that we were alone together. She laughed in my arms and hugged me tight again before letting go. "Darren would kick your ass if he saw us embracing like this," she muttered, as she playfully pushed my shoulder back.

I grinned at her. "Yeah, Lil too." I stepped back and admired my beautiful friend, practically my sister. "You and I aren't usually alone." I frowned as I considered that. "In fact, we've never been alone…not in my dreams…" I sighed as her expression softened. "God, are you here to tell me I'm nuts too? To tell me to back off from Lillian and live my life? Blah, blah, blah…"

She grinned wide, shook out her red hair and chuckled as I crossed my arms over my chest. "No, Luc. You've had a hard day. I'm not going to berate you for wanting to see a friendly face." Her expression turned serious before shifting to a playful scowl. "I'm here…to kick your ass."

Curiosity swelled in me as she broke into a grin, stepping aside so that I could see past her, to the board game set up on the middle of the living room floor, highlighted in a bright patch of sunlight. I looked back over to her and chuckled. Glancing at the game again, my chuckle turned into a hearty laugh. "You're going to beat me…at the game of Life? Seriously?"

Grabbing my hand, she led me to a side of the board. "It seemed fitting," she said over her shoulder.

I gave her a wry smile. "Nice."

She sat down cross legged on one side of the board while I took the other. I momentarily glanced at the other two empty sides. I gazed at her eyes, glowing warmly in the sunshine and let myself feel the peace of her remembered company. Sammy and I had always gotten along, but truly, as much as I enjoyed being with her right now, I wanted to see everyone.

I indicated the free space around the board. "We need more players. Do you mind?" She shook her head, still smiling, and I concentrated with everything I had at the spot on the floor to the right of Sammy. Hazily at first, then more solidly, Darren finally appeared and she smiled over at him. He glanced at us and then down at the board set between us. "Sweet!" He looked at both Sammy and I, while he raised a finger in the air. "I'm the doctor!"

Sammy rolled her eyes, but laughed. "You can't call the occupations, nimrod."

Darren gave her a level look. "And yet, I just did." She started to protest, but he leaned in and kissed her, cutting off her objection, just like he usually did. "Hey, sexy."

I grinned at the sight of them making out, happy that Darren wasn't going to bug me about bringing them here, that he was just going to visit with me. Twisting my head, I concentrated on the spot beside me. Nothing happened at first and I started to worry that nothing would. And then, so suddenly that it surprised me, Lil was sitting beside me, laughing at Darren and Sammy who were playfully smacking each other.

"Hey, beautiful," I whispered, as I leaned over to kiss her. She grinned breathtakingly and met my lips halfway. I paused after a few light touches to her soft, fragrant skin. "Are we fine?" I whispered, knowing how ridiculous that sounded, but needing her reassurance anyway. Our last meeting had been…intense. Her hand came up to my cheek and she bit her lip while she searched my face. "Luc…I…"

Suddenly a couch pillow smacked me on the side of the head. Irritated, I turned to glare at a laughing Darren. He held his hands out. "What?" He pointed at me. "You had a rough day and brought us here for some fun…right? Not some emotional outpouring of everything that's going on, everything we never got to say to each other," his hands mimed lips talking, "yada, yada, yada…"

I laughed and felt myself relaxing. Beside me, Lil relaxed as well.

"Yeah, let's just play." I decided then that any painful conversations I wanted to have with Lil over our intimacies lately, and with Darren over his brother, could wait. Tonight, I just wanted to have fun with my friends again.

Playing that dream game of Life with my deceased friends brought a smile to my lips that lasted the entire time. I held Lil's hand as we teased each other over the careers we received—her, a well-paid superstar, me, a struggling artist—and gave her a kiss when she got married. After seeing that, Darren commented that she was having an affair on her blue husband, which made us both giggle. For his part, Darren kept the mood in the room light, helping to give me a nice memory to take with me tomorrow, when I rejoined the harsh "real" world. I wished I could stay in this quiet room forever, playing board games with my friends—watching Lil gaze at me lovingly, watching Sammy laugh as she raked in the dough, and watching Darren complain about Sammy's "life."

"Seriously, another kid? Are you part puppy or something?" he grumbled when she landed on yet another "baby" space.

She grinned and shrugged. "I guess I'm really fertile. Besides, I like kids." She raised an eyebrow at him. "They help you win the game, you know." She cast a pointed glance at his car piece.

Darren scowled at her packed car on the game board. "For fuck's sake, Sammy…you've got five of the little bastards already. They don't even fit in the car." He smirked at her. "Couldn't you turn down your deadbeat husband every once in a while?" He motioned to the back of her car, where a lone blue person was surrounded by a sea of pink. "I mean, you put the poor, jobless jerk-off in the back seat." He grinned while Lil and I laughed. "How much love could there be?"

Sammy twisted her lips in an expression of both amusement and annoyance. "It's better than your situation." She pointed to Darren's car, where only his blue piece and a fallen over pink one resided. "And what exactly is your wife doing anyway, with her head buried in your lap like that?"

I laughed as I looked at Darren's car; it really did look that way.

Darren chuckled at her and grinned seductively. He flicked a glance at me and I knew he was about to say something that was going to get him smacked. When he did answer her, his voice was deeper and huskier. "That's just where I prefer my women."

Sure enough, Sammy's hand flashed out and smacked him across the chest. He grunted while she laughed at him. "Oh, come on, Cherry Pie," he jokingly told her.

She gasped at his nickname. While he'd told me once that he called her that because of her reddish hair, she had always chosen to see the dirtier side of the pet name, and usually smacked him whenever he said it. Although, the glint in her eye whenever he said it made me pretty sure the nickname turned her on. I was also pretty sure the name was repeated in their bed with far less violent results.

With an impish grin, she reached behind her to a container of dip that we'd been snacking on with some chips I'd conjured up. Dipping in her finger, she withdrew a glob and then swiftly flicked it at Darren. It hit his shirt and he looked down at the mess, surprised. His eyes snapped up to where we were all giggling uncontrollably. His surprised face turned devilish. "Oh, it's on now!"

Darren grabbed her wrist and pulled her on top of him as he lay down beside the board. He flipped her on her back and proceeded to run his hands up and down her sides while holding her legs firmly entwined in his. She screamed and squirmed as he tickled her. In between her fits of laughter and tears, she begged Lil and me for help, but wiping tears from our own eyes, we shook our heads. Neither one of us were going to get mixed up in their flirting.

Lil and I glanced at each other when our friends shifted to wrestling…or foreplay. She ran a hand over my forehead and brushed aside some of my hair. She looked torn about something. I was about to ask her "what" when she leaned forward and pressed her lips to mine. Her hand snaked around behind my neck, pulling me close as our mouths moved together. My heart surged and I cupped her face with my hands, my thumbs brushing over her cheekbones as the tips of my fingers twisted around her silky, pale hair.

Just as the kiss was deepening, another pillow dinged me. Seriously annoyed now, I glared over at Darren. He held his hands up in surrender under the intensity of my sneer. "Hey…I know how you two are when you get going…" he pointed down at the board game between us, "can we finish the game before the nakedness starts?"

Lil, her face still cupped in my hands, laughed, embarrassed, and pulled back from my fingers. I smiled and laughed with her, matching her tone, and then brought her over to my lap so I could put my arms around her and feel the life and warmth of the woman I loved while we finished our game. She giggled and settled down, grabbing my free hand and interlacing our fingers while she rested back on my chest. I kissed her head, the smell of her favorite shampoo suddenly assaulting me, while the ends of her long strands of hair tickled my arm. With a grin plastered on my face, I held her tight and leaned over to spin the dial—ready to finish my game of Life.

Chapter 11 – Happy Thanksgiving

Falling back into the pattern of school was practically seamless. Before I knew it, people were ignoring me just like the old days. Even Josh took a break from the sneering to simply turn away from me; maybe our conversation had finally gotten to him. I was so used to seeing anger on his face that I had no idea what the blankness meant.

A part of me reveled in the silence that permeated my day. A part of me longed for the friendships and polite acknowledgments that I'd gotten from this crowd for most of my life. But that was a long time ago, emotionally if not physically, and I shouldn't dwell. If it weren't for Sawyer though, I think I'd have faded into the wallpaper of the school, wrapped in my loneliness and regret.

Luckily for me, Sawyer did her best to bring me to life. Well, she did her best to make me smile anyway. Her parents hadn't caved yet on the whole after school visit thing, so all we had was our time at school and the never ending rides she gave me. We took advantage though, laughing and telling jokes and stories throughout the day. Sawyer had a knack for knowing just what mood I was in and skillfully turning it around, if needed.

She didn't talk much about her own moods, but I kept a close eye on her after any class we didn't share, looking for some sign that she'd been mistreated by the girls at school. I was a little shocked when she'd confessed that she was teased over being poor. I guess I'd just never noticed.

She was bright and warm and funny, and that got my attention more than what she was wearing. Of course, now that my attention was brought to it, I did see that she wore almost the exact same outfit every day: same jeans with the tears in the knees, same silver ring on her thumb, same Converse sneakers. Really, only the long-sleeve shirt or sweater got rotated. And over it all, she always wore my letterman's jacket. I was finally realizing that it really was her only coat. I was also realizing just what my handing it to her on that first day had meant to her. I'm sure she'd gotten some heat from the student body, and probably from her parents, too, over wearing a boy's coat, but it was something she didn't have that she'd desperately wanted, and a stranger had given it to her. If it were me, I'd probably feel pretty bonded to that person.

As we ate lunch in her car, I also noticed that, more often than not, she didn't have anything to eat, and I ended up sharing my lunch with her. It wasn't even a conscious thought on my part, I just automatically grabbed whatever I had and split it.

My mom and I struggled to make ends meet, although she refused to let me get a job and help her with the bills. She said I needed to be seventeen while I was seventeen, and I'd have a lifetime of working ahead of me. But we could still afford the basic necessities. Sawyer seemed to live just under that. It made me feel even more protective of her.

I'd thought about confronting Brittany, who seemed to lead the pack that teased her the most, but I didn't. I knew I wouldn't like it if Sawyer tried to take on Will or Josh, so I didn't attempt to fight her battles for her. Besides, she seemed to have a great handle on what was truly important in life. She understood better than most that bad situations weren't necessarily permanent ones, and life could get better.

I had less of a handle on that. I usually felt a little melancholy about my life. It was less intense when Sawyer was present, but it was still there, and when she left, it sometimes became unbearable. My dreams eased that ache, but added a different one, too. I'd missed my friends after our impromptu board game, which Sammy had readily won. When I had woken up the next morning, I'd stared at my ceiling for a good ten minutes, reliving the dream, committing it to memory…wishing it was real, wishing I could crawl back inside that dream and disappear—stay there forever. My dreams always felt so real. Sammy's laugh, Darren's dirty comments, Lil's sweet touches…they all felt more real than the bleakness of being nearly invisible at school. My head hit the pillow every night, ready to let go of my day, and spend some more time with them.

It didn't always work, I didn't always see them, but when I did, it was divine bliss…and pure torture. Because a part of me knew that no matter how real it felt, it wasn't. My friends were gone and buried, moved on to somewhere that I couldn't follow. And that sort of killed me.

I considered talking to the counselor about my dreams, about how I'd live in them if I could, but I never brought it up. I didn't bring up much around Mrs. Ryans. Sure, she asked a lot of questions and eventually got me talking about some of the tamer things in my life, but my friends were an issue I skirted around. She seemed to realize that, too. She'd try and casually slip them into conversation—so how are things going in the classroom? Anyone trying to pick fights with you? Did you ever fight with your friends…Darren or Sammy or Lil? What were those relationships like?

Ah…smooth.

I'd look down and shrug and give her the standard "I don't want to talk about it" answer of, "Everything was fine."

She finally did bring up the incident that got me sent to her in the first place—me being clearly out of it at school. She asked why I had done that, and in such a public way, and I'd shrugged at her and started to say "I don't know," when instead what slipped out was, "I didn't. I was drugged."

Her eyebrows shot up as high as mine. I really hadn't meant to mention that. Locking my jaw so I didn't spill any more, I watched her wide eyes take in my face. "You didn't?" She tilted her head as her eyes narrowed, appraising me, searching for the honesty…or the lie.

I straightened my posture and lifted my chin, meeting her squarely in the eye. I might have been guilty of a lot of things in my life, but this was one thing I wasn't guilty of. Feeling an odd sort of self-confidence, I decided to go with it. "No…someone slipped something in my water. I accidently drank it, when Sawyer gave me some Aspirin for my headache."

She tapped a pencil on her desk while she looked at me thoughtfully. I wasn't sure what she saw: a liar, a troubled kid, a victim. I didn't know what I wanted her to see, either. I didn't feel like any of those things. Finally, she dropped her voice as she spoke, "That's a serious accusation, Lucas. Have you gone to anyone about this?"

I shook my head. Without meaning to, I let out, "I don't have the best reputation. No one would believe me."

She sat back in her chair. Her face struggled with something, and I wondered if *she* even believed me. A surprising flutter in my stomach caught me off guard, and I realized that I wanted her to believe me. I almost needed her to. Her face finally settled into a professional mask and she leaned forward on her elbows. "Do you know who did it?"

I immediately shook my head again. A small slice of happiness burst through me that she seemed to believe my story, but I still wasn't going to mention Josh's name. That was a can of worms that I didn't need opened. Besides, I was letting him go…letting what he'd done to me go. Bringing it up, getting him busted—none of that mattered.

She narrowed her eyes at me again and I knew that she didn't believe *that.* I expected her to press me on it, but she surprisingly changed the course of our conversation. Maybe my admission made her believe I'd admit to more. "Lucas…can you tell me what you remember of the accident?"

My mouth dropped open as what she'd asked me took me back a step. She'd asked about my friends before, but never that, never about the actual wreck. It was such a shift from what we had been talking about, that my mind was too stunned to respond properly. Luckily, I was so used to the lie that it automatically rolled off my tongue. "Nothing." My senses recovered, and I bristled at her question. Why did everyone feel the need to ask that? "I thought I was in here for being wasted at school. What does…*that*…have to do with anything?" I knew my face was a scowl, but I couldn't seem to soften it.

Hers softened as she looked over my expression. In a quiet voice, she answered, "It's all connected, Lucas. Are you sure you don't remember? What were you doing right before the crash?"

Laughing, talking…living. I vehemently shook my head. "I don't know. I…I don't remember. I already said that!"

Her face still calm, even though I'd just yelled at her, she said, "What is the last thing you *do* remember?"

I clenched the chair, preparing to stand and storm out of the room. Heat and anger coursed through my veins, all with an icy edge, an edge of fear. I wanted her to stop. I didn't want to talk about this. Talking about it would be like grabbing a knife and cutting out my own heart. I wasn't capable of that. My throat locked up and I sputtered for words while tears clouded my vision. "I…I…I don't. Please…stop…"

A tear rolled down my cheek and she sighed softly when she saw it. "I'm sorry, Lucas. I know this is painful, but it's part of the process. You need to get this weight off of you. It's smothering you. Don't you see that?"

I shook my head as more tears followed the first. I swallowed, hating that I felt on the verge of screaming *and* sobbing. I could feel more awful tears and looked at the floor to try and calm myself down. Wanting it to end, I muttered, "Nothing, I remember nothing."

She answered me equally quietly, maybe bolstered by the fact that I hadn't fled the room yet. "They say beer was in the car, but you tested clean at the hospital…were you drinking, Lucas?"

My head shot up as the second most popular question passed her lips. I couldn't help the hurt in my face that she'd asked that. With everything we'd talked about and every connection I'd thought I'd had with her, I sort of expected her to instinctively know the answer to this. With an echo of betrayal in my voice, I answered her question more thoroughly than I usually answered anyone. "No…I wasn't. I took the keys because Darren was drunk, then I drove us home. I was completely sober." Hardness entered my voice as I shook my head, another tear falling. Bitterly I spat out, "You can take that or leave it."

She looked down at her desk before lifting her gaze back to mine. Compassion crossed her face as she slowly answered me. "You're defensive."

Her compassionate look heightened my irritation. I didn't want to talk about this. I didn't understand why she couldn't just let it go. Angry at myself for ever opening up to her, I spat out, "No one believes me anyway, so what does it matter what I say? If I do or don't remember? If I did or didn't drink? None of it matters."

Her eyes widened as surprise flitted across her features. "Lucas…it's *your* voice." She leaned in over her desk again, her springy, red curls brushing over some papers as she tried to get even closer to me, maybe to convey that she really was on my side. "It's the only voice that matters. You're the only one that was there."

My face paled as I caught the error in her sentence. With only a ghost of a voice, I muttered, "No, I wasn't the only one there…that's the problem." My mind flashed to my friends screaming in the car…Lil's head smacking the window. I felt my stomach rise.

"That's true." She leaned back in her chair and sighed softly. "All right, you are the only one that *survived*."

Her voice was soft and full of tenderness, but my stomach tightened and my head started to swim. I dropped my head and stared at my lap, wishing I could vanish. "I know that…" That was the one fact I was horridly aware of.

She leaned over again and surprisingly put a hand on my shoulder. "So…Lucas, one day you'll actually have to start living."

I looked back up at her gazing at me with a genuinely sympathetic face. My body started to shake with the restraint to not break down in her office. She'd hit too many sore points—blow after blow. I was depleted, I was exhausted…I was done. I needed out of her office. I needed one of my comforts, be it Sawyer or a dream version of Lil. Standing on unsteady legs, I whispered, "Are we done?"

She watched me struggling with multiple emotions and then nodded. "Yes, Luc. I'll see you Monday after Thanksgiving break."

I nodded absentmindedly as I backed out of the room. I'd nearly forgotten that I'd get a small reprieve from both her and the school for a long weekend. Of course, that meant no Sawyer as well. I clutched my stomach and hustled out of her office and out of the school, so I could feel the cool, crisp air across my clammy skin. I sat on a step outside the main doors and dropped my head into my hands, finally losing it.

Sawyer found me like that, what felt like an eternity later. I didn't notice at first. I didn't really notice the flurry of bodies walking past me and feet shuffling under my vision as I kept my head resting on my arms, hugging my knees. I really didn't notice anything until I felt Sawyer's arms slink around my shoulders. She pulled me into her and I sniffled, begging the torrent of tears to not start up again.

Sawyer kissed my head and rubbed my back, not asking what was wrong. She didn't need to. She knew I'd just come from the counselor. If I was this upset, she knew why. What else brought me to a blubbering mess besides my friends? Not much.

She kissed my head again and then laid hers down on my back as she continued rubbing circles on my jacket. She sighed softly and I finally felt the peace of her touch crawl into me. She whispered that everything would be okay and we sat in silence for long moments.

Eventually, I shifted my stance and she lifted her head off my body. I sheepishly moved to look at her, wondering how horrid my eyes were. She bit her lip as she looked over my expression, and then she shook her head and put a hand on my cheek. I sniffled again and closed my eyes, leaning into her touch, stealing her warmth and kindness.

"Ready to go home?" she whispered, and I tiredly nodded. I wanted to leave. I wanted to crawl into bed and never get out.

She helped me to my feet and slung her hand over my arm. She looked behind her and nodded to someone, and I glanced back, seeing Ms. Reynolds watching the two of us with a concerned expression. I turned away before she could respond to me. I hated a teacher seeing me this way. I hated anyone seeing me this way, really.

Sawyer drove me home in that comfortable silence and surprisingly shut the car off when she pulled in my drive. I looked over at her and blinked sleepily. "What are you doing?" My voice was still scratchy from crying so hard on the steps.

She put a hand on my arm. "I'm being a friend."

She opened her door while I half-heartedly opened mine. She grabbed my arm again while I reached into my bag and grabbed my keys. I wasn't sure what she was planning on doing, and I didn't want to get her in trouble, but I was eternally grateful that she wasn't leaving me yet.

I somehow managed to open the door and she pulled me back to my bedroom. I was so glum I couldn't even wonder why. She took my bag off my shoulder and then took off my jacket. She gently prodded me to sit on the bed and then she undid my shoes and took them off.

Confused, I watched her lift my legs onto the bed and then softly push me down until my head touched the pillow. I started to say something, but she laid down on the edge of the bed, facing me, bringing her legs up to mine and wrapping her arms around me. She pulled me into her shoulder and I felt the emotion re-bubble in me. I tried not to, but as my arms snaked around her waist, I felt the tears resurface. I dropped my head and let the tears fall onto her shirt. She shushed me, rocked me, and whispered that it would be okay, while I embarrassingly cried in her arms.

She stayed with me like that, gently rocking me, until my tears eased and sleep finally, and gratefully, took me.

I awoke with arms still around me. I wasn't sure how long I'd slept, but I was sure Sawyer was going to get in a lot of trouble for still being with me. Even though I loved the comfort of her arms around me, guilt washed through me. As much as it meant that she'd stayed, I didn't want her getting into trouble because of me.

Pulling back, I lifted my head from her shoulder and groggily spoke, "Sawyer, you should go. I don't want…" My scratchy speech cut off when my hazy vision cleared and I saw whose arms were around me. A small smile lifted the edge of my lip as I took in golden hair and pale blue eyes. With a stuttered exhale, I cinched my arms around her, pulling her as tight to me as I possibly could. "Lillian."

She rubbed my back and then ran her fingers through my hair, pulling my head into the crook of her neck. "Lucas…"

She kissed my head and laid her cheek on me as I took long, deep breaths, savoring the remembered feel of her beneath my fingertips as I clutched her tight, the remembered sound of her as she hummed softly in my ear, and the remembered smell of her as my nose rested against her collar bone. I immediately knew that I was still sleeping, possibly with Sawyer's arms still around me, but I didn't care. I had my girl and I gripped her with everything inside of me. I could feel the tears swell up as I remembered my emotional day, and I swallowed them back, not wanting to cry into yet another feminine shoulder.

She kissed my head again and then moved back to kiss my cheek. "Lucas…" She pulled back farther to plant a kiss along my jaw and I moved my head so our lips could touch. The emotion broke over me at feeling her soft lips move under mine. A small sob escaped me without my permission and her hands flew to my cheeks. "Oh, Lucas…" she muttered in the space between our kisses, "I'm so sorry."

Another sob hit me as my hands moved up to wrap into her long, blonde locks and she deepened the kiss. As her fingers brushed aside some stray tears, I let go of the emotion threatening to overtake me. I had my girl. My girl loved me. My girl was here with me. My girl was real, as real as anything else.

I relaxed into the sensation of moving lips and tender fingers and eventually my breath became uneven for a different reason. I leaned over her, pushing her gently back onto the pillows. Her fingers ran up to clutch my hair and she made a soft noise as she pulled me into her. One of my hands released from her hair to trail over her shoulder and slide over her breast. I gently cupped the molded shape of her bra before slipping my hand under her shirt. She sighed as my fingers slid up that creamy skin, and I sucked in a quick breath; her bra had vanished.

Her fingers tightened in my hair and her lips fiercely attacked mine as I stroked my thumb over the sensitive spot. With a throaty exhale, I lifted her shirt and shifted my lips to that delicate skin. She arched against me, her fingers urging my head closer. My lips covered her, my tongue swirled around her and I gently let my teeth scrape against her. She muttered my name and ran her leg up and down my calf. I placed a kiss between her breasts and then lifted her shirt to bring my attention to the other one.

That was when my world shifted.

Suddenly Lillian wasn't writhing beneath me. Suddenly she was standing near the window, chewing on her lower lip. I fell forward on the pillows when her body disappeared and it took me a second to adjust to the new situation. Real-feeling or not, that was a strange experience. I looked over to her staring at me with a worried expression, her pale hair catching the faint light of what looked like early morning rays.

"Lil?"

She gave me a sympathetic face and took a half step toward me before pausing. "I'm sorry, Luc." She shook her head. "This isn't why I came here."

My brows knotted together as I tried to understand the sudden change in the room. I'd been emotional when she first arrived, but she'd calmed me and then aroused me. I had no idea why she was now pushing me away. "Lil, what's wrong?" I patted the bed beside me as I rolled to face her. "Come back to me."

She looked like she wanted to take a step but was forcing herself not to. She shook her head and worried her lip so hard I was afraid she'd puncture herself. "I can't, Luc. I came here to comfort you. I know how hard today was, but we can't… We shouldn't…" She sighed and closed her eyes for a second, and for a moment, she looked just as tired as me. She tilted her head when she reopened them. "Luc, we shouldn't be together…like that."

I sat up on the edge of the bed, my breath hitching. "Why not, Lil? It's you and me…what could be more right than that?"

She shook her head sadly. "It's not helping you, Lucas. Look at how hard today was for you…you couldn't even talk about us." She shrugged her shoulders as she indicated me, and then herself. "This isn't helping you move forward."

"Is this because of the field? Because we almost…" She looked down, and I stood up, walking over to where she stood at the window. I gently placed my hand under her chin, lifting her head so she'd look at me. "You wanted to, Lil. We both wanted…"

She nodded. "I know…we were ready." She brought a hand to my cheek, rubbing her thumb back and forth. "But making love to me…won't bring you happiness in real life, Luc." She dropped her hand, her eyes misting over. "And that's what I need to think about—your happiness, while you're alive." Her voice choked up and she swallowed.

I put my hands on her waist, inching towards her. "Are you…breaking up with me, Lil?" I rested my head against hers, knowing my question was stupid—a dead person couldn't break up with you—but my heart raced anyway.

She exhaled brokenly and brought her hands to my cheeks. "Oh,

Lucas…no." She rocked her head against mine. "I'm not capable of that, not even in death," she whispered.

I lowered my lips to find hers and she returned my kiss tentatively. "Lillian…I…I…"

I love you. I adore you. Don't ever go away. I need you…stay with me, because I'll never love anyone but you. I wanted to say it, I wanted to finally pour my heart out to this warm, wonderful person in my arms…but I couldn't. For some reason, I just couldn't, and my throat completely locked up on me.

"I know, Luc," she whispered, as she kissed me a final time. She pulled back to look over my face. "I am glad that you're finally starting to talk to someone about some things, Lucas." She half-grinned. "Someone alive, that is."

"I really haven't said anything…"

She put her hands on my arms, rubbing them up and down. "Not yet, but you're trying. It's a start. You should tell her about the wreck, Luc. She's right, you shouldn't hold that in." I frowned and started shaking my head. I didn't want to talk about that. She sighed at my reaction. "Maybe it's time you opened up…to Sawyer."

Sawyer's name passing her lips gave me an odd, guilty feeling. I looked down and bit my lip, knowing dream Lil was well aware of everything that had transpired between the two of us. I felt her hand on my chin and reluctantly looked up at her. "I know, Luc. You're…close with her." Her smile was sad as she ran her thumb along my jaw. "That's the way of things, Luc. That's normal, that's what moving on should be. It's healthy and I…I want that for you."

Her eyes misted over and when a tear spilled down her cheek, I brought her face to mine, kissing her over and over. "No, no, Lil. I don't care for her like I care for you. We're just friends. I'm not with her and I won't ever be. I'd never do that to you." I pulled back as more tears spilled from her eyes. I had no idea whether she was sad because of my relationship with Sawyer…or because of what I'd just said. It spilled out as my own conflict ran through me, "Lillian, it's you I'm in lov--"

I jerked awake before the words fully left my mouth.

I squeezed my eyes shut, willing sleep to take me, willing my dream to return, right where I'd left off, desperate to finish telling Lil I loved her—to finally get that off my chest. I couldn't though. I was awake, and sleep eluded me. I gave up and opened my eyes, looking around at my reality. Being cold was the first thing I noticed. Even though a blanket was over my dressed body, a chill went through me. A chill that said *This is real, Luc. That was fake and* this *is real.*

I clutched the blanket and brought it farther up my chest. The second thing I noticed was that it was dark out. I gazed out the window, not able to tell if I'd only taken a long nap and it was early night outside, or if I'd completely zonked out and it was pre-dawn. A quick glance at my clock confirmed that it was the latter. I'd fallen asleep in Sawyer's arms and stayed asleep all night. My hand went to the spot on the bed where Sawyer had been comforting me. I wondered how long she'd stayed…and if she'd gotten in trouble for it.

I sighed and curled myself into a ball, feeling cold and alone and tired from too much sleep. My dream had started out so comforting but had turned on me and a pit of ice was firmly settled in my stomach. If Lil turned her back on me…I wasn't sure how I'd get through my life. I couldn't imagine night after lonely night without ever seeing her again. I didn't even want to imagine it.

The sounds of someone else awake, prodded me into movement. I stood and wiped the sleep from my eyes, yawning and stretching, all at the same time. I shuffled out into the living room and noticing the kitchen light on, made my way there.

I smiled as I watched my small mother, dressed in her bathrobe and fuzzy pink slippers, preparing a turkey. Her hands moved with practiced ease over the large bird as she filled one end of it with stuffing and then shoved it in an oven bag. With everything I'd been feeling lately, I'd completely forgotten that today was Thanksgiving. Mom always had to work at the diner in the evening (it was a busy night for the restaurant, as those without a family came in for some good food), so Mom always prepared our dinner early, always making a huge bird, so we'd have leftovers forever. I think my mom felt guilty about my Hot Pocket dinner habit.

She looked up at me when she noticed my entrance, then she glanced at the clock. "Morning, honey, you're up early."

I shrugged and walked over to the coffee pot to start a batch. "I guess that's what happens when you go to bed in the afternoon."

She blinked before returning to her bird prep. "Afternoon? You were deep asleep when I came home, but you were still dressed, so I covered you up." She paused before lifting the heavy bird to put it in the oven. "You fell asleep in the afternoon? Are you feeling okay, honey?"

I shrugged again and nodded. "Yeah, I'm fine, Mom. Just tired, I guess." She looked about to say more on the matter, but I distracted her by opening the oven door and commenting on her turkey. "I know you love turkey, Mom, but that bird is huge."

She grinned as she slid the heavy tray into the oven. "Well, I have a confession." I closed the door and she wiped her hands off on a towel draped over the handle. Her face looked excited and guilty. "Don't be mad…" she started and I frowned; when people started sentences that way, it usually never ended well.

"What did you do, Mom?" I crossed my arms over my chest and leaned against the counter, waiting.

She bit her lip, but smiled. "Well, I didn't want to say anything, because I was sure it wasn't going to happen." She shook her head. "In fact, I was positive it wouldn't, until I got a call last night at the diner." She grinned and her entire face lightened; for a moment she looked ten years younger.

I tried to keep my scowl, but smiled at seeing her so happy. "What are you talking about?"

She put a hand on my arm. "I invited Sawyer and her parents to dinner." She laughed softly. "They said yes."

My smile dropped. "You what?"

She scrunched her brows at my reaction. "I invited… I thought you'd like that? The two of you seem so close…"

I shook my head, trying to understand what had just happened. Sawyer's parents had firm rules, and didn't seem to like me at all. They'd agreed to come over? Come over… I'd get to see Sawyer today. I'd prepared myself for a long weekend without her, and here I'd get at least one more day with her, parents or not. I finally grinned and hugged my mom, who giggled like she was ten years younger. "No, I'm happy, really happy. I'm just shocked, I guess."

I pulled back and eyed my wonderful mother appreciatively. "Thanks, Mom." I shook my head in disbelief. "I can't believe you did that for me."

She shook her head and patted my cheek. "Oh, Luc…there isn't anything I wouldn't do for you, you know that." She went about prepping dinner and I smiled softly at her before finishing my task of making us coffee. She glanced back at me over her shoulder. "It wasn't easy though. Her parents were very…resistant."

I sighed as I filled the pot with water. "I don't think they like me."

She frowned. "They don't even know you."

I avoided her gaze and poured the water into the pot. "The rumors are everywhere, Mom. I'm sure they've heard them." I whispered that and studied the flowing water, like my life depended on me watching it enter the machine. Mom and I didn't usually discuss the torrent of gossip that surrounded me. In fact, we generally ignored that subject…a lot of subjects actually.

Her hand touched my arm. "Luc…look at me." Briefly closing my eyes, I turned my head to see my exact shade of eyes warmly absorbing me. "We'll just have to convince them that the rumors are just that…rumors." She patted my arm and then brought a hand to my cheek as my eyes misted. "You're a good boy, Lucas. Sawyer is lucky to have you, and they'll see that. I promise."

I sniffed and shook my head, smiling a little to release the emotion building. "Yeah, sure, Mom." She patted my arm a final time and then went back to her meal prep. I finished making the coffee, ignoring the emptiness of her promise and focusing on the sentiment instead. For a moment, I wondered why my mom was still alone. She was wonderful and warm and so open to loving someone. As I watched her from the corner of my eye, I hoped that her own loneliness wasn't because of me.

I helped my mom in the kitchen for the rest of the morning with the things that she felt my inexperienced hands couldn't mess up—mainly peeling potatoes and opening the can of cranberries. We worked in a comfortable silence, enjoying each other's company without feeling the need to fill the space with chitchat. We got dressed and cleaned the house, putting on some cheerful music in the process. Time passed and the kitchen filled with an aroma that made my stomach rumble. Mom laughed at the loud sound and popped a giant-sized cookie in my mouth, just as the doorbell rang.

Smiling around the edge of the huge snack, my empty stomach suddenly felt full of swarming butterflies as I realized who was here—Sawyer. I took the cookie out, taking a large bite, and eagerly made my way to the door. I opened it with my cheeks full of my treat and started laughing in my anticipation.

Sawyer's pale gray eyes were the first thing I noticed, followed by her huge grin and that straight, super-dark hair, held back from her face by two silver clips that gleamed in the noon sunshine. Then I flicked my gaze down at her hands, outstretched in front of her and holding a pumpkin pie. "Hi, Lucas! We brought dessert!" She giggled adorably, seeming to be as excited to see me, as I was to see her. I grinned and took the pie from her with one hand, while wrapping my cookie hand around her waist, pulling her in for a tight hug.

That was when I noticed she wasn't alone. A deep voice cleared their throat behind her and I opened my eyes, eyes that I hadn't even realized I'd shut, and looked up at Sawyer's father scowling at me. Oops. My getting handsy with his daughter was probably not the best way to make him feel at ease with me. I immediately dropped my hand from around her waist and straightened. With my "grownup" face, I handed the remainder of the cookie to Sawyer (who took a big bite with an even bigger grin on her face) and extended my hand out to him.

Swallowing the last of the cookie in my mouth, I said, "Hello, sir, I'm Lucas West." My seriousness faded as delight broke over me. "I'm so glad you came."

Sawyer's dad was intimidating. He seemed like he'd be right at home chopping lumber deep in the forest, and I wondered briefly what he did for a living. He was a good five inches taller than my six-two and much broader than me. His hair was a sandy brown and his eyes were a blue-gray color that complemented Sawyer's. I felt my grin slip as his lips twisted into a not-amused look, and I took a step away from Sawyer, just to be on the safe side. He harrumphed some sort of response and instead of shaking my hand, protectively placed his palm on Sawyer's shoulder.

I swallowed and felt like taking a step back until a voice beside him spoke. "We're delighted to be invited. Thank you, Lucas."

I glanced over at Sawyer's mother. I'd always pictured her to be an older version of Sawyer—super-dark hair and beautiful gray eyes—but she couldn't have been more different. Her eyes had a slightly more noticeable almond shape than Sawyer's and were a light golden brown. Her hair was a tawny color and looked nothing like Sawyer's, aside from the straightness. But her smile…that was an exact match.

She extended her hand out to me and I lightly shook it. "It's nice to finally meet you, Lucas. Sawyer has told us a lot about you." I glanced over at Sawyer; she looked beyond embarrassed, and was attempting to shake her dad's hand off her shoulder.

I suppressed a grin at Sawyer's irked face and stepped back, indicating inside. "Please…come in."

Sawyer's mom smiled and grabbed her husband's hand, urging him across the threshold. He seemed to follow her reluctantly, still skillfully keeping his other hand on Sawyer, his message coming across loud and clear—don't touch. I ran a hand through my hair as I shut the door behind them.

I caught Sawyer's eye as she ate the rest of my cookie. She rolled her eyes at her dad's firm grip on her and then gave me that wry smile I loved. While her parent's quickly eyed my home, I glanced at her outfit. I generally didn't notice what she wore, but I couldn't help but notice today, it was such a change from her standard jeans and t-shirt. Today, she was wearing a dress. It was simple, green and long-sleeved, but combined with her dark hair and light skin, it was beautiful. I grinned and mouthed, "I like your dress."

Sawyer and I were good at lip reading, doing it a lot during class, and she smiled and flipped up the knee-length hem in a quick curtsey. I started to laugh and her dad immediately swung his attention back around to me. Seemingly on autopilot, his hand pulled Sawyer back to him and she squeaked at the sudden movement. She turned her head to glare at him, just as my mom came out of the kitchen, swiping her hands on her slacks.

"Oh, good. Mark, Pam, you made it." My mom extended her hand out to the pair.

Sawyer's mom, Pam, took my mom's hand in both of hers and warmly shook it. "Well, it was very generous of you to invite us, Victoria. How could we say no?"

She glanced back at her husband, who cleared his throat and stepped away from Sawyer. "Yes, thank you." Sawyer's dad, Mark, had a voice as low and deep as his size, and he seemed to dwarf my mom as he shook her hand after his wife. His face had softened into genuine kindness, though, and I took that to mean that his issue was with me and not my mother. That was to be expected, I suppose.

My mom beamed as she shook their hands, happy to have company in her home again. "Please, call me Vicky, only my mom calls me Victoria." She glanced at Sawyer standing beside me after the introductions were finished. "Oh, Sawyer...you look beautiful, honey."

Sawyer blushed and looked down at the compliment. "Thank you, Mrs. West."

Sawyer and my mom had never been officially introduced, but they'd seen each other plenty of times, including that unfortunate time when I was whacked out in the nurse's office. There was enough familiarity between them that I didn't need to make any introductions. Besides, my mom adored Sawyer. Sawyer made me smile at a time when not much did. That was enough to practically make Sawyer family.

Mom looked over at me, a huge grin on her face. Noticing the pie in my hands, she grabbed it and ruffled my hair. I bit back the embarrassment as she merrily thanked me for holding it. She artfully thanked Sawyer's parents for bringing it, complimenting Mrs. Smith on her shoes and Mr. Smith on his tie. Both of Sawyer's parents had dressed up for the occasion, probably in the nicest clothes they owned. With the ease of someone used to throwing dinner parties, which we never really had, she ushered both parents into the kitchen to help her open a bottle of wine. She winked at me before she disappeared with them, and I grinned; Mom had just given me alone time with a girl. I started to wonder just how much Mom liked Sawyer.

I nodded over to the couch and Sawyer followed me. She sat down beside me, fidgeting a bit as she remembered she was wearing a dress and not jeans, and finally crossing her legs demurely in front of her. She leaned back with me on the sofa and put her hand over mine, lacing our fingers.

"I wasn't expecting to see you for a while." I said quietly over the music.

She shrugged. "I wasn't expecting it either." She glanced back at the kitchen. "They told me last night when I got back from your place. They were a little mad that I was late, but when I told them that you were…" She trailed off, and I blushed and looked down. What I'd been was bawling like a baby. Great, she'd told them that? Oh well, that was probably the least embarrassing thing they'd heard about me. She cleared her throat. "Anyway, after that, they told me about the invite, and I begged them to say yes." I looked over at her when I felt her squeeze my hand. "Surprisingly, they said okay." She grinned and leaned into my side.

I leaned back into hers, leeching her comfort as surely as her warmth. "Well, I'm glad they did."

A small frown turned her lips down. "Are you all right? After last night, I mean." Her free hand came up to cup my cheek. "You were really upset…"

I swallowed and looked away, down to the ring on her thumb enclosed in my fingers. My own thumb came up to stroke the cool metal. "Yeah, I'm fine. It was just…too much…"

I let that trail off, not wanting to go into details. Sawyer didn't ask them, instead, switching the topic to her overprotective parents and the list of rules she'd been given before leaving the house, one of which she was already breaking by being alone with me. I chuckled and she amended that with, "Well, technically they said I wasn't to be alone in your room with you, so I guess this is okay."

She squeezed my hand and I laughed and leaned in to whisper in her ear, "Then I suppose I shouldn't tell them you were in my bed last night."

She giggled and glanced back to the kitchen. "God no, they'd drag me out of here so fast, you'd see the smoke trails."

I sighed and looked over her face while she giggled. "They really don't care for me, do they?"

Her giggles subsided while she returned my gaze. "I told you…it's not you, Luc." She bit her lip and I could tell there was a big fat 'but' following that. I motioned with my hand for her to spit it out. She chuckled a little and shrugged her shoulders. "Well, come on. I have a history of poor choices when it comes to guys and, here I am, hanging out with a cute boy who just got suspended from school for being high and is surrounded by sordid rumors of drinking problems. You do the math."

She eyed me with that adorable half smile, and I grinned in spite of myself. Ignoring the hurtful truth in her statement, I focused on the one part I could make light of. "You…think I'm cute?"

She laughed so loud that we both glanced back to the kitchen, but my mom was doing a great job of running interference for us. We laughed and talked some more while my mom occupied her parents, but eventually Mom came out and motioned to us that dinner was ready. Our kitchen was too small for everyone to eat in, so we'd set up a card table and some folding chairs in the living room. After everyone loaded up their plates with delicious-smelling food, we all scrunched together at the table, Sawyer and I taking one side, while one parent each took the three remaining sides.

Sawyer and I laughed and bumped each other playfully at our close proximity, which made her dad scowl and clear his throat at us. Sawyer twisted her lips at him, but I straightened up and stopped fooling around. He eyed us throughout the meal, like he was waiting for me to do…something. Sawyer's mom watched us too, but skillfully hid it between polite conversations with my mom. Her dad didn't care about being polite; he was practically screaming "keep away" at me. I would have found it funny, if he hadn't been so intimidating.

For her part, Sawyer looked torn between accepting her parents' strictness and telling them off for it. I wasn't sure where the line was for her, but when her dad suggestively cleared his throat when she leaned in to ask me for the salt and pepper, I thought she was quickly approaching it.

Sawyer sat back in her chair after that and scowled at him. He matched her look for a second before shifting his eyes to mine. For a moment, I saw Sawyer's gray eyes staring back at me, and that momentary resemblance relaxed me some…until he spoke.

"So, Lucas…"

My body tensed at the possible list of questions he could ask me. Sawyer beside me tensed as well. He glanced over to her and shut his mouth, maybe changing his mind. He twisted his lips and, sighing a little, shrugged. "To be perfectly honest, we only agreed to come here today because Sawyer begged us."

Everyone at the table stopped eating, and an uncomfortable tension filled the room. I glanced at my mom, who was frowning at him. He cleared his throat and continued, "But, now that we're here, I think this is the perfect opportunity to say that…" he took a deep breath and turned to face my mom, "…your son needs to keep his distance from our daughter."

My mom's mouth dropped open in shock, her face paling at the directness of his statement. I felt Sawyer beside me start to shake in anger, and even Sawyer's mom closed her eyes and hung her head. Either Sawyer or my mom were about to lose it, I could tell from their looks and body language. Surprisingly, I lost it first.

"What? Why? Because of what happened with my friends? Because of the rumors about that night?" I shook my head. "None of those are true." Noisily throwing my fork down on my plate, I yelled, "I'm not a drunk!"

His intense eyes focused on mine, but the next words spoken came from Sawyer's mother and not from him. "No, Lucas. This isn't because of your…situation, not solely anyway." I shook my head, confused. She sighed and grabbed her daughter's hand, squeezing it gently. Sawyer looked about ready to smash her plate on the floor. "This is because of Sawyer's…situation," she said quietly, her eyes begging her daughter to calm down.

The anger in my body instantly evaporated, replaced by concern for my best friend. I looked over at Sawyer, who was shaking her head, tears starting to fill her eyes. "I don't understand," I whispered.

Sawyer jerked her hand away from her mom, who looked hurt by the rejection. Her dad's deep voice answered me, a surprising softness in it. "She's been through a lot this last year and she doesn't need someone…like *you*…dragging her back down."

I bristled at the derogatory tone in the word 'you', but it was Sawyer who flew off the handle. "He doesn't drag me down, Daddy." Her hands flew up in the air as she glared between her two parents. "I'm doing better, you even said so yourself!"

"That's because of your efforts, dear." Her mother reached over for her hand again, while my mom and I exchanged confused glances. I really had no idea what they were talking about.

Sawyer pulled away from her mother's hand again and shook her head, a tear dropping to her cheek. "No—it's because of him! I'm better because of him!" More tears fell and her voice started quavering. Not caring that her parents were denouncing me in front of her, I wrapped my arms around Sawyer and pulled her tight, my need to comfort her stronger than any stern warning her father could give me. She leaned into my side as her tears flowed freely. "You can't separate us, Dad, we need each other."

Her pleading tone tore my heart, and tears stung my own eyes. I wasn't sure what was going on, but I knew this moment was critical for Sawyer's and my relationship. If her parents forbade her from seeing me…I wasn't sure what would happen to me. "She's right…please?" I looked between her parents, begging clear in my eyes and in my voice.

Her father's eyes turned surprisingly sympathetic and nearly as tired looking as my own mother's eyes so often were. "We just don't want to see you hurt, Sawyer…"

I immediately answered for her. "I'd never hurt her, she means everything to me. She's my best friend."

My mom, finally getting over her shock, started to interject, but Sawyer's mom placed a hand on her arm, staring intently at her husband, who seemed to be turning over my words. Finally, he slowly said, "Just…a friend. You have no romantic interests in her?"

Sawyer straightened from my side and wiped a hand across her eyes. "Dad!"

I ignored her protest and held his eye, knowing that this was the make-or-break point for her father. This was the way I could keep her close…by pushing her away. "No…no, I'm not interested in her that way. I'm with someone…else. I have a girlfriend."

The entire room silenced as my words sunk in. Sawyer minutely inched away from me, shrugging my arm off of her. I couldn't look at her, but I imagined that her face was confused, maybe even hurt. I glanced at my mother instead who kept looking at Sawyer with bewilderment clear in her features. She didn't know what I meant, she never saw me with anyone but Sawyer. She didn't realize I meant Lillian. Sawyer's parents looked between each other with surprised faces. Sawyer's mom looked at Sawyer, concerned, but her father looked at me, pleased.

"Oh, well…that changes things a bit." He smiled and leaned back in his seat. "Okay then, Sawyer, if being his friend means that much to you, I suppose we can support it. You have improved and maybe he *is* why…" He thought for a moment, while I tried to understand what they were talking about. Just when I was about to ask a question, he smiled and leaned forward in his chair. "Okay, the short visits you had before would be all right—but short mind you." He pointed at me when he said that, and I swallowed and nodded.

I finally looked over at Sawyer, worried I'd hurt her, but she was eyeing her parents scornfully. "Well, thank you, Dad, for bringing that up here like *that* and completely embarrassing me." She stood and tossed her napkin on her plate. "The meal was wonderful, Mrs. West, please excuse me." With that, she left the table and walked outside, slamming the door shut behind her.

Her father sighed and looked over at her mother. "I suppose I could have handled that differently?"

Her mom twisted her lips at him. "You think, Mark?"

She started to stand, to go after her daughter, when I stopped her. "Do you mind if I…?" I nodded my head over to where Sawyer had gone, and her mom sat back down and nodded.

As I started to stand, her father put his hand on my arm. "I wasn't trying to insult you, son. I realize you mean a lot to her." He sighed wearily. "I'm just trying to protect her." His eyes aged dramatically as he gazed at me.

I swallowed and nodded at him before looking over at my mom. "I'll be back in a minute," I said to her as I stood. She nodded, faint red splotches on her cheeks from listening to her son be sort-of attacked right in front of her. She flicked glances at Sawyer's parents and I wondered if there would be words said when I left…probably.

Sighing, I made my way to the door. I closed my eyes before opening it, not relishing seeing the effect of my statement on Sawyer. She knew we weren't together like that, we talked about it often enough, but sometimes…sometimes it felt like we were anyway, and I really had no desire to hurt her by belittling our relationship in front of her family. It was just a means to an end.

I closed the door behind me and cautiously made my way to where she was sitting on the front step, arms around her knees. She didn't look when I sat down, only hugged her knees tighter. It was chilly outside and neither one of us had jackets on. Wondering if I should, I put a hand across her shoulders and pulled her into me. She sighed and laid her head against me.

"Sorry about that," I muttered, as I ran a hand up and down her arm.

She looked up at me. "My dad's the ass," she bit out.

I smiled at her and shook my head. "He just cares about you…that's all."

She leaned back and looked over my face. "I know," she whispered.

I wanted to ask her about the many parts of the conversation that I couldn't follow, but her eyes still looked overly moist, and I didn't want to make her break down. I wanted to make her happy, like she so often made me. I wanted to reiterate the good news that had come out of the whole debacle, that she could visit again, but she started speaking before I could.

"What did you mean…about seeing someone, Lucas? Do you…do you have a girlfriend?" Her voice was barely above a whisper and wavered on the end of her sentence.

I stared down at my shoes, not able to look her in the eye. I couldn't tell her about Lillian—about meeting with her in my dreams, about all the times we'd been intimate lately, and how it felt better to me than anything in reality, well, almost anything anyway. I couldn't tell her that, to me, Lil was still my girlfriend; we were still in love, still together. I couldn't tell her any of that—she wouldn't understand.

Still not meeting her eye, I whispered, "No, there's no one." *No one alive anyway.* "It was just something to say…to get him off our backs." I finally looked over at her. "I mean, he doesn't need to worry about you and me. We're just friends…right?"

She smiled weakly at me. "Yeah, right…of course."

I grinned and pulled her tight. "Happy Thanksgiving, Sawyer."

She chuckled and laid her head back down to my shoulder. "Happy Thanksgiving, Lucas."

Chapter 12 – Friendships

Sawyer and I did something that weekend that we'd never done before—she came over, and we watched a movie. Her parents had indeed relaxed her rules around me, since I'd sworn to not have any interest beyond friendship with her. I'd like to think that the decision was partly because they trusted Sawyer as well. She was the most trustworthy person I knew, and I really couldn't see what she could have possibly done to make them so overbearing.

I considered bringing it up while we sat close together on my couch watching some romantic comedy that she had picked up at the grocery store before coming over. I wasn't really interested in the movie, which showed more of an interest in showing off Matthew McConaughey's bare chest than any actual plot, but I was interested in spending time with her, so I kept my groans and eye rolling to myself.

We sat on the same cushion, our hips touching and my arm slung around her shoulders. She had her feet up on the couch and angled her knees into me, her head resting on my shoulder. If her dad had been here, he probably would have revoked her visitation privileges immediately; we did look a little too cozy for platonic friends. But that was just the way we were. We enjoyed the comfort of each other's touch, and when we were alone together, we often relished in it.

My thumb stroked her upper arm as I spaced out on the movie and instead thought about what to say to her. I wanted to know what was so mysterious. I wanted to know what she'd done that had uprooted her family and practically put a leash on her. I also wanted to respect her silence.

And Lord knows, I wasn't the most vocal one about my own secrets. I never talked with her about the crash. In fact, I never even brought up that night with her. The few instances she'd caught me crying about it were the only times it came up. Usually when I was with her, I was trying to push that part of my life away.

The bad parts anyway, I still wanted the good parts, the happy memories and most of all, the amazing dreams I'd been having with my friends. I still craved those and tried to bring them to me nightly. And Lillian…she hadn't reappeared to me yet, but I was ready for her to, ready to tell her I loved her. Maybe speaking of having a girlfriend out loud during Thanksgiving dinner had finally broken through that last barrier in me. I was ready to move forward…with her.

And I was well aware of the oxymoron in that. I was aware that moving forward with a dead girl wasn't actually possible. But it was real enough for me. Her passing had created a hole in me, and I was going to greedily fill it with her ethereal presence. Once I got her to reappear to me, that was.

I'd considered talking to Sawyer about her…but I couldn't. There'd be no point in that. I knew exactly what she'd say, exactly what anyone would say—'That's crazy, Luc. That's not a real relationship.' And Sawyer might actually make that conversation worse by adding, 'Is that why you won't be with me, because you're in love with your dead girlfriend and living out your fantasies with her…in your dreams?'

My stomach clenched at just the thought of hearing Sawyer say those words.

I knew the situation would hurt her…and I didn't want to do that. She meant everything to me. So our first real time together, not in school, and not under the pretense of "homework," was spent mostly in silence, each of us respecting the other's desire for privacy. And I loved every second of it, regardless of that ridiculous man's ridiculously buff body.

Poking fun at her movie choice and vowing to pick the next one, I parted ways with her a couple of hours later. A few hours after that, after having a late dinner with my mom, who'd conveniently "run errands" while Sawyer was visiting, I headed off to bed, hoping to meet up with the other woman in my life.

And I did…sort of.

I'd managed to bring myself back to that field just beyond my house. That field dappled in sunlight with a bubbling brook beside it. The air was warm and cheery, and a light breeze ruffled my messy hair. It was idyllic, and I was proud of myself for recreating it. Somehow I'd even managed to bring the bed back.

I sat on the edge of it and waited…waited for her to come to me. The sky darkened and I momentarily worried that I'd lose control and it would start raining. I didn't want to dream about the rain. I concentrated on the clouds, demanding that they open back up and drench me in sunshine. It took a while, but eventually a bright shaft hit me in the face and I blinked, suddenly blinded.

"Impressive, you're getting pretty good at this."

I smiled and brought my hand up over my eyes to look at Lil standing at the side of the bed in front of me. Only, it wasn't Lillian. My eyes opened wider as I took in the auburn hair gleaming in the sunshine. I'd been concentrating so hard on Lil that I really hadn't expected to see anyone else. In my surprise, I lost control of the one aspect of the dream I was currently using and crashed harshly to the ground as the bed underneath me vanished.

I grunted as I landed painfully on my back. Rubbing my backside, I scowled up at Sammy, who was laughing as she looked down at me. Shaking her head, she extended a hand and helped me up. She pointedly looked at the spot where the bed had been. "Not who you were expecting?"

I shook away my surprise and pulled her in for a hug. No, not who I was expecting, but a welcome friend regardless."Hey, Sammy."

She held me back just as tight. "Hey, Lucas."

We broke apart and she looked around at the romantic setting I'd provided. I looked around as well and felt myself blushing; Sammy knew exactly what had happened here, in my steamiest dream to date. She grinned when she noticed my face. "Thank you for getting rid of the bed." Laughing, she lightly shoved my shoulder away from her. "I don't think you and I will need it, but maybe Darren and I can use it later." She laughed again and the radiant warmth in it eased my discomfort.

"Where's, Lil?" I asked softly, once her giggles tapered back.

She sighed and kicked a rock in the grass. "Ah, Luc…she wanted me to come instead. Try talking to you…"

I sighed and sat down at the kitchen table…that was suddenly in the field where the bed had been a second ago. "About what, Sammy?"

Instead of taking the other chair, she walked around to my feet and squatted down in front of me. She picked up both of my hands and ran her thumbs over the backs while she grasped them. "You need to stop this, Lucas."

I stiffened and shook my head, both not wanting to stop and not wanting to hear another friend ask me to. "No…why?" I suddenly felt very alone. "Don't you guys want to see me?" I knew my voice was small and pathetic, but that was the way I felt.

I looked at my lap and felt one of her hands release mine to cup my cheek. "Of course we do, Lucas. We want to see you. We'd see you every night if it were up to us…."

"But…" I muttered.

"But, we're trying to do what's best for you. And this," she waved her hand around the dreamscape I'd created for Lil, "this isn't right."

I shook my head. "It's just a dream, Sammy…I know that. But it brings me comfort. Why can't I have that? Why can't I have you guys…and Lillian?"

Her hand returned to mine in my lap. "Because it's not just a dream to you, it's not just comfort. It's a date…with her. A date you were hoping would lead to…more." She raised her eyebrows as she gave me a stern look. "You're trying to continue the relationship you had with her in your head. Advance it even."

"I just want to tell her that I love her. I'm not trying to…" I shrugged my shoulders lamely. "I just want to finally tell her I love her. I never got to…"

Sammy sighed and brought her hand to my cheek again, running it down my face. "Do you honestly think she didn't know that?"

I closed my eyes at the reference to Lillian in the past tense; tears started to burn in them. I tried to swallow back the pain, but I couldn't. Lillian wasn't past tense…not here. Here, she was alive. Here, she was real. "I want to see Lil now, Sammy," I scratched out, my voice raw with barely contained emotion.

I felt Sammy standing and opened my eyes to watch her lean form grab the other chair and swing it around to me. She sat right beside me and grabbed my hand, much like Sawyer would have. "I'm sorry, Lucas…not tonight."

I squeezed her hand as my eyes watered even more. "Please?" I wasn't sure who I was begging—Sammy, Lillian, my dream world…or myself.

Sammy was the one that answered though. "She won't appear to you tonight, Luc. As hard as you try, it won't happen." She lifted just one corner of her full lips. "It's me or nothing."

I slumped against my chair before leaning my head over to Sammy's shoulder. I'd take her over nothing any day. She leaned her head against mine and murmured into my hair, "Are you disappointed that it's just me?"

I raised my head to look at her. "No, no of course not, Sammy." I swallowed and looked down. "I just…my last moment with Lil didn't end well, and I wanted to talk to her about it."

Sammy sighed and clenched my hand. "I know. Your last few moments alone with her have been kind of…intense."

I shrugged and averted my eyes. There was nothing I could hide from my friends. Not here. "Right, I suppose you've been getting into my dreams just like Darren? I suppose asking you not to would be just as ridiculous as asking him not to." I shrugged again and looked back at her, feeling my cheeks heat.

She laughed a little. "I would give you the privacy if I could, Luc, but you know I don't really have a choice." Her finger came up to tap my head and I got the reference. All of this was in my head; they all knew what I knew. I gave her a wry smile. Lil would know about me telling Sammy that I loved her just now. Of course, it wasn't a big secret. We both knew we loved each other; we just couldn't seem to say it.

Sammy rested her chin on my shoulder as I thought about my elusive girlfriend. "Darren does have a point, you know, about you pulling us to you." I looked at her from the corner of my eye, wanting to object again, but holding my tongue. Sighing, she raised her chin from my shoulder. "We love you, Luc, but you can't have a life like this, always living in your head with us." Her knuckle came up to stroke my cheek. "What future is there for you like that?"

I gave her a tired smile and shook my head. "That's what you guys don't seem to grasp. I don't care. I don't care about that life. I want you guys. I want my friends. I want to keep coming here, and seeing you and Darren…and Lil."

"You can't keep having…intense moments with her, Luc." Her golden eyes narrowed at me, a shaft of light hitting them, and making them seem to glow with the life I so readily remembered from her. "You're hurting her and making her feel really guilty." She shrugged while I frowned. "She feels really bad about the moments she's already let happen."

My mouth dropped. I'd never imagined making my girlfriend feel bad by touching her. "She feels bad…why?"

Frustration crossed Sammy's face, like she was speaking in a foreign language to someone who couldn't understand. And in a way, I didn't. What was wrong with me having an active fantasy life with my friends? I wasn't hurting anyone. No one even knew how often I hung out with them. The real world held no intrigue for me anyway. Everything I wanted was right here. Well, besides Sawyer, I guess. She was the only thing worth getting out of bed for.

"Because she wants you to move forward. She sees how you isolate yourself and shut down, barely talking to anyone, not saying nearly enough to your counselor." She raised her eyebrows and looked at me pointedly. "If it weren't for Sawyer, I think you'd be mute."

I shrugged and looked out over the shadows and light playing across the field. I briefly wondered if I should make it rain anyway. It would match my mood if Sammy and I were drenched. "I have nothing to say," I said flatly.

She let out an annoyed grunt and I looked back at her. Her brow was creased with definite irritation. It was an odd look to see on Sammy, who was rarely angry. "You're not the same person, Lucas."

My own irritation spiked. "Of course I'm not. I killed all of my friends—do you have any idea what that did to me?"

Her face immediately softened, her hand coming back to my cheek. "Yes…I do."

As her thumb stroked my face, I whispered, "Can I please see Lil now?"

She sighed and shook her head, tears brimming in her eyes. "I'm sorry, Luc…not tonight."

I woke up after that, wishing I could go back into the dream and twist it the way I wanted to, twist my friends the way I wanted to. But then it *would* be completely false. If I made my friends do and say what I wanted them to, well, then they really would be gone. I closed my eyes, wondering if I was completely insane.

It was early enough that I felt I could get up and start getting ready for Monday morning back at school. I showered, shaved and dressed in a long-sleeve tee and baggy jeans. I was styling my hair in the mirror when the photo tucked in the edge caught my attention. I pulled it out and looked over the happy image of the four of us. Things had been so different then. Darren and Sammy had been trying to convince Lil and me to road trip to L.A. over the summer. We probably would have. We probably would have all piled into Darren's car and made a memory that would have stayed with me 'til my death bed. I suppose that summer did leave a lasting impression on me, just not quite in the way I'd expected.

"Luc?"

I turned to look at my open doorway and saw my mom leaning against it, watching me. I gave her a halfhearted smile before gazing at the picture one last time and then tucking it back in the mirror. Still staring at my tired reflection, I heard her tell me that she'd made some coffee. I nodded at her reflection, noting her tired eyes.

I walked over to her and slung my arm around her shoulder, walking together to the kitchen to start our morning ritual. She smiled up at me and patted my chest. When it was ready, we drank our coffee in silence, me staring out the window, turning over the dream with Sammy, while Mom quietly worked on a crossword puzzle.

A horn honking startled me from my thoughts, and I glanced over at my mom. She was studying her watch and I could almost see her mentally tracking the minutes. I looked over at the clock, but neither one of us were late for our days.

"You okay, Mom?" I asked, as I stood to get my backpack.

With the impatient look of someone waiting for something, she smiled and said, "Of course, everything is fine, honey." She stood and kissed my cheek. "Have a good day, Luc."

I nodded and wished her the same. With one last hug before I slipped on my jacket, I wished my mom well and made my way out to Sawyer. I must have had a strange look on my face in the car, for Sawyer shot concerned glances at me the entire drive to school. Once in the lot, she finally twisted to face me as she shut the car off. "You okay, Luc…I mean, really okay? You seem…quiet."

I blinked, making myself let go of the night I'd had, and threw on my best "I'm fine" face. Her brows pulled together and I thought maybe I wasn't pulling it off very well. I shook my head. "I'm…" I started to say "I'm fine," but looking at her concerned face, I ended up saying, "Just a weird dream, that's all." I shrugged. "I'm just trying to process it."

Her face softened. "Oh. Do you want to talk about it?" She placed her hand over mine and rubbed her thumb across the back.

I smiled at her warmth, but shook my head. She wouldn't understand. "No…" I looked down and peeked up at her from the corner of my eye, hoping she bought my next sentence. "I don't…remember enough of it, to talk about it."

She nodded and squeezed my hand, not asking for any further details. "Well, just keep in mind that dreams are just dreams." She smiled warmly, as she unknowingly broke my heart. "They don't mean anything."

I felt my chest squeeze and looked away from her as I opened the door. She opened hers as well and met me at the front of her car, holding her hand out for me. I took it with my head still down, willing the tears to stay in my eyes.

Dreams didn't mean anything? But…what if dreams were all I had?

Although the Thanksgiving break had been a short one, it seemed to reenergize the school. There was a last day of school feeling around the campus, from teachers and students alike. Everyone seemed ready to let studying go and kick back and have some fun during winter break. When I walked by groups of people with my head down, I could hear them making plans for the upcoming mini-vacation a few weeks away.

I had no plans. I had no desire to make plans. All I really wanted was to keep seeing Sawyer everyday and if I couldn't do that at school, then at least I could look forward to her coming over to my house. I suppose in a way, those were my plans.

The students buzzed with holiday energy and more than a few took notice of me again in their excitement. Not that they found talking to me exciting, but their pent up energy needed some release, and tormenting me was one way to do that.

Will kept up his shoving, pushing and tripping, successfully sprawling me across the hallway one afternoon in such a nonchalant way, that it looked like I'd stumbled over nothing and decided to spread eagle on the floor for the hell of it. Yeah, the students in the hall when it happened had found that hilarious.

And of course Josh got over our intense conversation and started trying to stir things up again. He was prodded on by a few people around him, urging him to try kicking my ass. I stopped even looking at him. I couldn't stop him from outright attacking me, but I could control how I responded to him. It didn't hurt any less, listening to him verbally attack me without even acknowledging his existence, but it kept me in sort of a numb zone, where I didn't cry or yell or hit him. That was an improvement in my book, so I embraced the numbness.

Brittany continued tormenting me too, and, in her own twisted way, Sawyer as well. When I met up with Sawyer after art class, Brittany would toss derogative comments my way to her friends, then smirk at me suggestively when they were busy laughing. I had no idea what she hoped to gain by both flirting with and dissing me, but I wished she'd stop. I really wished she'd stop tormenting Sawyer. I'd come across Sawyer on more than one occasion with a hurt look on her face as some girls, led by Brittany, walked away giggling. I had the sneaking suspicion that my callous remark about not being her boyfriend was to blame.

The rumor mill was loving the fact that I was physically close to Sawyer but appeared to be emotionally distant from her—as Brittany had cruelly put it, "I was fucking her, when I didn't even care about her." Like most things about me, it couldn't have been farther from the truth and also like most things about me, it couldn't have been more readily accepted from the students at Sheridan High.

More than a few stared at us, shaking their heads and whispering, as we walked down the hall. Now, not only was I a drunk, I was a louse too. Perfect. Just what I'd always wanted to be when I grew up.

I kept my head down, stayed out of conversations, and ignored the bustle and buzzing around me. Besides Sawyer, I ignored almost everything, and I was getting exceptionally good at it. I also hadn't opened up any more in my counseling sessions. I was halfway through my treatment and figured I only had to show up for the next few weeks and things would get back to normal. Well, my normal anyway.

Mrs. Ryans seemed to notice that I was shutting down and shifted her tactics accordingly. She talked more about the incident that got me there, trying to get me to talk about Josh's involvement, which I wouldn't, and trying to get me to tell her what I'd been feeling during the incident. That had taken me aback at first. I mean, I was high, I wasn't really feeling anything. But then I realized that wasn't true, most of my feelings, beside the unfortunate come-on to Ms. Reynolds, had been about Sawyer.

I made the mistake of mentioning that to Mrs. Ryans, or Beth, as she still kept trying to get me to call her, and opened a new portal in my head for her to dig through—my relationship with Sawyer. I gave her the standard "we're just friends" speech, but she didn't seem to buy it. It probably didn't help that she purposely kept an ear on the gossip around school and had undoubtedly heard about the nastiness that swirled around us.

I didn't know what to say about that. I mean, we *were* just friends and the rumors were way off. But a nagging part of me remembered kissing Sawyer, remembered her lips on mine and wondered. It couldn't be more than friendship, though, not with my continued involvement with Lil (who was still avoiding me), but I didn't mention that to Mrs. Ryans. She'd probably lock me up in a padded room or something, and Sawyer and I were complicated enough without bringing my special brand of crazy into it.

Sawyer had started hanging out at my house every day after school. It was the highlight of my day. It wasn't as if we didn't see each other all the time, but there was something about being alone in my house, away from the scrutiny of the student body. It was relaxing and we let our guards down a little. We talked and laughed and watched movies and sometimes, if her parents let her stay late enough, she even let me make her my Hot Pocket dinner specialty. We didn't talk about anything overly deep, nothing about her secret, nothing about mine, but we talked about the rumors at school and the torments of Will and Josh and Brittany. We were bonded already, but going through that chaos together…I don't know, it bonded us even tighter. I felt surer of her than anyone, besides my mom, of course.

And we were comfortable together. We'd stretch out on the couch, my long legs taking up all the cushions, hers flopped casually over mine as we cuddled up under a blanket to watch a movie she'd rented—one that I'd approved first. We were lying that way, my arms wrapped around her as she stretched in front of me on the edge of the couch, my head back against the armrest, watching one of the Terminators, when my eyes started to drift closed. Fully content and happy with her in my grip, I let myself relax into sleep…

The sound of water falling filled my head, lifting my awareness. Each drop felt like a gong going off in my brain because it was so loud, or maybe that was because everything else was so silent. I wasn't sure where I was for a moment and couldn't remember what had just happened. All I was aware of was the dripping sound of rain on vinyl and metal, and then slowly, I became aware of the rushing sound of water pouring down glass. I shifted and opened my eyes. Immediately, I inhaled a sharp breath and my vision clouded, as pain vibrated through my skull. I brought a hand to the side of my head and felt the blood there. Then I remembered where I was and what had happened.

I was in the smashed remains of Darren's car. We'd just gone over the embankment and I'd had a rough ride down the steep hill, ending with a painful smack against the side window. I remembered that solid hit, felt the pain of my head whiplashing back against the glass; my neck remembered that too. But my window had remained intact and, besides the smear of blood on the side of my skull and the pain screaming throughout my jolted body, I was alive. Miraculously, I was alive.

My eyes refocused on the water streaming down the windshield like a surging river. The sudden downpour was still streaming hard around us. Wait…*us*… My hazy brain struggled to remember that I wasn't the only one in the car. I remembered Lillian hitting her head hard against her window, and wondered if that had hurt her as much as it had hurt me. Carefully, I reached my hand out for her. In the darkness of the dim lights from the dash, I could only see the outline of her body, slumped against the passenger side door.

"Lil?"

My hand brushed her shoulder but she didn't move at the contact. "Lil?" I carefully unbuckled my seatbelt and, even though every muscle in my chest and hips protested, I moved as close to her as I could in our bucket seats. "Baby, talk to me."

As my vision improved more, I glanced back at the empty rear seat, the open door, where I could just barely make out the scraggly underbrush and shadowy trees, before they disappeared into the dark thickness of night. I remembered Darren and Sammy's unbuckled bodies bursting through that door, the force of their impact breaking the inferior metal of the latch. Where were they outside? Were they okay? God, please let them be okay. My head throbbed and my heart raced as I turned back to Lillian.

"Lil, did you see where Darren and Sammy went? Lil?"

When she still didn't respond to me, I brought my hand to her cheek, her cool cheek. Concerned, I finally noticed the glass around her still body, her head resting against the boulder protruding through it, the slick wetness of her blood on the rock, turning it black in the darkness. Wind was coming through the shattered window, bringing rain with it, dampening Lil's blouse and shorts and washing the blood down her arms. So much blood. Flashes of her head smacking that stone assaulted me. She'd hit it so hard. Her fragile, fragile head had hit it so hard. There was so much blood…

My heart in my throat, speech barely still possible, I turned her face gently to look in her eyes. "Lillian, baby? Please…answer me…" Her head offered no resistance and twisted easily in my grasp. My wide eyes locked onto hers, but it was too late. No one was there to look back at me…

I woke with a start, screaming.

I had been in a cold, dimly lit car in dark woods, the sound of rain all around me, but now I was in a warm, dry, and brightly lit room, lying down on a soft couch with a TV flickering in the background, playing the end of a movie I couldn't remember. I wasn't registering that a dream was fading from me, and hopelessly confused, I had no idea where I was and what was real. Still sobbing, I clung to the last remnants of my nightmare. "No, no, no. Lil, talk to me! Please…please don't be…"

Hands and arms and hair flew around me, taking me into a tight embrace. Soothing sounds entered my ear as I broke down into remembered sobs. Lil's eyes—those beautiful, loving, pale blue eyes—empty…vacant…dead. I sobbed even harder, gasping for air. "The rain…I couldn't stop…so much water…I couldn't stop…the rock…oh God, her head…so much blood…there's so much blood…I don't know what to do…"

"It's all right, Lucas…let it go. It was a dream…you're safe."

It was a dream. I was safe. I recognized then that I was safe on the couch, wrapped securely in Sawyer's arms and not back there again. But she was wrong, it wasn't just a dream, it was a memory and *she* wasn't safe. None of them had been. My hands cinched around her waist as I buried my head in her shoulder, and continued my wracking, tortured crying.

"God, Sawyer, why won't this ever stop? I just want it to stop," I sputtered between my tears.

I felt her fingers wiping some tears from my face and when my sobbing subsided, I pulled back to search her eyes, for comfort or maybe for hope. She cupped my cheek as we locked gazes. Her eyes were moist and concerned, as empathetic as eyes could get. I reached up to grab her cheek and we held each other's faces as a few more tears silently fell from me. Swallowing, I rested my head against hers. "I just want it to stop." I leaned up so our noses were resting side by side; my heart was thudding in my ears. "Please…just make it stop."

Sawyer's breath was fast on my face through her parted lips and I found myself matching her pace. Not thinking of anything but pushing aside this grief, I found her mouth. She gasped as our lips met: soft, wet and slightly salty from so many of my tears. "Please…make it stop," I muttered around our lips. Her breath was still fast against my skin and her hand inched up to weave into my hair. She let out a soft noise, and the lingering pain of my nightmare faded as her reaction to me stirred something deep inside, something I'd thought was so buried it would never resurface in waking life. The warmth of desire flooded through me and my hand slid around to her neck, pulling her into me.

Our lips parted, and my tongue lightly slid into her, brushing up against hers. She moaned and an ache went straight through me, blocking out all remnants of my vicious memory. She tasted sweet, like the watermelon Jolly Rancher she'd been sucking on earlier. It was indescribably good and I wanted to taste more. I angled my mouth differently and deepened our connection, my hands twisting into her dark locks. She moaned softly again and the slight ache shifted to an almost painful need. I needed her. I'd always emotionally needed her…but this, this was entirely different.

Keeping her mouth close to me, I shifted her from our side-by-side position, so that her back was flush to the cushions. Never breaking the motion of our lips, I leaned over her, shifting more of my body on top of her. Her fingers dropped from my hair to run down my back and my body shivered in response. She made a noise in her throat and wrapped her legs around mine as I carefully adjusted my entire body over the top of hers; the blanket that had been draped over us dropped to the floor.

The need surging through me overran my commonsense, and before I could analyze what we were doing, I was pressing the most sensitive part of my body against the most sensitive part of hers. I was hard, I was ready, and I was aching so bad my legs were shaking. She gasped at the feel of me and her fingers clutched at my back when we connected. I groaned at the feel of her and moved my lips to her neck.

While I placed deep kisses up her neck to her ear, we started moving together intimately. It was the most incredible thing I'd felt (while being awake) in a long while, and it didn't take long for our movements to become more urgent, along with our breath. It was almost like my earlier despair had crumbled the dam between us, and we were finally letting the weeks of pent-up attraction spill over into our lips and bodies. Our desire to connect was an almost frantic one, with our fingers lightly tugging, and teasingly pulling at our clothing, while our hips moved in perfect, simulated rhythm.

She sucked on my neck, her teeth lightly grazing my skin, while my hands slid under her shirt to feel the softness of her stomach, the lace of her bra. She ran her hands under my shirt and up my back. The feel of her fingernails along my bare muscles sent electricity straight down my body, making me throb with the need to release.

I hissed in a sharp breath and pushed harder against her, wishing it was more. Our mouths met again, and each break of our lips brought a ragged breath or a soft whimper. I heard myself mutter "more" and "please." I heard her suck in an erotic breath and utter my name. I'd never heard so much passion and desire leaked into the syllables of that word. It crumbled me.

Driven by pure desperation and need, my hands slid down her body and tugged at her jeans, wanting them off, wanting that barrier between us gone. "Please…I need…more. Closer…please, closer." My words were breathless, coming in pants between our fiery kisses. Every inch of me felt electrified, oversensitive, and every rub, moan, and moment of flesh on flesh seared me…but I still needed more.

She whispered my name again, followed by her own pleas for more, and then her fingers moved between us. Stilling my hips, she unzipped her jeans. My heart pounding, our lips never stopping, I felt her push them down her hips, and then her fingers reached over to unzip mine. "Oh God, please," I muttered, as I helped her position mine the same as hers.

Freed from the restraint of one barrier of clothing, I resettled on her thighs. Her hands slid around to grab my hips, guiding me where she most needed me. With a ragged cry, her whole body arched against me as we pressed against each other, unimpeded by the thick fabric of our denims. I bit my lip and groaned deep, feeling the warmth of her body as the thin materials separating us slid together. It was bliss. A bliss I didn't know I could still feel while being conscious.

Vague cries and gasps and muttered pleas for more filled my ears, some from her, some from me. It was so easy to be with her like this, that I couldn't remember why we'd never done this before. I couldn't even think about all the lines of friendship we were crossing. I couldn't think of anything, really. My mind had shut off a while ago and only sensation, desire and instinct drove me.

Her own out-of-control needs seemed to be driving her as well. In one fast move and arch of her back, her hands went to her hips and she pushed her jeans down farther. My breath hitched with the anticipation of where this might go, of where I wanted it to go, and then I hastily helped her scrunch the bulky material all the way off her legs. With her jeans no longer restricting us, I settled more firmly in-between her thighs and pressed directly against her.

"Oh, Sawyer…God, yes," I muttered, as I was finally able to completely press all of me against her. I could definitely feel her readiness for me, for this. My heart surged and my breath could barely keep pace as our hips found a rhythm that was natural and appealing, and felt so much more connected than we physically were. With a loud cry, her head dropped back on the cushions and her hands ran back up my spine. She started to pant in an intoxicating rhythm and her hands came up to tangle in my hair. I watched her face intently, knowing she was close to coming and, oh God, how I wanted to do it with her. My breath came in a quicker pant as I pushed harder and faster against her.

She muttered my name over and over, followed by a faint "don't stop." She closed her eyes as her body stiffened and the beginnings of ecstasy washed over her. I wanted more. I wanted to stop grinding against her. I wanted to pull down her underwear and slip inside her. I'd never gone that far before with anyone, but I suddenly wanted it more than I wanted the air I was gasping for. I imagined how that would feel—her body wrapped around me: warm, wet, tight…

She cried out and clenched my back hard as her climax intensified. A moment of desperation washed over me as I ceaselessly moved against her. Grabbing her hips and pulling her into me, I unconsciously started shifting her underwear down. I wanted to be inside her so bad. I wanted to come so bad. And then, suddenly, and much to my surprise…I did.

My fingers curled around the edges of her underwear, twisting them, and I dropped my head to her shoulder. She held me tight against her, and a long cry escaped me as the euphoria ripped through my body. She ran her hands through my hair as a chorus of "Oh God" ran through my head and surely followed out of my mouth. I panted in her ear, struggling to control my breath, while she ran a hand tenderly down my back and whispered my name.

It was hearing her lovingly say my name that snapped reality back into me. Oh, fuck…no. What did I just let happen? What did I just do? Ugh, and kind of all over her. Did I just ruin everything?

Frozen in terror, I remained on top of her, my head glued to her shoulder, until our breaths returned to normal. Feeling genuine fear, I lifted my head to look at her. We stared at each other with frozen, shocked faces. We hadn't had sex, technically, but it felt like we just had. We'd been so connected and needy, almost desperate with how much we'd wanted each other. And I'd wanted so much more than just coming in my shorts. I'd wanted her in a way I'd never wanted anyone but Lillian.

Thinking of Lil made icy guilt flash right through me. This would kill Lil the next time I saw her…and she'd know; I couldn't keep anything from my friends. They knew what I knew…and they'd all know about this. I imagined Lillian would be crushed.

Finally, feeling horrid and guilty and a little gross, I lifted off of her. "I should…I'm gonna… I'll be back in a minute." She only nodded as I stood up and adjusted my jeans. Avoiding looking at her again, I went to my room. I changed my underwear and cleaned myself up; luckily most of the mess appeared to have stayed with me. Throwing on a pair of sweats that were lying on my floor, I ran a hand through my hair and sighed.

Great. If I hadn't been misleading before…I definitely was now. Why did I let that get so carried away? Why did I even start that, when I suspected she had real feelings for me? I thought of my dream. I thought of my despair and my overwhelming need to make it end. I sighed as the answer struck me—I'd needed the release. I'd been selfish, and taken something from her that I was pretty sure she'd let me have. I closed my eyes as I put my hand on the door handle, momentarily thanking my sudden climax from stopping me from going all the way with her. I wasn't sure if she'd have let that happen or not…but I had the feeling she would have. Because she liked me, because she cared about me…for some odd reason. I hoped she wasn't hurt by what just happened, but I didn't see how she couldn't be. God, now I really was a louse.

Sighing, I opened my door and prepared to face her. Shaking my head, I wondered how things could change so fast. In one night, I'd managed to hurt the two women who mattered most to me. I'd betrayed Lil and misled Sawyer even more. I wished I could redo the entire day. Hell, if I was wishing for redos, then I wished I could rewind time all the way to *that* night.

I walked back to the living room, where she was sitting quietly on the couch, perfectly put back together and playing with the ring on her thumb. I sighed softly at seeing her nervous habit return and she looked up at me when she heard the noise. I moved to sit beside her, keeping as much distance between us that I could without offending her. "Sawyer…" Oh God, I didn't want to have to say this… "I'm…I'm really sorry…about…that." She flushed with color and nodded, studying the floor. I swallowed and felt my cheeks heating. I hated this. "Do you want to talk about it?"

I really hoped she said no, and we could just pretend none of this ever happened. She looked up at me with analyzing eyes and I wondered if my thoughts were all over my face. They must have been, for after a moment of contemplation she finally shook her head. "I should… It's getting late, I should go."

I ran a hand through my hair and nodded as she stood up. I stood up next to her and debated grabbing her hand, or putting mine on her shoulder, or even hugging her, but everything felt weird and contradictory, so I didn't do anything. "Okay…um…I'll see you tomorrow morning, then?" I didn't mean for it to come out like a question, but it did.

She nodded, clearly deep in thought, and made her way to the door, where she grabbed her bag and jacket. I silently watched her slip them on and place her hand on the door. My heart squeezed at the thought of the strain I'd placed between us; we'd been so perfect. She turned back to look at me with her hand still on the knob. "Goodnight, Lucas."

"Goodnight, Sawyer," I whispered. *And I'm really sorry.*

Chapter 13 – Are We Okay? Am I Okay?

I awoke the next morning with a knot in my stomach. No, not a knot. A knot sounded too small and simple. What was bundled up in my stomach was gargantuan—a super knot, exposed to some otherworldly gamma rays and wreaking havoc on my digestive system with its super size and strength. A little dramatic, yes, but that's what it felt like.

Luckily, I hadn't had any dreams worth remembering the night before. Luckily, Lil and all my friends had stayed away. Maybe they'd sensed that I needed space. Or maybe it was just a fluke; dreams are usually random anyway, regardless of how much I'd like to think that I can control them. Yet another reason not to talk about them to people. It makes the argument of "How can you hope to live in a world beyond your grasp, always wishing and wanting it to come to you?" too valid of a point.

I didn't need other people nagging me on the one sore spot that I had with my dreams, my dilemma with them, if you will. It bothered me enough that I couldn't always have the conversations I wanted, that I couldn't always see who I wanted. That sometimes I had dreams I wouldn't wish on anybody…like my nightmare the evening before.

I shivered as I lay in my bed, staring at my ceiling, remembering the fragments of that dream. Unlike most of my dreams of my friends, I didn't know I was dreaming. Of course, that dream hadn't really been a dream. It was a memory. I'd been reliving events and thoughts that had really happened, right down to turning Lillian's head to make her look at me.

I closed my eyes and fought back the bile suddenly rising in my throat. That had been the most horrific moment of my life and I didn't wish to revisit it. Even still, the screams and tortured cries I'd made in that car echoed through my head. I don't know how long I'd yelled and shaken her, getting her blood all over me, but eventually shock had taken over my body and I'd sat back in my seat, shaking violently, watching the rain ease up on the windshield…waiting.

Looking back at that moment, I think I'd been waiting for death to take me too, not for someone to rescue me. I think I'd been shaking in that seat, praying for some internal injury to make itself known. Waiting for some part of me to bleed out, so I could close my eyes and join my girlfriend, wherever she had gone. And so, not knowing that Sheriff Whitney was coming, that he was close to being my savior, I had waited…to die.

I opened my eyes with that unwelcome memory burning my irises. Combining it with the super-knot in my stomach and the bile I'd already been fighting back and, well, I lost all control. I scrambled to the bathroom and nosily heaved into the toilet.

Perfect…just how I liked to start my day.

Panting, and urging my body to calm down, I rested my head on my arm over the cold seat. My other hand squeezed my stomach in a massaging fashion, trying to ease the pain of that discomfort. I closed my eyes as my breathing and stomach settled. Feeling a light touch to my shoulder, I glanced behind me. My mother leaned over me, concern clear in her haggard features.

"Are you all right? Are you sick?"

I sat back on my heels, shaking my head. "No, I…"

I didn't know what to say. I didn't want to talk about my dream. I never talked about that to anyone. All I ever told people, even my mom, was that I remembered leaving the party and the next thing I knew, I was waking up in the hospital. God, how I wished that were true. But it wasn't, and I couldn't tell her about dreaming of my memory of finding Lil dead…that would lead to too many other conversations I didn't want to have.

Throwing on a weak smile, I shook my head again. "I'm fine…bad Hot Pocket."

Her face twisted in parental compassion, and probably a little bit of guilt for what I constantly fed myself with. Her hand came up to my cheek, cupping it. "I'm sorry, Luc. I really shouldn't buy that stuff for you."

I sighed that my stupid cover was making her feel bad about herself. I seemed to be really good at making her feel bad about herself. I hated that. I stood up, feeling a little wobbly, and put a hand on her shoulder, drawing her in for a quick hug. "I'm fine…really. It was just a weird moment, but it's gone now." I hoped it was gone for a while.

She returned my hug, her face never relaxing out of concern. "Oh…all right. Do you want to stay home? Should I call the school?"

I seriously considered that. But…as terrified as I was to see Sawyer again, avoiding her for a day would probably only make this…thing…between us worse. No, I needed to get this awkwardness behind us so we could have our amazing friendship back again. I relied on that friendship too much.

Shaking my head, I reiterated, "No, I really am fine."

She finally conceded, reaching up to kiss my cheek before leaving me to shower away my troubles. Or try to anyway. The soothing feeling of hot water and sudsy bubbles sliding over skin only did so much to ease the soul. But being clean, and eventually dressed, did lighten the pit in my stomach. Now it was only a typical bundle of nerves and not the radiation-enhanced version I'd had upon waking.

Sipping coffee with Mom in the kitchen later, I waited for Sawyer to appear. And waited…and waited. I started to worry that *she* was going to avoid me. She'd only said she'd see me this morning…she didn't say she'd come get me. I'd just gotten so used to being picked up, I guess I kind of expected it now. Pretty selfish of me really.

Mom looked at her watch and frowned. Another few minutes and I'd have to take the bus or be late. God, I really did not want to climb back on that damn bus. I shifted in my chair and spun the coffee cup in my hands, trying to appear unworried. Surely she wouldn't ditch me?

"Um…Luc?" Mom began, glancing at her watch again.

"She'll be here," I muttered, more to myself than my mom.

"Well, she's never late and you're going to be, if she doesn't get here soon..."

I stopped fidgeting and stared at my mom, meeting her gaze. "She'll be here." My voice sounded confident, but I wasn't. How badly had I damaged us?

Mom stood, ruffled my hair, grabbed my coffee cup and walked over to the sink. "Okay," she said as she rinsed out our cups. She glanced at her watch again and shook her head. "Sorry, Luc, but I have a...meeting before work." She shrugged and looked really guilty. "I can't give you a ride today, honey...if she doesn't make it."

I stood up and threw on an unworried smile. Walking over to her, I slung my arms around her and brightly proclaimed. "Have a good day, Mom...and don't worry, she'll be here."

She sighed and cupped my cheek as her eyes took me in. I waited patiently for her to finish and then she grabbed her purse, kissed my cheek and left me alone in the kitchen...with that gargantuan knot making a reappearance.

I paced for a few minutes and then decided the enclosed space was just making me feel worse. The bus had gone by not long after my mom had left and my options for getting to school on time were dwindling. I supposed I could run there...if I really needed to. Or maybe I'd just skip first period.

I stepped outside and breathed in the crisp, cool December air. It had rained during the night and everything was slick and damp. Deep puddles filled in a low spot on our lawn and the edge of the road by the sidewalk streamed like a narrow river. Leaves dripped their stores of excess water and the whole world felt heavy and damp. I was not looking forward to being out in this.

Just as I had mentally accepted that she really wasn't coming, a familiar Camaro pulled into the drive. A frazzled Sawyer waved at me through the window, urging me to get my butt in the car already. I started from where I'd been stupidly staring at her and briskly walked to her car, getting in and shutting the door behind me. She was off before my door had even finished closing.

"Sorry I'm late," she muttered as she sped down the wet streets, the sound of the rain splashing up under her car nearly as loud as the roar of the car's engine.

"It's okay...I'm just glad you came." I cringed at my choice of words and stared out the window. The town sped by and I clutched the handle of the door, part nerves from driving so fast in the rain, part nerves from the tension I felt in the car.

"Why wouldn't I?" she shot back, a flatness to her tone that I didn't like hearing.

She'd ignored the suggestiveness of what I'd said, so I ignored it as well and looked back at her. She focused hard on the road, too hard for it to not be intentional. Her hands were white as she gripped the wheel and she was breathing shallowly though parted lips. I sighed at her obvious discomfort. I didn't want us like this.

Just as I was about to speak, to apologize for my behavior last night, we reached the school lot and she parked, shut off the car, and opened her door, all in practically one move. I had trouble adjusting to her swiftness, and scrambled to pick my bag off the floor and open my own door. By the time I'd successfully done both, she was ten paces in front of me, walking fast towards the main building.

"Sawyer, wait," I called as I hurried to catch up. The lot was full of cars, and no one was around. We only had a few moments before the bell was going to ring; we'd barely have time to get there, and we definitely didn't have time for the conversation I felt we needed to have. I suddenly got the feeling that that was exactly what she'd planned this morning. Her being late wasn't an accident.

She said nothing and didn't slow her pace, but my long legs caught up to her easily enough and we made the final steps to the doors in an uncomfortable silence. I watched the way her hair streamed behind her, unrestrained by any clips or rubber bands. I remembered that silky length wrapped in my fingers yesterday, remembered her breath in my ear…remembered the noises she'd made and how she'd clutched my back when she climaxed beneath me. The way she'd held me tight when I did.

She cleared her throat and gestured to the door and I woke from my thoughts, my face heating as I realized we were at English already. In my spacing out, I'd missed the entire trip up here. I pulled open the door as I let my heated memories fade; I really needed to not think about her like that.

Ms. Reynolds smiled at our joint entrance, and the bell rang right as we sat in our seats. Ignoring the people around me, and Ms. Reynolds perkily asking how everyone did on their last assignment, a five page paper we were supposed to write on the person who inspired us most (I think she was trying to prep us for our college), I stared at Sawyer.

Unlike most days, Sawyer didn't look back at me. She'd slung my letterman's jacket over the back of her chair and was chewing on the end of a pencil, intently listening to the teacher. Nothing in the slump of her body or the casual way she ran her thumb over the edge of her notebook showed any signs of turmoil, but every once in a while, just her eyes would flick over to me, and I knew. I knew she was making herself not return my unblinking gaze. She was making herself ignore me.

When nothing had changed halfway through class, I couldn't take it anymore. I needed to talk to her; I needed to know if we were okay. It was unfortunately a silent reading period, and everyone had their nose in a book. It was too quiet for me to whisper a conversation to her.

Ms. Reynolds was preoccupied with reading our essays at her desk, her red pen flying across the papers as she worked, and aside from the rustle of turning pages among the students, she was making the only noise in the room. Sawyer was twirling a lock of hair around her finger as she read quietly and I stared at my book without even seeing the tiny typed letters on the page.

Wanting to curse for having to resort to fifth grade measures, I grabbed my pencil and quietly tore a sheet out of the notebook still open on my desk. I wrote a question in it and folded it as silently as I could. I extended my note enclosed hand out to her, but her eyes remained on her book. Worried that she'd just plain blow me off, I coughed and exaggerated the "take it" motion with my hand.

She finally pulled her eyes away from whatever fascinating novel she was reading, and stared at my hand. She flicked a glance to my eyes and I could clearly see the reluctance on her face. I gestured again, my brows drawing together as I worried. With a soft sigh, she finally reached over and took the note from my hand. She unfolded it while I bit my lip. With a shake of her head, she picked up her pencil and wrote something next to my question. Then she refolded it and handed it to me, not looking at me. I took it immediately.

In my messy scrawl I'd written, "Are we okay?"

In slanted, elegant script she'd responded with, "Yes."

My mouth dropped and I looked over at her. That's it, that's all I get? A one-syllable answer to cover all the tension between us? She met my eye and I gestured to the paper and shook my head disbelievingly at her. She shrugged and started to turn back to her book.

Irritated, I wrote, "Are you avoiding me?" Deciding to not leave her with another yes/no question, I added, "What's wrong?"

She took the note, read it, and responded with, "No. Nothing."

Sighing, and wanting to scream in frustration, I wrote, "Talk to me!" I nearly ripped the paper I wrote it so hard. I harshly handed it to her and stared while she sighed and wrote a reply. It was a long one and I relaxed.

"I don't know what to say to you. Last night shouldn't have happened for several reasons, but I'm not trying to avoid you. I promise."

I frowned down at the paper and glanced back at her. She was worrying her lip and twirling the ring on her thumb. I frowned more as I wrote, "You seem mad at me. Are you? Do you hate me for what I did?"

Her brows drew to a point when she read that. Shaking her head she replied with, "No, I don't hate you. I'm mad at myself. I shouldn't have let that happen."

Incredulous, I wrote back, "You? I'm the one that started it. I'm the one that kissed you." As I wrote those words, I really hoped our note didn't get confiscated and read out loud. Ms. Reynolds wasn't the type to embarrass students like that though. Now, if we were in Mr. Varner's class…

"You were hurting. You needed…something. I should have pushed you away, found another way to comfort you. I'm mad at myself. I know better than that…"

I didn't know what she meant by that last part, but I was so stunned that she was angry at her own conduct that I ignored it. I didn't blame her for getting carried away when I practically attacked her, especially when I was pretty sure she had feelings for me. It was all my fault. I was the one with the lapse in judgment. I was the one being misleading, again. I told her as much and she sighed and stared at me a moment.

I bit my lip as her wrist performed the delicate act of cursive writing. "You were…impaired. I understand. Will you please stop apologizing? You're just making me feel worse."

I understood what she meant by impaired. She didn't mean drunk or high, she meant overwhelmed by grief. I suppose I was. It still didn't excuse what I'd done and I felt like falling at her feet and begging her forgiveness. I just wanted things to return to normal.

I hastily scrawled back, "I'll stop apologizing if you stop being mad at yourself and avoiding me—because you *are* avoiding me. I just want *us* back. Please?"

She closed her eyes briefly. When she opened them to glance at me, they seemed excessively moist. I swallowed when I read her response. "Okay. I'm sorry if I came off that way. I really was just late this morning, but I guess I do feel sort of weird around you, kind of guilty and…angry. I'll stop. We'll brush this aside and just be us again. Okay?"

She held her hand out to me as I read the note and I automatically grabbed it. My eyes were overly moist now too. I'd made her feel guilty and angry. I couldn't grasp that the anger she felt was only towards herself. A part of her had to hate me a little. If anything, she had to hate me for pulling back from a relationship with her. I knew she wanted that, well, I was pretty sure anyway. But I was…taken. I was with Lil and we could only be friends. I wished I could tell her that.

Instead, with one hand I wrote, "So, we're okay then?"

She took it, read it and nodded her head, smiling at me. I relaxed back in my seat and smiled halfheartedly. I wanted to believe that, I really did, but a part of me just couldn't. I held her hand for the rest of class, praying that it was true.

The rest of the day went by with an odd sort of tension between us. A tension that anyone not in the loop would notice. Outwardly we were the same. We walked to classes together. We talked about trivial topics with our heads close together. I even held her hand during break, needing to feel close to her, even if eyes were watching.

No one else probably noticed the strain in our faces, the slight edge of discomfort in our voices and the almost panicked way we gripped each other. And no one else definitely noticed the quiet lunch we had in her car. No one else was there for that, and the odd feeling between us only intensified in that small space. And, of course, in the closeness of confinement, my mind had started wandering to touching her again.

As she ate half of my sandwich, I watched her lick some crumbs off her upper lip. I instantly imagined that tongue along *my* upper lip. As she leaned over and her hair fell over her shoulder, I imagined that curtain of dark hair enclosing our faces, brushing against my shoulder. As her fingers wrapped around her water bottle, I imagined them wrapped around me. And as she tilted her head up to take a long drink from that bottle, I imagined…far more intimate acts.

I knew I wasn't helping matters any, and turned away from her to stare out the window. My body had started responding to the fantasies I'd allowed it, and I berated myself for mentally going there. It was wrong on so many levels—wrong to Lil, wrong to Sawyer. But still, you can only control what your body does and feels so much. Some things are just instinct.

I was so lost in my inner fog for the remainder of that long day that I barely noticed any of it. By the time Sawyer and I parted ways, her for purity club, me for counseling, I couldn't remember a single face I'd seen or assignment I'd been given.

The only thing in my head was Sawyer…and guilt…and confusion. As I sat down in my chair and stared at my hands, I started wondering if counseling was the best place for me. I started wondering if maybe I should finally open up to Mrs. Ryans. Just the thought brought back super-knot though.

Still staring at my hands, I heard her merrily greet me. I returned the greeting and my lip lifted to a tiny smile when she asked me to call her Beth. I studied the lines and creases of my fingers as silence filled the room around us. I wanted to say something, but the behemoth in my stomach had me in a strangle hold—I couldn't speak. I awkwardly shifted in my chair and concentrated harder on my thumb, mentally outlining the unique lines that only belonged to my skin.

Mrs. Ryans started speaking to me, asking me questions that only required either a nod or shake of my head. She usually started out that way, to loosen me up, I think. No matter my good intentions throughout the day, no matter how much I wanted to talk to her sometimes, by the time I sat in this chair across from her, my throat always closed up. She seemed to sense that and eased me into conversations. I'd been silent a lot lately, but today, I was nearly mute.

As half the session went by without so much as a peep from me, and without me even looking up at her, she finally sighed and I felt her hand reach over to touch my shoulder. I finally looked up at her with the contact.

"I want to help you, Lucas, but I can't do that if you won't talk to me." Her astonishingly blue eyes seemed to brighten with concern. "Please. I'm used to a little resistance from you, but this…" She indicated where I was rigidly sitting with my hands fisted in my lap. "I can't help you, if you completely shut down."

I tried to relax my stance and unknown aches told me I'd kept my rigid posture for a while. I hadn't even noticed. Her pale, red eyebrows drew together as she removed her hand from my shoulder and sat back in her chair. "Things are different today," she surmised. "Something happened?"

I stiffened back up as she crept closer to the truth. Her eyes took in my response and she spoke in a low voice, "Did someone else bother you?" She knew I was picked on. She knew someone had even drugged me. I shook my head—that wasn't my issue today. She sighed and then a thought seemed to lighten up her speckled cheeks. "Is it Sawyer? Did you have a fight?"

I closed my eyes and exhaled. Part in nervousness that she'd guessed correctly, part in relief that she'd guessed correctly. I felt that knot start to loosen and I swallowed noisily a few times, trying to loosen my tongue as well. Finally I sputtered, "Yes…no…I don't know."

I opened my eyes to find her watching me with an elated expression that she tried to keep even. She was excited I was talking, even if I wasn't making much sense. She leaned over her desk, her red hair moving over her shoulders as she did so. "Can you tell me what happened?"

I nodded, so she'd know I was going to respond, and then I mentally made myself relax in my chair. I listened to the quiet jazz she played in the background and noted how everything else in the room was silent. She normally took kids during school hours. I was her exception. She'd told me once that she stayed late with me so we'd have more privacy. She was aware that her flimsy Japanese screen did little to block out conversations, and she'd fit me into her life this way in the hopes that I'd open up to her if no one was around to hear. I swallowed again and hoped I'd be able to do that today.

"I…we… I sort of…made out with her…and I'm really scared. I'm really scared that I've destroyed our friendship…" My words were halting, starting and stopping and seeming to take forever in coming out, but she sat patiently and waited for me to be done.

She infinitesimally raised her eyebrow at my admission. I'd sworn up and down in earlier sessions that there was nothing between us and now I'd let it slip that maybe there was. Evening her face she said, "Why are you worried about it being destroyed? You both seem to care about each other. Maybe you're just finally moving closer. That's natural, Lucas."

I shook my head and wiped my hands on my jeans, ignoring the fluttering sensation in my stomach. "No, we aren't like that." I sighed. "Well, I'm pretty sure she likes me like that." I ran a hand through my hair nervously. Both dreading and wanting to finish my thought, I whispered, "I was having a weak moment and…I took advantage of that fact." I shook my head again, in anger this time. My voice heated as self-loathing ran through me. "I needed the comfort and I stole it from her…and I sort of feel like a bastard."

I waited for her to agree with me, my head down. That's exactly what I'd felt like today—a bastard. One of those guys that jerked girls around simply because they could. I felt horrid. She surprised me by instead saying, "You have feelings for her as well, you know."

I looked up, already shaking my head at her, but she continued, "Everything you've told me about her…" she shook her head, her curls bouncing merrily, "that's not a man describing a friend, that's a man describing the woman he loves."

In my surprise, it spilled out before I could stop it. "No, I can't like her. Lillian's my girlfriend, and I don't want to hurt her." I immediately shut my mouth as I realized what I'd just said. I could feel my face pale and I begged the fates that she somehow hadn't heard that.

No such luck. Her brows drew together. "Lillian?" She looked past me, over my shoulder, and I could see pieces of the puzzle that was me snapping into place for her. With an expression that clearly said "I understand you better," her eyes came back to me and she asked, "Lucas…are you afraid to hurt Sawyer, or are you afraid to hurt Lillian?"

"Both," I whispered, wishing I could vanish.

She nodded, like she finally got it. "So, you won't let yourself be with Sawyer, acknowledge the love you feel for her…because you still feel loyalty to your ex-girlfriend. You're still bound to her."

I bristled at her summarization and answered before my head could shout at me to stop. "She's not my ex! We're still together. I still see her and--" I cut myself off, wishing that earlier knot would return and cinch off my throat. This was exactly why I didn't want to open up to her. I couldn't talk about this with her, she'd think I was nuts.

Her expression guarded, she slowly said, "You still…? What do you mean you *still* see her?"

I immediately stood up, needing to get out of there. "I have to go." I made to head for the door.

She stood up as well, hastily reaching across her desk to grasp my arm, stopping me. "No, stay. Please…stay and talk to me. Do you still see Lillian?"

I shook my head, tears forming. She'd put me in a padded cell and pump me full of anti-psychotics if I told her the truth. "No…I…no, I know she's dead."

Her hand ran under my arm to my elbow, supporting me. With a gentle squeeze she asked, "Then what do you mean?" I hesitated, starting to buckle under the strain of hiding this. She saw my internal debate. "You can trust me, Luc, you can tell me."

I stepped away, breaking the contact. Scared beyond belief, I decided to let it out…or maybe *it* decided for me. "I dream of her and it's real…as real as anything in this world. And in that way…we're still together." My voice was shaking and tears dripped to my cheeks as I waited for her to tell me I was crazy.

I'd been backing up while I was speaking and I eventually bumped into the door handle. My hand automatically clutched it, seeking escape. Her face fell into sympathy as I twisted the knob. As I pulled open the door she shook her head at me and my body tensed.

"Luc…oh, Lucas…that's not real."

I swallowed back the tears and fled into the hallway.

I was running and wiping tears off my cheeks when I heard her behind me. "Luc, wait. Please." I kept going, fighting the natural instinct I had to obey a request made from an authority figure.

I slowed as I made my way to the section of the hall where the purity club was just letting out. Feeling panic creep into me, I stopped, not knowing which way to go. I could hear Mrs. Ryans's heels clicking up the hall as she caught up from behind me, and I could hear the light laughter of students as they left the packed classroom in front of me. My breath was coming in stuttered pulls, like I'd just run a marathon and I could feel the burning sensation of a massive barrage of tears starting to form. I was gonna break down; it was more a question of where than when.

Sawyer's black hair entered my vision as she exited the classroom, a big smile on her face as she talked to a young, blonde girl. She hadn't seen me yet, but I was positive that the moment she looked into my eyes, I'd start to cry. I didn't want to cry again in front of her, especially over Lillian.

I backed up and ran into Mrs. Ryans. She looked over my panicked face as I stared at Sawyer and pulled me into a classroom. I broke down the minute the door closed. She held me and let me cry all over her. I hated it. I hated feeling so weak in front of a teacher-like figure. She only held me close and rubbed my back, though, making soothing sounds and not commenting.

When I'd finished, I pulled away from her, wiping my nose on my sleeve and turning my face away from her. I sat on a nearby desk and sniffled, getting my breath and emotions under control. Mrs. Ryans sat on a desk near me and waited patiently for me to more-or-less put myself back together.

When I did, she quietly said, "Lucas…can you talk about her now?"

I knew which *her* she meant and the beginning of a sob rose to my throat. I shook my head and looked at her, my eyes begging for the torture to be done for one day. She seemed to understand my expression and nodded. Her next words made that sob escape however. "I'm very proud of you for telling me. I know that was hard." As my eyes let out more embarrassing tears, that I hurriedly brushed away, she brought a hand to my shoulder. "We'll leave it for another day, okay?"

With a shaky exhale, I nodded, a numb sort of relief filling me. Relief that the burden of my hidden secret was lifted, relief that she hadn't outright called me nuts and relief that I didn't need to open up any more today; my fresh wound hurt enough. She moved her hand from my shoulder to my knee and patted it a couple of times.

"I do have an assignment for you though."

With an even shakier voice I muttered, "What?"

She smiled at me. "I want you to take Sawyer to the winter dance."

Shock flew through me, like she'd just asked me to jump out the window. The winter dance was the last official school function before winter break. It was semi-formal and open to every student. I'd gone last year with Lillian and the others. It had been a fun night with lots of holding and kissing and…

"What? I can't… Sawyer and I can't…" I sputtered on my words and couldn't finish.

A somber expression marked her features. "This is important for you, Lucas. I want you to go and I think Sawyer is the best person to go with you. Of course, who you take is ultimately up to you…but I do want you to go, regardless of your escort."

"But…I don't dance." Even I knew that objection wasn't going to get me anywhere.

She smiled with one corner of her lip. "It's not about dancing, Lucas, and you know that." Her face got serious again. "It's about you reconnecting with society, with your peers. It's about you stopping this shut down. It's about you living…in *this* world."

I bristled and pulled away from her hand on my knee. I waited for her to further comment on my dream life, but she didn't. She only held my gaze and I knew we both knew what she was talking about. I shook my head and she sighed, but shrugged. "I can't make you go, Lucas…but I do think it would help you." She stood up and put a hand on my shoulder. "Think about it." Her eyes drifted over my worn features. "Think about if what you're doing now…is making anything in your life better." Her voice was soft and concerned, full of genuine compassion and I found myself nodding.

I stayed in that classroom after she left, my body swirling with so many emotions, I could only feel numbness. My chin lifted when I heard the door open. Sawyer's head popped in, looking around. She spotted me still sitting on a desk and walked into the room. "There you are." Her brows creased together as I blankly stared at her. I wasn't sure what I looked like, but I knew how I felt: empty, alone…tired.

She sat beside me, not breaking our eye contact. Her hand came up to brush some hair off my forehead and then she ran her fingers down my cheek, brushing away a tear I hadn't even realized was there. Her thumb continued stroking my face as we gazed at each other.

"Tough session?" she whispered. I could only swallow and nod in answer. The hardest one yet. With a sigh, Sawyer brought her arm around me and pulled me in for a tight hug. "I'm sorry, Luc." I exhaled as she said the words, feeling like she was apologizing for more than just my meeting with Mrs. Ryans.

Feeling the tension between us slip away, I hugged her back just as tight and whispered, "I'm sorry, too." She nodded in my shoulder and I knew she knew exactly what I meant by that.

She drove me home and stayed with me for a while, going over our Philosophy homework while slyly watching to make sure I was really okay. Other than homework, we didn't talk much. I didn't tell her about my session, and she didn't ask. We didn't talk any more about what had happened between us; that was over and dealt with. And I definitely didn't ask her to the dance. It was such a crazy idea that I couldn't even entertain it yet.

I didn't really want to reconnect with society, with my peers. They didn't want to reconnect with me, either. At least the rejection was mutual. I didn't see the point of it, and I didn't see the harm of having a better life in my dreams, crazy as that was. For now, going to a silly high school dance seemed the crazier suggestion.

Dances were apparently in my thoughts when I fell asleep that night though. I blankly looked around at a gymnasium fully decked out for a dance, complete with blue and white crepe paper, generic popular music in the background and a revolving disco ball suspended from the ceiling, throwing sparks of light across the laminated floor. I looked down at myself, taking in the black slacks and white button-down dress shirt. I ran a hand through my hair and felt the product styling it back into more manageable waves. I looked around the empty room, feeling the lonely expanse of it. Where was everyone?

The room suddenly felt…thicker. The scent of lilies and vanilla hit me and I closed my eyes, remembering the fragrance Lillian used for special occasions. Dances, dates, nights when she snuck into my bed to be intimate with me… The memories assaulted me, and I swallowed and sat on the bleacher behind me. Panicky nerves shot through me. She was finally reappearing to me. I was about to finally see her again…and she'd know. She'd know I was unfaithful to her. She'd hate me. She'd finally hate me…and I deserved her hatred.

I felt her presence get even closer and my whole body tensed. I couldn't do this. I couldn't look at her and break her heart without even having to say a word.

Her high heeled shoes filled my vision as I regretfully opened my eyes. I swallowed but didn't look up at her. I didn't want to see those achingly beautiful pale eyes fill with tears.

She wasn't just going to let me ignore her, though. She squatted down and looked up at me. I avoided looking at her face, my gaze instead going to her dark blue silk dress, the spaghetti straps clinging to her pale shoulders. I swallowed again.

"Lucas," she whispered.

I closed my eyes briefly and then made myself look up to hers. Her hands stroked my knees as she squatted in front of me, a small smile playing on her peach lips. A trace amount of smoky eye makeup highlighted the brilliant blue irises that were gazing at me lovingly; only the slightest hint of moisture was in them.

"I'm sorry," I immediately choked out.

She shook her head, the tight blonde curls of her intricate up-do bouncing as she did. "Don't, Luc…it's okay."

A tear dropped to my cheek as I swallowed and spoke the words I was terrified to say. "I…I feel like I cheated on you." My voice quavered and I swallowed again, looking down at my hands pressing against my stomach.

Her hands came up to grab mine and I looked back at the hazy image of her in my watery vision. "That's ridiculous, Luc." She shook her pale head again. "You can't cheat on me…I'm already gone…"

I shook my head and grabbed her face. "Not to me…not to me…" I brought her lips to mine, needing her comfort. "I'm so sorry. It won't happen again, I promise," I whispered against her mouth.

She pulled back and sighed brokenly. "I *want* you to do this, Lucas. I want you to move forward with Sawyer." Her lips came up to a small smile and I felt my heart seize. "I'm telling you it's okay."

I stroked her cheek, brushing aside a tear as it spilled from her eye. "Then why are you crying?"

She swallowed, her smile slipping. "Just because I know it's right…doesn't mean it's easy."

I searched her face, not wanting to listen. "I can't be with her, Lillian…" She shook her head, like she knew what I was going to say next. "I can't be with her…because I'm in love with you." I searched her watery eyes as I reverently whispered, "I love…*you*."

Her eyes closed and tears fell from both of them. "Oh, Lucas…" She reopened them, pain and joy clear in her face. "I love you, too." She leaned in to kiss me and I pulled her tight, never wanting to let her go.

Chapter 14 – A Moment of Happiness

I awoke the next morning with a feeling in my chest that bordered on genuine happiness. I stared at my ceiling and absorbed every detail of the dream I'd just had: the way Lillian's hair caught the sparkling light of the disco ball, the way the silky dress she wore clung to her body when we danced, the way her lips repeated over and over that she loved me too.

We'd finally said it. We'd finally moved past that last barrier between us and exposed our hearts to each other. It was no great surprise, but we hadn't been able to make that leap in real life. Being able to do it at all, even in a fantasy world, gave me a nearly euphoric feeling.

I stretched out my muscles while a long grin spread on my face. The dream had lasted much longer than most dreams I'd had of late. It was like neither one of us had wanted to let go of that peaceful moment. We'd recreated the last dance we'd been to when she'd been alive, minus the swarm of people. It had just been Lillian and me on the dance floor, and every song had been a slow one. Her arms had wrapped around my neck and mine had cinched tight around her waist. I'd told her nonstop that I loved her, that I needed her, and she'd run her fingers through the back of my hair and kissed me repeatedly.

I closed my eyes, remembering the feel of those lips on mine. I didn't care what Mrs. Ryans said—it *was* real. As real as lying awake in my bed, as real as plodding through school, and as real as hanging out with Sawyer.

I opened my eyes and sighed. Sawyer. While our relationship had coalesced back to normalcy by the end of the day yesterday, I couldn't help but think that we were on the edge of something. That, if I let that happen again, I'd push her to the point where there was no saving our friendship. She'd been unbelievably patient with me up until this point, but I could see the strain of my mixed signals getting to her.

I couldn't imagine being in her position; liking someone who seemingly flirted and acted like they liked you back, only to have them push you away from any real intimacy. But, we couldn't be like that…even if I did share her feelings, which I wasn't sure if I did or not. I mean, how could I be head over heels in love with Lillian *and* have my heart ache for Sawyer? I couldn't. I didn't. What I felt for Sawyer was immense comfort and limitless friendship—my body wanted to translate that into a physical relationship because I was a seventeen-year-old virgin. That made more sense.

I got out of bed and ran a hand down my face. I wouldn't take it there again though. I'd be the friend Sawyer deserved and keep my physical distance. I'd return us to a more normal guy/girl relationship of at least a foot apart at all times. Then my hormones would be kept in check and she wouldn't get hurt anymore. I could at least do that for her.

And for Lillian.

I made my way to the bathroom to shower and shave, all the while thinking of Lillian again. I'd hurt her. She may have tried to stoically brush it off as "that's real life and you should embrace it," but I could see it in the slight tremor of her lip and the few tears she'd let slide down her cheek. I'd abandoned her, betrayed her, and she'd been devastated. I'd never do that again. I'd never bring her pain again. I'd never let her go…we were going to be together forever.

As I sat down for my coffee with Mom, a smile was still with me and she delighted in seeing it. She commented on it and I only told her things were fine. I didn't want to tell her that Lillian and I had finally moved up in our romance. She'd tell me that was impossible and I needed help…etc, etc, etc. I didn't want to hear it. I felt good, and I was going to keep that feeling, even if that meant being vague or even outright lying to people.

Sawyer surprised both my mom and me by arriving a few minutes early and coming inside. Mom stood up and gave her the chair she'd been sitting in, then poured her a fresh cup of coffee. Sawyer politely thanked her, twisting the ring on her thumb, and my mom leaned back on the counter, beaming at the two of us.

Mom believed Sawyer was making me happy and wanted to foster that, wanted us to be together, or maybe she thought we already were. To a casual observer it did look that way, especially with her still wearing my jacket. But we weren't, and even though she did make me happy, happier than any living person, she wasn't the one making me smile into my coffee cup.

"You seem…better today," she said quietly, once we were finally driving to school.

I grinned and flicked the disco ball hanging off her rear view mirror. It caught the early morning rays and threw tiny dots of light across her dashboard. It reminded me of my dream so firmly that I let out a contented sigh and leaned back in my seat.

"Do I?" Even I could hear the bounce in my voice and I laughed as I stared off into the window. "I guess I just had a good night."

"Oh." Her voice was genuinely surprised and I looked back at her. "That surprises me. Usually when you have a bad session, it takes you a couple of days to get…well, to smile again, honestly." She shrugged, her concerned look not leaving her.

I sighed as I thought back over talking with Mrs. Ryans yesterday. I'd messed up. I'd said way too much and broken a wall I hadn't meant to break. I was hastily trying to repair that wall now; plastering the fragments before it completely fell apart on me. She knew I dreamed of Lillian. She knew I considered that a real relationship. She'd surely assign me medication now…but that didn't mean I had to take it. I didn't have to do anything I didn't want to. Well, besides go in the first place.

I shrugged and told Sawyer the one thing we'd discussed that I could share. "She surprised me more than anything. She wants me to go to that stupid winter dance." I shook my head. "I haven't been to a dance since…" I bit my lip and looked back out the window. "It just took me back that she'd ask me to take you to something like that."

"She wants you to take *me*…to a dance?"

I spun my head back around to her at the incredulity in her voice. She was studying the road. Her hair was pulled back into a neat and orderly ponytail, giving me a perfect view of her expression. She was trying to keep her face neutral, but I'd studied her features long enough to know when she was excited. Her eyes flicked along the road, probably not even seeing it, and a merry glow seemed to spark in the grayness. The very edges of her lips were curled up in a slight smile and her hands had tightened on the wheel.

Oh God, she wanted to go. I'd never imagined that possibility. Not that I'd imagined going at all, but still, I'd pictured Sawyer being as resistant to the very idea of it as I was.

"Do you…would you want to go?" I whispered, praying she said no…and meant it.

She bit her lip, her eyes sparkling even more as she sat up straighter in her seat. "I didn't get… I missed..." She stumbled around for words before finally shaking her head and sighing. "Yeah, I've always…" She bit her lip again and a light flush ran along her cheeks. She giggled nervously and simply said, "Yeah."

She flicked a quick glance at me, noticed the look on my face, that must have been somewhere between humor and horror, and frowned. "But you don't want to…" Her eyes went back to the road. "No, of course you don't want to. That was something you shared with…" She shook her head. "Oh, that's why you were upset..."

I fixed my face and started to say something, but she cut me off. "I'm sorry…of course you don't want to go. That was stupid of me to think that you might…"

Her face flushed deeper and she fixed her eyes straight ahead. My thoughts stuttered and no coherent words came out of me. I shut my mouth and looked out the window as we made the final turn into the school parking lot. I'd never imagined the conversation playing out this way. I thought I'd tell her crazy Mrs. Ryans's plans and she'd laugh them off with me, agreeing that the woman was loony. I'd never considered that Sawyer would actually want to go with me.

I watched her worry her lip as she parked the car. Of course…she *was* a girl. As different as she seemed from other girls, as mature and pragmatic as she could seem sometimes, she was still a girl. And I knew from a year of being with Lillian that girls liked dances. They liked getting decked out to the nines in slinky dresses and professionally done up-dos. They liked the loud music and cheesy balloon arches and getting posed photographs taken. They liked seeing their men dress nice and act more gentlemanly than teenage boys generally did, bringing them flowers and taking them out to a nice dinner. They liked standing close and pressing their bodies right up against their men, nearly promising more intimate acts later, if they were taken care of in the right way.

I sighed as she shut the car off. If I did this for her, asked her to go, that last part might be a problem. Not that I would let anything happen between us…again, but it would violate my new "foot apart" rule if we slow danced all night. I looked back to her as she started to open her door. I supposed I could put that rule on hold, for one night.

"Sawyer," I said, stopping her from finishing cracking open her escape route. She looked back at me, a faint redness still along her cheeks. "Would you like to go to the dance with me?"

Her flush deepened and she let out a nervous laugh. I kept my face steady and even, so she'd know that I was serious, that I was seriously asking her. Her eyebrows rose as she took in my face. "Are you being serious?" Her voice matched her eyes.

I nodded and let a smile creep into my lips. "Yes."

She twisted in her seat to face me, her escape route momentarily forgotten. "You didn't seem like you wanted to go. Why ask me?"

I shrugged. "Honestly, I don't want to go." Her face darkened and I quickly added, "But you do…and after everything…"

My words drifted off as I looked over her softening face. The early light of morning backlit her dark hair and her face glowed at me like an angel. I swallowed as I looked over her features, resisting the urge to cup that porcelain cheek. Keeping a distance with her might be harder than I first thought. She tilted her head as she watched whatever emotion was sliding across my features. I swallowed again and looked down, pushing back the odd feeling that had started to build in me.

"After everything you've put up with from me, I could at least put up with this…" I looked up and met her eyes again, "…for you."

She swallowed as she searched my face. I made myself calmly watch her, unblinking, unworried about the delightful tension building in the car. She locked her gaze to mine, leaning forward slightly. My eyes flicked down to her lips before I caught myself and forcefully looked back up at her eyes. Her hand raised and she brushed some hair off my forehead. I wanted to lean into her touch and made myself not react. I also made myself not pull away, either. She didn't know about my new rule. She didn't realize she was breaking it. I couldn't just initiate something like that without warning her first.

When I didn't react or touch her back, she pulled her hand away and set it in her lap. "Okay," she said slowly. "I'd love to go with you."

She grinned and then turned to open her door. The tension left the car with her and I stayed in my seat a moment, wondering how so much had changed so fast. Wasn't I dead set against going just yesterday?

She stood outside her car waiting for me, delight clear in her eyes. Shaking my head, I opened my door and joined her. She held her hand out for me and stepped within the one foot radius I'd mentally set as a "do not enter" zone. I didn't take her hand and stepped back. Surprise and confusion washed over her face and I sighed, knowing I'd have to talk about this with her sooner or later, and sooner was probably a better idea.

She started to take a step towards me and I put my hands out to stop her. She shook her head at my gesture, hurt clear in her eyes.

"I've been thinking," I started, glancing around to see if any students were this far back in the lot with us. A few were and were watching, but I needed to do this, for her sake. I swallowed and continued, "I…don't want to hurt you any more than I know I have." She looked about to argue, and I held my hands up higher. "No, I know you think you were as much to blame as me for what happened the other night, but the truth is…"

I paused, wondering what to tell her. I'd started this conversation without thinking about how I could explain keeping her away from me without hurting her even more. She'd given every appearance that she liked touching me, liked being close. If I suddenly shoved her back and told her I didn't want her physically near me…well, I couldn't see how that wouldn't hurt her. Unless…unless I played the one card every guy my age has. God, I hated to play it. I wasn't a Neanderthal…I did have control. Usually.

I half smiled and shrugged. "I'm just a guy. You're a really pretty girl and when you're around me, my body reacts to…" My cheeks heated, but I made myself say it, "I've never had sex with anyone and I really want to…and when you're touching me all the time, I forget that we're only friends and all I can think about is that you have breasts and that I'd like to…" I swallowed, wanting to crawl back in the car. "I'm sorry. I can only control myself so much. I think we should keep some distance between us from now on."

Oh, God. I wanted…to die.

Her face had dropped in shock so many times while I was speaking that it was nearly comical. She sputtered on what to comment on first. "Distance? From me? You like my…? You want to…? Wait, you're a…virgin?" She shook her head in disbelief as I closed my eyes, wanting to skip forward to the part where this was just a fact between us, and we never talked about it…ever again. "You…you think I'm pretty?"

I opened my eyes and smiled at the awe on her face as she took that in. Only meaning to tell her that of course she was pretty, I found myself whispering, "I think you're beautiful." My voice came out nearly reverent, and I mentally slapped myself. God, I might as well shove my tongue down her throat. It would be just as misleading. A warmth settled in me at that thought, and I shook my head to break it.

Her eyes had moistened and her mouth dropped open again. Sighing at how my morning was not going as seamlessly as I'd imagined—maybe Sawyer and I had crossed that line of friendship too many times already?—I shoved my hands firmly in my pockets and motioned with my head to the main building. "We're going to be late," I muttered and immediately started walking.

She fell into step beside me, and with her gaze never leaving mine for more than a few seconds, we made our way to class. On the way there, I noticed things I hadn't before—signs for the upcoming winter dance were everywhere. Handmade posters were taped up every few feet down the hall, a large banner hung over the window on the staircase and 8x10 notices were plastered on every classroom door, urging students to buy tickets to the last dance of this year. Now that I'd agreed to go, I couldn't seem to escape it. Interesting how I'd blocked all that out before.

Sawyer kept her distance from me but bounded to her seat with a grin on her face. I had no idea what was going on in her head. Was it really just about getting dressed up and having fun together, or was she imagining having her arms around my neck all night? I flushed as I thought about how close she'd be and for how long. I wondered if maybe I should talk to Lil to reassure her that nothing was going to happen. I was just being a good friend and making my counselor happy. But, knowing Lillian, she would tearfully smile and tell me that I should let something happen, that I should be with Sawyer and not her, or something equally ridiculous. It didn't seem like she was going to break things off with me, but she was sure insistent for me to break things off with her. Like I would ever do that.

I carefully walked past Will on the way to my seat. When I looked up at him though, he was busy in a conversation with Randy and didn't even notice me. Randy glanced up at me and then hurriedly shifted back to his intense conversation with Will. They seemed to be arguing about the last football game.

The season had ended before Thanksgiving break and our team...hadn't done well. I'd run into Coach in the hallway after the final defeat and he'd actually scowled at me. Like the fact that Will tended to drop the ball, and the other team took advantage of that and scored a lot was somehow my fault. He'd muttered that I'd probably let him down for baseball too and then stormed off down the hall. I hadn't seen Coach since, but got the feeling that when spring rolled around, he'd be all over me to try out. I had no plans to.

Sawyer had filled me in on bits and pieces of the football games, since she went to most of them. It had surprised me at first when she'd admitted that she did...I hadn't gone to a single one. She'd said that she went with the Safe and Sound Club. A bunch of them went to every game, trying to dissuade the ranks from the debauchery of post-game partying. Games were Friday nights and before that fateful Thanksgiving dinner, we'd generally parted ways Friday afternoon until Monday morning. It had never occurred to me that she would go to the games without me. She'd said she wouldn't if her parents didn't insist on it. Apparently they wanted her to reconnect with the community as well.

She had laughingly told me about how awful the games had been. I think she'd been attempting to cheer me up, let me know I was missed. And in a microscopic way, it did make me happy. A small part of me enjoyed the fact that my absence was noticed in some small way. At least to Coach, if not the rest of the team. For the rest of them...well, I think they'd rather take the loss than have me play with them. And Will had been especially stormy around me when loss after loss had started being attributed to him. He'd started acting like my being a better player was a character flaw that needed to be humiliated out of me. As I sat down, I was grateful that his conversation with Randy had kept him out of my hair, for one morning at least.

Sawyer had an adorable grin on her face throughout the entire class. She seemed to find my multiple mortifying revelations endearing. I still felt flushed with embarrassment. I really hadn't wanted to say any of that, especially the being a virgin part, but I couldn't tell her the real reason why I needed space, and it seemed as good of an excuse as any. Maybe if I hadn't added that last part about her being beautiful, she wouldn't look so thrilled.

We worked on reports for the books we were supposed to have finished yesterday and Sawyer gave me small, knowing smiles every few minutes. I couldn't help but grin back at her, but I did wonder if any of my admissions had been for the best.

I walked her to the front doors after class and as we separated she leaned into me, but never actually touched me. With a laugh she jokingly stated that she was headed off to her workout, huffing over to the Science building for one class, only to turn back around afterwards and head right back up to the second floor. I laughed with her and wished her luck in her Chem. test.

When I saw her again she was huffing and getting her breath back, but her face was still excited, darn near elated. I mentally sighed, but returned her beaming smile for her benefit. She'd been running later than usual and had just made it in the door when the bell rang. When I asked her what she'd been doing, she shyly admitted that she'd been talking to Sally Hoffen, the Safe and Sound Club president, about the dance. They'd been going over hair styles and dress ideas. She was telling me she was concerned about how she'd afford a nice enough dress when I interrupted her.

"You told Sally that we're going together?" I hadn't meant for my tone to be rough, but in my surprise it kind of came out that way. I rarely talked to anyone besides Sawyer, so it always kind of threw me for a loop that she kept up conversations with other people besides me. Again, I can be a little self-absorbed.

Her happy face fell as she looked over mine. I instantly felt bad for bursting her excited bubble and was trying to apologize when Mr. Varner slammed his hand down on my desk. I jumped about a foot and turned to stare up at him with wide eyes.

"Mr. West, Miss Smith…do I need to separate you two lovebirds?" His eyes narrowed as he flicked his gaze between us. Among the giggles running through the classroom, I heard someone dreamily sigh.

"No," I muttered, slinking back in my chair.

He crossed his arms over his chest, and even though I wished this were a dream and I could whisk him away, he remained standing in front of my desk. "What were you talking about anyway?" His eyes flicked around to the students listening intently, and my face heated. "I've always wondered what's so vital that students choose to tune me out." His hands made a go ahead gesture and he sat on the edge of the desk in front of mine—the girl there nearly swooned out of her seat. "So, go ahead…we're all ears."

Sawyer flushed bright red while I shook my head. No way was I fessing up to him, I'd rather have detention. Unfortunately, the girl with Mr. Varner's rump on her desk decided to be teacher's pet. I could only imagine what favors she thought she was winning. "They were talking about going to the dance together, Mr. Varner," she said brightly.

He smiled at her and then looked back to us with a tilted head. "A dance…how touching." He stood from her desk, making her sigh, and stepped up to mine, leaning over the edge. "I'll be going to that little dance as well, Mr. West." His eyes flicked down me contemptuously. "And if you so much as whiff of alcohol…you're gone."

My eyes narrowed and I felt myself starting to stand. I wanted to knock that smug look off his face, and with the surge of embarrassment and anger running through me, I thought I could do it. When I was in a half crouch, I felt a hand on my arm and looked over at Sawyer, who was shaking her head at me emphatically.

Mr. Varner smirked and stood up straight. He raised two fingers at me. "Two strikes, Lucas."

I clenched my hands into fists and made myself stay seated and quiet while he sauntered back to the front of the room. The students around me started giggling and whispering, and I knew the rumor mill had just ground out a new story. Maybe in this one I'd actually slug the bastard.

I was still steaming about the incident with Mr. Varner when Sawyer and I were huddled around her locker later. I kept my back to the lockers and didn't look at them. This morning had started out so well, but it was steadily spiraling downward. I tried to let the heat slide off of me as I rested my head back on the cool metal. I looked over when Sawyer slammed her locker shut.

"He's such an ass! I don't get what girls see in him." She gave me a pointed look. "Does a chiseled face really make up for poor social skills now?"

I grinned at her peevishness, feeling my own die down. "Chiseled?" I teased.

She returned my grin and then frowned a little. "Are you mad that I told Sally?"

Her face concerned, she leaned against her locker. I watched her shoulder compress against the locker that should have been my girlfriend's and sighed. I wished Lil was here. I wished I was asleep and could see her. I started out of my odd desire and shifted my focus back to Sawyer.

I shook my head at her. "No, it just surprised me, that's all. Sometimes I forget that you have a life without me."

She smiled and started to reach out for me, but then stopped herself. I was glad she had, but found myself with an actual ache at the loss. This was going to be a *lot* harder than I had thought. "I don't have much of a life, if it makes you feel better."

With a grin she started walking down the hall towards Math and I fell into step with her. She looked over at me with a seriousness on her face that I knew pretty well. She was about to say something beyond her years. "You could have it too, you know."

I scrunched my brow, confused. "Huh?"

She shook her head. "Have a life. Have other friends."

Ice flashed through me, but I threw on a smile. "Why would I want other friends, when I'm perfectly content with you?" I shifted my grin to a crooked one and bit back what I was really feeling. No one in this school wanted a friendship with me. No one but Sawyer. She was all I had here. Really, she was all I had awake.

Sawyer seemed to hear my silent words as we walked among the crowds that I felt watching and whispering about us. My upcoming appearance at a school function would be well known by the end of the day. "I know I've mentioned this before, Luc, but not everyone here is against you."

I scoffed at that, not meaning to sound angry and bitter, but clearly hearing it in my own voice anyway. "Right, nothing but warm fuzzies here." I looked around at the people I'd known since practically kindergarten. I didn't know what Sawyer saw, but all I saw were heads bent together in gossip, and I was tired of being gossiped about.

Sawyer sighed. "Well, there's Randy, and that's just one instance."

I stopped in the hallway as her casual remark settled in my system. Was she joking? She looked around when she felt that I wasn't beside her anymore and then looked back at me, her eyebrows raised. I stood a couple of paces behind her, my mouth dropped open in what could only resemble the expression of a mentally impaired person. "Randy?" I said incredulously, while I heard the kids lining the hall quiet. "Are you serious? You know what Josh had him do to me. You think he wants to be pals?"

My tone was getting louder and louder as I spoke, and Sawyer glanced around the hallway before stepping close to me, well within my one foot zone. I was so irritated that I didn't care, though. Quietly, she whispered, "Yes, Lucas, Randy. If you'd pay a little closer attention, you'd see that he feels really bad about drugging you. " I started to pull away, but she grabbed my arm, dragging me closer. "Josh tricked him into doing it. Randy told me that Josh told him it was a liquid laxative. Randy didn't know what would happen. He just wanted you to suffer a little bit. He didn't know you'd get suspended."

I jerked away from her arm, pulling apart. I was sure it looked like we were having a lover's spat, but, regardless of my actions, Sawyer wasn't the one I was angry with. No, I was mad at everyone else—all of them, all of my harassers, all of the whisperers and all of the lookey-lous. "When did you…?" I shook my head, not really caring when she'd had this heart-to-heart with one of my tormentors. "Well, that's so much better. I'm glad he only wanted to send me to the john for a few hours." I threw my hands up as my voice got loud again. "God, what a relief, Sawyer!"

Her face flushed and, with an irritated shake of her head, she stormed off down the hall. Closing my eyes and cursing my dramatics, I hurried after her. Everyone watched us leave. I grabbed her elbow right as she slipped into the door. She looked down at where we were touching and then up to my face. Red blotches still marked her cheeks and I sighed, hating that I'd hurt her. Ignoring every person in the classroom, ignoring the teacher writing on the white board, ignoring my own desire to keep a distance between us—ignoring it all, I pulled her into a tight hug.

"I'm sorry. I'm an ass, I'm sorry," I whispered into her hair.

She nodded against my chest and returned my tight embrace. I sighed as I kept my eyes closed. Here I was, just a few hours after telling her that I needed physical space, holding her tight, like I was afraid she'd vanish if I didn't, while every eye around us watched. I was trying to avoid misleading her, and I was trying to avoid more gossip about us…and I was failing miserably. A giggling titter filled the room and I finally broke apart from her, feeling my cheeks heat. Her face was flushed as well as she looked around the semi-filled room and awkwardly adjusted her bag on her shoulder.

I motioned to our seats and we gratefully sat down. A few eyes followed us before turning to look at each other. The whispering started again. I got out my book and flipped through the pages, not seeing any of them. I heard Sawyer beside me do the same and snuck a glance at her. She was staring at her desk, but met my gaze when she felt my eyes.

"I'm sorry," I mouthed again, and she nodded.

The bell rang, the teacher turned from where she'd been writing equations on the board and everything fell back into normalcy. Well, as normal as things ever got for me. I thought about Sawyer's comments during class. I ignored my over-reaction to them and really focused on what she'd been saying. I couldn't believe it. I didn't see how anyone in this school would want anything to do with me. It wasn't like anyone ever approached me, other than to ask me the questions I'd answered so many times, I was sick of it. I'd stopped answering them a while ago. And Randy…that one was definitely off. No way was he looking to be my friend. No frickin' way.

Things got back to normal with Sawyer during lunch in her car. We relaxed back in her seats and ate our sandwiches and she commented that her dad had finally gotten a job with the logging company, so things were looking up for her family. She happily bit into her very own PB&J when she said that. I blinked at her in surprise when she did. I hadn't realized her dad was out of work. I knew things were tough for them, but never really knew why, and had never asked.

"That's great, Sawyer. I didn't realize he was looking." I grabbed a corner off my own ham and cheese sandwich and curled it into a ball before eating it.

She watched my habit before responding. "Yeah. He and Mom both quit their jobs when we moved out here. They've both been looking, but times are tough…" She shrugged and looked really guilty. I wondered why, until I remembered that her parents had dropped everything and moved out to the middle of nowhere—from Portland she'd told me once—because of her.

"Do you want to talk about what happened, Sawyer?" I asked quietly while she spaced out, gazing over my shoulder.

She brought her eyes back to mine and shook her head, snapping out of her mini-trance. "No." She smiled and her face got animated again. "I want to talk about the dance." She was grinning from ear to ear and I couldn't help but grin with her. She was so excited about this stupid dance.

I rolled my eyes, but then laughed and we started going over the details. The dance was the last Friday night before the school broke for the holidays. It was a winter wonderland theme, of course, and both guys and girls were expected to wear nice dress clothes. Sawyer was a little anxious about that, not being able to afford anything even remotely nice yet, even though her dad was now employed. I told her my mom had a couple of nice party dresses that would probably fit her if she wanted to wear one. She looked at me oddly and said she'd have to look at them first. Then she smiled brightly and started going on about corsages.

We were talking about having dinner at my place to save on cash—she made me promise that we wouldn't be having my Hot Pocket standard—as we walked to our next classes. I shook my head at her as we parted ways. For someone who seemed almost anti-social at times, she sure was digging this.

As I walked to Science, I was surprisingly grateful to Mrs. Ryans for even bringing up the idea. Maybe it would be good to get out in the real world. As I opened the door to Astronomy, I reconsidered.

Josh was glaring at me, and I quickly ducked my head and broke eye contact. We hadn't had any confrontations in a while and I was trying to keep it that way. I heard his laughter and resisted the urge to look as I sat down.

Keeping my eyes straight ahead, I started daydreaming about Lillian to distract myself; I couldn't wait to see her tonight. I was in the middle of reimagining slow dancing with her in my dream, my fingers low on her waist, hers running through the back of my hair, when a wadded up piece of paper smacked me in the side of the head. Irritated, I looked over before I could stop myself.

Josh was laughing, sneering cruelly while Randy held down his arm, stopping him from chucking another piece. Brushing it off, I exhaled slowly and stared straight ahead again.

"Hey, Luc," I heard Josh say from the other side of the room."Heard your date to the dance went off on you." I closed my eyes and focused on my breath, focused on not reacting. It hadn't taken very long for that tiny spat to twist into high school dramatics. Josh, apparently enjoying my attempt at non-reaction, continued, "Hear she only agreed to go in the first place to be your designated driver. At least one of you is smart," he added.

My head twisted around as I visually drove nails into his body. That? That was the way he was going to spin our fight in the hall? I gripped the edge of my desk, my fingers digging into the hard, wooden top, urging the flare of anger he sparked in me to die down. He started rocking with laughter at my reaction and I started shaking from the restraint. Biting my lip to not tell him to go to hell, I made myself face the front again. The laughter from his side of the room grew even louder.

Fortunately the bell rang and the teacher started class. I knew it was too late, though. I knew the student body would take that pathetic gossip and run with it. By the end of the day, the very idea of me going to the dance with Sawyer would be akin to me going with a breathalyzer attached to my arm; someone to keep me in check, since I obviously couldn't do it on my own. I sighed as I listened to what had once been my favorite subject. What else could I have expected from these people? Definitely not friendship. Sawyer was so wrong about that.

As soon as I could, I darted out of that class. Even though I'd sat in the back, I got out into the fresh, chilly air before everyone else. I heard Josh snigger as I left the room.

Practically speed-walking to my next class, I pictured an irate Darren beside me. I imagined restraining him from turning around and beating the shit out of Josh, much like the time I'd had to restrain him from wanting to go after some senior who had said Sammy had a fat ass. Personally, I thought the guy was just upset that

Sammy had turned him down, but Darren had taken it as a personal attack on his girlfriend. He'd been determined to give the guy a broken nose…in the middle of American History. I'd dragged him out of the room with both arms locked under his elbows as he'd yelled threats at the imbecile.

Picturing restraining hot-headed Darren from fighting helped calm the inner beast within me, and I felt more relaxed with every step away from Josh. For as much as I understood his anger, as much as I tried to ignore the hurts and insults, a part of me just wanted to kick his fucking ass! Much like Darren had done when he'd finally run into that guy at a party a few weeks later.

Using Darren's remembered temper to moderate mine, I was calm again by the time I stepped through the doors into art class. Josh was behind me for the day and I could let him go. I was easing a smile onto my face and working on my latest project, when I felt Mrs. Solheim come up beside me. She praised me for my work and then chirpily said, "I hear you're going to the dance, Tom. That's great!"

She walked away before I could respond, and I shook my head as I watched her; her loose pants and flowing tunic were a myriad of contrasting colors that was almost dizzying to look at. How had my spacey art teacher heard that already? News traveled so fast around here.

I waited outside of art for Sawyer to get out of choir. I'd tried to go to one of their concerts once, but she'd told me she'd rather not have me there, so I hadn't ever heard her sing. She'd explained it away as her having a solo that she'd never be able to get through, if she knew I was listening. I was dying to hear her sing, especially if she was good enough for the teacher to have her sing by herself, but I respected her wish and stayed away. Looking back on that, I wondered if it had more to do with keeping me away from her parents than with her nerves. Or maybe it had been a combination of the two.

I waited for a while and frowned. She was taking a long time to get out of there. Remembering the flood of gossip that had started, I began to worry about her. Brittany hopped on anything she could to tease her, and I'd handed her a nice little bouquet to choose from. I started walking over to the room just as her black hair came out the door.

She immediately looked over to me and started walking my way. She walked tall and straight and didn't look behind her. I did. Brittany, and the group that usually flocked around their queen, was just exiting the building. They were looking over at Sawyer and laughing. Brittany looked past Sawyer's back, to where I was scowling at her. The smile fell from her lips, and she glared back at me. Then her lips twisted into a look that clearly said "come get me." I was not about to.

Ignoring her, I focused back on Sawyer as she walked up and adjusted the bag on her shoulder. "Everything…okay?" I asked, glancing at Brittany's retreating form, her hips swaying in such an exaggerated way that it was clear it wasn't a natural walk. She confirmed that by looking over her shoulder at me. She muttered something to the girl beside her, which made the other girl laugh and look at me, too. When their joint laughter died down, her friend faced front while Brittany sneered and teasingly ran a hand down her ass.

I shook my head at her odd, mixed attitude towards me and turned back to Sawyer, who was watching her as well. I was about to ask her what Brittany had done, when she interrupted me. "I can never tell if she wants to screw you…or kill you." She turned back to me with furrowed brows.

I shook my head and sighed. "I know…I can't either. What did she say to you?"

She shook her hair out, her face relaxing as she did. "Doesn't matter. I don't know what her problem is with me, and I can't control what she does or says…" She exhaled and let a warm smile touch her lips. "But it's still up to me how I react to it, right?"

"You sound like my counselor now."

"Well, maybe I've discovered my calling in life."

I laughed. "Being my counselor? Do you think that would be a lifelong job?"

She giggled, staring at me with adoration clear on her face. "I hope so."

I swallowed at the look in her eye and then nervously chuckled. "Well, don't expect it to pay much."

She laughed and shoved her hands in her pockets. For a second, I missed that I couldn't hold her hand, but it was for the best. I shouldn't be so friendly with her, if it wasn't going to go anywhere other than, well, friendship. I shoved my hands in my pockets as well, and we made our way to our next activities in comfortable silence.

Chapter 15 – Leave Me My Happy Fantasy, That's All I Ask

I hesitated with my hand on the door handle, a hard ball forming in my stomach. Yesterday's session had been horrible—emotional and draining. I didn't want a repeat of that day. I didn't want to confess any more of my secrets to the person on the other side of this door. Of course, I did still have a couple more weeks left of sessions, and if I ever wanted back into the purity club with Sawyer, I had to do this. As my hand slowly twisted the handle, I wondered if that was even the real reason I still kept coming here day after day.

I opened the door and stepped through, the familiar jazz music coming to my ears. Mrs. Ryans sat at her desk, her hands resting comfortably in her lap, waiting for me. Her springy hair was swept up in a clip, and only a few loose curls brushed her shoulders. Her ice-blue eyes warmed at seeing me and she motioned to the chair on the other side of the L-shaped desk that made up her work space.

I glanced at the computer behind her as I sat down, watching her screen saver of colorful lines twisting and bending in on themselves; a constant progression of being turned inside out. It reminded me of how I felt coming here, like every session was turning some piece of me inside out, and eventually I'd just be a messy pile of goo on the carpet.

"Hello, Lucas."

Her warm, low voice brought me back to the moment and I pulled my eyes away from her computer to meet her gaze. I swallowed a sudden bundle of nerves and nodded my greeting back to her. She looked over my face, and maybe seeing the tension there, frowned slightly. Almost immediately the frown vanished and she started in on the easy to answer questions, loosening me up.

When I felt more at ease, she skillfully started turning the conversation to harder questions, questions I didn't want to answer. "How have you been feeling lately?"

I shrugged. "As well as I usually do, I guess." She raised her eyebrows at me and nodded, encouraging me to expand on that. I shook my head and found a smile creeping onto my face, remembering my dream last night of Lillian. "I actually woke up happy today…really happy." I didn't mention that school had sort of ruined my buzz; just being truly, purely happy at least once today was pretty impressive for me.

She must have thought so as well. "That's great, Lucas." Her face brightened as she said that, and I could tell she really meant it. "Was that because you dreamed of Lillian last night?"

The smile immediately fell off my face. I felt that knot return, and I shook my head no. I'd let too much of that slip; I couldn't risk anymore coming out. She frowned as she looked at me. "Really? You didn't talk to her last night? To tell her about your day maybe?"

I swallowed. That was exactly what had happened last night. We'd talked while we'd danced. I'd told her everything that had happened to me since our last meeting. I'd told her everything in my heart, things I'd never tell a living person. My hopes, my desires…all the things I wanted for the two of us. She'd listened and smiled, only a trace of sadness in her features when I talked about what our life could be like—together forever in my head.

I shook my head again, and Mrs. Ryans compressed her lips. Looking down at her desk, she twisted a pencil in her hands. After a moment, she looked back up at me. Not able to take her gaze, I averted my eyes. "Luc, I'd really like to help you. You can talk to me about her…it's okay."

Quietly, I said, "There's nothing to tell. I…I didn't see her." I swallowed again and risked a glance back at her. She didn't appear to be buying my lie. Feeling a need to turn the conversation, I told her, "I asked Sawyer to the dance."

She blinked at me, and then a huge grin lit her face. "That's wonderful, Lucas. Truly, wonderful. I think you guys will have a great time."

I smiled and relaxed back in my seat. "Yeah, maybe." A huge grin plastered my face. "Sawyer is so excited to go. I'm still not sure about the whole thing, but the look on her face when I asked her…" I laughed and slowly shook my head, looking at my lap. "Whatever happens there will be worth it, after seeing that look."

I raised my eyes to hers; she was still smiling warmly at me. "I never would have thought a stupid dance would be so important to her, but you should see her…she glows." A soft chuckle escaped me as I thought about her delight when we'd discussed flower choices. She'd settled on a corsage of daises, of all things.

"Well, most girls do like dances. I'm sure you and Lillian went to a few?" I absentmindedly nodded, still thinking about the way Sawyer's eyes had lit up when she mentioned swinging by the diner so my mom could see us all decked out.

I heard Mrs. Ryans ask her next question and found myself answering it instinctively. "I didn't know I'd be going along with your crazy plan when she came to me last night, but, no, Lillian will be fine with it. She wants me to be with Sawyer…" I froze as what she'd asked finally filtered into my head. She'd asked if Lillian had had a problem with me going to a dance with another girl. I'd been thinking about other things and had answered reflexively. She'd just set a word trap for me and like an idiot, I'd fallen right into it. She'd completely caught my lie.

"So you did see Lillian last night." She kept her face and voice neutral, but I thought I could detect concern.

I shook my head. "I don't want to talk about her. She's not a part of this…of me being high at school, which is *why* I'm here." My tone was insistent and desperate. I wanted to stop all these side conversations we'd been having. None of them had anything to do with Josh slipping me drugs.

She shook her head at me. "Lucas," she said softly. "I told you before, that is what you did to get here…it's not why you're here."

My face hardened. "Yes, it is. The only reason I'm here, is to complete my sentence so I can get back into the club. I'm only here because I was drugged and got busted."

She leaned back in her chair and crossed her arms over her chest. "And why do you want back in the club?"

I frowned. "Because…I…I want to…help out…the school."

She raised an eyebrow at me, once again catching my lie. "You have shown no interest in being a part of this school, of being a part of this community even. Why do you really want back in?"

I sighed, knowing I needed to fess up. "To be with Sawyer."

She nodded, like she knew that. "But…you don't want to be with her. " I shook my head, about to argue and she quickly amended. "As more than a friend. You want to maintain that distance because of Lillian. Because in your mind, you're still with her. Because your guilt and shame and…need, won't let you release your friends. You're holding on so tight…you're drowning. You speak to no one. You barely look at anyone. You disassociate from everything. Someone drugged you…and you've done nothing. Your body is still in this world…but you're slowly leaving it. Do you see how it's connected? Do you see why you're really here?"

My face pale, I muttered, "No, why?"

She laid a hand on my arm and sighed. "A part of you wants to reconnect, Lucas. A part of you wants to be with Sawyer. A part of you wants to belong to *this* world. A part of you wants to live, Lucas. You just have to be willing to let that part out."

I didn't know what to say to that, so I said nothing. I did nothing. I stared over her shoulder at her computer and watched the twisting lines again. I felt my stomach clench in icy familiarity and I focused on keeping my breaths natural and even. I heard her sigh at my reaction. I wasn't sure what she wanted from me, but I had nothing left to give her today. She seemed to understand that, and the remainder of our session was a quiet one, with her talking and me listening, nodding occasionally and muttering one word answers when it was appropriate.

When our time was up, she walked over to me and put a hand on my shoulder. "I know your required time here is almost up, but I'd really like to keep seeing you." She smiled encouragingly while my heart dropped. "I'd like to help, Lucas."

I stood up, saying nothing, but thinking, *Not a snowball's chance!*

I left the room and went to go find Sawyer. Purity club was having an "event" day, meaning they were stalking other clubs and sports practices to recruit more members. It was almost like some odd cult, led by Ms. Reynolds. It was working though; the club had tripled in size since Sawyer and I had joined at the beginning of school.

I found them loitering around the basketball team in the gym. They were passing out t-shirts to the players, and being ridiculed by said players behind their backs. But, not by all of them though. Some had thoughtful expressions and kept the shirts, slinging them over their shoulder or quickly stuffing them in their gym bags. Some of those people cast quick glances at me when they did that and I wondered if I was a walking advertisement to join the club. '*Don't let this happen to you'*.

I sighed and rolled my eyes. I spotted Sawyer mid-eye roll up in the bleachers, talking with Sally again. Sally was short and wide, with frizzy nondescript brown hair. Her style was kind of granola, like she probably was also in the Save the Earth Club. But she had one of the nicest smiles I'd seen in a while. I'd known her for a long time, but never really *known* her. She was currently making Sawyer laugh though, so I instantly liked her.

I made my way over as members of the club started to say goodbye and leave the gym. Sawyer spotted me and waved. I hesitantly walked up to her, not sure if my being here was me technically participating in a club activity or not. I wasn't welcome to join, but I wasn't sure if I was "banned" either. Sally only gave me a soft smile when I stepped up to them though. I saw the tightness in the smile and thought she probably didn't approve of me hanging around but was nice enough to not say anything directly to me.

I looked away and muttered, "Ready, Sawyer?"

I heard her stand and cheerily say goodbye to Sally. She was still buzzing about the dance; they'd apparently been talking about it. As she hopped off the bleachers, I glanced back at Sally. She nodded politely at me, but had an odd look on her face—almost compassionate *and* disapproving. Like she understood how hard things were for me, but still didn't like me or what I'd done. I could understand that.

As Sawyer and I walked away, I shook my head and sighed. She asked if I was all right and instead of my usual answer of fine, I told her that Sally didn't like me.

She shook her head. "No, she does."

I gave her a blank look. "She said that?"

She frowned and her eyes shifted to the corners as she ran through past conversations in her head. "Well, no, not outright." She looked back to me. "She's never said anything bad about you, though."

I smirked that, in her logic, not saying anything mean was akin to liking. "That's because she likes *you,* Sawyer." Pointedly I said, "Believe me, she doesn't trust me and she doesn't like me. If you told her you were going with someone else to the dance, you'd see it. She'd probably do cartwheels."

Sawyer sighed as she opened the gym door. "Not everyone's against you, Luc."

I sighed as I followed her out. "So you keep telling me…"

I was anxious to go to bed after Sawyer left for the night. I desperately wanted to see Lil. Wishing for bedtime made the evening go by exceedingly slowly. Especially since Mom was working and I had no one to help me pass the time. I ended up crawling into bed at six and staring at my ceiling, willing sleep to claim me. When it didn't, I considered popping an Ambien…but, remembering my promise to Sawyer and her face when we'd talked about it, I didn't.

Eventually my body did succumb to slumber, and I drifted away to unconsciousness. I floated in a hazy realm, not really knowing where I was or when I was or even what I was. Then my world seemed to solidify and I had the distinct feeling of cool air brushing across my cheek, followed by the sound of gravel crunching under my shoes. I smelled crisp, clean air and heard a train rumbling in the distance. I smiled as I realized where I was.

I turned. Behind me was a rundown-looking, split-level home with a large rectangular paved driveway and a basketball hoop prominently hanging over the garage. The house had seen better days, but being busy parents with two rambunctious boys had made home repairs fall by the wayside. Two rambunctious boys…and me, I suppose, since I was as much a part of this household as the actual sons, Darren and Josh.

I looked over the house, reminiscing. I hadn't been to the home in real life since the accident. Darren's family still lived there, I just wasn't welcome anymore. Looking at the picture perfect memory I'd created, I smiled as I took in the second story window with a shutter missing. Josh had tried sneaking out one night. He'd stumbled and pulled off the decorative wood, and both he and the shutter had tumbled to the ground. They'd never repaired the window, using the money to repair Josh's arm instead. I moved my eyes over to the gutter that was half pulled away from the home. Darren had been convinced that he was Spiderman when he was eight, and had tried climbing up the house to prove it to me, since I'd told him he was full of crap. He'd realized he wasn't Spiderman the minute the gutter gave way under his weight, and he'd fallen to the ground and twisted his ankle.

I took in the other features I knew so well, as well as my own home. The bare spot on the first floor roof; we'd worn down the shingles from years of us jumping from there into their collapsible pool. The dent in the garage door where Darren had accidently backed his Geo into it. The long scratch along the side of the house that Darren and Josh had made when they'd tried to haul a full size ping-pong table down the narrow rosebush-lined path that led to the front door. The only thing they'd successfully done that day was scratch the home and trample some of their mom's beloved flowers.

No one in the house had been happy that night. Still, I'm sure Darren's mom would have taken a thousand of those nights over the one night I had given her months ago. A long sigh came out of me as I thought about the last time I saw her. It was at Darren's funeral. She wouldn't even look at me. I couldn't bring myself to talk to her or to Darren's dad. I'd watched them from the back of the ceremony, wondering how much they hated me. I didn't see how they could feel anything less than loathing for me.

It had certainly been that way for Lil and Sammy's parents. Sammy's mom had slapped me at Sammy's funeral. My mom had nearly slapped the woman back, but Sammy's mom had broken down into sobs and had to be carted off by Sammy's older brothers. The entire family had left town not long after.

Lil's parents had also moved, gone back to where they had originally moved out here from. Her parents had been more reserved around me, not seeming to hold any anger, just regret. They regretted bringing her out here in the first place. They regretted fostering our relationship. And they regretted trusting me. The last thing her father had said to me was, "How could you not be more careful."

Since I asked myself that same thing every day, I could only hang my head at him and say, "I don't know." Her parents had left with her baby sister not long after. The only ones left were Josh and his mom and dad. I didn't see the latter two people;

we all avoided anything that might bring us into contact with each other. As for Josh…well, him I couldn't avoid until I graduated.

A voice in front of me snapped me out of my melancholy. "Catch."

Instinctively I looked up, right as a basketball headed for my chest. I caught it, my head snapping to Darren in front of me, laughing. I laughed as well and bounced the ball a couple times. He squatted to defend the basket behind him and I crouched down as well, moving the ball from one side of me to the other.

"Hey, Darren, good to see you."

He shifted from one foot to the other, watching my movements. "Yeah, well, I get bored just hanging out with two girls all the time…thought I'd surprise you."

I chuckled at the thought of him, Sammy and Lillian all hanging around some ethereal place, waiting for a doorway to my dreams to open. A part of me knew that wasn't how it worked, knew that they weren't real people, waiting around for me. But it eased my heart to think of them that way, to think of them with full and complete lives, even when I wasn't around. Much like Sawyer, as I'd fully realized today.

He grinned and I suddenly moved with the ball, twirling around him when he got close to me. Coach was right though, Darren had good hands. He snaked out and tore the ball away from me, twisting and shooting before I had barely even registered that the ball was gone. It swished through the hoop and he pumped a fist in the air.

He pointed over to me as he went to grab the ball that was starting to bounce over into the grass. "You still suck, Lucas." He laughed as he reached down to pick the ball up. "You'd think you'd make yourself better in your dreams."

I exhaled slowly as I took his place, crouching in front of the basket. "I'm all about realism," I muttered sullenly.

He dribbled the ball and cocked his head at me. "Is that why you and Lil still haven't done it?"

I straightened at his comment and he darted past me, scoring another basket. He laughed as he scooped up the ball and tossed it to where I was still standing in the same spot. I caught it and gave him a glare. "We're going to, Darren…soon."

I dribbled the ball and changed places with him. He crouched down, ready for me and I immediately tried to fake him out and get around him. Didn't work. He anticipated the move and ducked under my hand to catch the dribble before I could. Deftly, he twisted and backhanded the ball into the basket. Show off.

I scooped it up as he laughed at me again. "You'll never score, Luc." Knowing he meant that in more ways than one, I forcefully chucked the ball at him. He grunted when he caught it. "Hey," he muttered.

I stood under the basket with my arms out. "What's really on your mind, Darren?"

He idly bounced the ball as he stared at me. Finally, he sighed and shrugged. "I just think it's stupid, Luc." I crossed my arms over my chest and leaned back, waiting for him to explain that. He sighed again and held the ball under his arm. "You held off on having sex with Lil in real life, but you're trying to get her to go all the way with you in your dreams? You're demented, man."

I glowered at him as irritation sparked in me. Why did he always have to go there? "Thanks." My tone was flat, not amused in the slightest. Sniffing, I raised my chin and added, "Why shouldn't we? As you always say—it's just sex. Why make such a big deal out of it?"

He looked at me incredulously, like I'd just asked him the most outrageous thing he'd ever heard. "Uh, because she's dead. Because we're not talking about you guys holding off at junior prom because she thought it was too cliché. She's a corpse, dude."

I blanched at his harsh choice of words. "So are you."

One edge of his lip twisted into a wry grin as he brought a hand to his chest. "Yeah, but we're only talking. We're not screwing."

I looked away from him, wishing he would drop this and just hang out with me, just be the best friend I needed him to be. My real life was hard enough. I didn't need that filtering into my dreams too. "I want to, Darren." Quieter I added, "I always wanted to."

I felt him come up to me and put a hand on my shoulder. Reluctantly, I looked back at him. His face was firm, but deeply sympathetic. "But you didn't, Luc. You guys decided to wait…and you ran out of time." He shook his head, a sad smile playing on his lips. "You have to let that go."

I shook my head, my brows furrowing. "No, I can't… I don't…" I shut my mouth and paused, collecting myself. "This way I can be with her. We can pick up right where we left off. It will be like nothing bad ever happened." I knew my eyes and voice were pleading with him, and I wasn't sure why I needed his support on this so badly. Maybe I was just tired of being chastised by people on the subject.

He sighed and dropped the ball on the ground. It bounced just once and then ominously stuck to the ground with a dull thud. Darren ran his hands through his hair and grunted. "But bad things did happen, Lucas. And you can't just wish them away." He waved his arms around him, indicating his house and the driveway. "Dude, all of this is just in your head. If you have sex with her, it will just be in your head!" He gave me a pointed look and poked a finger in my chest. "You'll wake up all alone in your bed, wishing you had something more."

I stepped back and pushed his shoulders away from me. I felt my jaw tighten as I answered him. He was hitting too close to home, and fear started to mix with my irritation. "So…it will feel real during."

His face remained sympathetic, but his tone betrayed his own rising temper. "But, Luc…it's not. She's dead, man…let her go, let us all go." He stepped forward and put his hands on my shoulders like he wanted to shake some sense into me. "You're going to die a virgin because you can't let her go. Wet dreams will be the extent of your relationships, and that's not fair to the *real* people who love you. And she does, you know. And you do, too."

I smacked his arms away and raised mine up in the air. "What the hell are you talking about?"

"God, I never realized what a fucking moron you are." He shoved my shoulder again. "Sawyer, idiot. You want to be with Sawyer. You know that…right?"

I bristled, suddenly furious that everyone was trying to tell me how I felt. That everyone was after me for wanting to be with *my* girlfriend. What was so wrong about wanting to be loyal to my girlfriend? Couldn't people just leave me to my fantasy life? Couldn't my fantasy life leave me to my fantasy life? I stepped back and made to move around him. "Why can't we just get together and hang out like we used to, Darren? Why do you always have to get after me?"

His hands reached out to stop me and I turned to face him. I thought his eyes were misted over, but I couldn't really tell through my own angry fog. "Because I'm your best friend. And sometimes that means I have to tell you things you don't want to hear."

I shook my head, my anger fading as sadness filled me. "Your brother, your whole family, the school, God, the whole town…nothing there is easy for me. I just need you to accept that this is how I want things…and be my friend. I need this, Darren. I need you guys."

His eyes definitely misted. "I know, Luc. And if I thought it would help you, I wouldn't say anything. But, you're scaring me. You're scaring all of us. You lived, Luc..." he clutched my shoulders, a tear dropping to his cheek, "…so live."

The icy fear I'd felt before returned, and I suddenly didn't want to be there anymore. I backed away from him, feeling more like I was at a counseling session and backing away from Mrs. Ryans than backing away from my best friend. As much as I tried to recreate my old life, I suddenly felt like I hadn't recreated it at all. "I've gotta wake up now, Darren. I'll see you around."

His face pleaded at me as another tear dropped to his cheek. "Wait…Luc…"

My eyes opened and I stared at my ceiling, still seeing Darren's stricken face. I closed my eyes and felt the tears well, but I forced them back and made myself get up. It was still late at night, not as much time had gone by as it had seemed. I stood and ran a hand down my face, wanting that dream to fade out of my memory. I'd gotten too used to retaining them though. It was such a habit in me, pulling in every moment of the dreams so that I wouldn't forget them, that I couldn't stop myself from doing it now. The conversation was embedded in me, like it or not.

I stood and made my way to my door, wanting some water. I stopped when my eye caught the picture that was always tucked in my mirror. I stared at Darren's face in it and wondered if my dream version of him was as close to the real Darren as I thought it was. Unfortunately, I had nothing to compare it to. Darren and I had never had a conversation about sleeping with a dead girl in real life. In fact, the only conversations we'd had about sex were him teasing me for my lack of it. He'd never understood why Lillian and I had let opportunity after opportunity pass us by. Sometimes I didn't either, but we'd thought we'd have more time. We'd thought we'd have all the time in the world. We were so wrong.

I tore my eyes away from the picture and made my way out to the hallway, needing that water now. I stopped just outside my door and paused, every fiber of me shooting with anticipatory energy. I heard a voice coming from the kitchen. Immediately, I looked back at my mom's door. It was late, or early depending on your definition, and Mom should be home from the diner. Her door was closed and her light was off. I couldn't tell if she was in there or not.

I turned back to the hallway and listened harder as I crept along the wall. I didn't know who was in our house, or whether or not they meant us any harm, all I knew for sure, was the voice was deep—a man's voice, and oddly…familiar.

I paused in the living room where I could hear better, my entire body tense. A softer voice answered the man's and I recognized it as my mother's. I relaxed as I realized she was talking to someone she knew. That probably meant the person wasn't going to attack us. Curiosity propelled me forward though. Who was she talking to at this hour?

The voices were too low to make out the words, but the tone was soft, relaxed, and occasionally a soft, feminine laugh echoed back to me. The overall vibe I sensed was that she was having a friendly conversation. I inched even closer, hating that I was kind of spying on her, but not able to stand not knowing. I had a sudden respect for cats and their dreaded sense of curiosity.

Just when I thought I heard the man say something with my name in it, followed by a long sigh and an, "I don't know," from my mom, I clumsily bumped against the end table next to the couch, knocking over a picture frame on top of it. I immediately righted it, but by the silence in the kitchen, I knew they'd heard. Feeling guilty and stupid, I darted back to my room.

Leaning against my door, I heard the front door open and close. I exhaled softly and leaned my head back against the wood, wondering what that had been about. I heard my mom coming up the hall and I froze, careful to not make a sound, so she'd think I was still sleeping. Her shuffling feet paused at my door and I felt her lean close to it.

"Luc? Are you awake?" she asked softly. I stifled a sigh, torn by wanting to lie with silence, and wanting to be honest and confess. "Lucas?" she said again.

I did let out a sigh this time and turning, opened the door. I kept enough from my mom already; I really couldn't handle keeping anymore. "Yeah, I'm awake," I muttered, as I guiltily looked down at my feet.

"Is everything okay?" she asked and I looked back up at her. She was still wearing her diner's uniform and her hair was still pulled back into a falling-apart ponytail. She looked tired and worn, but a faint trace of happiness was around her too. Nothing obvious, just a crinkle in the lines around her eyes and a slight lifting of her lip, even as her brow bunched together in concern…probably nothing no one but me would even notice.

Her identical eyes flicked over my face and I quickly answered her. "I'm fine…just couldn't sleep." She nodded and brought a hand up to my cheek. She was about to speak when I interrupted her, "Was someone here? I thought I heard a guy's voice." I blushed a bit at admitting that I'd been listening, but again, curiosity.

Her face paled and she dropped her hand from my cheek. She opened her mouth a couple times before answering me. "Uh, oh…that was…" Her eyes went over my face faster, and if I didn't know any better, I'd swear she was searching for a lie. "Um, Jake…from the diner." Her face relaxed and she casually tossed a hand in the air. "I had trouble starting my car and he followed me home, just to make sure I was safe." She smiled and patted my shoulder. "I offered him a cup of coffee before he drove home. I'm sorry if we woke you."

I frowned as I looked over her face. That seemed genuine enough. I'd met Jake a few times. He was a cook there and always went out of his way to help anybody who needed it. Him trailing my mom home, just to make sure she made it back safely, was exactly something he would do. But still, something about the set of her jaw and the glint in her eye was screaming at me—*don't ask anymore, just believe me.*

I sighed, thinking my dream had just thrown my senses out of whack. My mom wouldn't lie about something like that. She might try to hide how difficult her life was from me, but she would never flat out lie. Not to me.

Guilt washed through me that I couldn't be more honest with her. I leaned forward and pulled her in for a hug. "You didn't wake me, Mom." I sighed again. "Sorry to spy on you…I just didn't know who was here." I tightened the hug and whispered into her hair, "It's my job to keep you safe, right?"

She returned my hug and then pulled away. She brought her hand up to my cheek again and shook her head. "No, it's my job to keep *you* safe. No matter how old you get…you'll still be my child, and I would do anything for you." She leaned into me, her face suddenly intense. "You know that, right?"

I blinked at her expression and nodded. "Yeah, I know, Mom."

She nodded and relaxed, giving me a kiss on the cheek. "Try to go back to sleep, Lucas. You need your rest."

I watched her head down the hall to her room and then turned and closed my door. I had no idea if I wanted to go back to sleep again or not. I didn't want to fight again with Darren. I hated that. Our time together was a precious thing to me and I hated to waste it spatting like catty girls. I shook my head and sighed. Well, even picking a fight with Darren was preferable to the numbness of my everyday existence. I'd take the chance in the same way I took a chance every time I closed my eyes.

There was always a risk when I dreamed, always a possibility that a pleasant one could morph into a nightmare. Like the one I'd had that had driven me to that regretfully passionate moment with Sawyer. A moment that still plagued me, both by how fond the memory was, and how horrid the memory was. I hated hurting or confusing Sawyer. She was my best "living" friend.

With what felt like the hundredth sigh tonight, I crawled back into my bed and laid my head back on my arms. I stared at the familiar cracks and fault lines in the plaster. Lines I couldn't really see in the dark room, but knew were there. Spacing out as I mentally traced the lines, I heard a voice beside me quietly say, "You really should fix those one day, Lucas."

Smiling widely, I turned my head. "Hey, Barbie."

Lillian's pale eyes, gray in the darkness of my room, seemed to glow at me with life. She lightly smacked my arm. "Don't call me that."

I grinned and leaned in to kiss her. "How about…I love you instead."

I pulled back to stare at her and she bit her lip before shaking her head and sighing, "I love you, too."

She leaned into me, wrapping her hands into my hair and pulling me on top of her. My hands wrapped around her trim waist and ran up her spine. A shiver ran through me as our suddenly bare bodies pressed together, and with a deep moan, I lost myself in the depth of her sweet kiss.

Chapter 16 – D-Day

I was frustrated. No, I think I'd left frustrated behind me a few days ago. Now I was moving past that, into deeply, chronically agitated. I'd been having more and more frequent dreams of Lillian lately…and they weren't going like I'd planned, or even like I'd imagined they would.

This morning, much like several other mornings, I'd awoken with a start from a dream about her. It had been an intense one, much like several other dreams I'd had with her. We'd been in my room, panting with desire, and she'd told me that she loved me more than anything. I'd told her I loved her, too, and wanted her desperately. She'd said "yes" and moved me on top of her, our naked, writhing bodies lining up perfectly.

That was when I woke up. That was when I *always* woke up. We'd yet to make it past this point.

I smacked the pillow beside me hard and cursed the fact that I couldn't control the dreams like I wanted to. I couldn't stop myself from waking up right at the critical moment and it was beginning to irritate me beyond belief. I wanted to be with her…why couldn't I be with her?

I got up, showered, shaved and got dressed for my day. It was Friday. It was *the* Friday—dance day. D-day. I knew what school was going to be like today. It would be a heightened version of what this entire week had been. With the upcoming promise of a break from school on the horizon, and the hope of a romantic (for the girls) and possibly deviant (for the guys), night coming up, the student body had been energized.

There had been a constant chatter around classes. I tuned out most of it, but still caught phrases like: Who are you going with? What are you wearing? Do you think he'll kiss me? Do you think she'll put out? Pretty standard pre-dance conversations. I kept my head down and pushed it all out. Especially when I heard my own name whispered on more than a few occasions. Those I tried to ignore, but it still seeped in: Lucas will be there, think he'll be sober? Think he'll spike the punch? Will Sawyer really stop him from getting drunk? Does Sawyer drink too? Should she drink while she's pregnant?

Yeah, there were still pregnancy rumors floating around about us. That would be a pretty miraculous pregnancy, if it were true.

Thinking about my virgin status brought my mind back around to Lillian. I couldn't figure out why the dreams were snapping away from me. I'd never lost them so consistently in the same place before. It was like she had on an ethereal chastity belt and I wasn't being allowed to cross it. I didn't even have anyone I could talk to about it. My mom? God, no. No way. Sawyer? I think that conversation would only hurt her feelings and make me horribly uncomfortable. My counselor? No, she didn't need any more ammo. She was already firmly on the "live your life" soapbox, her and Darren both.

I sighed and made my way through the living room. I couldn't even talk to my best friend about it. Not when he was so dead set against it happening in the first place. He thought it would hurt me more. I didn't see how that was possible. What could hurt worse than the aching loneliness I struggled through every day? Honestly, I thought finally making love to Lil would be the best moment of my life.

I tried to push out how sad that statement actually was as I walked into the kitchen. A full pot of hot coffee met me, along with a note:

Had an early meeting. See you later tonight at the diner. Can't wait to see Sawyer all dressed up! Love, Mom.

I half smiled and poured myself a cup. Mom, being a typical mom, was excited about seeing Sawyer and I all dressed up like miniature adults. Sawyer had come by last weekend and tried on a few of Mom's dresses. She'd been reluctant at first, not even wanting to put a few on, but eventually she warmed up and tried on a couple of Mom's more elegant looking ones. Mom never got rid of her party clothes. Many of them she'd had since before I was born, but she reasoned that eventually, she might have some reason to wear them and nice dresses were expensive. As I'd watched Sawyer twirl around my mom's bedroom in a couple of those dresses, I'd thought my mom was pretty smart.

I sipped my coffee in silence and spaced out as I stared out the window, waiting for Sawyer to come get me like she did every morning. Our no-touching policy had been more or less going okay. We didn't hold hands anymore and didn't hug or sling an arm around the other. Honestly, I missed the contact, but it wasn't fair to either her or Lil to keep up with the…well, I guess flirting, really.

Not that we'd been perfect. Occasionally we slipped. Once, while watching a movie with her (and watching her more than the movie), my hand had acted on its own and reached over the half-cushion between us to grab her fingers. I hadn't meant to do that, but once she'd turned and smiled at me, lacing our hands together, I hadn't been able to pull away without offending her, and we'd spent the remainder of the movie that way.

Then there were the occasional moments where I just needed her to touch me, needed her comforting caress—bad memories, bad dreams, bad encounters with used-to-be friends or, more often than not, bad counseling sessions. Well, maybe not necessarily bad, but…hard. Wounds and scabs were being lifted and scoured, and I hated it. I hated going and hated speaking, yet found myself saying more and more every session. And Mrs. Ryans's favorite subject…was Lillian and me. She pried for insight into our relationship daily.

Seeing Sawyer's car in the driveway pulled my thoughts away from my girlfriend, and finishing my cold coffee, I grabbed my bag and coat and made my way out to Sawyer. She beamed at me as I opened the door and sat down.

"Good morning, Lucas."

I grinned at her happy face, her midnight hair pulled back into an adorable ponytail, showcasing her perfect cheekbones which were highlighted in a rosy pink from the chill in the air. I shook my head at her, knowing her grin was because she was picturing us at the dance that night. As I returned her greeting and we pulled out of my drive, I hoped all the teasing she'd endured lately was worth it. I'd only caught a few glimpses of it, but it was enough to boil my blood and make me worry for her. But she'd brushed off Brittany and her group of tormentors with a chipper shrug, assuring me that we were going to have fun.

As I watched the school loom closer and closer in the windshield, I began to wonder. I pushed aside the dread in my belly when I heard Sawyer giggle beside me and nearly bounce out of the car once we'd stopped. She waited for me at the hood and a true smile spread across my face as I joined her. We would have fun…somehow.

The buzz around school was just what I'd expected. The students were so into the upcoming event that I was virtually ignored. Aside from an odd look by Randy and a suggestive look from Brittany, I got through my day pretty much unmolested. Josh didn't even look at me. Of course, the huge fight I'd heard him have with his girlfriend in the hallway during break might have had something to do with that. I'd only caught the words, "Why don't you take your whore to the dance?" before she'd stormed off, and he'd chased after her. I suspected that maybe Josh had gotten caught with his hands on someone else's merchandise again.

Mrs. Ryans had poked and prodded in our session, but she'd held back in places she didn't usually hold back, almost like she didn't want to ruin my night by bringing me to an emotional edge. We'd talked a lot about the dance and about what it meant for me to sort of reenter society. I confessed my fear about the whole matter, and she assured me that it was worse in my head than in reality. She'd again encouraged me to continue to see her after my time was up, and told me I could call her during winter break, if I needed to talk to anyone. She'd even handed me her business card with her cell phone number written on the back. Maybe that was what had opened me up. Maybe that's what had made me ask this as we were parting ways:

"Do you think life ever makes mistakes?"

I'd been looking down, staring at the sharp, right angle of her desk when I'd asked that. At the silence that greeted my question, I raised my head to find her looking at me with an odd expression, hopeful, yet sad as well. Finally she nodded her head and quietly told me, "Sure, all the time." She sighed and looked down at the pencil in her hands before meeting my gaze again. "Some people live who shouldn't…and even more people die who shouldn't."

She gave me a pointed look when she said that and I nodded. Something about the sentence nagged at me though, picking at a hard-to-reach corner of my brain, but I tried to brush it aside when I saw Sawyer again. Her bubbly excitement eventually drove all the painful thoughts of my friends away, and with her giggling that she'd see me in a few hours, she dropped me off at home.

And so, before I knew it, my day was over and I was prepping myself for the big night. It was an even bigger deal for me than just a dance—this would be the first Friday night that I'd actually left the house in a really long time. Thinking about that, in-between dressing and trying to manage my unruly hair, my stomach starting doing little flip-flops. I pushed aside my fear, as best I could, and after I'd finished getting ready, I sat and waited for the time to pass by. It took a while, which the clock on the wall ticking ominously with every achingly long second, reminded me.

It felt odd waiting for Sawyer to pick me up. It felt odd for two very different reasons. One, it felt like I had rewound to this morning, and I was waiting for her to pick me up for school again. The fact that we actually were going back to the school wasn't helping. Second, it felt odd that I wasn't driving to pick her up. Not that I wanted to drive, not that that was even a possibility—I didn't think I could even gather the courage to start a car. But still, it was the sort of event where a guy should really be doing the picking up.

The one bonus of her coming to get me, I suppose, was that I didn't have to face the wrath of her father. Maybe wrath is too strong of a word, but she did tell me that he had…reservations…about us going to a dance together. Sawyer had to all but promise him that she wouldn't be opening her legs for me. She hadn't exactly put it like that when she embarrassingly told me, but that was the impression I'd gotten. It made me flush just thinking about it, and I wasn't sure why. Maybe because we'd finally be breaking our no-contact rule tonight. Breaking it repeatedly. We'd be close, really close…all night.

I wiped my sweaty hands on my black slacks and picked up the corsage box, tossing the clear plastic back and forth in my hands, the intricate daisy creation inside it, shifting back and forth. I really shouldn't be nervous about holding her all night. It wasn't like anything was going to happen. I'd even finally had that conversation with Lillian, to assure her that we were just going as friends and it didn't mean anything. She'd looked away from me after I'd told her that, and apologized that she couldn't be there with me. I'd held her and kissed her, and told her she was with me everywhere I went. She'd looked at me sadly and told me I shouldn't be with her, told me I should be with Sawyer, since she was alive and could give me the life I deserved. I'd told her to stop being ridiculous, and kissed her with as much ferocity as I could muster.

She always tried to slip that into our meetings. That what we were doing wasn't right, and that I shouldn't be saving myself for her when I had a living girl right in front of me. I hated when she said that. I hated that even after pouring our hearts out to each other, she still wanted me to end things. I wished she'd understand that I never would.

Lights splashed along the kitchen window and I looked up from the table to see Sawyer's car in the drive. I exhaled slowly and stood while I watched her car shut off and her dome light pop on when she opened her door. How cute. She was going to come to the door to get me, just like an actual date. My stomach flopped again.

Forgoing the warmth of a jacket for style, I grabbed my corsage box and opened the door for Sawyer. I held my breath when I took in the sight of her. She looked…like a goddess. She was wearing my mom's deep, navy blue, velvet, long-sleeved party dress. I wasn't sure what my mom had worn it to, but it was a touch sexy. It was long, nearly draping onto the floor, but not quite reaching it thanks to dark blue, open toed high heels that she'd also borrowed. The dress flared slightly around mid-thigh, with a slit down the middle starting well above her knee, well above the school's policy on short skirt lengths. I hoped they'd overlook it, since it was technically a dress. It hinted at a pair of very shapely legs above the opening and highlighted the very shapely calves when her movements offered a peek.

But that really wasn't what made it hot. It was the fact that the velvet material clung to every curve of her, and I couldn't help but notice something that I'd never noticed before, something her loose t-shirts and worn jeans had hidden quite well. Sawyer…had a really nice body. I felt mine responding, just taking her in, and I changed my initial description—the dress wasn't just a touch sexy, it was the sexiest thing I'd ever seen. I tried really hard to forget it was my mom's.

Collecting myself, I stepped outside and closed the door. "You look great," I told her. Understatement much?

She laughed and bit her lip, eyeing me up and down. "You look great too."

I knew I came nowhere near her perfection, what with my basic black pants and lighter shade of blue dress shirt that complemented her dark shade. We'd opted for no tie, thank God, and I had on basic black dress shoes. Honestly, I could have been going to church and not a semi-formal, but this was how Sawyer wanted me, and tonight was mainly for her. A thank you, if you will, for putting up with me.

She ran a hand along the side of my hair, fixing a messy piece that hadn't been cooperating with me, and I felt my body react even more to her slight touch. *Great.* And we hadn't even started dancing yet. Maybe having her borrow my mom's clothes was a bad idea.

Wanting to be a gentleman, and shut parts of my body off, I gallantly offered her my arm and walked her over to the driver's side of the car. She laughed delightfully as I helped her sit down. The slit of her dress fell open and I could see a smooth expanse of inner thigh before she adjusted it. My body really liked that. Feeling like a moron, I moved around to the passenger's side. I got in with a frown on my face and stared at her gripping the wheel in her beautiful dress, her thumb ring gleaming in the dash lights. It really wasn't very gentlemanly to let her drive. I really should…

"Lucas, you okay?" she asked.

I snapped out of my thoughts, my stomach starting to squeeze at the very idea of switching places, and threw on a smile. "Yeah, I'm just not feeling like a very good date." I blushed a bit at calling myself her date and indicated her driving, to cover my momentary embarrassment.

She looked at herself behind the wheel and nodded. "Oh, do you want…to drive?"

I felt all the blood rush from my face at hearing it said out loud. Thinking it was one thing, having it presented as a viable option, quite another. I felt my stomach lurch and I heard my heart pound so hard, I was sure she could hear it, too, in the quiet space. Her eyebrows shot up and her hands went to my cheeks, stopping me from repeatedly shaking my head no, which I hadn't even realized I'd been doing. I was breathing heavier as I stared at her intently.

She slowly brought me back to a more relaxed state, holding my face and making me keep staring at her. Her gray eyes bored into mine—loving, concerned, friendly and maybe, somewhere in the depths, something a little more. She'd applied a dark, smoky eye shadow with long, thick, black mascara, and the stunning grayness seemed to pop out at me. Eventually, I felt calm and nodded against her hands, gently releasing them from my face and ignoring how warm her touch had made my skin.

"I'm fine," I muttered. "I better stay over here, though." I shrugged, feeling stupid.

She smiled and fixed my stray piece of hair again. "Okay…sorry for asking. That was stupid."

I looked down, shaking my head. "No…it's okay." I noticed the box in my palms and opened it. With a smile, I grabbed her wrist and slipped the flowers on. She stiffened when I first touched her, but smiled when she realized what I was doing. She admired her wrist once the flowers were in place, then she laughed and gave me such a loving look that an ache went straight through me.

I swallowed and shifted my eyes away from hers, sweeping them over the intricate up-do of her shockingly black hair instead. It had been meticulously curled and pinned into place so that most of it was held up, exposing her slender neck, but a few long pieces were left free, and dangled down to tickle the hollow between her shoulder and her collar bone in an intimate way. I swallowed again and forced my focus to the more innocuous windshield. This was going to be a really long night.

She started the car and we pulled away, heading for the diner. My mom was excited to see us and had offered us a free meal in exchange for stopping by. Since I really had no expertise in cooking, and Sawyer had had no interest in my Hot Pockets, we'd both agreed.

We pulled up to the diner a few minutes later, and I smiled as I saw my mom in the large window, talking to a silver haired man sitting alone in a booth. I frowned as I watched her laugh and lean over closer to him. The man laughed as well. I was frowning because I recognized the man. Sheriff Whitney. She was chatting with the sheriff.

I sighed, not relishing eating while he was there. Painful memories snuck up on me, and I brutally beat them back. Not tonight. Tonight was for Sawyer, and this moment was for my mom. I wasn't going to let my moodiness ruin the evening for either of them.

Sawyer noticed my frown. "Hey, we could go somewhere else if you want. Back to your place?"

I looked over at her; the perfect heart-shaped arch of her lip was painted in a pleasing shade of pinkish-red. "No, this is fine. I just wasn't expecting…" I shook my head. "This is fine. Mom is dying to see you anyway." I brushed a stray piece of hair away from her eye, tucking it behind her ear. My eyes swept over her face as my thumb absentmindedly stroked her cheek. "You won't disappoint her, either. You're beautiful," I whispered.

Oh my God, Lucas, I berated myself. *Get a grip.* I immediately pulled my hand away from caressing her face and cracked open my door. Yeah, tonight was going to be a *really* long night.

I told her to stay where she was before I slid out of my door, and grinning like a moron, I skipped over to her side to let her out of the car. It was old-fashioned and odd, since she had driven, but it made her laugh and she rewarded me with a huge smile, so it was worth it. I held my hand out for her and she grasped it, lacing our fingers as she stood up. I hadn't stepped back when I pulled her from the car so we were standing closerthanthis when she stood up. My heart started racing as that velvet encased body pressed against me. With a content smile, she looked over my face, her eyes flicking between mine. Mine weren't so gallant anymore and stared blatantly at her stained lips.

She leaned forward, and I instinctively leaned down. "Luc," she whispered.

"Yes," I said breathily.

"Are you going to let me get out of the car?" She gave me a wry grin, her oh-so-cute dimple showing itself.

I blinked and realized that my body was trapping her in the open car door. I blushed and let out a nervous laugh as I stepped aside. I heard myself mutter, "Sorry, you just look really…good," as we walked hand in hand to the small diner.

She laughed. "I never realized you had such a fetish for cocktail dresses."

I playfully scowled at her as I opened the diner door. Immediately upon entering we heard, "Oh my God! You're adorable! Aren't they adorable?" My mom came up and gave each of us a hug as she beamed at us. As I watched eyes around the diner laser beam onto me, I felt my cheeks flush. Not a lot of those eyes thought I looked adorable.

Mom broke off from hugging me to engulf Sawyer. "Oh, Sawyer, dear, you're beautiful, just beautiful." She looked over her shoulder at the sheriff sitting at the booth next to our display, his gaze firmly on me. "Isn't she beautiful, Neil?"

I blinked as I watched the sheriff twist his silver head to glance at Sawyer and smile. Had my mom really just called him by his first name? I knew they were friends, well, I mean, I knew they talked, but first names seemed a little disrespectful and it surprised me. His smile shifted to my mother. "She's lovely." His gaze shifted back down to Sawyer. "Your dress is beautiful on her, Vicky."

I shook my head. Did he just call her by her shortened name? The weirdness just wasn't going to stop. Before I could comment on it, and really, nerves had already locked up my throat, Mom was ushering us to a booth that she'd reserved for us, making elegant place cards with our names on them out of comment cards. I smiled at her attempt to make our diner meal a fancier experience, and helped Sawyer scoot into her side of the booth before I slide over into mine. Sawyer's dress hitched up her thigh a little when she slid across the vinyl and I suppressed a groan. Were the fates trying to kill me tonight?

Mom beamed at us as she read off a list of specials like they were five star cuisines. We ordered an appetizer of chicken strips, burgers for our main course and milkshakes for drinks. Mom laughed and rumpled my hair, immediately apologizing and trying to fix it. I sighed and shooed her off with a smile on my face. I watched her head over to a small circle of waitresses and animatedly tell them something. She looked back at us over her shoulder, and I knew she was bragging. I smiled as I watched her; she suddenly seemed ten years younger, laughing and smiling with her friends. Those friends were respectfully listening to her, but on occasion they gave me odd, appraising looks. I could almost see their minds trying to match the portrait Mom painted of me with the gossip that ran like wildfire around this town. The two probably didn't mesh well.

Feeling like I was being put on trial right here at the table, I stopped watching the group and shifted my attention back to Sawyer. She was watching me with a concerned expression, and I did my best to relax my face. Her hands reached out over the table for mine, and needing the comfort, I reached back for her. We laced our fingers and her thumb started stroking the back of my hand. I ignored the guilt that the small gesture gave me. Tonight was for her, and she enjoyed contact. Tonight, I wouldn't pull away—she could have all she wanted from me. Well, up to a point at least.

I blushed as I thought about the intimate moment we'd had a few weeks ago. In my head, I pictured that happening again tonight…with her in that dress. My blush deepened as the image clearly flooded my brain and my clothes were suddenly very uncomfortable. Taking a deep breath, I thanked God we were sitting down. I needed to get this under control…and fast.

"You all right, Luc?" Sawyer tilted her head at me, some loose pieces of her hair dangling over her shoulder.

I smiled and laughed, some of my tension easing. "Yeah." I looked down at the table and shook my head. "I'm great."

She seemed about to question me further when my mom showed back up with our milkshakes. Mom eyed our clasped hands as she set our drinks down. I thanked her as I let go of Sawyer's fingers to grab my cup. I watched Mom as she smiled at us and then walked over to the sheriff. They talked for a moment while I watched them intently. His eyes flicked over the two booths separating us, staring at me unabashedly and I lowered my head, not wanting to watch anymore. It didn't matter if he was here. I looked up at Sawyer, merrily sipping on her shake. She was all that mattered tonight. I reached over and grabbed her free hand again.

We chatted easily and Mom soon brought our appetizers and main courses. We laughed while we ate, making the meal as fancy as we could with our flimsy paper napkins and plastic basket of fries. Pretty soon our meal was done and Sawyer got up to fix her lipstick. I smiled, watching her backside as she walked to the bathrooms. That dress really was amazing.

My focus was suddenly shattered as someone sat down in the booth with me. My face paled as Sheriff Whitney sat in front of me. I tried to speak, but my throat locked up again. His aged eyes bored into me. I could tell he was gauging my sobriety and I felt my jaw tighten and my chin lift up. Perhaps noticing the defiance in my eyes, he shook his head and smiled softly.

"How are you doing, Lucas?

I shrugged and mumbled, "Fine." I was a little surprised any speech came out of me.

He nodded and cocked an eyebrow at me. "You're…okay tonight?"

I let out a long exhale, calming myself. "I'm fine," I repeated.

He was silent for a moment and then sighed. "I'm just trying to look out for you, Lucas. Your mom and I both worry about you." I bristled at him mentioning himself in the same sentence with my mom. Why did she feel the need to confide in a man who brought back such horrid memories in me? If there was one person I wished I wouldn't see anymore, it was this man. Because even though he was asking about my current level of awareness, and not that night's, and even though, through everything, he'd been nothing but nice to me, all I heard in my head when I looked at him was *They're all gone.* I knew it wasn't right, but I sort of hated him for it.

I didn't say anything to his comment and he eventually sighed again and stood up. "Well, have fun tonight, Lucas." He started to walk away but then turned back to me. "And stay sober."

Okay, that wasn't what he said. He'd said, "And be careful," but *stay sober* was what I'd heard. I nodded and stared down at the crumpled up napkin in front of me.

I looked up when I felt a hand on my arm. Sawyer stood by my side, concern on her face. Not wanting to see that look on her anymore tonight, I smiled and stood up, wrapping my arm around her waist. The velvet slid under my fingertips as my hand came to rest on her hipbone. I tried to ignore how much I liked that, as I cheerily said, "Ready to dance?" She grinned and nodded, and with quick goodbye hugs to my mom, who looked about to cry, we made our way back to her car. I helped her in again, avoiding looking at that enticing slit up the middle of her dress, and then we were off for a night of…fun.

I took a deep breath as we pulled into the familiar, but foreign, parking lot. I hadn't been here at night in so many months that I'd almost forgotten how different it could look. The oversized florescent lights spaced sporadically around the lot bathed it in an odd purplish-pinkish wash of color. The edges of the lot stayed pitch black. I knew in the daytime an empty field surrounded the lot on one side. In the darkness though, all you could see was a sea of nothingness encroaching on the lot, almost as if, at any moment, that inky night would extend its reach and swallow the high school whole.

I turned my head away from the dark boundaries of the lot as Sawyer picked a parking space directly under a pink light. That may be a little over-the-top of a description. I guess I was a little nervous. As I stared out the window at the fancily dressed people walking arm-in-arm to the large, square-like lump of a building that the gymnasium was enclosed in, I realized I wasn't a little nervous, I was bordering on terrified.

A light touch on my arm brought my attention to Sawyer. She was relaxed back in her seat watching me with a small smile on her lips. Her hand stroked my arm as she spoke to me. "It will be okay, Lucas. We'll have fun." She looked out the windshield to glance at the dressed up couples then swung her eyes back to me. "Just ignore them and focus on me." Her hand reached up to cup my cheek. "Tonight is about you and me." Her voice was nearly a whisper and my heart started beating faster for a completely different reason.

I gave her a tiny smile and nodded. She was right. This was something she really wanted and I really wanted to give that to her. What the rest of the world thought…was irrelevant. Sawyer was all that mattered tonight. I owed her a good time. I owed her a lot.

I gave her a look that clearly said, *Please let me pretend you need my help*, and opened my door. Getting out, I watched her watch me from the window, that small, satisfied smile still on her lips. I opened her door and extended a hand to her. She giggled as she let me help her up again.

It was chilly outside and neither one of us had opted for coats, so we hightailed it to the gym. Well, as fast as Sawyer could hightail it in that dress and those heels. We approached the front doors with a crowd of people and I felt Sawyer's hand tighten in mine. I looked over at her, but her face showed no strain. If she was nervous for any reason, I couldn't tell.

We heard the thump of the music before our feet had even crossed over the doorframe. It was loud pop, some sort of top forty hit that must have sprung up over the summer, since I'd never heard it. I hadn't done a lot of listening to music in the past few months. Sawyer, beside me, was humming along, so at least one of us was keeping current.

We checked in at a small table set up near the doors. Oddly, it was being run by purity club members. They had buttons and flyers for people to take and were telling everyone to have a safe night. That was met with a lot of eye rolling and grunts of acknowledgement, but it didn't dampen the members' spirits. I think a general sense of gloom only spread over the three perky people behind the table when Sawyer and I walked up to it.

Sally happened to be the one checking us in, and she gave me a discerning look that was just as obvious to me as the sheriff's had been. Some rebelling part of me wanted to start acting drunk, but I didn't. I stood straight and calmly met her eyes. I tried to remember that this girl was Sawyer's friend and was only looking out for her friend's best interests. I also was looking out for Sawyer's best interests, so I sort of felt bonded with Sally…even if she didn't approve of me.

She finally nodded us off, telling Sawyer she was gorgeous and wishing us both a "safe" night. She emphasized safe more than she had for any of the other couples, and I felt my cheeks heat. Honestly, did these people think that I'd walk into the gym messed up…again? I already had one strike; I had no desire to get kicked out of here.

The obligatory photo op was setup across from the check-in table and Sawyer squealed with delight when she saw it. I smiled at her response and pulled her over there. We stood in line behind a couple that was obviously practicing for where their night was predictably headed. There was deep throat kissing and ass grabbing and general sounds of moaning. It made me really uncomfortable to watch them, and I was grateful when it was their turn. When they stepped up to the fake flower arrangement in front of a bland black and white background, Sawyer leaned into me and whispered, "Do you think they like each other?"

I looked down at her and chuckled, while the ass-grabby couple cemented their love in an 8x10 glossy. I laughed out loud when I saw that the guy was indeed cupping the girl's ass throughout the entire photo session. Even though the couple were freshmen, I was suddenly reminded of Darren and Sammy, and I stopped laughing and looked away.

Sawyer tugged on my arm when it was our turn. Now, I may have been overly sensitive to the mood of the people around me at this point, but I swear it got pin-droppingly silent when we posed beside our flower-potted pedestal. I knew that wasn't actually possible with the loud, thumping music coming from the open room next door, but it felt like every human within a twenty foot radius of us stopped breathing. I know I did.

Sawyer nudged me in the ribs. "Hey, relax. You're gonna break my hand."

I started when I realized how hard I was gripping her. I met and held her eyes, letting the comfort I found there wash over me, easing the tension in my hand and my body. I heard the click and saw the bright flash of light and Sawyer and I both turned to the photographer.

"That was perfect," he said merrily, ushering us aside for the next couple.

"But we weren't even looking at you?" I asked, feeling a little stupid.

He grinned and shook his head. "Trust me, kid, it's perfect."

Sawyer bit her lip and a flush crept over her face. She smiled up at me and nodded her head to the ordering table. I shrugged my shoulders and followed her. If that was fine with her, then I guessed I had no complaints. After I got a packet ordered for her, we made our way to the main gym where I could see the twirling lights and gyrating bodies.

As we stepped into the room, I couldn't help but notice how similar the gym was to my dream version of it the night I'd finally told Lillian I loved her. Aside from the swarm of bodies, it was so similar, that I nearly expected Lillian to walk up to me and ask for a dance. My heart squeezed as I took it all in—the crepe paper plastered with glitter snowflakes, the blue and white balloon arches, the stray balloons that had floated up to the high ceiling, the suspended disco ball throwing sparks of light everywhere.

"Oh, Lil…" I muttered as I looked around, wishing she was here.

"What, Luc?"

I looked down at Sawyer beaming up at me. Guilt forced me to shove aside the painful thoughts I was starting to wallow in. I threw on a smile and shook my head. "Nothing," I attempted to say lightheartedly. She frowned, but then I slipped my arm around her waist and pulled her into my side and she smiled again, resting a hand on my chest as she twisted in my arms. It was closer than we generally were with each other, especially in a crowd this size, but her dress and body pressed against me was sweeping all negative thoughts from my mind and I clung to that, desperate to make this night memorable for her.

We moved to a less crowded spot and slunk back into the shadows to people watch for a bit. It was dark where we were and not too many people glanced our way. Eventually, she laid her head on my shoulder, and I felt her sigh contently. I rested my head against hers and enjoyed her warmth. A few eyes passing close did some double takes, and I knew that before long, everyone would know we were here. It didn't matter. Aside from dancing and talking and hopefully laughing, Sawyer and I weren't going to be giving them a show.

As the music thumped around us and the swarm before us grew in size, encroaching on our peaceful spot and forcing us farther back into the shadows, I started to relax. My thumb lazily drew a large circle over the soft velvet covering Sawyer's hip and her fingernails started lightly stroking back and forth along the fabric of my shirt. It was perfect. It was peaceful. And for the first time since Mrs. Ryans had suggested it, I started to think us being here was a great idea.

Then Sawyer's hand shifted from lightly running over my chest to lightly running over my stomach. Her head was still resting on my shoulder and I was pretty sure she was absentmindedly watching the people before us dance, maybe not even fully aware she'd moved her hand, but I was.

Her pinky lightly grazed over the button on my slacks and I closed my eyes. It felt really nice. I remembered those hands running up my bare skin and my hand tightened and squeezed her hip. The continual movement of her hand was making a wonderful tension start in my stomach and I kept my eyes closed, focusing solely on where she was touching me.

Her hand dropped fractionally, subconsciously, and one finger barely touched the top of my zipper. I groaned as my body instantly, and not subtly, responded.

Chapter 17 – No Big Deal

I immediately stepped back from her, breaking all of our contact. She started as she looked back at me, and I threw on a tight smile. She frowned. Great. I didn't know how to explain that she was turning me on without embarrassing us both, and possibly doing that misleading thing that I was so good at. I mentally cursed my stupid, hormone-driven body and wished that, just for one night, I could shut off that part of me. Sometimes being a seventeen-year-old guy was a pain in the ass.

Not knowing what else to do, I extended my hand to her and nodded my head to the dance floor. It was packed, but the song was fast, so we wouldn't actually have to touch each other too much. And right now, at least until I could calm down a little bit, I needed space.

Her face brightened as she nodded her head, her loose curls bouncing along her shoulders. She reached over for my hand and my eyes drifted down to the v-neck of her dress. It plunged deeper than anything I'd seen her wear before and the top of her cleavage showed. There was more than I'd imagined on her, and my already-buzzing body replayed the memory of my fingers running over those breasts, feeling the soft firmness as I cupped them through her bra…

Oh, good God!

I closed my eyes for a second, breaking my inappropriate focus, and pulled her out to the dance floor. We'd be more exposed to gossipers out here, but at the moment I'd rather have that kind of exposure than the kind my body was starting to make. I could hide in the light-splotched crowd until my blood flow returned to normal.

The driving beat engulfed us and the driving bodies surrounded us as we parted the sea and moved to a central location in the pack. I caught a few heads turning and whispering to others around them as we passed, but I ignored it. I let go of Sawyer's hand as we found a place with a little room to move.

I wasn't really a dancer, but what guy in high school is? The others around me were doing the, "Yeah, I'm only out here to please my girlfriend in the hopes of getting lucky later," dance, so I copied them. Sawyer however…could move. I found my eyes drifting over her body as she frolicked around to the upbeat song. She sang along and moved her hands through her hair, dislodging a few long pieces, which only made it look even better. A slight flush crept into her cheeks as the heat of the crowd and that long-sleeved dress started to get to her. She was intoxicating to watch.

I realized this wasn't helping my situation at all and shifted to look out over the crowd. I noticed sets of eyes staring at me, but many more sets were staring at Sawyer. Most of those sets were guys, and most of those had a glint in them as they watched her body move. A sudden surge of possessiveness washed over me, which actually startled me with an icy wash of astonishment. Was I possessive of her? She wasn't mine, by any stretch…but, I didn't want her to get hurt. And as I glared back at a few male eyes, all I saw were jerks and assholes who'd stomp on her heart if given the chance. Hell if I was going to give them that chance. They'd have an easier time getting through her overprotective father than me.

A few guys glared back at me, but most turned away and focused on their own dates. A calm, satisfying peace went through me as their eyes left my beautiful friend. *Not tonight, boys.* Tonight, this angel, for some reason, was mine. A smirk was stuck on my lips for most of the songs after that.

Finally, a slow song started playing and Sawyer smiled and reached out for me. I wasn't sure exactly how my body was going to respond to hers being so close to me, but I couldn't deny her what she wanted. Not tonight. Praying that I could stay in the even-flow I'd managed to obtain, I smiled and grabbed her waist, pulling her into me.

My fingers slid over the crushed velvet of her dress. The contours of her body beneath it were only too obvious. I slid over the lean muscle of the sides of her stomach, around her curved hipbones to the lowest part of her back. As her arms laced around my neck, a few of my fingers disobeyed me and rested along the very top of her backside. She either didn't notice or didn't care, as she gazed at me adoringly.

She sighed and tilted her head as we stared at each other. She pulled me tighter, her chest resting flush against mine. Her breasts pressed firmly against me made me swallow repeatedly as I searched my brain for something else to think about. Not helping the situation any, she started running her hand through the back of my hair, bringing our faces mere inches apart.

My eyes drifted to her lips and I knew…I knew this was going to be a bad moment if I didn't do something to distract myself—and soon. Quickly thinking of anything to say to her, I sputtered out, "So, Miss I'm-secretly-obsessed-with-school-dances, how is it you've never been to one before?" She'd let that slip during our planning sessions for tonight and it had surprised me. For someone so into it, I figured she'd been on the dance committee at her old school.

She sighed and looked away, our bodies naturally pulling back from each other. I exhaled a quick breath in relief but couldn't quite understand her reaction. She was worrying her perfectly painted lip and staring out over the crowd of intimately dancing couples, but she didn't seem to be seeing any of them. I idly wondered what exactly was replaying itself in her head.

"It's okay, Sawyer…to talk to me." I immediately recognized the oddity of me saying that, since I never really opened up to her. She raised an eyebrow as she twisted back around to face me, and I thought she probably caught the oddity of it too.

She didn't call me on it though, only shook her head. "I didn't have a date." I frowned at her anticlimactic answer. Surely there was more to it than that?

"Why didn't you go alone…or with a group of friends?" I knew that some of the girls around here did that occasionally. It seemed socially acceptable for girls to that—girl power and all. If a group of guys did that, well, there was a certain social stigma to it.

Sawyer looked down before quickly looking back up at me. "I didn't have a whole lot of girlfriends back there and the school instituted a one guy, one girl policy anyway. It had the parents in an uproar at first, but what can you do?"

She was still worrying her lip and looking like she really wanted to fess up to something. I wouldn't normally have pushed, but she looked like she wanted to talk about it, she just wasn't quite there yet. I squeezed her waist, drawing her tight to me again. "Hey…tell me."

She sighed again as she looked over my face. I thought her eyes were starting to water, but I couldn't really be sure in the swirling light patterns that flashed along our bodies. She opened her mouth and shut it, then opened it again. I waited patiently until she finally spoke.

"The boy…the stupid one I told you about…" Her heart was in her eyes as she flicked them over my face. Her voice dropped so low, I had to lean in to hear her over the music. "He…" I nodded at her and rubbed the small of her back, silently encouraging her to open up to me. She swallowed and then finally did. "He was supposed to take me to junior prom last year."

She looked away, her eyes definitely shining as she glanced around at the crepe paper and loose balloons. "I was so excited to go." She turned her head back to me, the sad smile on her lips making me hold her tighter. "He was the most popular guy in our class, and my class alone was about three times the size of the entire student body here." Her head motioned around to the suddenly sparse feeling gym. A surge of jealousy flashed through me, but I forced it down and made myself concentrate on her story.

"He was handsome and athletic and funny and charming," her eyes locked onto mine, "and he told me he loved me." That jealousy sprang up in me again, but her lower lip started to tremble, and it shifted to sympathy, instead. "I thought I loved him. I adored him. God, I practically worshipped him."

She looked down at our tightly held together bodies and her voice dropped again. I lowered my head to rest against hers, so I could hear her in the noisy room. "Two weeks before the dance, I gave him my virginity." She looked up at me and I forced myself to not close my eyes and dwell on the sudden sadness that swept through me. Sadness that she wasn't at the same level I was, that she'd been with someone like that before, that someone else had ever touched her that way. But I made myself keep eye contact as her voice quavered with her next words. "I loved him and gave him every part of me…and he…" her voice and face turned to a mean sneer that I'd never seen on her, not even when she talked about Brittany, "…he gave me a three on his fuck-o-meter."

My mouth dropped open and a hard flash of anger burned me. "He *what?*"

The moisture in her eyes built up to flood level as her face softened into sadness. "He was playing some stupid game with his friends, something his brother had picked up at his fraternity." Her eyes looked over the crowd again as her arms tightened around my neck. "He got points for sleeping with different types of girls. I was a low type."

She swallowed and lowered her head. I brought my hand up to her chin and made her look at me. Our feet slowed to stillness as I held her in my arms. "No, no you're not. You're not a low anything. He's an idiot."

She sniffled and swallowed back her tears, a light smile playing on her lips. I stroked my thumb along her cheek before returning my hand to her waist, pulling her in for a hug. She returned the embrace, laying her head on my shoulder, her mouth facing my ear. Without us looking at each other, she continued.

"I found out about it, when I overheard some girls laughing about me in gym class. They said there was a chart in his locker and I was on it, so I busted it open to see for myself…and it was true. He'd slept with a half dozen other girls while I thought we were a couple, and he ranked them all higher than me. Needless to say, I didn't go to the prom with him. I barely went to school after that. I just couldn't take the hurt and humiliation. I couldn't bear to look at his charming, beautiful face."

I held her tight, my hands coming up to wrap over her shoulders, wishing I could wrap myself around her heartache. I'd never loved someone who'd used me like that. I almost couldn't imagine the torture that must have been for her. "I'm so sorry, Sawyer," I whispered.

She sighed and sagged against me. "Do you know what the stupidest part is? I still loved him. I spent weeks wondering what *I'd* done wrong, why he didn't love me like I loved him. A part of me wanted to rush over to him and tell him I forgave him for everything, beg him to take me back. But I started seeing him hanging on other girls…and I couldn't. I knew I didn't compare. I knew I had no chance. I knew I was worthless."

I immediately pulled back from her and put both hands on her cheeks. "No, you're not. Don't ever say that." I shook my head, disbelieving that the warm, wonderful person between my hands could ever think they were anything but perfect.

She closed her tear-filled eyes and leaned her head against mine. In a whisper she continued with her painful reminiscing. "I didn't handle it all very well and I…I did something outrageously stupid." Her voice lowered even more, to where I could barely make out the words over the blasting song lyrics. "I…got…really drunk and…"

She stopped herself and peeked up at me. Biting her lip, she shook her head against mine. "I freaked my parents out. They pulled me from the last few weeks of school and eventually dragged me out here. They thought I'd do better in a smaller environment, even though it cost them their jobs, their friends. They gave up their entire lives back there…for me." A tiny smile lit her lips. "I try to never forget that, even when they're being impossible about *our*…friendship." I smiled with her and dropped my hands to her waist again. She pulled her head back, and her voice took on that wisdom-soaked tone that was too old for seventeen. "This town, this school, was a chance for me to start over, and I've never taken that for granted, even when things here have been hard."

She grabbed a loose piece of her super-black hair, holding a strand up for me. "I did this to remind myself that I can be anyone I choose to be." She looked at the strand and smiled. "I'm traditionally a mousey-brown kind of color. My mom gets a kick out of coloring it for me every few weeks. It's the one thing we splurge on."

The smile on my face faded as I thought over everything she'd confessed to me. I ached with sympathy for her and admired her for her strength at the same time. Maybe our situations weren't exactly similar, but she'd certainly dealt with her fair share of torture and ridicule. And here she was, starting over in a new town, determined to make it through each day in any way she could, much like me.

My hands slid up to her shoulder blades again, hugging her to me, our heads resting together. My heart warmed as I held her tight, never wanting to let her go, never wanting her to get hurt again. The music swelled around us and my hand came up to cup her cheek. We melded closer together and now every inch of her was pressing against me, head to foot. We'd stopped bothering to move with the music a while ago and were just standing still together on the swaying-with-bodies dance floor, holding each other.

"I'm so sorry, Sawyer." I rocked my head against hers as my thumb stroked her cheek, wishing I could stroke away her pain. "I wish I'd been there. I wish I'd known you." I exhaled softly and ran my finger along the edge of her face. I could see her eyes start to water again as she stared at me. "I wish I could have saved you from that."

My hand moved around to the back of her head, holding her in place against me. She lifted her chin so our noses rested side-by-side and her breath lightly fanned over me. "I'd never let anyone hurt you, Sawyer. I'd never hurt you. I love you," I whispered, my words not making it any farther than the centimeters away from me that she was.

I didn't know what I meant by that phrase anymore. I couldn't think of anything, other than the overwhelming feelings I had for her. I couldn't process anything farther than naming that feeling. Her watering eyes threatened to drop that moisture as she held my intense gaze.

"I love you too," she whispered, a tear finally making it down her cheek. I didn't know what she meant by that, either. There were so many different levels of love—it was too exhausting to think about it…so I stopped.

My hand came back to her cheek, stroking the tear away with my thumb. Her lips parted, her breath picked up pace, and my eyes drifted down to the perfect heart arch. I found myself closing the distance between us, my lower lip brushing her upper one. We paused like that, my breath faster, my heart starting to race and my body starting to react again.

"Lucas," she whispered, her lips moving against mine as she spoke.

My throat closed and my nerves spiked. The pounding in my chest intensified to a level that I thought might be dangerous for me, and the only coherent thing screaming in my head was *Kiss her!* Her body pressed against mine, our lips lightly touching, her thumbs stroking the back of my neck as mine rubbed against the fabric of her dress. It was all too much for my body—too emotional, too sensual. I couldn't help it and I couldn't stop it, especially since I'd been struggling with my hormones all night anyway, and her hips pressing against mine were only exacerbating the situation.

She gasped and glanced down at where our hips were touching and I knew she knew. I knew she could feel me becoming aroused by her. Embarrassed beyond belief at what I'd been trying so desperately to hide from her being exposed, I stepped back, quickly dropping my hands to my sides. Surprising me, she stepped forward, pressing herself up against me again, and I sucked in a quick breath.

"Oh…Lucas…" she whispered again, her hand coming up to my cheek, her lips stopping just short of touching mine.

My heart thudded in my ears as I debated crossing that line again, debated caving to the feeling I'd been fighting back all night, debated letting her in. Finally, I stopped fighting this feeling I'd been losing against all evening, anyway. Hating myself, I leaned forward the infinitesimal amount needed to connect our lips; my hands automatically slipped around her waist.

The kiss was different from any kiss we'd experienced before. For one thing, I was in better control. I wasn't having an emotional breakdown and I wasn't high off my ass. The kiss was light and languid; we felt each other, we absorbed each other, we learned each other. There was so much emotion in the movement, that I nearly expected tears to spring to my eyes.

We broke apart after a moment and as my eyes lazily opened, I focused on the shape of her mouth as she pulled away from me. My eyes slowly lifted up to hers, right as hers lifted to mine. I could see the questions in her depths; I could see the desire too. I didn't know what to do. I didn't know what was right. All I knew was that her firm body, wrapped in luxuriously soft velvet, was still making my body react. All I knew was that my breath came faster as I gazed at her. And all I knew was that I missed the warmth of her lips on mine. And I needed that. I needed her back on me.

Maybe finding an answer to her unasked question, she leaned back in at the exact same time that I did. Our lips met in the same place as before, but this time with slightly more urgency. My hand trailed up her spine, straight up the back of her neck to tangle in some loose strands of her up-do. Some silky tendrils threaded through my fingers as I moved my hand all the way up to scrunch into the back of her hair, pulling her into me.

I didn't care that we were being quite public. I didn't care that everyone in school would know about this after break. For once, I didn't care about the gossip that surrounded us. She was what I cared about—her mouth, her tongue, her breath, her body…her heart.

I couldn't stop kissing her. I couldn't believe she was letting me. I couldn't believe *I* was letting me, but I couldn't stop. Part of my brain was screaming that it was wrong, really wrong, but as her soft lips moved across mine, all I could think was that it felt so…right. My body was saying that I needed this. That this moment was perfect and my brain should just shut up…and for once, my brain listened.

Just as her hands were weaving through my hair and our kiss was deepening, we were suddenly yanked apart. I stumbled as I was forcibly pulled a foot away from her. She stumbled as well at the sudden movement. Panicked, I looked over to a smirking Mr. Varner, who had one hand on Sawyer's shoulder and one hand on mine, prying us apart. I blinked at seeing him holding us; I hadn't been physically pulled away from a girl since the seventh grade.

"There is no foreplay on the dance floor." He leaned into the both of us. "If you want to have sex, you drive your car to the river, just like all the other kids." He chuckled at that and looked me over, concentrating on my eyes. If he'd had a flashlight, he would have flicked it back and forth over my irises, making sure they dilated properly. I glared back at him, showing him that I wasn't under any influences. He smirked again and shook his head before turning and leaving us to our slow dance.

I looked back at Sawyer, reason returning to me as I did. I shouldn't have been kissing her. It was still really wrong and misleading, and I'd sworn I wasn't doing that tonight. Why couldn't I ever keep my silent promises to her? Instead of clutching her tight to me again, I kept our distance. I avoided looking at her eyes as guilt washed through me; guilt for her and guilt for Lillian.

Finally, I looked over my shoulder at the punch bowl on the snack table and muttered, "I need a drink. Want one?"

With a soft voice, she answered me, "Sure…I guess."

Studying the spot in the corner of the gym where the punch bowl was, I extended my hand out to her without looking her way. I felt her grab it and interlace our fingers. Embarrassment and guilt prevented me from looking at her just yet. None of that should have happened. I weaved us through the throngs, grateful for the bodies around us that gave me an excuse to not have to engage her yet. I heard a buzzing current of whispers follow us along and I could only imagine the stories I'd just provided this crowd:

"Did you hear? They were practically screwing on the dance floor. I heard Luc was so wasted Sawyer had to hold him upright. Then Mr. Varner came by and Lucas picked a fight with him. God, he was only trying to be a responsible teacher and Luc went off on him—you know they had a threesome, right?"

I sighed and rolled my eyes at all the possible forks the gossip stream could run through. I set my jaw and tightened my grip on Sawyer as I pulled us through the crowd. They'd pick the worst one and run with it—that was just the way it went. The most hurtful comments, the most tortuous situation—whatever was the best scandal, that's what people would believe. Guilt calmed my temper as I thought through what Sawyer knew of hurtful gossip. She really was a lot like me…and here I was, dragging her back down into the mud, when she was trying to get her life back together again.

I let go of Sawyer's hand when we reached the six foot table with a huge bowl of some pink liquid. Sawyer stepped beside me, but I kept my face forward, staring at the stupid bowl, the water slightly sloshing inside from the bass of the hip-hop number pounding in the room. Her hand came up and I thought she might swing me around to look at her, but she only reached down to the table, to grab a couple plastic cups from a large stack of them.

No one was manning the station, so I ladled some punch into a cup when she handed me one. Without looking at her, I handed the full cup back to her and grabbed the empty one. I filled it as well and sighed, hating how I was ruining her night. Sure, we'd been inappropriate, and I knew we'd need to have a conversation about that, but I couldn't just ignore her for the rest of the night. Hadn't I promised that I'd make this night memorable for her? That we'd have fun? I knew I wasn't being much fun at the moment.

We stepped away from the table, and I finally turned to face her. She was holding her cup in both hands and staring at the liquid inside, one thumb stroking the ring on her other one. I sighed and she looked up at me.

"Sawyer…" My throat suddenly parched, I took a huge gulp of punch, nearly swallowing half the cup in one gulp. That was when my entire night shifted. That was when everything in my body shifted.

My throat burned as the huge amount of liquid I'd consumed traveled down the length of it. I didn't know what I'd just had, but I knew a large portion of it was alcohol. Some idiot had actually spiked the punch bowl. A year ago I'd have thought it was funny, but a lot had happened in a year. Now, as I coughed and sputtered on the potent liquid, everything that had happened in that year rushed in on me. More specifically, everything that had happened on *that* night rushed in on me.

It was the alcohol. The smell. The taste. Whatever was in there was sending my senses into overdrive. It was the same as that night. It was the exact same stuff Darren, Sammy and Lil had been drinking at the bonfire party. I hadn't actually drunk any myself, but my mouth had been all over Lillian, and what she'd tasted, I'd tasted.

The memories flooded my brain as my vision started to swim with the suddenness of the alcohol hitting my system. I stepped back from Sawyer and she grabbed my half full cup and set it on the table with hers. Confusion and compassion were clear in her face as she reached out for me. My mind filled with images of prancing around a fire and lying with Lil on the beach. The remembered taste of alcohol on her breath, on her tongue, assaulted me. I couldn't shut it off.

My stomach rose as I took another step back from Sawyer. I couldn't control my body. That one dose of alcohol was enough to bring back every horrid and wonderful detail of that night, and I generally tried to keep those memories buried deep within my subconscious. My mind drifted forward in the sudden torrent of reflections—to the onslaught of rain, to the faint yellow stripe in the road, to the squeak of the windshield, to Darren's laugh, to the beer can being passed back and forth, the smell of it reaching me whenever Lil handed it to Sammy.

I leaned over and clenched my stomach, my breath embarrassingly fast, nearly out of control. I was having a panic attack in the middle of the dance, a dance where people were already watching my every move. But my breathing was really the least of my problems. My stomach clenched with a terrible familiarity as Lil's face clouded my eyes.

I looked around, knowing I didn't have much time. Sawyer's wide eyes caught mine for a second and she put her hand on my back, asking what was wrong. I couldn't answer her. I couldn't even speak because my stomach was in my throat, closing off speech. Unfortunately, it wasn't going to stay there.

A wastebasket on one side of the punch bowl table drew all of my attention and I darted over to it, leaving Sawyer a few paces behind me. With both hands on the edges, I leaned over and nosily lost my stomach, that vile liquid leaving my system in not one, but three short heaves.

I panted over the edge of the basket, feeling my stomach descend to its normal level. The sound of laughter hit me over the music. I closed my eyes and felt my cheeks heat. Throwing up in the middle of the gym was not exactly the best way to stay inconspicuous. Embarrassment flooded me, and regardless of wanting to give

Sawyer a good time, I suddenly wanted to be gone. Maybe trying to rejoin the world hadn't been the best idea after all.

I felt Sawyer's hands lightly rubbing my back as she leaned over to ask if I was all right. I nodded, still able to hear chuckling going on around me. The can reeked of alcohol now, and leaning over it was going to make me lose it again, so reluctantly, I straightened and faced the music, so to speak. I turned, wiping my mouth with my sleeve, and was met by Sawyer's concerned gray eyes. She ran a hand across my cheek then put the back of her hand against my forehead, like she was checking to see if I was sick.

I shook my head and muttered that I was fine then glanced behind her at the packed gym floor. Several sets of eyes were staring our way; some of the students were bent together in conversation with their partners, others laughed outright. Two individuals, cracking up louder than necessary, caught my attention. Josh and Will were on the edge of the floor, just a few steps away from me, standing together and holding their stomachs they were howling so hard.

Josh got himself under enough control to give me a twisted sneer, and I had the feeling he was either responsible for the punch bowl or had known about it. Either way, he was enjoying my embarrassing reaction. I glanced around the room, full of people that I didn't even feel like I knew anymore, and turned away, needing out of there.

Sawyer grabbed my arm as I twisted away from her. "Where are you going?"

I glanced around at the masses, their residual laughter still echoing loudly in my ears. "I need…quiet."

She nodded, understanding, and grabbed my hand, leading me from the room. She led me through a set of open doors into the hallway. The bathrooms were on one end of it and a swarm of students were down there. She pulled us to the other end where the coach's office was. No one was in that end and it was peacefully quiet. The hallway turned into a short T, with the guy's locker room on one side and the girl's on the other. We stopped as we rounded the corner to the short side of the T by the girl's locker room. I leaned back against the wall and closed my eyes, wanting to be back at home.

A warm hand came up to cup my cheek and I nearly sighed out loud from the comfort in that touch. "You all right, Luc? What happened?"

I cracked open my eyes, not sure how to explain my latest meltdown. Sawyer's eyes held a depth of emotion that made it hard to think clearly. I wanted to confess everything to her. I wanted to tell her everything in my heart and in my soul, but fear locked my throat up. Talking about that night was so hard.

"Luc," she whispered. "You can talk to me."

A corner of my lip lifted at my words coming back to me. Guilt washed through me. She'd confessed something really hard for her to talk about tonight…I should do the same. Maybe once we got past that hurdle, everything else between us could be talked about.

"I remember everything…from that night. Every horrid, intricate detail. I wish I could forget." My throat threatened to seize up on me and my heart started racing again. She only stared at me expectantly, though, and I flushed, realizing that I'd never actually said that out loud. I looked down and stammered a few times while she stepped closer, resting her hands on my chest.

"It was the punch. Josh, or someone, spiked it and it reminded me…it reminded me of…" My voice trailed off, my throat closing.

"It reminded you of that night…the night of the crash?"

I looked up at her, my face softening with relief that she understood. "Yes," I whispered. "I just couldn't take it. I couldn't stop the memories of the wreck from coming, and I hate thinking about what happened…" I stared at her, my face paling as I wondered if I'd just said that out loud. Apparently I had.

Her hand came back to my cheek, her eyes darting between mine. "Do you…remember, Lucas?" she whispered.

My mouth fell open and I wanted to scream, *"Yes!"* Instead, I floundered for any syllables.

"Holy crap! You did show up."

Sawyer and I turned our heads to look at the voice encroaching on our privacy. It belonged to Brittany, who was sauntering out of the girl's locker room, alone. She was stumbling a bit, like she'd had a few cups of the punch. Her honey hair was twisted into a perfectly put together mass of cascading curls and her dress was short and tight. She looked like a million bucks, but I wouldn't have gone near her if you'd given me two million.

"Leave us alone, Brittany," I muttered, my voice cracking as emotions surged through me.

Ignoring Sawyer, Brittany sneered at me. "You think you're so great," she slurred as she stepped into Sawyer, causing her to back up a step. Sawyer's face flushed as she glared at Brittany.

Trying to move away from where Brittany was now trapping me against the wall, I muttered, "What are you talking about?"

She put both hands on either side of my body, leaning into me. I instinctively pressed against the wall to get away. "The locker room is empty. We could finally get this…tension between us over with."

I flicked a glance at Sawyer. Her face darkened and her hands clenched into fists. Not wanting a fight, I gently pushed Brittany away from me. "What do you want with me, Brittany? I don't get you."

She stepped back and crossed her arms over her chest. Beside me, Sawyer relaxed her stance, and I thought maybe I'd averted World War III. Brittany gave me a condescending look as her eyes swept the length of me. "You…all those years you acted like you were so much better than me."

I tilted my head, not understanding. Besides our make out session, I'd barely noticed her. I certainly had never looked down upon her. I just had had other things come up, especially when Lil and I got together. "What are you talking about?"

She stepped up to me again. "You know exactly what I'm talking about. You were all over me…hot to trot, and then you got all sanctimonious and wouldn't even touch me, like I was beneath you or something." Her lip twisted in a sneer. "Mr. High-and-Mighty quarterback and his Barbie doll prom queen." She scoffed at me. "Like you didn't want to fuck me." Her lips curved into seductiveness.

I rolled my eyes and sidestepped away from her, closer to Sawyer who was listening intently. "I didn't ever want to…fuck you, Brittany. Not even close."

"Whatever, Lucas. I remember what you were like, and I'm sorry but…" she ran a hand down my chest and I pulled away, "the way your hands ran up and down my bare body," she flicked a glance at Sawyer and I suddenly realized with a surge of annoyance why she was bringing this up, "the way your tongue probed my mouth—you wanted me."

I roughly pushed her back, angry that she was trying to hurt Sawyer by bringing up something that hadn't really meant anything to either one of us. She stumbled at the sudden movement, and I thought she might fall, but she righted herself at the last moment.

"If I'd wanted you…I'd have taken you. God knows it wouldn't have been hard…half the team did."

Her face paled as she truly glared at me. With a new hardness in her voice, she raised her chin and said, "You can't talk to me like that. You're not a god around here anymore." She laughed once with no trace of humor in it. "You had it all, but now, well, you've sunk all the way to the bottom of the social barrel. Hell, you're underneath the barrel, and I find that very…" she smiled, and not in a pleasant way, "…satisfying."

I grabbed Sawyer's hand, ready to leave Brittany's vitriol. In my irritation, I couldn't help but snap back, "And yet, you're *still* trying to get me to screw you."

She sniffed haughtily, stumbling a bit where she stood. I momentarily considered turning her in for being drunk on school property, but immediately discarded it. Regardless of what she'd do to me if the roles were reversed, I wasn't going to start turning people in out of spite. Just as I pulled Sawyer's hand to leave the hallway, Brittany angrily brushed by me, bumping my shoulder in the process.

I turned to watch her leave. She paused at the corner to the main hallway, one hand on the wall to steady her. She looked back at me, that suggestive smile returning to her lips. "Even I don't mind dumpster diving every once and a while, Luc." Her eyes lingered down my body before flicking to Sawyer. Then with a throaty laugh, she disappeared down the hall, presumably to rejoin the dance.

I rolled my eyes and shook my head, turning over my shoulder to look at Sawyer. I had an apology for Brittany's comments ready on my lips, but the look on Sawyer's face caused it to completely evaporate. Her face was pale white, and her eyes were starting to water as she stared at the spot where Brittany had just stood.

"Sawyer?" I said quietly, suddenly very nervous, but wanting to know what she was thinking. I stepped in front of her line of sight, and she blinked and looked up into my eyes.

I was just about to ask her if she was okay, when she spoke in a shaky voice. "Did you…date her?"

I exhaled slowly, hating Brittany for so callously bringing up that brief, pointless encounter. Trying to exude nonchalance, I said, "No. We just made out once." I shrugged in what I hoped was a casual manner and added, "It didn't mean anything."

Her eyes widened and her mouth fell open a little bit. Her cheeks regained some color as her eyes narrowed at me. "Didn't mean anything? Do you know how much crap she gives me because of you?" I cringed and started to apologize, but she cut me off. "With how she torments me, it obviously did mean something, at least to her. Why didn't you tell me you had a history with her? No wonder she hates me, Lucas."

She shook her head and if I didn't know any better, I'd swear a flash of jealousy went through her face. But that couldn't be—she was so vastly different to me than *that* sour woman. She couldn't possibly be jealous of that meaningless encounter when she and I had so much of…something.

I put my hands on her shoulders. "No, really, it was nothing. I don't know why she's latched on to you…or me. I think it all goes back to Lil, really. She just hates to lose, and I really didn't pay much attention to her, especially once Lil and I started dating." I felt like I wasn't doing a very good job of explaining. My hands moved up to her cheeks, almost begging her to understand how little Brittany meant to me. "But it was nothing, Sawyer, just two kids messing around. It was no big deal."

After I said that, she batted my hands away from her face and her eyes narrowed in anger. I took a step back, surprised at her reaction and wondering what I'd said to make her mad.

"No big deal?" she said quietly, a seething undercurrent to her tone.

Not sure what I was doing wrong, I cautiously said, "Yeah. It was just making out…no big deal." I shrugged and raised my arms slightly, hoping she'd get that I meant that.

Her face got even stormier, and I suddenly got the impression that I was digging myself into an even deeper hole. I just wasn't sure why. Her finger suddenly came out to poke my chest. I frowned at the movement and at her words. "Just when I think that you're different than all the other guys, you go and say something like *that*, and you sound just like them."

I blinked, hopelessly confused. "Sawyer, I don't… What did I say wrong?"

She pulled her finger back, crossing her arms over her chest and looking away from me, towards the girl's locker room. Vague sounds of music and people laughing drifted from the other hallway to us, but I didn't care about the embarrassing debacle that had driven me out here just a few minutes ago. I didn't even care about the odd exchange with Brittany. All I cared about was this woman before me who seemed to be mad at me for some reason.

Not turning her head to look at me, she spoke in a tight, controlled voice. "Nothing. You said nothing wrong, Lucas. I was just wondering…if maybe you *came* in your shorts for her, too." She looked back at me then, her eyes angry, hurt and on the verge of tears. "I was just wondering if *that* was 'no big deal.'"

Chapter 18 – Me and My Big Mouth

I closed my eyes as icy comprehension flooded me. Oh, crap. She'd taken my words towards Brittany and applied them to *our* intimate encounter. I hadn't caught the warning signs in time, and had stuck my foot in my mouth, or up my ass…or maybe both. I'd made it seem like fondling a woman's breasts was as casual an encounter to me as shaking a woman's hand—meaningless, trivial and mundane. But what Sawyer and I had done together couldn't have been farther away from those words.

I heard her sniffle and choke back tears, and then I felt the velvet of her dress brush against me as she stormed past. I opened my eyes and grabbed for her elbow, but she pulled away and turned the corner, out of my sight.

"Shit. Sawyer, wait," I called after her as I sprinted to catch up.

Turning the corner, I glanced at the far end where kids were still loitering around the bathrooms. Sawyer was only a step or two in front of me, so I caught up easily, running around in front of her to make her stop. She paused well before touching me and made a move to the right, which I blocked. She tried the left and I blocked that as well. As I repeatedly asked her to stop, she finally sighed and stood still, looking up at my face.

I swallowed when I saw the slightly black tear streaks down her cheeks. I reached out to wipe one away. "I knew you were mad at me for that. I knew you were more upset than you let on."

She pulled away from me, swiping her fingers under her eyes to dry her cheeks. "Of course I'm upset, Lucas. I want to be with you. But I don't know what you want." I tried to touch her again, but she brushed my hands away. Her cheeks flushed and her voice trembled. "You think I'm pretty, and I obviously turn you on." She gestured at my pants and I felt heat and embarrassment creep through me as she continued. "But you won't be with me." She raised her hand to indicate where Brittany had disappeared down the hallway. "And now I know why."

She lifted her chin, trying to look strong, but it trembled and at that moment she looked more like a heartbroken little girl than the wise woman I was used to seeing. Her next words brought more tears to her eyes and broke my heart. "It obviously didn't mean to you what it meant to me. You obviously don't feel the same as me. *I* was obviously 'no big deal.'"

Her tears released and I couldn't take it. I grabbed her and held her tight to me. She struggled for a moment against my embrace then stopped and sagged against me. "No, Sawyer. I promise it wasn't like that…not with you."

I felt a light sob in her body as I pressed against her and I had to swallow my own tears at hurting her. Wasn't I just vowing to protect her from all the jerks and assholes of the world? Who knew I'd be the biggest one?

"No, I was just a release for you because you were having a bad day—that's all I've ever been to you," she cried into my shoulder.

I held her head to me and kissed the top of it. "No, no that's not true…well, it is true but that's not--"

Her head broke away from my grasp as she pulled back to look at me. "It is true?"

Her freshly re-streaked face tore me, and my hands came up to brush the black, smudgy tears aside, trying to fix her beautiful makeup. "You and I are nothing like what Brittany and I were." I grabbed her cheeks again, making her keep eye contact with me when she tried to turn away. Swallowing, I let my heart pour out—not conscious of my words, only needing her to know how I felt about her. "It's true that I find comfort in you, Sawyer. So much comfort...if you only understood how much. But it's more than just peace that I find in you...I care for you. You mean so much to me. You mean everything to me. I like you. Really, I *do* like you."

She pulled back from me, grabbing my wrists and lowering my hands from her face. Perplexed, she murmured, "You *like* me?" Confusion swept through me, but before I could ask her why she questioned my statement, she clarified. "You told me that you loved me...again, and then you kissed me...again."

I looked away when I realized that in pouring out my feelings for her, I'd understated them. I'd told her on several occasions that I loved her, the most recent a few moments ago on the dance floor. But now, here, when it really mattered, I switched it to "like." I could see how that was confusing. Hell, it was confusing to me, and I was the one who'd said it. "Sawyer..."

She interrupted me, ducking down to meet my wandering gaze. "And I can see in your eyes that you mean it, and that you're not talking about the friendship kind of love, either. But then you pull back, and I don't understand why." I gazed at her helplessly, not sure what I could possibly say to make her understand. She still held my wrists in her hands, almost like she was trapping me. And I did sort of feel that way, trapped by both her body and her words.

But then she switched her grip so our fingers laced together. Still standing a good foot apart from me, she whispered over the sounds coming from the busy end of the hall, "I know you've been through a lot, Lucas, and I try to not take it personally when you pull away, but I'm confused." She shook her head, the loose strands of her messy up-do brushing across her shoulders. "I don't know what you want from me or even how you really feel about me." She shrugged her shoulders and spoke the words that I didn't know how to fix. "You're confusing me."

"Sawyer, I..." I had nowhere to go with that sentence and let it die between us.

She looked at me expectantly, her eyes flicking between mine, willing me to tell her why we weren't together. I wished I could. But how could I explain why there could only be friendship between us? Especially when I pushed the limits of that friendship so often.

In my silence, she came up with her own excuse, one that tore me. "Are you using me? Just like that asshole at my old school?"

That jerked me out of my turmoil as a surge of anger sliced through me. How could she compare me to that lowlife? I'd never hurt her like that. The anger spike died down when I realized that I *had* hurt her. Maybe unintentionally, and maybe not as directly as her jerk-off ex, but I had hurt her. Tenderly, I brought one of our laced-together hands up to stroke the back of her cheek. "No, Sawyer, never."

She swallowed and took a step towards me, closing the distance. "If you're not using me, then why do you pull away? If you like me, then why can't we be together?"

Her lips trembled when she spoke, and another tear dropped to her cheek. I think it was that tear that finally broke me. I felt my own eyes water as I felt the horrid words rising in my throat. The words that I knew would hurt her and confuse her even more. The words that I knew would hurt me and confuse me even more. The words that I knew would make me sound like a lunatic and forever change her opinion of me. They were coming though…it was too late to hold them back, much like the tear rolling down my cheek.

"Because I'm cheating on Lillian, and I can't let that happen anymore." A light cry escaped me and I swallowed to hold it inside.

Sawyer's mouth dropped open as confusion clearly showed in the crease of her forehead. Her tone was low and flat when she spoke. "What? What do you mean?"

Feeling her pull away from me, even though she wasn't, I dropped her hands and grabbed her forearms, my fingers digging into the soft velvet encasing them. "I'm sorry, but I'm in love with Lil. I don't want to hurt her anymore. Either of you."

She stepped back from me, her eyes searching my face as she tried to understand what I was telling her. I wanted to rewind the conversation. I wanted to rewind the night. I'd never have kissed her on the dance floor. I'd never have misled her again, and then none of this would be happening. She wouldn't be looking at me like I was damaged. Then I'd never have had to hear the next words she spoke to me.

"You're saying that in the present tense. She's gone, Lucas. You know that…right?"

Feeling more horrid tears slide down my skin, I nodded and took a step towards her. Even though she stayed where she was, I felt her pull farther away. "I know. I do know that, but I still love her." My words came out faster as I tried to explain. "I dream about Lillian, about what it was like to be together and it feels…just like it used to. I've found a way to still be with her." My eyes searched hers, frantically, willing her to understand. "Don't you see? It's not that I don't want to be with you—it's that I'm still with *her*. She's still my girlfriend."

Her face took on a look of incredulity and concern, and I hated seeing it. "But…that's crazy, Luc. That's not real."

Desperation crept into my voice at the thought of her looking at me differently from now on. "It feels real." I shook my head as my hands tightened their grip on her arms. "Who's to say what's more real, if life and dreams feel the same?"

Her hands came up to grab my face. Her grip was tight too. "You can't think like that. You can't live like that."

I smiled. It felt like an odd thing to do, but I wanted her to see that I liked my dream life and I wanted to keep it. "I do think that." Her thumbs started stroking my face, the metal of her ring feeling cool against my tear-streaked cheeks. I felt my odd smile getting wider; I probably looked as crazy as I sounded. "I've found a way to spend time with her again, with all of them. I almost always know it's a dream now, and I can almost control them. I'm getting really good at it. Well, better anyway, but I think with more time I'll be good."

She looked about to protest, her face a mask of concern now, but I beat her to it. "No, I know what you're going to say, but you're wrong. I *can* live this way. I can try. I have to—it's better than anything out there." I nodded my head over to the rowdy laughter I could hear building on the other side of the hallway from where we were standing.

Her face paled and she dropped her hands from my cheeks. "Even me?" She took a step back from me.

I closed my eyes. Once again, I'd stuck my foot in my mouth. Once again I'd forgotten that she didn't realize how important she was to me, that she was lumping herself in amongst the people I could barely even look at anymore. She was so above them all to me. Couldn't she see that?

Opening my eyes, I gazed at her heartbroken face. "No, Sawyer. I…I didn't mean it like that."

I stepped up to her, wrapping my arms around her waist, drawing her in for a hug that I felt we both needed. She didn't resist me, but she didn't hug me back either. I swallowed back some awful tears, praying that my callous words and actions tonight hadn't permanently damaged us. So much for giving Sawyer a memorable experience. Although, maybe I had succeeded on that point, just not in the way I'd originally intended.

Resting my head on her shoulder, I exhaled into the crook of her neck. "Honestly, Sawyer, you're my only reason to wake up."

Just as I felt her arms come up to my back, the laughing that had been going on at the far end of the hall was suddenly right next to us. I raised my head from Sawyer's body, wondering who was bugging us now. I felt my grip on her tighten when I received my answer.

Josh. Josh had decided to disturb our heart wrenching moment.

Swiping a hand across my wet cheeks, I glared at him; I was not in the mood for any more tormentors tonight. I hadn't sustained eye contact with him in a while, and he seemed amused that I held his stare. From behind him, I heard Will chuckle. My glare switched to Will when I heard him seductively say, "Hey, juvy. I like your dress." He eyed Sawyer up and down and I pulled her slightly behind me.

Sawyer didn't exactly need my protection though. From over my shoulder she told him to fuck off. His eyes on her turned mean and I put even more of my body in front of her.

"What do you want?" My eyes flicked between the two of them, but also took in the crowd gathering behind them, clearly expecting a showdown.

Josh crossed his arms over his chest and sneered at me. "Did you like the punch? We made it just for you."

I wasn't too surprised that my suspicions about the punch bowl were correct, so my expression didn't change any. My words took on a heated tone however, as I spoke loud enough for everyone in the hall to hear. "You drugged me and now you spiked the punch? You trying to get kicked out of here?"

Josh smirked, his dark eyes glancing behind him at the gathering masses. Will beside him shifted uneasily, glancing down at Josh and then the people filling the hall, before looking back up to me. Josh took a step towards me and a hush went over the tittering crowd. I could hear a flush from the bathrooms in the distance it was so quiet. Keeping his voice low and cold, Josh said, "No, I'm not trying to get *me* kicked out."

Taking another step into me, his finger came up to poke my chest. I stood still, making myself not react to his goading. "But you need a little punishment, so, yeah, I had you drugged by poor, stupid Randy…and you can't do anything about it, because no one here believes a goddamn thing you say." He was whispering heatedly, right in my face. I could see the crowd behind him bunch their brows, trying to catch a few words, but they weren't. His confession was only being heard by me, and I had already known it.

I shoved him away from me, my control momentarily slipping. His size was nothing compared to mine, so I ended up pushing him into Will. The crowd made a "here we go" noise as Will helped right him. Then Will took a step forward, like he was gonna whale on me in Josh's place, but Josh held him back with a hand on his chest. Will was more my size and a fight between us would be more evenly matched strength-wise, but he seemed to be letting Josh take the lead on this fight. Maybe he understood that this was something Josh and I needed to work out. Or maybe he just had a follower mentality and wasn't up to taking the initiative. Yet another reason he sucked as quarterback.

Sawyer, behind me, was *not* a follower however, and tried to sneak around me to put her own two cents in. I twisted to put my hands on her shoulders, stopping her. Josh glared over at her, his eyes narrowing at the evident bond between us. One thing that always seemed to flare Josh's temper was Sawyer and I, like he wanted me wallowing in darkness, struggling to hold it together each day, and any glimpse of happiness that I showed was an irritant to him.

Keeping his hard eyes on Sawyer, Josh sneered, "Even your *girlfriend* thinks you're a drunk." His tone inflected harshly on the word girlfriend and he almost looked like he wanted to spit at her feet. I think he would have, if we were outside. Sawyer bristled in my arms and I held her still, wondering how to get us out of this without fists flying. Where had all the chaperones gone anyway?

Josh held his hand out and stared at it, like he was reading a letter. "You were…impaired. I understand." He looked up at me, his face gloating. He was talking loud enough for everyone to hear now and a buzz went through the crowd.

I looked back at Sawyer as his words triggered a memory. He was miming reading a letter, and he was implicating Sawyer, whom everyone assumed was my girlfriend. Recognition flared in Sawyer's face at the same time it did in mine. Sawyer had written that in the note we'd passed back and forth in English, the day after our "incident" on the couch. She hadn't meant it like Josh thought she did, but it sounded bad, really bad.

He'd seen that? Where had he seen that? Didn't Sawyer have that note? I searched her face while she furrowed her brow and stared out over the hall, her eyes flicking back and forth like she was trying to remember what had happened to that incriminating evidence.

Anger flashed through me at the thought of Josh's eyes on that intimate conversation. And if he'd read it, that probably meant a good chunk of the school had read it too. Sawyer looked back at me, color flushing her cheeks, and I knew she'd just realized that, too. I tried to remember what that note had said, but all I could remember was what we were talking about—our moment of near-sex. I cringed at the thought of gossip about our sacred moment flying around the school.

My self-imposed rule of not ever engaging Josh again vanished in my anger and embarrassment. But more than that, it vanished because I knew how much Sawyer would be hurt by the idea of those words swirling out of control. I didn't want Sawyer hurt or harassed by Josh. I'd do anything to prevent that.

Releasing Sawyer, I walked up to Josh and shoved his chest again. He was more prepared for it this time and shoved me back. The crowd behind him buzzed with energy and tightened ranks, effectively cutting off Sawyer's and my escape to the gym. Irritated at the entire evening I yelled, "I wasn't drinking, Josh!"

Everyone in that hallway knew exactly what I was talking about. Everyone knew I was talking about the night of the crash. The room silenced, expecting an answer to the questions I always dodged. Aside from Josh and me scuttling back and forth, you could have heard a pin drop.

"Oh, come on, Luc—no one buys that!" Josh shoved me again, pushing me into Sawyer. She stumbled, and I twisted to prevent her from falling. I turned my head back to Josh when he added, "There's a witness anyway, Luc. Someone saw you slamming back beers, so you can stop acting like such a fucking innocent!"

A buzz of noise went through the crowd and Will, beside Josh, crossed his arms over his chest and met Josh's eye, nodding. Several other heads were nodding too. Not all, some faces looked surprised, but the majority was not startled by Josh's proclamation. This was apparently something most of the student body had already accepted about that night. I was surprised by it, as I'd yet to hear it.

My face felt like all the blood had rushed from it as I stepped away from Sawyer and up to Josh. He ran a hand through his dark hair but didn't back away.

"What…who?" Even before I said it, I knew. Who else in this school would spread lies and gossip about me, all in the hopes of bringing me down a peg? Who else, but that jealous little bitch? My face twisted into a sneer as I answered my own question. "Brittany."

Josh smirked. "Do you remember seeing her there now?"

I ran both hands through my hair and grunted in frustration. I heard Sawyer say something behind me, something about Brittany being a cunt, but my focus was all on Josh and that damn smirking smile on his face. "God, Josh! She's lying! You know she's a liar. She's always made up crap about me, trying to start shit. She wasn't there! She's mad at me for ignoring her or something. She was jealous of Lil, because after I met Lil, I wouldn't touch *her* anymore!" I knew I was ranting as I yelled at Josh, but I couldn't hold it back anymore. "She wasn't fucking there! No one from school was there!"

Josh stepped up to me, his face as dark as the black on black outfit he was wearing. He poked a finger in my chest again. "How convenient for you."

I ran my hand through my hair again, ruining any semblance of order, and gestured at my chest that he seemed to love poking. "Damn it, Josh, you know me." I frantically patted myself as I shook my head. "Do I drink? Have I ever been a drunk?"

He shoved me back, his hands clenching like he wanted to do more. "That night—yes! There was beer spilled all over you, Luc! My cousin was at the hospital—he says you reeked of it!"

"It was open in the car, Josh, but it was Darren's, not mine." I threw my hands up in exasperation and felt Sawyer's hand come up to rest on my shoulder, trying to calm me down. It worked a little bit and in a quieter voice I added, "Why…why do believe the rumor and not me?"

Josh stepped right into my face, his eyes wild with fury and hatred. I barely even recognized the kid I used to know. Seething, he screeched, "Because you got away with it! You got away with killing them all! You didn't even get so much as a fine for the open beer can! You got away scot-free and everyone knows why!"

Feeling tears sting my eyes, both from anger and sadness, I yelled back, "What the hell are you talking about?" Sawyer's hand tightened on my shoulder and I heard her say something about leaving, but Josh was in my face and that's all I could focus on.

Not backing up an inch, he yelled, "Your mom, Luc! You got away with it because your mom is fucking the sheriff! He covered for you, fixed your test at the hospital—all for his whore!"

That was when I saw red. That was when I didn't care about getting kicked out of school. That was when I didn't care that Sawyer was standing right behind me, that Will was on the other side of Josh, looking ready to assist if needed, or that a large mass of witnesses was behind them. That was when I didn't care that I'd made myself a promise to never let Josh get the better of me.

That was when Josh got the better of me.

My fist came around and solidly connected with his jaw. I had size and strength behind me, and his scrawny frame was no match. His head jerked around with the hit and he collapsed to the floor. My hand throbbed from the connection but I ignored it, keeping a tight fist for when he stood back up, for when we finally finished this. I stood over him, breathing heavy, as pure venom poured through my veins.

"Fuck you!"

He looked up at me, slightly dazed but grinning broadly; a trail of blood dripped from a cut across his bottom lip. He'd wanted a fight with me for a while now and he was finally gonna get one. He was small, but he was fast. He sprinted back to his feet and socked me in the gut before I could block it. The crowd behind us started chanting for a fight and I knew this was gonna end with me being evicted from the school forever.

I pushed him back as the wind was knocked from me. He made to tackle me, but he was suddenly grabbed from behind. As I panted to get my breath back, I looked over at Randy holding Josh's arms behind his back. Will glared at Randy, but made no move to separate the two of them. Josh cursed and tried to pull away from the large linebacker, but if he wasn't a match for me physically, then he definitely wasn't a match for Randy.

Ignoring the look from Randy that clearly said, "Get the hell out of here," I stepped right up to Josh's seething face. Rage drove me to my next words and I wasn't even aware of saying them.

"Fuck you and your lies!" I glanced up at the sea of faces watching, always watching. As hatred filled me, I didn't even see the distinctness that made them individual people. I only saw a blur of gossiping, heckling, cruel, humanoid blobs in various shapes, sizes and colors. My mind flicked back over the countless times they'd laughed at me, stared at me, tormented me…I was sick of all of them.

"Fuck all of you and your lies! You want to hear what truth sounds like?" I stepped back from Josh and gestured my hand over the suddenly quiet crowd. "Here's some truth—I wasn't drunk that night and I remember the whole fucking thing! It wasn't alcohol that screwed me up, it was the stupid weather. The goddamn rain ruined everything." My voice cracked and the indistinct shapes watered as my enraged eyes filled with tears. "That damn rain came out of nowhere and hit hard, like someone turned on a fucking shower. I slammed on the brakes to stop and lost control of the car. I fucked up—completely sober and they all died because of it!" I gestured at myself with both hands while I screamed at the crowd. "And I wish every day that I'd died with them!"

Josh stopped squirming against Randy and stared at me blankly, his anger seemingly sapped. Mine wasn't yet. I stepped in his face again. Randy let go of Josh and shoved his hand against my shoulder, warning me to stay back.

"You can't hurt me, Josh…because I already wish I were dead."

I backed away from him as icy realization hit me. I'd said too much. I'd said way too much. I felt Sawyer's hands on my back and her sweet voice finally reentered my head. She was begging me to leave with her. I took another step back and looked at Josh again and then the hushed crowd. "So just leave me alone," I whispered. "All of you."

I turned to head to the locker rooms, needing to run away from this mess and hide for a while. Immediately Coach stepped out from around the corner. His arms were crossed over his school-colored polo shirt and his hard eyes took in me and then the crowd behind me. I knew I was busted. I knew he'd heard and probably seen that entire fight. My face fell as I realized I was about to be tossed out of here, for good this time.

He narrowed his eyes at me as he barred my way. "Problem here, West?"

"No, Coach, I was just leaving." I knew he wasn't going to buy that, but what else could I say to him?

He nodded and pointed through the crowd to the gym. "Exit's that way."

My mouth dropped open as I stared at him. There was no way he hadn't heard me yelling, and there was no way he'd missed the crowd chanting "fight." Plus, he'd already looked over at Josh, and his cut lip was a dead giveaway. Was he really just going to let me walk?

As I stupidly stared at him, Sawyer tugging ineffectually on my arm, his eyes softened. He put a hand on my shoulder. "I'm so sorry I misjudged you, Luc," he whispered. I could only blink away tears and nod, as I finally let Sawyer pull me through the crowd that had started to disperse at the arrival of a teacher.

She pulled me past a confused Will and a sympathetic Randy. I heard Randy mutter something as I passed by him, but I was too dazed to register the sound and kept my eyes glued on Sawyer's heels in front of me, leading me to freedom from this horrid night. Before we disappeared into the gym, I heard Coach's booming voice yell, "Not so fast, McCord. I'd like a word."

As we hit the loud music and swirling lights of the gym, I was a little startled to see the party still going strong. I felt like my entire world had just started rotating the other way. Josh's words seared my brain, and I could hardly focus on placing one foot in front of the other as I followed Sawyer.

She stopped mid-gym and turned to me, her hands coming up to cup my cheeks. Her eyes were wide and concerned as they flicked between mine, but my head was swirling with so much residual anger and pain that I couldn't tell her I was fine. I couldn't tell her anything at all. Her mouth moved and I heard vague speech, but heated words echoed in my head and I couldn't hear hers.

"Your mom is fucking the sheriff! He covered for you…for his whore!"

Sawyer's face directly in front of me started to get hazy around the edges as I started sucking in faster and faster breaths. I could see her mouthing, "Breathe, Luc," over and over, but still couldn't hear her over the music and Josh's voice in my head. Her image started to swim, and panic started to take me. I backed away from her hands holding my face and looked around the gym, looked for something to ground me. All I saw were faces I didn't know—staring at me, laughing, talking, and whispering.

Their imagined voices filtered into my head. "See him throw up…drunk…loser…saw him pounding beers…his mom screwed…" I put my hands over my ears to stop the flood of whispers that I was translating into horrid gossip.

I turned, and ran right into Ms. Reynolds. Her wide eyes took in my expression and she grabbed my shoulders. "Luc? What's wrong?" I could only shake my head, barely able to breathe, let alone speak.

I broke away from her grasp…and ran. I bumped into quite a few startled couples, but it didn't stop me. I didn't stop until I burst through the main doors of the gym and darted out to the parking lot. I sank to my knees on the concrete, letting the cold, crisp air fill my lungs. It burned, but felt good as I gasped it down. My breath finally evened out as my panic attack started to subside.

Grief welled in me, and I put my head in my hands and let the tears fall. What a mess I'd made of tonight. I'd only wanted to show Sawyer a good time and here I was, dramatically bawling on my knees in the parking lot.

I don't know how long I stayed there, my slacks getting wet from the cold ground, but eventually I heard two sets of feet hurrying my way.

One paused behind me while the other ducked down to my side. Arms encircled me and Sawyer's comforting smell hit me. My hands dropped from my face and reached around her waist. I rested my head against her shoulder and she kissed me before leaning her head against mine. I swallowed repeatedly, sucking in the guilt and grief while she rocked me and urged me to let it out.

When I felt more in control, I raised my head to look at her. Her eyes glistened with sympathy as she returned my gaze. "I'm so sorry I ruined your night," I whispered.

She kissed my temple. "Don't…don't worry about it. Are you okay?"

I choked back more tears and shook my head. I wasn't sure what I was, but I was nowhere near okay. From behind me I heard, "Do you want some help getting him home, Sawyer?"

I looked over my shoulder and saw Ms. Reynolds standing behind us, shivering in her light dress as she vigorously rubbed her bare arms. Sawyer glanced at me and I gave her a wide-eyed, pleading look. She understood and shook her head at Ms. Reynolds.

"No, I can handle this, thank you."

Ms. Reynolds didn't look convinced, but only nodded her head as Sawyer helped me stand up. Wanting her to leave us, I tried to throw on a smile. Ms. Reynolds frowned even more, so I stopped trying to look happy. She sighed and looked over at Sawyer. "Call my cell if you need anything, Sawyer. Oh, and tell your parents I'll come over next week sometime."

I furrowed my brow at that, and Ms. Reynolds shifted her attention to me. She patted my arm, but looked like she wanted to hug me. "Everything will be okay, Lucas. Have a good break…all right?"

Feeling stupid, I nodded. She turned around and briskly walked back to the warm gym. Turning to face Sawyer, I couldn't think of anything to say to her but, "Do you *know* Ms. Reynolds?"

She turned her lip up that *that* was the first thing I'd chosen to comment on. "She's my mom's second cousin…or something. She agreed to keep an eye on me for her."

I looked away and nodded, finally seeing why Ms. Reynolds always seemed to put so much personal attention on her, calling her parents if she skipped pep rallies, frequently keeping her for a few minutes alone after purity club. Sawyer had a spy.

Sawyer's hand grasped mine and she pulled me toward her car. I glumly followed, hating just about everything that had happened tonight. The pounding music from the gym had faded to nearly nothing once outside, and by the time we got to her car, the night was quiet. I handed her the car keys, having held them for her, since that fabulous dress didn't have any pockets.

She opened my door and helped me in like I was a toddler. I hated that she felt the need to mother me after everything that had happened between us, but I silently sat there as she buckled me in and then got in on her side.

She took her corsage off her wrist and looped it around one end of her rearview mirror. I watched as she adjusted some of the bent and broken flower petals, thinking those crushed flowers summed up our night pretty well. Melancholy swept over me and I stared out the window while she started the car.

She didn't move the car though, and I looked back over at her after a few long seconds idling in the parking lot, the heater on high. "Sawyer?" I asked quietly.

She didn't answer me at first, only warmed her hands with the blasting heat before turning it down to low. She plucked at a sleeve of her dress and then twisted in her seat to face me. Her expression serious, she calmly asked, "Did you mean it?"

Not knowing what part of the evening she was referencing, I gave her a questioning look. "Mean what?"

She looked down for a split second before lifting her eyes to mine again. There was moisture in the grayness and I hated seeing it. I started to reach out for her face, but her words froze me solid. "Did you mean that you wish you were dead?" Her eyes flicked over mine as my stomach dropped. "Do you really wish that you were dead every day?"

That moisture built, welling into a small sea before breaking over the dam and trailing down her cheek. I watched it slither down her skin, wondering how to answer her question in the most honest and vague way. Whenever anyone asks that, the answer they expect to hear is no. No, of course I didn't mean it. I was exaggerating, or it was a heat of the moment thing. But for me…

I pulled my gaze from her cheek and met her eye. Shaking my head, I whispered, "No. I didn't mean it. I don't wish I were dead…"

Not *every* day…

That was the defining point for me, but it wasn't one I was about to share with her. The fact was, I did think about death. How could I not after what I'd endured. Immediately after the crash, I had longed for it. I hadn't wanted to live in a world without my friends. I never shared that desire with anyone, but it was in me…buried. And on bad enough days, it sometimes resurfaced.

Sawyer nodded and a light smile lit her lips. She exhaled and her head came down to rest against mine. Her hand came up to grasp my cheek and she nodded again. My hand came up to the back of her head and I shifted her to my shoulder, pulling her to me for a tight hug.

As we embraced in the pinkish light of the fluorescent bulb above us, the only noise in the car coming from her radio, a nagging thought crept into the back of my head. A remembered conversation with my counselor, a feeling that somehow I was missing something horribly simple and all this suffering…didn't need to be happening.

But as Sawyer pulled away from me, saying that she'd drive me home now, the feeling passed and a rolling wave of intense anger hit me. I had no desire to go home. Not when my beloved mother…was possibly a lying whore.

Chapter 19 – The Intervention

Sawyer's eyes widened as she looked at me, and I realized I had a mean sneer on my face. I adjusted it into what I hoped was a calmer look. Her brow brunched at seeing it, and I thought that maybe I was failing. I began to shake my head at her. "No, I don't want to go back there."

She still seemed confused, but then understanding hit her and her mouth dropped open. Her eyes narrowed at me, partly concerned, but partly irritated, too. "You don't want to go home? Because of what Josh said about your mom?" She put a hand on my arm and leaned into me. "It was probably just another stupid rumor." She shook her head, her softening curls brushing her velveteen shoulders. "No more truth to it than Brittany seeing you drinking that night."

I swallowed and closed my eyes at that remembered revelation. No wonder so many people believed the lies about me. Brittany was popular—Queen Bee, top of the herd, big fish in a very tiny pond—people were prone to believe the things that she said. No wonder no one believed my halfhearted attempts at denial.

I opened my eyes and shook my head, tiredness and sadness winning out over my anger. "I just can't be there right now, Sawyer. I just can't be somewhere where she is." I swallowed again and gave her pleading eyes. "Can I…can I stay with you tonight?" I whispered, not knowing how she'd react to that after our heated moment at the dance.

She sighed and her hand came up to run down my face. She must have noticed something in my features. Maybe that my anger had faded into melancholy, maybe that I was barely keeping it together, maybe that there was no way I could handle being alone right now. For whatever reason, she bit her lip and nodded. "Yeah, all right. You'll have to sneak in, though."

I nodded and relaxed back in my seat. She looked me over for another moment before twisting back to the wheel and starting to drive. We turned the opposite direction of my house from the parking lot, and I felt a moment of guilt that Sawyer went out of her way to come get me every day. Just another thing I had to apologize to her for. As gloom settled over me, I wondered why she bothered with me at all. What did I give her but confusion and heartache? She should be with someone else, someone who could give her what she wanted. Someone who could love her the way she deserved to be loved. Someone not…broken.

I sighed out the window as I watched the town go by and felt her hand come over to grab mine. Feeling like our no contact rule was so shattered at this point that it didn't even really matter anymore, I grasped it back hard. Her thumb stroked circles into my hand, urging me to relax, and I let my grip loosen a little bit.

"Hey, you want to talk about…anything?" she asked, giving me concerned glances while she drove.

"No…nothing to say, really."

She sighed, and I looked over at her. Her face was frustrated and she was biting her lip. I knew I'd said a lot tonight that I usually didn't say, and she wanted to talk about it. She wanted to delve into me and open all of those scars so she could help me heal, much like Mrs. Ryans, but she was respectful enough of our friendship to still not press me about it. I appreciated her for that and felt bad at the same time.

Just when I was about to ask her what she wanted me to talk about first, she changed the subject on me. "Did you hear Randy?" she asked, raising an eyebrow at me.

I frowned and tried to think back to what she was talking about, but all I could remember about the evening was Josh. Josh and his cruel words.

I shook my head, and she clarified. "He apologized, Luc, for drugging you. He said it over and over." She looked to the road quickly and then back to me, narrowing her eyes. "You didn't hear that?" I shook my head again and she sighed, a soft, sad smile coming to her lips before she turned back to the road. "I told you he felt bad. I told you not everyone is against you. I mean, you saw the way he was holding Josh back." Her eyes came to mine again, warmth in the gray depths. "He was trying to help you, Lucas."

A surprising flash of jealousy swept through me at the look in her eye when she talked about Randy. I rolled my eyes and stared out the window. We were driving into the countryside, the houses spaced farther and farther apart. Sawyer apparently *did* live in the middle of nowhere. As more guilt filled me over how far she went to help me each day, bitterness entered my tone.

"Yeah, nothing but helpful…Randy."

She slowed the car and pulled over to the side of the road; the only thing around us were empty grass fields. I looked around at where we were and then looked over at her, confused. She didn't acknowledge my confusion, only twisted in her seat to face me.

"He tried to apologize to you at the dance, and I know he's wanted to, even before that." Her tone got that sage sound to it and I sighed at hearing it. That made her furrow her brow. "He feels really horrible for getting you suspended, but he hasn't been able to say he's sorry, because you always blow him off."

I raised my eyebrows and was about to protest, but she shook her head and didn't let me finish. "Maybe not intentionally, Luc, but you walk around with your head down, not really noticing anything or anybody." Her face softened and she put her hand on my still wet knee. "I know you're doing it to protect yourself, but not everyone hates you here." She looked down and shyness entered her voice. "Some of us even love you," she whispered.

Her adorable look calmed my nerves, but her words brought a buried ache to the surface. People laughing, teasing, tormenting me…none of them cared. She was wrong. I shook my head at her, and my voice came out harder than I intended it to. "You don't know what you're talking about. You've only been here a few months. I've been around these people my whole life."

She looked up, surprised at my tone. "I know…"

Irritated at myself for snapping at her, I added, "I thought you hated these people…isn't that what you said?"

She shrugged and looked away, tucking a loose lock of hair behind her ear.

Her face looked torn, like she didn't want to continue this conversation but felt that we needed to have it. I didn't really want to have it. I wanted her to agree with me that everyone sucked and hold me in her arms all night while I cried over my miserable existence. But, then again, maybe I was just wallowing in pity.

"That was before I got to know some of them." She peeked up at me out of the corner of her eye. "The people in the club aren't so bad, and other people have approached me at the games and stuff." As I cocked my head at her, she faced me and smiled. "They ask about you, you know, because they know we're close. They ask if you're okay."

I had a snappy retort on my tongue, but swallowed it when what she'd said registered with me. "They…ask about me? If I'm…okay?" I don't know why, but it shocked me that anyone but her would care enough to ask about my mental state.

Her face softened even more and she brought her hand to my cheek, sweeping her thumb around my eye. "Yeah. Some people just don't know what to say to you, others are giving you your space to grieve." She dropped her hand as my mouth fell open, shocked. She cringed. "But you don't talk to anyone, Luc, no one but me. You walk around with your head down and ignore everybody. It makes you unapproachable. People just aren't sure what to do around you."

I looked away, absorbing that. So my isolation was my fault now? I sniffed and softly said, "Now you really sound like my counselor." I shook my head, still not looking at her, still picturing all the people I encountered in my day. I didn't see any of them the way she described.

"Which people ask about me?" I whipped my head back to her, a frown on my lips. "The people who whisper about me and ridicule me? The ones who laugh when Will trips me or urge Josh to kick my ass…*those* people?"

She sighed, her hand holding mine, clenching it tight. "No, Luc." She leaned into me again, momentarily resting her head against mine. "You are only seeing what you want to see…not everyone's like that." She pulled back to look at me, her eyes soft with compassion.

Her words baffled me. I couldn't understand how we could view the same school so differently. "Why would I want to see that? Why would I *want* people to hate me?" I whispered, heat entering back into my voice.

She stared at me for long seconds before finally sighing and sweeping some unruly hair off my forehead. Shaking her head she said, "I don't know. Maybe…because *you* hate you."

My mouth dropped open again and she swept her hand around to my cheek, cupping it again. I sputtered for something to say, but couldn't focus. I couldn't find any argument with that. I did sort of hate me. I didn't really blame anyone else in the school for feeling what I did. But she was wrong…there was no compassion for me in that school. No friendship to be had but hers.

Blinking sudden tears from my eyes, I swept my gaze out over the windshield at the empty fields around us. The emptiness suddenly felt metaphoric in a horrible way. "Why are we out here?" I whispered, speech finally returning to me.

She dropped her hand from my face and pointed to a tiny light suspended in the near darkness, yards up the road from us. "That's my house." She looked back to me, her eyes apologetic. "Sorry, but you're gonna have to get out here and sneak through the fields."

I nodded and looked out over the dark expanse between us and the light. I wondered how often I'd trip and fall along the way.

She let go of my hand and pointed again to the house. "My room is downstairs, basement level." She looked over my frame. "I'm pretty sure you'll fit through the window. I'll open it so you'll know which one."

I nodded and moved to crack my door. She grabbed my hand as I pushed it open. "Lucas." I looked back at her expectantly, and she bit her lip. "I'll see you in a little bit."

I nodded and headed out into the darkness. I closed her door behind me and then watched as she pulled away, her taillights driving into the distance. Up the road, she swung into the driveway of her home, the headlights splashing onto an older style, two-story farmhouse. Well, I guess three-story if she lived in the basement level. I hoped I would fit through the window. Sneaking through the house didn't sound like fun.

Bracing myself for a few trip-ups through the long, dark grass lying between us, I inhaled a deep breath and headed out to meet back up with her.

By the time I got through the field, and to the dark corner of the house where Sawyer had indicated that her room was, I did indeed have two or three splotches of mud on me, including a rather embarrassing one on my ass. I brushed myself off the best I could and cautiously approached the house. I ducked down into a crouch and then shook my head and straightened back up. Being shorter wasn't going to make me any less visible, and really, looking like a lurker would only increase the chances of Sawyer's parents calling the cops if they happened to spot me.

Walking over the soft, shorter grass of her lawn, I studied the dark rectangles of the bottom level windows. On the very back corner of the house there was one that had been opened for me. I glanced up at the first and second story windows, but everything was still dark inside. No giant-like shadow pacing on patrol, protecting the virtue of the teenager within. Although with what Sawyer had confessed to me tonight, *my* virtue would be the only one left in the house. Super.

I crouched down at the window and began to slide it farther open. It squeaked horribly and a "Shhh!" answered me from inside. Trying for silence, I carefully pushed it open the rest of the way. Most basement rooms have those odd half windows that push out and make access nearly impossible, but these windows had been converted to more traditional, although still smaller, windows. Either her parents or the previous owners hadn't wanted whoever lived in these rooms to be trapped if there was a fire. The unwelcome side effect of that was evident, as my body just slipped through the opening—a fire escape also served as the perfect "afterhours" boys' entrance.

I hopped down into Sawyer's room and smiled as I looked around. It was only sort of what I'd expected it to be. Her furniture was white and, although clearly hand-me-downs, the items were elegant and sophisticated, made for a grown-up. But the curtains and bedding looked like a set for a pre-teen, with shades of hot pink, neon green, and lavender. The walls were all painted in an infant-like shade of pink, almost like her dad was trying to keep her his baby girl through latex. By the half dozen posters of various rock groups tacked up on those pink walls, it would seem that her dad was failing.

CDs and their cases littered her desk, which had an older CD player on it along with her school bag. A bookcase beside her bed was overflowing with books—classic novels, romances, and that writer who wrote those mysteries where all the titles started with a different letter in the alphabet. She had up to M, as far as I could tell. Unlike my room, there were no clothes laying around the floor. She must have kept all of them neatly in her drawers or in her closet. Her bed was neatly made, a faded, white teddy bear sitting on her pillow.

She grabbed that teddy bear as she watched my eyes linger on it. A faint blush crept into her cheeks as she muttered, "Barney. I've had him since I was two." She immediately put "Barney" inside her dresser and a corner of my mouth lifted at her embarrassment. Turning back to me, she handed me a pair of sweats and a really big t-shirt. I took them and cocked an eyebrow.

With a pointed glance at my muddy slacks, she said, "I thought you'd get a little dirty walking through the fields, so I grabbed some of my dad's laundry." She shook her head and smiled wryly at me, her dimple showing itself. "You look like you found every mud hole."

"It's dark out there."

She nodded and went over to close the window I'd stupidly left open. "I know…sorry."

I nodded and smiled back at her, finally noticing that she had changed out of her dress. She was wearing lounge pants with the word "juicy" across her bottom. That's what got my attention. She had also slipped on a long-sleeve t-shirt, taken her makeup off and removed the pins from her hair, the dark, freed curls dangling around her shoulders. Apparently, I'd taken a while getting here.

She looked over my face taking her in and explained, "My dad didn't really like that dress, so I got out of it as quick as I could." She rolled her eyes. "He was waiting for me in the kitchen." A small smile lifted her lips as my eyes widened, wondering if he'd come check on her while I was here. Almost reading my mind she said, "He won't come down here. He saw me getting ready for bed, so he won't worry about me sneaking out…not that I would."

I quietly nodded, still a little scared to make any noise at all. She laughed at the restraint on my face and then pushed me towards her door. I automatically tensed when she opened it, but it only led to what kind of looked like a tiny living room. There was a love seat and an old TV and a small stack of movies, all of them romantic comedies, a couple with Matthew McConaughey.

From there, she pointed to a room across from the couch. "The bathroom is there." She gave me a friendly push and was grinning when I looked back at her.

As I walked across the room, I noticed the stairs that led up to the main floor. I felt exposed walking through the line of sight of those stairs, like any minute her dad was going to run down them and fillet me alive. I briefly considered not changing my clothes, so I could make a run for it if needed, but I *was* pretty dirty, and didn't want to be rude by messing up Sawyer's house.

I changed and got ready for bed, nerves creeping up on me at the thought of staying here with Sawyer all night. I'd never spent the night with a girl before, not even Lil. Not a full night anyway. Not that I had to stay in Sawyer's bed with her or anything. I could crash on her floor, or better yet, the loveseat in the living room. Feeling more secure with that idea, I splashed some water on my face, grabbed my dirty clothes, and made my way back to her room.

I paused before walking through her doorframe, exhaling a quick breath. She looked up when she saw me, and rested a book that she'd been reading on her knees, the letter L mystery, from what I could make out on the cover. She flicked the corner of the pages with her thumb and bit her lip. I thought she looked as nervous about this as I was. I set my stuff down on a chair at her desk, leaving my shoes on top of my muddy pants, and pointed with my thumb at the door.

"I can… I can stay out there…"

She frowned and shook her head, patting the bed beside her. "That couch is awful, really." Looking down shyly, she added, "You can stay…with me." She peeked up at me and I could clearly see the hope in her eyes. Knowing I shouldn't encourage that hope, I nodded and sat down on the bed.

I lay back on the pillows, adjusting my oversized clothes and propping my bare feet up, so my knees stuck up in the air just like Sawyer's. She put her book on her nightstand and shut off the lamp beside it. Darkness swept over the room, and I looked over to the lump I knew was her.

"Thank you for doing this for me," I whispered into the darkness.

I felt her rustle beside me, still not able to see much but a vague outline of her shape. "It's all right, Lucas. I know tonight was hard for you."

"It was hard for you too," I whispered, the words barely audible. She must have heard me, for her hand reached over and grabbed my arm. Her fingers trailed down me until she reached my hand and I laced us together.

I felt the bed move as she shifted her body. I couldn't see her knees in the air anymore, so I thought maybe she'd switched to her side to face me. I shifted as well to face her. The night between us made it seem like we were the only two people in the world. A warmth and comfort spread over me and I scrunched closer to her in the small bed. I felt the edge of her body, her knees touching my thighs, and sighed softly.

"Luc?"

Her voice was directly in front of my face, the minty smell of her toothpaste washing over my skin. "Yeah?"

I felt her sigh and the shape of her head started getting clearer to me as my eyes adjusted. She was silent, not asking me anything, and I studied the darkness, wishing I could see more of her. Just when her features started to get clearer, when I could tell that she was biting her lip, she spoke.

"Is…Is Lillian the only reason we're not together?"

I tensed, not sure how to answer that. Finally, feeling that if anything, I owed her the truth, I said, "Yes." Seeing her brows knit together, but feeling safe wrapped in the night around me, I added, "I still see Lillian, Sawyer."

I felt a smile come to my lips as I thought about Lillian and how close we'd been lately. How any moment now, we'd be pushing past that last physical barrier in our relationship. "We're just like we used to be." I searched Sawyer's face, changing from an indistinguishable black to a faded gray as more light filtered through my eyes. Her face held a blank look as she listened, a forced blank look, and I decided to be as honest with her as I could. "I really hurt her, when she found out about what we…when we…"

Her eyes looked down, and I knew she knew what intimate moment I was referring to. "You should have seen her face, Sawyer. I wrecked her." I bit my lip and shook my head, feeling the sudden tears sting my eyes. My voice trembled when I spoke again and Sawyer lifted her gaze back to mine at hearing it. "I won't do that again to her." I brought a hand to her cheek, hoping she could see the apology in my eyes, hear it in my voice. "I can't let anything else happen between us. I can't cheat on her anymore."

She swallowed and her eyes clearly glistened, apparent even in the darkness. "But, we're not…having an affair or anything. She's gone, Luc."

I dropped my hand from her cheek and turned my head and body away from her, looking up to her ceiling. A spattering of glow in the dark stars spelled out 'I love you' right over her bed. I sighed, wishing those words were as simple as they looked. "I have to be faithful to her, she's my girlfriend." My head turned back to her. "And…yes, I know how that sounds. I know I sound completely crazy, and that's why I never talked about this with you before. But it's still true…it's how I feel."

She was silent a long moment and then she propped herself up onto an elbow. "Okay, Luc. I don't really understand it and I don't agree with it…but, I haven't gone through what you've gone through, and I don't know how I'd react."

Her voice and face took on that seriousness that I'd gotten used to over the past few months, and I automatically paid even closer attention. She looked down at the inch or two between us and then looked back up to me. "Just don't…don't use me. If you don't feel it, that's fine, but don't…don't go there anymore. Please."

I sat up on my elbow as well, twisting to face her. I resisted every urge I had to cup her cheek again. "I'm so sorry about what keeps happening between us, Sawyer. I'm not sure what…" I bit my lip and shook my head. "But I'm not like that asshole who used you…and I really am sorry…for everything."

Her eyes still glistening, she nodded her head and sank back to her pillows. Releasing our fingers, she rested her head on her curved-back arm. I copied her position and we stared at each other in silence for a few long moments. I felt peace and sleep crawl up on me. After another few silent seconds, she quietly said, "But you do like me?"

I smiled in the dark, reaching over to squeeze her free hand. "Yes, Sawyer. I like you…a lot."

She smiled and looked down, then sadness passed over her face and she turned away. I muttered that I was sorry again and she swallowed and nodded, looking up at the stars over her bed. For a moment, I imagined that she was thinking the exact same thought that I'd had about love a few moments ago. I squeezed her hand again and she finally looked back at me.

"Are you cold?" I asked quietly.

She shook her head, but shivered involuntarily. I gave her a wry grin and then moved to pull the covers back. I climbed underneath and held my arms out for her. I wasn't sure what I wanted her to do, I just needed her close. She looked over my face and gesture, and then gave me a soft sigh before crawling under the covers. She twisted, so her back faced me, and I wrapped an arm around her, keeping her warm, keeping her safe, and I prayed, not being misleading again.

I felt her body relax into mine and I rubbed her arm, wanting to encourage the comfort that she always gave me.

"Luc?" She twisted her head around to look at me.

"Yeah?"

She bit her lip, and I thought she was debating whether or not to ask me something. Finally she whispered, "You talked about the crash tonight. And you've mentioned…bits and pieces before. Do you…do you want to talk about what you remember?"

I tensed up, but made myself not react negatively to her words. Memories rushed through me though. Memories of that night and memories of yelling at the students earlier. Both memories were equally horrid. I looked down and shook my head. "I'm sorry, Sawyer. I can't. I just can't. It's…too hard."

When I looked up, I could feel my tears, and knew they were close to spilling over this time. She nodded and immediately said, "You don't have to. If you're not ready…you don't have to."

I felt myself instantly start to relax. Swallowing, I found her hand again and squeezed it. "I'm sorry if I ruined your big night, Sawyer."

She twisted in my arms, her head turning all the way around, so she was directly in front of my face again. "You didn't, not really. I still had fun with you…for most of it anyway." She shrugged and then gave me an apologetic face. "I wanted to show you that school could actually be fun." Her eyes met mine, looking genuinely remorseful. "I feel like I failed."

I pulled her tight against me. "I had a good time with you…" I smiled and she twisted around so her back nestled into my chest again. I brought my knees up, so hers curled around me, and lowered my head to rest it against her shoulder. Peace and love and warmth flooded through me. "I had a good time with you, Sawyer…it was everyone else that I had a problem with."

She nodded and clutched my arm, bringing it around, so the back of my hand rested against her heart. We were silent after that, all words momentarily spoken, and then sleep found us and we gave into it.

The sound of music entered my consciousness first: hard, thumping music that reverberated through my chest and ear drums. It was loud, much louder than was needed for the large rectangular room. I looked up at the disco ball suspended from the ceiling, spinning so fast the swirling lights were making me nauseous. I looked down at the popped balloons littering the floor, the floor swarming with people, with what looked like the entire student body. I had no idea why I was back at the gym, back at the dance, and why the crowd of people didn't seem to be dancing. They seemed to be forming a tight circle around two people moving back and forth inside it.

That was when shock went through me. That was when I saw myself between the cracks of bodies. Darren walked up beside me, crossing his arms over his chest and looking at the other me moving around someone else in the circular opening that the student body had left us.

I relaxed, registering a dream in progress. "Hey, man," I said over to him.

The music around us suddenly softened and I clearly heard him when he spoke back to me. "Josh was in fine form tonight." He twisted his lip and shook his head, his dark hair matching the dark mood in his eyes. "I'm going to have some serious words with that kid next time I see him."

I nodded and looked back at the circle, which included Josh as well as me. We were apparently engaged in a screaming match, although I couldn't hear it. The sound of the music, while quiet around Darren and me, was blocking out all other noise.

Sammy came up on the other side of Darren, leaning around him to nod politely at me. I nodded back and watched, slightly confused, as she turned her golden brown eyes to watch the show with Darren. I wasn't sure why I was dreaming about this. This was a moment I didn't want to relive.

As I was contemplating trying to change the location, I felt Lillian step up to my side and grab my hand. I stopped my efforts and turned to smile at her, squeezing her small fingers. She gave me a tiny smile in return and turned to watch the show as well.

I glanced between the three of them, not sure why they were so intently watching this when they knew what had happened—they knew everything in my head. Finally, I turned to look as well, my curiosity mixing with apprehension as I watched an angry version of myself yell at Josh. I hated seeing myself like that. I hated hearing it too, but unfortunately, I had to—the music had suddenly stopped when I'd focused fully on the fighters.

"It's not true! Whatever you think you know, it's not true!"

Josh's angry, scrawny form stepped up to mine in the circle, shoving me back against the wall of eager listeners. The faces watching us held a look of cruel delight; they were eating up my torment. Sawyer was nowhere in sight.

"Everyone knows it, Luc!" He looked over the crowd and they all started nodding and murmuring agreements. He came back to shove a finger in my chest. "Your mom is a whore and screwed you out of trouble! Because you are a no-good, worthless drunk, who slaughtered my brother!"

My body in the circle paled and cowered, scrunching down among the wall of bodies, looking defeated. But the other me, the me who was watching, was enraged again. I took a step forward, ready to pummel the living hell out of my dream version of Josh, when Darren suddenly put a hand on my shoulder, stopping me.

I looked over at him, but he was still intently staring at his brother. I exhaled a slow breath and turned to watch as well. The dream version of me sank to my knees, despair all over my face. "I'm sorry…I did kill him. I did get away with it."

Josh stepped up to me, hands clenched at his sides. "So, you admit you're a murderer?"

I watched myself lower my head and then nod. I felt sympathy for that dream version of me, which was an odd thing to feel. I hadn't killed my friends the way that Josh implied…but I had killed them, and I did sort of feel like a murderer. I felt Lillian's grip on my hand tighten.

Josh sneered and looked over the crowd. With a triumphant voice, he boomed, "He admits it! He admits that he killed them ruthlessly, coldly." He looked back to me while the crowd booed their opinion of me. When it quieted down, he spoke in a low voice, "Well, what do we do with you now?"

The crowd started voicing their options, most cruel and most wanting revenge. I swallowed as I watched the entire student body, and a large section of the faculty too, try me for my crimes against humanity.

Josh listened to the suggestions and then came up with one of his own. "I think we do the only fair thing." He squatted down and lifted my drooping head. My eyes widened, both on me and on the dream version of me, as I watched his hand swing back, a jagged rock the size of a softball enclosed in it.

"Eye for an eye…right, Luc?"

Once I realized what Josh was going to do, I broke free from my friends and darted to the crowd, trying to worm my way through. My friends let me go, but it didn't matter. The mass of bodies eagerly thirsting for my blood were impossible to get through. I pulled and struggled and even punched, but it was no use. They were as effective a barrier as concrete.

From over the din, I heard Josh sneer, "You want to die every day? Well, today's your lucky day!"

Through the breaks in people's bodies, I watched in horror as Josh brought that rock around to the side of my head. My dream version of me did nothing, only continued to stare at Josh with pathetically empty eyes. I turned away and closed mine when I heard the sickening connection, the wet thud as my brains were bashed in.

The crowd around me erupted into cheers and I sank to my knees, no longer able to stand. I felt my chest heave and my stomach rise, and I wrapped my arms around myself, trying to keep it together.

Then the gym was quiet, and my friends were the only bodies left in the room. Sammy and Lillian squatted down on either side of me while Darren stood before me. I looked up at him, wondering if my face now matched my pathetic dream version's face.

He sighed and squatted down, placing a hand on my shoulder. "The dance was awful, Luc."

I swallowed as I looked between the three of them. True, the dance had been bad, but nowhere near what I'd just envisioned. I steadied my breathing as I locked eyes with Lillian. Her hand came up to stroke my cheek and she gave me a sad smile.

I nodded as I held her gaze. "I know. I tried."

"You didn't try hard enough, Luc," Darren said. "You handled that badly."

I looked back up to Darren. "I handled it the best I could, Darren." I looked back to the empty gym floor behind me, almost expecting to see my blood everywhere. "I handled it better than that."

"Did you?" he asked and I twisted to give him a sour face. He shrugged. "You let them vilify you. You let them pick on you. You let them make you a victim." His eyes flicked over to where Josh had just killed me.

I bristled and stood up. "I told them what happened. I told them about that night. Doesn't that count for anything? Isn't that what you all want from me?"

Sammy stood and put a hand on my arm. "It's a start, Luc. But you did that to push people back." She shook her head, her auburn hair flashing red where the lights hit it. "You did that to force people away, not bring them closer."

I shook my head, not understanding. "I spoke…isn't that enough?"

Lillian put her hand on my other arm, her pale hair a sharp contrast to Sammy's. "No, Luc. You need to stop being defensive and start letting people in. Like Sawyer."

I pulled away and stared at the three of them, irritated and a little scared. "What is this? Some sort of ethereal intervention?"

The three of them looked between each other and then back to me. There was a solidarity in their silence that unnerved me. Finally Lillian was the one that spoke, and she did it like she was speaking for the group. "Lucas, we're worried for you. We want you to be healthy and happy…and you're not."

I shook my head and grabbed her hands, holding them up to me. "I'm happy. I'm happy here with you." I looked over at Darren and Sammy. "With all of you."

Darren clapped my shoulder. "But your real life is suffering because of it, Luc. Holding us tight is pushing everyone else away."

I shook my head again, but Sammy spoke before I could argue. "Look at Randy, Luc. You didn't even hear his apology…and I'm sure there are others who want to befriend you, people that you don't even see."

Darren took up her speech. "Because you go through every day in a daze, only thinking about how to pass the time, so you can come here again to be with us."

My mouth dropped open as I stared between the two of them. "So? What's out there that is better than what's in here?"

Aside from watching myself get stoned to death, of course.

Lillian's voice was soft in my ear, but struck me to my core. "Sawyer."

My head snapped back to her, my eyes watering. Knowing my physical body was currently spooning with Sawyer, I felt guilt creep through me. "No, Lil. I told her no."

Her answering smile was a sad one. "Exactly, Lucas." One of her hands released mine to come up and touch my face. "You can't push away a chance at real love for the twenty minute encounters you get with me."

Her pale blue eyes watered, but I was the one who finally broke down. Tears streamed down my cheeks as I responded to her. "Those twenty minutes are worth it." I looked over all of them, desperation clear in my face and voice. "You're all worth it. Please…"

They all looked at each other again, Sammy's tears flowing as freely as mine. Darren sniffed and stared at the ground and a soft sob escaped from Lillian. I suddenly got the feeling that this wasn't just another "Lucas must live" speech. I suddenly got the feeling that they were giving me a goodbye speech. Ice shot through every nerve in my body.

"Don't do this…" My voice was barely a whisper, but they all turned their attentions back to me. "Please," I added, my voice strained with tension.

Sammy stepped up to me, throwing her arms around my chest. "Oh, Lucas. You know how much I love you, right?"

I swallowed and shook my head, momentarily dropping Lil's hand so I could clutch Sammy's arms. "No, please…no."

The tears dripped from her cheeks as she started to sob. "I'm sorry, Lucas. You need to let us go if you're ever going to heal." Her hands grabbed my face. "I love you too much to let you slowly fade away because of us."

She kissed my forehead and I felt the burn of it run through me. I started panicking. "No, please, Sammy. I'll do anything…anything. Just stay…"

She sobbed again, resting her head against mine. "You were the best, Luc…and I want you to be that man again." Then she vanished and I was clutching air.

"No! No, please, Sammy." I tried to mentally bring her back, but nothing was happening. I couldn't control anything.

Darren stepped up to me, his eyes watering as he watched my frantic face search for his disappeared girlfriend. His arms came around me in a hug and I momentarily forgot my horror at Sammy leaving. A new horror struck me.

My mouth dropped open again as I clutched his shoulders. "NO! You can't leave! Not you!" My voice broke. "You're my best friend, and best friends don't leave!"

He shook his head, tears finally making it to his cheeks. "I already left you, Lucas." His eyes flicked over the sob-filled room, sobs I realized were coming from me. "This isn't real, man."

I clutched at him, trying to physically restrain him from abandoning me. "No…no, I won't let you. You have to stay."

A soft sob escaped him as he ignored my attempts to keep him in place and hung his head. "We should have done this a while ago. Maybe it would have been easier for you back then." He lifted his head as I vigorously shook mine. "And that's what matters, Luc. You." His hands came up to grasp my face. "You're the only one left. Don't forget that you lived. I love you, Luc."

Feeling him slipping, I started repeating "no" over and over. It didn't matter…he faded right before my eyes. A sob tore through me and I felt a piece of me shatter. Darren had been my best friend since we were five years old. There wasn't a monumental moment in my life that he hadn't either been a part of, or that I hadn't told him about, even after his death. I couldn't comprehend a lifetime without seeing his friendly face.

Arms swept around me then, and my sobs started coalescing together into one long grief-filled wail. If I couldn't comprehend a life without Darren, then a life without Lillian…

I spun and pulled her to me, determined to make her stay. I needed her. She was my air. I couldn't function without her. I was frantic in my desire to keep her near me, pulling at her clothes and hair and arms. She calmly shushed me and tried to still my body. Her hands came up to my face and she cupped my cheeks, making me stare at her, making me calm down.

When I could breathe more normally, I whispered, "Please, not you…please. Don't leave me…"

She closed her eyes, tears falling. "Luc…"

I shook my head, panic flaring. "No, no, no… I can't do this on my own. It's too hard. I need you, Lillian. I'll change, I'll be better…I'll do anything. Just stay… I need you to stay. I love you. I love you so much."

Her eyes opened and she kissed me softly. "I know you do, Luc, and I love you, too. That's why I have to do this. But you won't be alone. You'll wake up, and Sawyer will be in your arms…waiting."

I rubbed my forehead back and forth across hers, not wanting to hear it. "No! I don't want to wake up! I want to stay here with you. Please?"

She shook her head against mine. "And that's exactly why I'm doing this…why I'm not staying."

I pulled back to stare at her, my eyes wide with the pain slicing through me. "But why? We're so close…we've gotten so close." I kissed her over and over, hoping I could convince her just how right this was. "I want you…forever. You're mine. I want to show you. I want to make love to you."

She pushed me back, making me stop. "No…it's not real. It won't help you. You need to be with someone real."

Tears dripped repeatedly from her face and I could tell this was killing her to say these things, but right now, my pain was so incomprehensibly great, that I couldn't even care about hers anymore. "How can you do this to me? You said you'd never break up with me…you lied."

She swallowed, a sob escaping her. "Lucas…don't…"

I gripped her arms hard, feeling like I had a way to make her stay…even if it was a manipulative one. "No, you promised. You said you'd never leave. You said you'd always stay by my side. And I *demand* that you keep that promise." My voice broke as I horribly twisted the tender words that she'd spoken over our time together. Twisted them into weapons—weapons designed to hurt, weapons designed to stake her to me with guilt.

She sobbed again as she met my eye. "Oh, Luc, don't…" She shook her head. "Darren's right, we're already gone. I can't break up with you if I'm already gone…"

I shook her arms, knowing that I was probably bruising her. "And yet you are. I'm not breaking up with you! You're the one betraying me!"

A look flashed across her face once I'd said that, and I immediately recognized my mistake. I'd misfired my weapon, because she wasn't the one who had betrayed the relationship. That had been me. A moment of anger seeped into her features as she knocked my hands away from her arms.

"No, I didn't betray you. I never would. But I can't stay here with you. I won't do that to you…or Sawyer." There was strain in her voice as she spoke, and a clear note of jealousy as she said Sawyer's name again.

The guilt swept through me, taking my momentary strength with it. I engulfed her in an embrace. "I'm sorry…please don't go. Please don't walk away from me. I need you. I need to be with you. Please…"

She stiffened and then relaxed, wrapping her arms around me and threading her fingers in my hair. "I'm sorry too, Lucas. I love you…always, but I can't be this person for you. We can't be together…not while you're still alive."

Then she vanished.

Chapter 20 – Fixing a Mistake

I jerked awake, simultaneously gasping for air and begging for Lillian to stay. Silence and darkness answered me as I struggled to reject reality and return to my fantasy, or my nightmare, depending on how you looked at it. Losing all of my friends in rapid-fire succession punched a hole straight through me. My chest ached as badly as it had the night of the crash. It was like it was happening again—like I was losing them all again. Only this time, it felt permanent. I knew I'd never see them again.

Panic seized me, and my gasps for breaths turned into a full-on attack. I couldn't breathe. I struggled with the physical discomfort, but it was nothing compared to the hole ripped open in my chest. That wound was still searing along the edges, like acid had been poured over the top of me, eating me alive.

I twisted and turned in the bed, clutching at anything I could—cool sheets, silky hair, soft skin. I heard a vague voice shushing me and asking what was wrong, but the pounding of blood rushing through my ears was too intense to really pay attention to the voice. Besides, my friend's voices were vibrating through my skull:

"You need to let us go if you're ever going to heal. Don't forget that you lived. I love you…always, but…we can't be together…."

I turned and jerked on the bed while small hands tried to still my shaking body. Unfortunately, Sawyer's bed was smaller than mine, and in my near maniacal twisting I fell right off the edge, landing painfully, face down, on the hard floor. I groaned as what little air I had inside of me was forcefully pushed from my lungs. Taking small breaths when I could, I stayed where I was on the ground.

Sawyer immediately sprinted to my side, her arms encasing me. Her worried face looked me over and then looked upstairs; my fall hadn't exactly been quiet. Her face returned to me but I couldn't make out her features anymore. She was blurry, like a mirage, as my eyes filled with unstoppable tears.

"We can't be together…"

I choked and sputtered, trying to sob and speak at the same time. The only words I could understand coming from my mouth were, "don't leave…please…don't leave me…" Sawyer gathered me in her arms, pulling my limp body to my knees and rocking me, quietly reassuring me that she never would. I didn't know how to tell her that I didn't mean her. I didn't know how to tell her that I'd just lost everyone I loved…aside from her.

After what felt like an eternity of embarrassing blubbering, I numbly dropped my head to her shoulder. I felt drained, empty inside. I had nothing left now, nothing to look forward to, just long days of various forms of torture, and endless nights of…nothingness. They were all gone…and I knew I wouldn't be able to call them to me anymore.

"We can't be together…"

Sawyer sat on her knees before me, holding me tight and stroking my back. When she felt my breathing return to some normalcy, she pulled back. Her hands dried and cupped my cheeks, and her eyes glistened with sympathetic tears at the look on my face. I imagined that if the look was anywhere near how I felt, then I probably resembled walking death. Well, kneeling death anyway.

Swallowing, she started stroking my cheeks. "Oh, Lucas…I'm so sorry," she whispered.

I scrunched my brows and tilted my head. My grief soaked brain couldn't comprehend what she was possibly sorry for. Interpreting my confused look, she shook her head and said, "You dreamed of the crash again? You dreamed of what you remember?"

I shook my head at her, for once actually wishing that I'd had that dream again. That dream would have been downright cheery compared to the one I'd had—the one that had just altered my future from this moment forward. I found my voice creaking out of me as I answered her question that wasn't really a question.

"No…Lillian broke up with me. She left me…they all left me." I felt more tears drop from my eyes to splash on Sawyer's fingers. I didn't care. What did I care about embarrassing tears anymore? What day from now on would have anything but embarrassing tears?

In a sort of overwhelmed trance, I watched her mouth fall open. I wondered if she felt sympathy for me…or if she agreed with my friend's decision. Good for them for leaving my insane ass. I bristled at the idea of yet another person deciding what the best path for me was—I'd been perfectly happy with my delusional life—and awkwardly stood up, before she could respond.

"I need to go home. Can you take me?"

She stood, putting a hand on my arm and looking out the window. It was still fairly dark outside, but the sun had risen and amber light was starting to brighten the world. She turned back to me and nodded. "My parents probably won't be up yet. I'll just leave a note telling them that I wanted to return the dress as soon as possible."

I nodded, barely hearing her as my thoughts swirled. I wasn't sure why I wanted to be home, but honestly, I didn't know where to go to make this despair that was building inside of me end. Home seemed as good a place as any.

I changed back into my dirty clothes while Sawyer dressed in the bathroom. When she came out, she looked me over and then gave me a swift hug before grabbing my mom's dress and telling me she'd meet me outside by her car. I felt myself nod in response, but my entire body slumped down. I felt defeated. I felt like that dream version of me that had gotten his head bashed in by Josh. Only this time, my best friends had done the bashing.

When Sawyer disappeared up the stairs, I crawled out the window. I glumly walked over to her car, opened the unlocked door and got inside, not really caring if her parents spotted me out here or not. She came out her front door a few moments later and joined me. I could feel her eyes on me, but I ignored them, studying the muddy stains on my knees instead. One kind of looked like the rock Josh had killed me with last night.

She cleared her throat. "Luc…"

I didn't respond and she sighed then started her car. I didn't look up as she turned her car around and started out to my house. I didn't even look to see if her parents had heard her car start and turned on their bedroom light, wondering what their baby girl was up to. I just couldn't find it within myself to care anymore.

"We can't be together..."

Time flashed forward in an almost surreal way, and what seemed like only seconds later, she was shutting her car off in my driveway. I blinked and looked over at her. She looked worried and I wondered if I still looked like death...or maybe like the undead would be a better description. Like my body was being animated by some mindless creature, for certainly my soul was gone. My friends had succeeded in ripping that to pieces. What months of torture at the hands of Josh and the townspeople hadn't accomplished, my friends had managed in one night—they'd shattered me. Broken my spirit and left me billowing in the wind...alone.

Sawyer said my name again and again, but I still didn't respond. I didn't know what to say anyway. Was there anything I could say that wouldn't hurt her further? Was there anything I could say that wouldn't hurt me further? I grabbed my mom's dress from the back seat and turned away from her, opening my door.

She mildly surprised me by opening hers as well. Some tiny speck of my brain wanted her to rush home before her parents discovered she was missing...the majority of my brain didn't care anymore. She followed me to my doorstep, saying my name a couple more times. Each time the syllables crossed her lips, more tension crept into her voice.

I remained silent until I walked into the living room, unceremoniously tossing my mom's dress on the couch. It was my mom who broke my silence. She stormed down the hall when she heard the front door open. Her eyes were wide and red as she met mine. I gazed at her blankly, remembering all the vile things Josh had yelled at me about her. I didn't know if they were true...but I had a horrid fireball twisting in my stomach that told me they were. That expanding ball burned away some of my melancholy, as it thawed some of the ache around my heart.

I narrowed my eyes at her as she stormed right up to me. "Mother," I said flatly. She ignored my tone and flicked her eyes up and down, like she was searching me for injuries.

"Are you just getting home? Where have you been?" Her hand flashed back to my bedroom. "I just went to check on you before I had to leave on an errand, and your bed hadn't been slept in." A tear rolled down her cheek as her voice hitched. "Do you have any idea how terrified I was, Lucas? Where were you?"

I heard Sawyer behind me shift and clear her throat. She started to say my mom's name, but I cut her off. Ignoring my mom's question, and the tears on her worn face, I calmly said, "Isn't it a little early for errands?"

That startled my mom and she pulled her head back, appraising me. "I...I just had something I had to..." Her hand came up with a parental "listen to me" finger wag. "Don't distract me by changing the subject—where were you?"

I decided to set the tone for this conversation by being honest. Maybe if I was truthful, Mom would be too. "I spent the night at Sawyer's house...in bed with her." I heard Sawyer gasp behind me at how I'd phrased our innocent sleeping arrangement.

Clearly not expecting my admission, Mom paled and glanced back at Sawyer. Mom stuttered a bit as she considered what to say on the matter. Curious, I let her flounder for words, not clarifying what we'd actually done…or hadn't done.

"Well…I don't… You can't… You're too young." Her face turned considerably pinker as she looked back at Sawyer. I didn't look with her, but I was pretty sure Sawyer was bright red. The anger-despair mix in my belly prevented me from feeling guilty about that. Mom turned back to me. "You're both too young for that, Lucas. We should…sit…and talk…"

Her voice trailed off as I smirked. "About what, Mom? Sex?" I shrugged, not feeling the embarrassment those words would have normally given me. I felt Sawyer put her hand on my arm. She'd apparently caught up to where I was going with this conversation.

"Luc…don't. Not like this…" I heard her mutter. My mom heard her too and shifted her gaze.

I brought her identical eyes back to mine with my next comment. "What can you teach me about sex, Mom? Especially about *not* having it?" I crossed my arms over my chest and leaned back on a hip.

Sawyer begged me to stop this, but I couldn't. If I shut off the flood of anger I was feeling towards my mom…the grief would wash back in, and drown me.

I sniffed and waited for her answer. Her face paled again as she looked over mine. She licked her lips and smoothed back her ponytail. All signs of guilt. My eyes narrowed further as her actions confirmed my suspicions. "What are you talking about, Luc?"

I leaned into her and she took a step back. "What errand were you running?" I took a step towards her, ignoring Sawyer's plea for me to step outside with her. "Did you have another early morning meeting to get to?"

Sudden memories of her anxiously waiting for Sawyer to pick me up, or her dashing out of the house nearly an hour before her shift flooded my brain. The pieces were starting to fit. "You look tired…anymore late night visitors keeping you up?" That memory flooded me, too, and I wondered who really was here that night…and if that had been the first time, or just the only time I'd heard it.

She took a step back, shaking her head and stammering. "What are…? Why are you...? What are you really asking me?" Her voice was barely audible.

I took another step towards her. Sawyer begged me not to say it, but I needed to know. I needed the truth. I said it.

"I'm asking you if you're fucking the sheriff. If you're the whore that everyone thinks you are…"

I really hadn't been sure if the rumor Josh had ruthlessly spouted was true or not. Lord knows, lies spread like wildfire around here, but the pieces had started fitting together more and more with each passing second—the morning meetings, laughing with the mysterious late night visitor, the looks that passed between my mom and the sheriff at the diner, the familiar use of their first names, odd, too-friendly touches, his frequent visits over the summer, the way he always called me Lucas, when he referred to everyone else by last name…the way he said he'd look out for me the night of the crash.

If it was true, then it all made sense now. And as I watched my mom's face pale to a near ghostly white, her mouth dropping open and her eyes starting to water, I knew that it *was* true. My mom was sleeping with the sheriff. No, sleeping was a misnomer; my mom was screwing the sheriff, no sleeping involved.

Her momentary shock wore off and her face suddenly hardened; her hands clenched into fists like she wanted to hit me. She took a step towards me until she was right in my face. I didn't back down. "You do NOT talk to me that way, Lucas Michael West!"

Sawyer pulled my shoulder back and I could hear her crying. I ignored it and focused on the woman before me who had been my shining example of what a human should be. She looked faded to me now. "But it's true! Isn't it! You're sleeping with him and that's why I'm not in jail!"

She held her breath as she took a step away from me. I could see the debate in her eyes. She'd lied about this for so long, that she still naturally wanted to lie about it. Fire burned even hotter in me that she'd even consider lying to me now. She looked over my heated expression and finally let out a long exhale. Stepping back again, her shoulders slumped in defeat. Barely above a whisper, she murmured, "Yes, Lucas…it's true."

My mouth dropped open and a slice of pain went right through me. Even though I knew…it was hard to hear. I shook my head, feeling Sawyer's hand on my shoulder turn comforting. In a softer voice I said, "How could you? How could you lie to me…all this time?"

She dropped her head, and as more amber rays lit the room, I could see a sparkling tear drop to the floor. "Lucas…you wouldn't understand."

My fists clenched as pain shifted back to anger. "You're right, I don't. Did you start something with him just to keep me out of trouble? Was that the deal?"

Mom's head shot up and I heard Sawyer ask me to be gentle. I ignored it and focused on the suddenly irate eyes before me.

"No! There was no…deal. I didn't ask him to do anything, Luc." She flung her hands out to her sides. "We were together long before…"

My eyes widened, and she stopped talking. "You were together before…? How long have you…?" I couldn't even comprehend that my mom may have been lying to me for…years.

Her entire body slumped and she sat heavily onto the arm of the couch, her hands momentarily coming up to cover her face before dropping into her lap. "We've been seeing each other for five years, Luc…" Her eyes aged another decade as she looked up at me.

I felt all of the blood drain from my face. I thought I might drop to the ground, but Sawyer ducked under my shoulder and somehow I remained upright.

Five years? She'd been lying to me since I was twelve? Slowly shaking my head, I could only say, "Mom…he's married…"

She averted her eyes and a sob escaped her. Sawyer patted my chest as I watched my mom's tears fall. The fire in my stomach twisted into something putrid and painful. I felt like I might be sick. I felt like I wanted to run. Why was everyone I believed in letting me down?

"I know, Luc…that's why I had to lie." She looked back up at me, her eyes begging for my understanding. "I hated to do that to you, but you were so young. I couldn't tell you…"

Sawyer murmured that she should leave us alone, and I grasped her hand, hard. I couldn't take her walking out that door right now. Sensing that, she stayed. Drained and confused, I couldn't take standing in place any longer, either. I shuffled over to the couch, dragging Sawyer with me, and sank down heavily into the spot farthest from my mom. She immediately turned on the arm to plop onto the cushion, twisting to face me. Sawyer knelt at my feet, resting her head on her arm over my legs, giving me what comfort she could. Unconsciously, I put my hand on her back, drawing warmth from her, since I felt like I had none of my own left.

A horrid, silent tension built in the room as everyone looked at me, waiting for my reaction. Feeling numb, I could only blankly stare at my mom. Not knowing what else to comment on, I picked the one thing that seemed the most irrelevant. "He's so much older than you, Mom…like fifteen or twenty years."

She blushed and looked down at the cushion separating us. "I know, Luc. That doesn't matter to me." She looked back up at me and whispered, "I love him."

I shook my head and looked down to Sawyer, who was looking up at me with wet, concerned eyes. I stroked her back while I thought of my mom getting it on with a man who could almost be my grandfather. It wasn't a pleasant thought and it did nothing for my stomach. I could barely believe that this was reality. It felt like life was the dream, the nightmare. The one person who had been my example of morality my entire life was having an affair with a married man. It blew my mind. I knew my dad was a louse, but my mom...? Maybe I'd put her on a pedestal, but up until know she'd deserved one. Up until now, she'd been a saint.

I looked back over at her. "It's like I don't even know you…" I whispered.

Her eyes were pained as she softly sobbed my name. "Lucas…"

I shook my head, ignoring the ache in my heart, concentrating on the fire. "What about his wife? How could you do that to her?" I pictured the sheriff's gray-haired spouse, home alone, watching the windows and waiting for her faithful public servant to return to her. I wondered if she knew that her public servant was routinely "protecting and serving" my mother.

My mother sniffed and met my eyes. "I'm not proud of this, Lucas, and we certainly didn't plan to fall in love…" She shook her head as another tear fell to her cheek. "It doesn't excuse it…but his wife has been really sick for years. He takes care of her the best he can, but there hasn't been anything between them for a long time." Her eyes gave me that pleading look again.

"They're still married, Mom. He should divorce her if he wants to be with you."

She sighed. "It's not that simple, Luc. He does love her…in a way, and she's very frail." A clearly adoring look washed over her. "He doesn't want to risk her health by turning her world upside down. We keep it quiet and discreet, so she can live out whatever life she has left in peace."

I gave her a blank stare. "Oh. My. God. You're one of them." She blinked at me and I gestured at her disdainfully. "You're one of those women that believes everything the philanderer says…because he 'loves' them, and surely he'll eventually leave his wife." I couldn't even hide the contempt leaking into my voice and Sawyer tightened a hand on my knee. "Don't tell me you seriously believe that line?"

My mom's gaping mouth shifted from Sawyer, to me, and then back to Sawyer. Finally she looked up at me and sputtered, "It's not a line. He does…he does love me. He's been good to me." Her eyes hardened as they swept over my face. "And very few men in this world have been good to me!"

I turned away from her clear reference to my long-absent father. His leaving had scarred my mom in ways I probably couldn't imagine. Although, with how my chest still felt like the insides had been scooped out with a dull spoon, I was beginning to understand the pain of being abandoned.

Seeing my reaction to her words she whispered, "He's a good man, Lucas…maybe you could give him a chance?"

My head snapped back to her. "Oh yeah, a real shining example." Even as I said it, I could feel the hypocrisy in my words. Was I really getting after a man for cheating on his significant other? Hadn't I done the same? Hadn't I betrayed Lil by making out with Sawyer? Sure, we hadn't technically had sex, but it was one of the most intimate moments of my life…and I'd hurt someone I loved by doing it. Who was I to condemn the sheriff? Or my mom…

I closed my eyes as thoughts of Lillian swarmed through me.

"We can't be together…"

I felt the despair creeping back, my eyes starting to sting, and I frantically grabbed at the lingering fire in my system—anything to hold back the crushing pain. My mother's irritated voice helped stoke that fire, and I reopened my eyes to find her glaring at me. "I don't expect you to understand…you are only a *child*. But someday, you might."

I bristled at her condescending use of the word *child* and felt my hand clench the fabric of Sawyer's shirt. Her hand came up to stroke my arm in response and I relaxed my grip, never taking my eyes off my mom's.

Her face softened as she slumped into the couch. "Where did you hear about it?"

Keeping my voice flat, I told her, "At the dance. People know…they *all* know…" I wasn't actually sure how widespread the rumor was, but it sure explained why people didn't believe I was innocent. They believed my mom's lover had covered it up…they just hadn't had any proof.

She closed her eyes. "Oh God..."

I looked over the defeat on her face, and thought about how the town viewed me, how Josh viewed me—a monster, a horrid creature that had slain my friends and walked away with absolutely no consequences. Staring straight ahead of me, I whispered, "Are you why I didn't get in trouble?"

I heard her answer me but didn't look over, instead keeping my eyes focused on the empty space on the wall above the television set, a spot that used to hold pictures of my friends, before Mom had taken them all down. "Oh, Luc...you tested clean at the hospital..."

I finally did look over at her. She was worrying her lip and searching my eyes. Her small hands were clasping each other so tight, they were nearly white.

"There were a half-dozen things he could have charged me for." I shrugged my shoulders, irritated and pained at talking about that night. "We had an open beer in the car, Mom. He should have given me a MIP at the very least, reckless driving at the most, or even, I don't know, manslaughter."

Her gaze turned sympathetic and she stretched her arm across the space between us to touch my shoulder. I made myself not pull away. "Lucas...you just lost your friends, he didn't feel like he needed to punish you even more."

Then I did pull away, giving her an exasperated look. "Mom?"

She let her hand drop to the couch and she hung her head. Sawyer squeezed my knee again as my mom whispered, "I don't know, Luc...maybe." She looked up, more tears falling from her eyes. "I didn't ask him to."

So there it was. I wasn't being punished for my horrific crime because my mom was spreading her legs. A part of my brain knew I wasn't being fair, a part of my brain knew I was oversimplifying things, but the fire in my stomach pushed all of those rational thoughts aside. My despair crept up my chest to merge with the fire shooting through my veins.

"I murdered all of my friends and got away with it because of you!" I heard my mom and Sawyer start to object to the word "murder," but I cut them off. "No wonder everyone hates me!" Rage, fear, panic and depression, all flooded into me, and I stood up and turned to face them on the couch. Feeling like nothing was real anymore, I glared over at my mom. "It wasn't supposed to happen that way!"

Sawyer stood and placed her hand on my chest, begging me to calm down. My mom stood and put a hand on my arm, her eyes begging for me to relax as well. "I know, Lucas...none of it was supposed to happen."

I took a step away from both of them, running my hands through my hair. I felt like I was going to explode. Everything I knew was falling apart. I hated this...I hated life. I wanted my dream life again, but even that was gone from me now. Everything was gone...

"We can't be together...while you're still alive..."

That was when my brain snapped. I swear, I felt the exact moment that some neuron misfired and a section of my head imploded, as the emotional strain heaped upon it finally broke me. It was a profoundly intense experience, and in that breakage, a moment of clarity hit me. Words from my counselor that had been nipping away at my subconscious suddenly blossomed into life right before my eyes. They mixed with Lillian's last fateful words and suddenly, I understood what I'd been trying to grasp. Suddenly, I knew exactly why everything in my life was such a challenge—why everything was so hard.

"Do you think life ever makes mistakes?"

"Sure, all the time. Some people live who shouldn't…and even more people die who shouldn't."

I knew Mrs. Ryans had meant to stress the latter half of that sentence, but it was the first half that had plagued my brain. It was the first half that now made perfect sense to me when put in combination with Lillian's words. Of course, it was all so obvious now. Some people *live* who shouldn't. I was never meant to have survived that crash. Life had made a mistake.

One that I could fix.

Letting my hands fall to my sides, I looked from one woman to the other. Clarity and determination filled me. I could fix this. I could correct life's mistake. I could find peace. Fixing my gaze on my mom, I calmly told her, "No…my living wasn't supposed to happen. I was never supposed to have survived."

Her mouth dropped, her face going whiter than it had all morning, and she sputtered for words. I didn't let her find any. I immediately turned to Sawyer, thrust my hand into her jeans pocket and wrapped my fingers around her car keys. Before she could react, I jerked my hand out of her pocket, told her I was sorry, and bolted for the front door.

I heard both of them tell me to wait as I jerked the door open. I heard the tension and concern in their voices and I heard a long sob as the door slammed shut behind me. But it didn't matter, it was too late. An error had been made, a grievous one, and I couldn't let it go unresolved.

It all made sense now. Why I couldn't fit in at school. Why I could barely talk to anyone, save Sawyer. Why at times, I barely even felt human anymore. I'd survived something I wasn't meant to. I actually *had* died that day in the ravine. My soul, my spirit, my life-force—whatever you want to call it, had moved on, but somehow, my body had walked away. I'd been drifting aimlessly, torn between the two worlds. I'd tried to fill the void in my life by recreating my friends in a dreamscape, but that was only a patch, and they were right anyway. I couldn't continue on like that. I needed to fix what life had messed up. I needed to be with them…fully.

"We can't be together…while you're still alive…"

Soon Lil…very soon…

I scrambled down the front steps, flipping the keys to get to the one that looked like a car key. I found it and clutched it hard, feeling the unforgiving metal bite into my skin. I opened an unlocked car door and blinked when I realized I'd automatically opened the passenger's side. I'd been so used to not driving that it was now going to have to be a conscious decision to do it. I swallowed and stared at the steering wheel. Of everything I was going to do today, this would probably be the easiest. My heart still spiked though.

I slammed shut the door and turned to sprint to the other side. That's when Sawyer caught up to me. She pummeled into my body, knocking both of my shoulders back until I sat down onto the hood of the car. My mom stood a few paces behind her, fear in her eyes and tears on her cheeks. I started at my new position and glared up at Sawyer.

She was glaring, too, but I saw the fear behind it. I saw the abject terror brimming behind her watery eyes. "What are you doing?" Her voice was forced, like she really wanted to yell at me.

I stood up and put a hand on her shoulder. She pulled back from me, trying to keep her glare, trying to hold onto her anger so she wouldn't break down. I completely understood that feeling. I'd done it myself only moments ago. Checking my emotions, I was a little surprised that both my anger and my fear had dissolved. I felt nothing but peace. I hoped Sawyer would understand why I had to do this…she really was the best thing I had here, but I couldn't stay. I wasn't meant to.

"Sawyer…I have to do this. Please, try and understand." My voice was as calm and peaceful as I felt, but Sawyer only gaped at me, looking hopelessly confused and scared. I brought my hand to her cheek, her tears falling now.

My mother broke out in a sob and jabbed her finger at Sawyer. "I'm calling Sheriff Whitney! Do NOT let him leave until Neil gets here, Sawyer!" She turned and dashed into the house, and I knew the timer on how long I had to leave had just been set. I could fight off Sawyer and my mom…but the sheriff?

"Lucas…" Sawyer muttered, her hand coming up to my chest, clutching at my stained dress shirt. I remembered then that I was still dressed nice and a small smile touched my mouth. Fitting. I should be dressed nice for this occasion. It was sort of a special day. At least I'd look good when I saw Lil again. Now I sort of wished I'd gone with a tie after all.

Sawyer frowned at my smile and I rested my head against hers. With as much conviction as I could, I whispered, "I finally understand. It hurts so much. Life…it hurts so much. I don't feel like I belong. Ever since the crash, I haven't felt like I should be here, and now I know why." I pulled back to look at her. The pain in her eyes made me ache, but it didn't change my resolve. No matter what, I had to right this wrong. I had to set life back on its correct course.

"Luc…I don't understand. You're just where you're supposed to be…" A sob escaped her and I clutched her close to me, shifting us, so she was facing the car and I was free from it. Her hands went up to my cheeks as our heads stayed pressed against each other. I closed my eyes. I would miss her so much, but she was better off with someone else anyway, someone completely a part of this world.

"No, Sawyer. Life, God, fate…I don't know, but someone made a mistake, and I was never supposed to have survived that crash. That's why my dreams feel so real, that's why I'm so drawn to them. I'm supposed to be with them, with Lillian."

Rain started falling then, and not the soft, gentle rain of a spring storm. No, it was the heavy, hard rain of a winter onslaught. The drops around us were huge, and within seconds, the tops of our shirts were drenched. I inwardly smiled at how similar this rain was to that fateful night. It was like the universe understood my intent, and was helping me to fix its mistake. Even more peace and self-assurance went through me. This was right…this was meant to be.

Sawyer eyed me cautiously, the rain dripping down her face only highlighting those wide, worried, slightly almond eyes. "What are you saying, Lucas?" One of her hands dropped from my cheek and trailed down my arm, the arm with the hand currently death-gripping the car key.

Knowing my time was almost up, and knowing Sawyer was about to make her move to stop me, I leaned forward and brought my lips to hers, giving her the one last thing I could, even though she deserved so much better. Her hand came back up to my face as our mouths moved together. She held me close and a sob escaped her. I tasted tears along with the natural sweet taste of her as the rain mixed the two liquids and washed over our bodies. I knew she could feel the goodbye in my kiss. I felt it, too. I knew this would be it for us, and I prayed that the next few months for her weren't too painful. I never wanted to hurt her…and that's all I ever seemed to do. Yet another reason she was better off without me.

Mentally steeling myself, I did something I wasn't proud of, but it needed to be done…for her sake. She needed to let me go. She needed a better life with a better man. That thought echoing in my head, I brought my hands up to her shoulders and shoved her back, hard. Shock was on her face as she hit the side of her car, missing the hood and falling heavily to the hard ground. I didn't stay to make sure she was okay, I didn't have time. I dashed around to the driver's side door, and once inside, immediately locked it and then stretched over to the passenger's side, locking it as well.

As I sat up, Sawyer was standing at the driver's door, tears streaming along with the rain. She clutched at the door handle frantically, screaming my name. I put my hand on the glass and stared at her remorsefully. I regretted ever causing this beautiful woman pain and I hoped she knew that. I hoped she knew how I felt about her, that she knew she was the only thing that had brightened my life over the past few months, and that I did indeed love her. I still had to do this though…

She put her hand on the glass, flexing her fingers like she was trying to lace our hands together through the cold, wet barrier. I removed my hand and, out of habit, buckled my seatbelt. I paused with the key just touching the ignition. A brief moment of fear, mixed with determination and anticipation, coursed through me. It settled into peace almost instantly. This was right…I had no reason to fear it. Her eyes widened as she watched my fingers insert the key, and then she started pounding on the glass, maybe trying to break through the door.

"What are you gonna do, Luc?" she yelled at me, her face frantic.

I stared at her terrified eyes for a brief moment before answering her. "I'm only fixing a mistake." I turned the keys and started the car, never taking my eyes from Sawyer.

Her hands pounded ruthlessly on the glass as the engine roared to life; I was sure she'd have bruises tomorrow. "What are you gonna do?" she yelled again, the tears welling in her eyes almost indistinguishable from the heavy drops falling around her.

A moment of grief welled in me. She was the only one I'd truly miss, the only one that had never let me down. No, all of the letting down in our relationship had come from me. "I'm sorry," I mouthed to her.

She shook her head, muttering, "No, please…don't." From the corner of my eye, I saw the front door of my house open and knew my mom was soon to be flying down the stairs and throwing herself on top of the car if need be. I didn't want that.

I slammed the car into reverse, peeling out of the wet driveway in my haste. My mom ran to the spot I'd just been, screaming at me. Sawyer covered her mouth with her hands, shaking her head in horror. And then I took off, leaving them both in the driveway, in a downpour, looking terrified and distraught. I felt bad for the fear they had, and for the pain I knew they'd both go through once I'd finished this, but I had to finish it. I was never supposed to have survived that crash. That's why everything had been so hard lately and why my dreams had felt more real to me than life. I wasn't supposed to be here. One day, I was sure they'd both see that.

I drove more steadily than I'd ever believed I could. The rain sheeted down my windshield as I flew out of the city limits, out onto that fateful highway. The onslaught brought on memories of that night. They tumbled through my brain, one after another, each one only solidifying my decision—I was never supposed to have survived. I saw that now. The tiny disco ball on Sawyer's rearview mirror gently swung back and forth, like it was agreeing with my conclusion.

I wasn't sure if I'd be able to find the same exact spot in the road where I'd gone over the rail. It had been dark and pouring that night, but then, like a flaming neon sign, the bend came into focus. It seemed to glow at me. Faint, black lines on the asphalt from Darren's Geo were suddenly huge landing lights, showing me exactly where I needed to go over the edge. The exact point of contact was highlighted by a makeshift memorial that some of the kids at school must have created. It was supposed to be honorary, for the lives lost, but it was about to be a bull's-eye for another life, one that *needed* to be lost.

As I drove past the bend, I could see that the weakened guard rail I'd busted through the first time had been replaced. It looked strong and sturdy now. But I was no longer in a cheap, Styrofoam beginner's car. I was in a revved up muscle car and given enough speed, I'd slice through that metal like butter. And this time, my goal was speed. This time, brakes were the last thing on my mind.

I turned the car around so I could approach the bend from the same direction I had that night. I wanted everything to be the same, I wanted to perfectly recreate that moment—set the timeline straight. If I could have, I'd have stayed out here until nightfall, so it would be just as dark as the first time. I didn't have that kind of time, though. Either my mom, Sawyer or the sheriff would find me before then. I would just have to settle for the hazy, gray overcast light of this rainy morning. Oh well, it helped me see exactly where I needed to go anyway.

I stopped the car a half mile from the bend and stared at it. My demon. It was like staring down at the darkest part of myself. This is where my life had turned one eighty. This is where my life had ended. This is where my life would end. I unbuckled my seat belt.

This time…it would end.

Chapter 21 – Back to the Beginning

Moments passed as I stared at the metal railing barring me from my fate. I felt nothing inside of me but conviction, a cold resolve that everything would be better after I went through with this. I'd be truly reunited with my friends. Sawyer would be freed from her mothering need to take care of me, free to find a satisfying relationship with someone who could love her the way she deserved to be loved. I hoped, whoever he was, that he appreciated the amazing woman in his arms. And my mother could live out her years with Sheriff Whitney…Neil. With their secret already out, they could be more open with each other. And without me around to worry about and stress over, she could fully and completely love him. It made me smile that my mom wouldn't be alone.

I revved the engine a few times as rain splattered on the empty stretch of roadway, soaking it. No one had passed me or come up behind me as I sat, stopped, in the middle of my lane. It was still early in the morning, and this road was little traveled anyway. The familiar, soothing scent of lemons washed over me and I inhaled deep, glad that this calming scent would be the last thing I took with me. The wipers swished noisily back and forth, and I tore my eyes from the guard rail to watch their rapid movement, taking in every minute detail of my last moments on Earth.

I wasn't worried about the pain. I would take whatever I had to take to get my end result. Whatever mortal pain was necessary to transfer from this state to the next. Any physical pain could hardly compare to my months of emotional pain anyway. What were shattered bones and bleeding cuts compared to your heart being torn and shredded into thousands of pieces? Nothing…absolutely nothing.

A song on one of Sawyer's chick rock CDs (that I actually secretly liked) came on, and I turned it up. Ironically, it was a song about surviving a suicide attempt. I didn't like to think that what I was doing was suicide—I was merely fixing a mistake, but I suppose that's not what my official death record would say. The town would run rampant with rumors of how I'd driven off and dramatically taken my own life.

I sighed and hoped my mom wouldn't have to hear too much about it, that people would be kind to her over her loss. Maybe she and the sheriff could move away once his wife passed on from her illness. They could heal each other. I smiled wider as I pictured the great life they could have together.

As the haunting but beautiful lyrics drifted through my brain, I turned my attention back to the guard rail. I blinked, startled, when I noticed a car there that hadn't been there before. A car that I knew very well. A car that was currently blocking the predetermined path of my demise. I blinked again, not understanding what my mother's station wagon was doing parked in front of my bulls-eye. How had she found me so fast?

Then the station wagon door opened and a figure stepped out into the rain. I immediately understood how I'd been found, as I watched Sawyer shut the door, her clothes and hair drenched from the downpour. Sawyer and I nearly had the same mind at times, and if anyone could guess where I'd go to end my life, it would be her.

I should have realized that earlier and not spent so much precious time ruminating. I should have pieced it together that the Safe and Sound Club had probably been out here, on more than one occasion, to maintain the shrine that was sort of their reason for being. Even though Sawyer and I had never talked about this spot, of course she'd know exactly where it was.

She stood in front of the car door defiantly, arms over her chest, and I clearly understood the message, even from this distance—"You want this, you'll have to go through me to get it." I revved the engine, hoping she would move. She didn't. She didn't even flinch. I did it again, letting the car surge forward a few feet. Nothing. She didn't even react. Well, maybe she did lift her chin higher. She wasn't going to budge on this.

I cursed and slammed my hand on the wheel. She was ruining everything! She'd never let me down before. Why was she doing it now? I glanced at her corsage still hanging from the rearview mirror. Where before, I'd seen the broken petals as symbolic of our horrid night at the dance, now they seemed to mock my desperation. Gritting my jaw, committing myself to the action, I revved the car and slammed on the gas. I hated to take her with me, but I *had* to do this, I couldn't stop myself.

The car propelled forward, the rain forcefully smacking the windshield. She still didn't move. I was going to plow right into her. I imagined the car slicing her in two and tears stung my eyes. I imagined the life leaving her body and I felt a sob rise. The haunting lyrics of living through the pain played on through the car's speakers, searing me. The pleasing scent of lemons always present in Sawyer's car choked me. I loved her…I couldn't kill her.

I knew to not slam on the brakes in this downpour, so I gently eased them down, the car slowly responding. I was still going too fast to stop in time from hitting her though, so I turned the wheel, heading for the edge of the road. The car hit the gravel and I jerked the brakes down, spinning a bit on the loose rocks, but stopping without sliding.

My heart racing at what I'd nearly committed to doing, I cursed and slammed my hand against the wheel repeatedly. I looked out the window at Sawyer on the other side of the street, still standing in front of my mother's car, watching me. Her eyes were wide and she was ghastly pale, shaking uncontrollably. She'd thought I wasn't going to stop. And she still hadn't been going to move. If I was going…she was going.

I jerked open my door, angry that she'd throw her life away for me, and slammed it shut behind me. She straightened at my approach, dropping her hands to her sides, fists clenched for a fight. I shook my head as I walked right up to her, the rain drenching me, running down my face.

"What the hell do you think you're doing?"

Her eyes narrowed as she glared at me, the gray depths matching the stormy clouds above. "What am I doing?" She thrust a finger into my chest. "What the hell are *you* doing?"

I batted her finger away, frustration rising in me. I needed to do this. I needed to do it now…while I still could. "Get out of the way, Sawyer!"

She crossed her hands over her chest again, thrusting her chin out at me.

"No! This is insane, Lucas! I'm not just going to *let* you do this!"

I threw my hands into my wet hair, feeling like I wanted to yank it out of my scalp. She was messing up everything! And I'd been so close. "Ahhh! It's already done!" I jerked my hand over to the railing, indicating the ravine where my dead body should already be lying. "This is what was supposed to happen. I'm just fixing an error!"

She shoved her hands into my chest, knocking me back a step. Her face got right into mine, fiery and frightened. "Fixing an error? You lived for a reason, Lucas!"

I threw my arms out to the sides. The water droplets flying from my hands smashed into the droplets falling from the sky. The violence in the air around me only added to my conviction—today was a day for destruction. "No! There is no reason!" None to stay alive, anyway. I had plenty of reasons to stop.

Sawyer, her face paler than I'd ever seen, stepped forward and grabbed my cheeks. Fear outweighed the fury in her voice as she spoke over the pounding rain. "This isn't the way."

I shook my head in her hands, my own anger ebbing. "It has to be. I can't move forward, I can't go back…this is it for me." My eyes flicked over to the ravine again, hoping she'd understand, hoping I understood.

She shifted my head back to her when I started to stare longingly at the point of impact I so wished to meet up with. "No! You have to stay here. It *will* get better." Her eyes searched mine frantically as she swallowed and worried her lip, marked with beads of water. "Please, believe me."

I pulled her hands from my face. They seemed so small and fragile at the moment, and I wished she hadn't come out to witness this. It would be better for her if she'd found out after the fact.

"I remember everything, Sawyer, and it's killing me. I wish I could forget! I'd do anything to forget. I remember the rain, I remember losing control. I remember slamming into that guard rail and going right through it. I remember everyone screaming and then I remember…silence….and blood. So much blood. How do I forget that? How do I possibly forget that? How do I move on?" I took a step back from her, staring at the guard rail again. "How does any of *that* get better?"

She let out a soft sob and I turned my eyes back to her. I so wished she hadn't come. "Please, Luc! I don't know how, but you have to find a way!"

I put my hands up to my chest. "But that's just it—I don't want to anymore. I don't want to go on. I'm done!"

She threw herself at my body, her hands wrapping around my waist, her wet hair sticking to my arms like tethers trying to bind me to this world. "No, you have to stay. I *demand* you stay!" I couldn't help but note the similarities between her words and the words I'd spouted at Lillian. It wouldn't work for her anymore than it had worked for me, though. It was too late.

I tried to push her off of me, but she clawed and pulled in a ferocious attempt to stay attached to my body. We struggled with each other, until both of us were panting from the exertion; the rain never stopped its relentless soaking.

Eventually, I managed to firmly grab onto both of her wrists and hold them in front of me. Her eyes begged me as surely as her voice. "Please, you have to deal with the pain—we all do!"

Exhausted and frustrated at the physical and emotional battle I hadn't been prepared for, I snapped back, "What the hell do you know about pain, Sawyer?"

Her eyes hardened and she gave me a glare that would have sent any other boy heading for cover. I matched her look though, not backing down from this fight, not when what I wanted was so close to me, just a few yards over her shoulder.

Without a word, she twisted her wrists in my grasp and shoved her arms forward. Her clothes and skin were so wet that the fabric of her long sleeves bunched up around my fingers, the material sliding up her arms to her elbows. I looked down, confused…and then I stopped and stared, my mouth wide open.

"I may not understand exactly what you feel, Lucas, but I understand pain!"

I couldn't answer her; I was still staring at her arms. When she'd twisted them in my grasp, she'd turned her palms up to me. When she'd shoved her arms forward, my grasp on her shirt had exposed her inner arms. And for the first time, I completely understood why Sawyer always dressed in long-sleeved clothes. I remembered back to her habit of unconsciously playing with her long sleeves, and thought that maybe it wasn't an unconscious habit after all…maybe it was a reminder. A reminder, of the thick, three inch long scars running vertically down each wrist.

I relaxed my hold on her and ran a thumb down each telltale mark. She tried to pull away, but I had enough of a grasp on her to not let her keep hiding herself from me anymore. I thought back to her panicked look when Ms. Reynolds had been holding her wrist, and thought that this was something she probably hid from everyone.

My own pain momentarily forgotten, I looked back up to her tear and rain streaked face. "What did you do, Sawyer?" I whispered.

She shook her head remorsefully. "Something so stupid…I can hardly believe it sometimes." We both relaxed our positions until I was holding her fingers, lacing them with mine. "After that jerk of a guy used me…I couldn't deal. One night, sitting home alone, I just decided enough was enough…my life would never get better. I'd never love like that again, and nothing but pain awaited me." She shrugged as her eyes flicked between mine. "I didn't want to live another day in that agony, and I couldn't see a way out of it. I busted into my dad's liquor cabinet, busted into my mom's medicine cabinet, and started chasing sleeping pills with whiskey shots."

Her eyes lost focus and looked through me, back into her past. I gripped her fingers tight as she continued with her nightmare. "When that didn't work fast enough for me…I found a box knife in the garage. I sat on the floor and sliced each arm." Her gaze returned to mine. "I didn't even think about it…I didn't even feel it." Her lip twisted wryly. "I gave myself a trio of death…one of which was sure to claim me."

She blinked and shook her head, her voice starting to waver. "My parents came home, sometime after I passed out, and found me…bleeding all over their garage." She sniffed and heavy tears ran down her already wet cheeks. "They barely got there in time. A few more minutes…" She sighed. "That's why they don't give me much leeway now, why they moved us to the middle of nowhere. They're scared I'll try that again."

She dropped one of my hands and brushed the tears and rain off my cheek, mixing them into my skin as she softly stroked me. "But I'd never, ever try that again. Because I see now…that things *do* get better." She stepped closer to me so that our bodies were touching. I vaguely noticed that the rain was starting to let up, only a few droplets splashed on her cheeks and black hair as she lovingly gazed up at me. "I see that because of you, Lucas…because I fell in love with you."

She leaned up and brushed her lips against mine. I felt the crushing grief enter me as her lips touched mine. Grief that maybe I couldn't go through with this…grief that maybe I'd have to endure this nonstop pain even longer. I couldn't. I couldn't imagine another day feeling this way. A sob escaped me as our mouths moved together.

"I can't… I can't…" I mumbled between our kiss.

Her hands came up to my cheeks, her scars still visible to me in my watery peripheral. "You can…I'll help you. I love you."

I saw a patch of stale sunlight illuminate the top of my mom's car behind her and knew the storm was passing, moving on to another location. Panic seized me; it felt like my window of opportunity was closing. Like if I didn't do this now, while the conditions were similar to that night, then I'd never be able to do it…

I shook my head and stepped back from her. The rain around me was shifting to a gentle shower. I was running out of time. My breath started coming in sharp pulls—I had to do this. "I'm sorry…I'm not as strong as you, Sawyer." I backed away farther and her hand snaked out to grab the wet dress shirt clinging to my shaking body. She grabbed the top and pulled, trying to keep me near her, her eyes wide.

"You are! You're stronger than you think." She shook her head, her hair sticking to her neck. A patch of brighter sunlight hit her and for a moment, she truly did look like the angel she was. I'd miss her so much.

"You're wonderful, Lucas." Her other hand came up to clutch at my shirt, pulling me into her. "You're warm and funny and loving. You belong here…with me."

My voice came out in a sob as I tried to remove her fingers from my clothes. "I'm not supposed to be here…" I successfully removed her hands and clenched them in mine, wanting her to understand that I needed to do this, and I needed to do it alone. "Please…leave, Sawyer. You shouldn't have to see this."

Dropping her hands, I turned to sprint back to the Camaro. I'd find another way around her if she wasn't going to move. The rain was stopping, I needed to hurry. But Sawyer wasn't about to let me go without a fight. As I turned, she flung her arms around my waist, physically restraining me with everything inside her small body. I twisted in her arms, struggling to break free. "Stop, Sawyer, let me go!"

She sobbed into my back, her voice nearly muffled from our struggle. "No,

I'll never let go, Luc!"

We struggled together, but I was stronger than her. I eventually pulled us both into the middle of the highway. I started to panic as we became more exposed to the open road. It would serve my purpose if a car flew around the corner and struck *me*, but I didn't want to see Sawyer get hurt. Panic gave me the extra edge I needed to break away from Sawyer's adrenaline-filled grasp. I finally extracted myself and gave her a shove, merely intending to stall her to give me the time I needed to get back to the car.

As I ran, I watched her harshly land on the ground. Her hands behind her broke her fall, but it still looked like it had hurt, and for a second, I debated turning around to help her. But I felt sunlight on my face and not raindrops, and I twisted back around to the still running car. I didn't have time to help her.

As I opened the door, I heard from behind me, "Don't you love me?"

She had yelled that and the sound of her question echoed throughout my entire body. I closed my eyes and inhaled deep. Turning, I opened my eyes to see her standing in the middle of the road with her arms outstretched. Her face held more fear, anger and love than I'd ever seen on anyone.

"Yes," I said, simply.

Her hands clenched into fists as she stared across the road at me. I flicked quick glances up and down the street, praying that she'd move before she got hurt. Seemingly in sync again, her words echoed my thoughts. "You said you'd never hurt me." She pointed to the embankment I was aching to go over. "*This* will hurt me, Lucas!"

I slumped as I watched her. That would be my only regret, and she knew it. She was digging her finger in the one wound that made this an almost difficult decision for me. I would miss her, and I had no desire to hurt her. I couldn't see a way around that though…and it was too late to stop.

"Please…forgive me," I begged.

She stalked over to where I was standing in the open door. A part of me relaxed that she was now safe, a part of me worried that since she'd succeeded in making me pause, she would now succeed in making me stop, and then I'd fail. I didn't want to fail. I couldn't live like this anymore…I didn't want to.

She stepped right up to me, pressing her wet, shivering body into mine. "No, I don't forgive you. I'll never forgive you for this."

My face fell as she confirmed that my biggest regret was a warranted one. "But…but you understand." My hand reached down to her wrist, lifting it.

She understood the reference and shook her head, lifting her other wrist level with the first. "These were mistakes that I somehow managed to live through." She shook her head again and then grabbed my face. "Don't make my mistake."

Confusion flooded through me, as the sound of dripping water filled my ears; water dripping from leaves and branches, not the sky. The storm had stopped. The sound was reminiscent of that night, of the water dripping in the car. I shivered, and not from the cold.

"Mistake?" I whispered, not understanding the simple word. The only mistake I saw was my life being allowed to continue. I was supposed to die. It was fated, and you don't mess with fate.

My eyes had drifted to the ravine and she brought my attention back to her. "Yes, Luc…mistake. You were meant to live. You were saved." She shook her head, her face soft with compassion. "You were spared…just like me."

I was shaking my head, fresh tears falling, but she continued before I could object. "Would you rather *I* was dead, Lucas? That I hadn't survived?" I violently shook my head and drew her into me. No, I couldn't imagine that fate. She exhaled into my soaked shoulder, her arms going around my neck. "That's the same way I feel about you." Her hand twisted into my slick hair and she pulled back to gaze at me intently. "You're my miracle. Don't take that from me."

I felt something crack in me and I wanted to object, but words failed me. It felt like the window had fully closed, snapped shut, never to be reopened. I'd missed my chance. Despair crept into those cracks and a soft sob escaped me. Sawyer lovingly stroked my cheek. "I love you, Lucas. Heart and soul, I love you. I can't imagine a world without you in it. Please…stay."

I still couldn't answer; sobs were stealing my words. The grief I felt within me welled to such a painful point that I thought I might break apart. I'd never see Lil again. I'd never see any of them again. As my determination failed me, I started to feel the icy cold that I'd been standing in for a while. My body started to shake in earnest as the wet clothes stuck to my wet skin, creating a coldness on the outside that matched the coldness of my hollowed out inside.

Sawyer stroked my shaking arms, ignoring how her own wet body was shaking just as badly. "Stay here," she whispered. "Stay here with me. We'll figure it out together."

The coldness and loneliness overwhelmed me, finally broke me. I sank into the seat and lay over my knees, sobbing. She knelt down with me, her hands caressing my back. She murmured words of love and encouragement while my pain came out in wails. When I could breathe through the torture, I mumbled into my knees.

"They're gone…they're all gone."

She murmured in my ear in response. "I know, Luc. But I'm not gone. I'm right here…and I'm not going anywhere. Neither me nor your mom are going to leave you." As she spoke, I felt her reach over me and shut off the car. My sobbing increased.

It was an empty promise; no one can say they are never going to leave, not with life being as unpredictable as it could be. I understood that better than most. But the words gave me the faintest glimmer of something anyway. Something that nearly felt like everything was going to be okay, and I struggled to hold onto it, to absorb it into me so it could outweigh the crushing sadness. But it was a slippery emotion, and I failed to fully grasp it. I bent over and continued my sobbing.

I heard words escape through my tears, although I had no control over them. "They abandoned me…Lil abandoned me…."

I heard myself repeating it over and over in a nearly maniacal way, and Sawyer continued her soothing tone and soothing movements, repeatedly saying, "They didn't, Luc…they died. No one left you…they were taken from you. There's a difference…"

"Oh God, Sawyer…they're really gone…" The crying started in earnest at that point.

I don't know how long she comforted my crying body, but eventually, in the distance, I heard a siren approaching. I didn't look up from my lap as the siren got louder and louder. I mumbled more words, some coherent, some not, and Sawyer gave me comforting responses in return, always assuring me that she was here, and that she wasn't leaving.

Her hands rubbed warm patches into my back as my head rested on my knees. The siren stopped and I heard a door open in the distance, but it sounded foggy, like I was hearing it through a tunnel. I thought maybe I was going to pass out from the strain, but somehow consciousness stayed with me. And then, through that haze, I heard a voice calling my name in a panic. I lifted my head, not sure who was calling for me. I ruefully noticed the blue patches of cloudless sky above me, marred by only a few gray swatches of stormy clouds now, and those not looking like there was a drop of rain left in them. I'd failed. Some tiny, tiny part of my brain felt relief in that as Sawyer held me.

The person continued yelling my name, and Sawyer's body was jerked aside to make room for my mom. Sawyer stepped back, her stormy eyes never leaving my face, as my mom squatted in front of me. She threw her arms around me and squeezed so tight I couldn't fully inhale. I let her. Guilt filled me as she began to sob. The guilt increased tenfold when she started to sob apologies.

"I'm so sorry, Luc. I'm so sorry I lied." A figure stepped behind her, placing a hand on her shoulder.

I looked up from my mom to the sheriff standing by Sawyer in the open car door. His face was solemn, his steel eyes watery. He blinked a few times and shook his head. "I'm sorry too, Luc. We should have told you."

I dropped my head and shut my eyes. I hadn't wanted to see their pain. It was so much easier to imagine them years after the fact, when they were already over me. But my absence would have been just as painful for them as the death of my friends was for me. Maybe worse, since they'd have the added guilt of feeling like they'd pushed me over the edge…which they hadn't, not specifically anyway. It was multiple small events that had made this seem the only way out. As I shifted my focus between my mom, the sheriff and Sawyer, clarity filled me again, a less dramatic clarity than before, but no less profound. I didn't want to hurt the people who loved me. I didn't want them to feel the pain I felt. I didn't want them to feel responsible for my death, the way I felt responsible for my friends'.

I didn't want…to die.

I slung my arms around my mom and held her to me. While she sobbed, my eyes locked with Sawyer's. "I'm sorry," I said softly, speaking to both of them.

They both nodded, my mom on the verge of an emotional breakdown in my arms. Finally Sheriff Whitney pulled her back. She turned and embraced him in a way I'd never seen her embrace anyone. I stared at them a moment, at the obvious love between them, and thought maybe my mom was right. Maybe I was too young to understand their situation. I inhaled deeply, releasing it slowly. Well, maybe I was too young to fully understand it, but I wasn't too young to condemn it solely on principle. Who was I to judge where two people found love?

A sob rose in me, as my thoughts drifted back to my love…Lillian. Sawyer resumed her squatting position in front of me, her hands rubbing my wet, shaking legs. She looked over my face with concerned eyes. "Lucas?"

The sob broke free as a wave of guilt and grief washed over me. I might have been able to halt the desire to end my life—and even that was still sort of teetering back and forth—but the desire to live wasn't exactly bringing me sunshiny feelings. No, I wasn't being overwhelmed by some sudden need to seize the day and make the most of each moment. I was still crushed—devastated and feeling alone. I still hated myself…and what I'd done.

"I killed them, Sawyer…all of them."

Tears fell from my eyes and she cupped my cheeks. "No…it was an accident, Luc. Let it go, baby." She flushed a bit after she said that, and I smiled for a micro-second before grief swept over me, crushing me.

I knew if I was going to survive this day…I'd need help. I scooted forward a bit and reached into my back pocket. Finding my wallet, I pulled it out and gave it to my mom. She took it with an eager expression, wanting to help me in any way possible. She raised an eyebrow and in-between tears I told her to call Beth. She looked at Sawyer, confused, and Sawyer, her mind in line with mine again, thankfully explained for me.

"His counselor…Mrs. Ryans. Her card must be in there somewhere."

My mom nodded and immediately pulled out her cell phone while Sheriff Whitney watched the road, ever cognizant of the potential danger of so many cars pulled alongside the highway right at a sharp corner. I heard my mom's animated voice, talking rapidly and emotionally to someone on the other end of the phone. I tuned it out and focused on Sawyer, focused on my peace. I tried to make the comfort I used to get from her return to me. It was harder to do now; I had much more painful memories attached to her than before. But watching those pale eyes stare back at me unblinkingly, watching the beautiful shape of her lips, the arch of her brow, the spot where I knew my hidden dimple lay buried, eventually, I found a small level of comfort. Knowing that that was probably all I'd get today, I soaked it in.

"Thank you," I whispered, my voice so hoarse it was nearly comical.

She didn't laugh though. Instead, tears leaked from her eyes. "You're welcome…don't *ever* try that again."

A small smile crept into my lips and I nodded. Exhaustion overtook me and I lowered my head to hers. She ran her fingers back through my hair in a soothing, repetitious pattern, and we waited. Waited for me to feel well enough to live.

A numbness settled into me and I was vaguely aware of voices talking about me in the background. I stared without really seeing, my head a blank slate for once. I became aware of being removed from the car and shifted into the passenger's seat, although I had no idea who'd actually moved me over. Then the car restarted and I was leaving this cursed place. I was going home.

A hand came over to grasp mine and I clenched it, not knowing whose is was. A soft, comforting voice filled the car and I only caught the soothing, feminine tone, not the actual words. Within moments, we were pulling back into my driveway, where a strange car was already parked along the street, waiting for us. My mom's wagon pulled up next to us, and I looked over at her haggard face staring at me through the window. She stepped out of her car and opened my door, helping me out.

I blankly watched her as she grabbed my hand and helped me stand. She was drier than me, but looked just as worn; her eyes were red and her face was sickly pale. The sheriff came up to help her, having driven himself to our house, and the two of them clumsily got me inside. They walked me to the couch and sat me on it. I sort of felt like a rag-doll, an empty shell that people could move around and dress up to look human, but I wasn't really sure if that's what I was anymore.

I heard Sawyer's voice enter the house and I instinctively turned to look for her. She was walking through the door with Mrs. Ryans…Beth. She was animatedly telling her something. Beth nodded and eyed me with a furrowed brow. In my numb haze, I couldn't make out the words, but I could picture them well enough. Sawyer was replaying the events that had happened on the highway. I didn't care. I didn't care what Sawyer said to her. I had no secrets anymore.

Mom anxiously went up to Beth, grabbing her hands and making a pleading noise. I couldn't tell what she was saying either, but I figured she was begging the professional to save her damaged son. If I could have felt any emotions at the moment, I'd probably have felt really guilty about that.

Beth nodded and tried to remove her hands from Mom's grasp, but Mom was holding her tight, like she was her lifeline or something. Eventually the sheriff had to walk over and remove her, pulling her into the kitchen. Sawyer eyed me on the couch and looked torn as to whether or not she should join me. I watched her curiously, not knowing what I wanted since I wasn't letting anything fully enter my consciousness. Beth brought a hand to her shoulder and told her something. Sawyer nodded at her and then turned to wait in the kitchen, giving me one final supportive glance before she left.

Beth came over and sat in a chair next to the couch. She didn't say anything, just smiled at me. I stupidly smiled back, just like that doll again, mimicking life, but not really meaning it. She inhaled a big breath and let it out slowly. I did the same. "Lucas…" she said softly. I nodded and waited. "How are you?"

I looked down, numbness still the overriding feeling in my body. Knowing nothing would hurt me right now, I looked back up at her and spoke more honestly than I usually did. "I tried to kill myself today."

She gave me a sympathetic smile and nodded. The pride on her face that I'd admitted something extremely painful, freely, was evident. "I know, Lucas," she whispered. "I'm so glad you called for me."

I exhaled and it felt like my first true exhale in months. I felt pieces of myself reenergizing with that exhale. Rebooting, like I'd turned myself off, and the computer within me was resetting itself. I hoped whatever bug was in my system cleared itself out with this restart.

For the rest of the morning, I talked. Beth occasionally asked me questions, but mainly it was just me talking. I told her everything. I held nothing back, no bit of darkness, no edge of insanity, no self-hatred—nothing. As my emotions came back to life…it hurt, and I had several panic attacks that Beth calmly helped me to breathe through. Then I'd break into crying spells and she'd rub my arm and tell me to keep going. Eventually though, I told her everything I'd bottled up since the accident.

At some point, I lay down on the couch and threw my arm over my eyes. I occasionally heard people talking quietly in the kitchen, or objects moving around, and I knew every person in there could hear what I was saying. I still didn't stop, though. I spoke of the party we'd gone to that night. I spoke of Darren and Sammy, our friendship and their eternal bond to each other. I spoke of the accident and my horror regarding it. And I spoke of Lillian.

She was the most painful to talk about, but I did. I spoke of every aspect of our relationship. How intimate we'd been in life, but how we'd never taken that last leap into admitting our love out loud, and how we'd never physically shared that love with each other. I admitted even more intimate details of how we'd nearly done both of those things in my dreams. I went into an embarrassing amount of detail over how close we'd gotten to almost consummating our relationship. I'm sure I blushed a few times, but Beth only nodded and encouraged me to continue, and I did because I needed to talk about it with someone…alive.

Hours later, when my words ran dry, I remained on the couch while Beth went to talk to my mom for a moment. I nodded at her, too exhausted to speak anymore, although I did manage a thank you before she left the room. I was drained from an overly emotional couple of days. Or had it only been one day since the dance? It felt like years.

I felt rubbed raw, inside and outside, but a small smile was on my face as I stared up at the ceiling. I still felt a horrible sadness and an aching pain—that didn't magically go away or anything—but I did feel lighter. And for the first time in a long time, maybe for the first time since the crash, I felt something stirring in me that almost resembled…hope.

Sawyer came out and sat on the edge of the couch while the adults talked about me in the kitchen. I grabbed her hand, and blinkingly gazed up at her. I could feel the need for sleep filling me and she seemed to see that in me, too. She bent down and brushed some hair off of my forehead before she kissed it. Her black locks swept over my chest, and the familiar, comforting scent of lemons washed over me as she gave me a swift hug.

Leaning down, she whispered in my ear, "Get some sleep, Lucas. I love you."

I felt a love-filled ache building in my chest, and I slung my arms around her, pulling her tight to me. "Stay with me," I barely squeaked out, my throat raw from talking and tears. She nodded, and brought her legs up onto the couch, her arms wrapping around me. Despite our still slightly damp clothes, she was cocooning me in her warmth and in her love. I closed my eyes, feeling slumber rapidly approaching.

Before I completely gave into it, I twisted to bury myself even more into her sheltering embrace. My head fell into the crook of her neck, and I kissed her warm skin. "I love you, too," I whispered, before passing out from exhaustion.

I had no dreams that day and was relieved for it.

Chapter 22 – How Different the World Can Look

Sawyer didn't leave my side much during break. Either I was at her house, in her dorm-like room downstairs, or she was hanging with me at my place. It had taken a bit of effort to get that kind of clearance for her; her parents had been furious when they'd woken up the morning of my "attempt" and discovered her gone. It had taken my mother going over there (with Sheriff Whitney no less) to convince them that Sawyer had saved my life and shouldn't be punished for it. Of course, none of us mentioned that I'd spent the previous night in bed with her. Leniency only went so far, after all.

After that revelation, her parents were far more encouraging of our relationship. They engaged me more when I came over, and I tried to be engaging in return. Sometimes it felt forced, like when we were all seated at dinner and they started discussing what Sawyer had done for me. I could tell they were proud of her, and even though they were respectful to me, avoiding any of the actual reasons I'd made the attempt, an icy ball knotted my stomach. Only Sawyer's hand on my skin made it melt.

The free time we spent alone together was usually spent talking. Once she and Beth had finally gotten me to open up, I couldn't seem to shut up. I went over every aspect of the crash with Sawyer. She constantly assured me that it had only been a horrid accident that could have happened to anyone. I also went over every dream of mine with her—every nightmare *and* every fantasy. I'd wanted to skip over the ones with Lil, but with a warm hand on my back, Sawyer had encouraged me to not leave her out, since she'd been so vastly important to me. So I didn't. I went over every intimacy and every desire I'd ever had. Sawyer's cheeks flushed and she studied her hands…but she listened.

Surprisingly, it helped. I'm not sure why. I don't know why the simple act of sharing your burden with someone else makes it lighter, but I certainly felt that way. I completely lost the desire I'd had to drive out to that bend…or even to see it again, really. That's not to say that everything in my life was instantly perfect, but I no longer felt the need to "fix the mistake" as I'd so naïvely put it.

I cringed whenever I thought about what I'd almost done, what I *would* have done if Sawyer hadn't stopped me. I'd been so sure. I'd been absolutely positive that what I'd been about to do was the correct path for me. I'd had no reservations about ending my life, and that knowledge gave me chills. The fact that Sawyer knew, and had gone through a decision as chilling as mine, bonded us in a way that surpassed the relatively short amount of time we'd known each other. It was as if our shared tragedies had fast forwarded us into a relationship that felt as if it had been going on our entire lives. She was my best friend. No one understood me like her and no one else probably ever would. And as our talks started ending with passionate kisses, I began to understand that she would be my friend *and* my lover. She would be my first…I was positive of that.

When my healing time of peace with Sawyer was over and the New Year came around, we went back to school. I was nervous the first day. I'd left a mess behind from the night of the dance, and I had no idea what to expect from people. But Sawyer clenched my hand, and vowed never to leave my side, even when we had to be apart.

The first person we saw from that night was Randy. He was standing outside of the main building, kicking a clump of grass showing itself through a crack. I let out a long exhale when I saw him, but then straightened and made myself approach him. I'd suffered worse lately; I could handle this.

He looked up when he felt us standing in front of him. His eyes widened as they met mine, and I realized that it had been a long time since I'd willingly looked him squarely in the eye. In fact, it may have been the first time all year that I'd purposefully held someone's gaze. He started talking immediately.

"Hey, Luc, I'm so sorry about…the thing in Astronomy…" His voice trailed off and I made myself not cringe. The "thing" he referenced so simply had made me look like an idiot and gotten me kicked out of school temporarily.

Deciding that none of that mattered, I tightened my hold on Sawyer's hand and let a soft smile reach my lips. "It's okay, Randy. I understand that you didn't know what you were really doing to me…and I forgive you." I clapped a hand on his shoulder and walked away.

I exhaled a quick breath as I entered the main building. Looking back, I saw Randy eyeing me through the door. He still looked really guilty, but he did have a slight smile on his lips. He nodded at me through the door and I turned my attentions back to Sawyer, who was beaming up at me.

"You did great." She rested her chin on my shoulder as she looked up at me. I smiled and leaned down to her, resting my head against hers.

"Because of you," I whispered.

She frowned and shook her head, not wanting to take credit for me opening up. I smiled and cut off her objection. "I wouldn't be here if it weren't for you, so I'm going to give you all the credit today."

She sighed and rolled her eyes, and I leaned down farther to press my lips to hers. Her fingers reached up to brush my cheek as our lips moved softly but intently together. I could feel the stares of kids in the hall, but I pushed them out of my mind. Sawyer was mine, and for once, I wanted them all to know that. I wouldn't hold anything back from her again.

Our make out session was abruptly interrupted by a hand on my shoulder. I broke off from her to look up at Coach. I cringed, remembering the last time I'd seen him. "Get to class, lovebirds," he gruffly barked at us.

Sawyer blanched at his tone, but I was used to his rough demeanor. Looking down at my feet for a second before deciding to hold his steely gaze, I said as stoically as I could, "Coach…am I in trouble?" I *had* punched another student after all, and deserving or not, there had to be some sort of repercussion for that.

Coach's lip curled wryly. "For kissing? No, I think I'll let that slide." He pointed a finger into my chest. "Just this once though."

Sawyer giggled nervously as I slowly said, "No…for punching Josh at the dance."

Coach gave me a pointed look and crossed his arms over my chest. "I don't know what you're talking about, Luc." I stammered and open and shut my mouth a few times. Coach glanced up and down the hall. "It's like I told the principal, the fight was over by the time I got there." His eyes flicked back to mine. "I didn't see or hear anything…so how would I know who got punched?"

A stream of stupid disbelieving noises left my mouth. He didn't hear anything? I was one hundred percent positive that that wasn't the case. But then, the coach was fair, if hard. He'd probably heard Josh verbally lead me straight into that fight. Who knows, maybe he felt like Josh got what he deserved. I did.

Coach put a hand on my shoulder, his face brightening. "Well, we can always talk about this later…when you show up for baseball practice in a few weeks." He clapped my shoulder and winked at me. As I watched him walk away, I was certain I would be on the baseball team this spring.

As Sawyer and I walked up the stairs to class, I made myself pay attention to the people around us. One of the things Sawyer and I had talked about at length during break was my habit of shutting down, of tuning out the world around me. She completely understood the desire, saying she'd done the same thing at her school, but it was warping my perception of people. I couldn't change the past, and I couldn't change what certain people believed of me, but as I opened my eyes and looked around, I saw that more people really did look at me with concern and curiosity than outright anger. It was an eye opening experience for me.

I made myself give tight smiles and small nods to people I used to know very well. More often than not, I received a smile and nod in return. There were still whispers and gossip swirling as I walked down the hall, but what I noticed now was that the talking didn't always stop when I walked by. As I paid more attention, I could hear that a lot of the conversations people were having…had nothing to do with me. I flushed a bit at how self-absorbed I could be. But when you feel awful about yourself, it seems like the entire world has their backs to you, whispering about you…condemning you. But how often was that really the case? Probably not as often as I'd believed. As I studied people in the halls, I started to understand that truth more and more. Mainly, I saw people going on about their own lives, wrapped up in their own dramas. Most only registered me with a cursory glance.

That's not to say that *everyone* was talking about their own lives. A few heads were bent together in harsh whispers that stopped and turned into unblinking stares as I walked by. I even caught a few words in reference to my "revelation"—that I remembered the crash, and my version of those events greatly differed from all the gossip. I was both relieved and pained to know that the truth was circulating amid the lies. I hoped the tide would start to shift now.

As we entered the classroom, I noticed the several sets of curious and thoughtful eyes. Those eyes took in my hand holding Sawyer's and I noticed a few smiles among the faces. I made myself meet every eye and smile back. That surprised quite a few of them and I started to wonder just how much I *had* shut down lately.

Ms. Reynolds gave us a warm greeting, her hand touching Sawyer's shoulder, her eyes studying mine. I gave her a genuine smile and a friendly nod. Sawyer's distant cousin had always been kind to me and I hadn't forgotten that. She spoke with us for a moment before class, asking how Sawyer's break went and how I'd been. I wasn't sure what she knew, but being family, I thought she probably knew a lot about what had really happened to me after I'd left the dance. I told her I was "better" and she gave me a warm smile in response.

Sawyer and I made our way to our seats, parting to go down our separate aisles. I stopped at Will's desk when I noticed his foot slip out to trip me. Inwardly, I smiled—some things never change. I twisted to face him and he sat up straighter, defiance in his eyes. I let my inward smile show on my face. I'd dealt with much worse than tripping, it seemed silly and childish to me now. A slight laugh escaping me, I pointed at his foot.

"Do you mind not tripping me anymore? It's kind of stupid…don't you think?"

A couple students seated near him laughed, Randy included. Will flushed and looked around, retracting his foot. "Whatever, Lucas," he glowered. Feeling magnanimous, I clapped his shoulder as I walked by. He seemed startled by that and turned to watch me walk back to Sawyer.

She was again beaming at me as I sat down. "I love you," she mouthed.

"I love you too," I said, loud enough for those around me to clearly hear. Her eyes looked around and her cheeks filled with a light, rosy color. It was beautiful on her. "Come here." I leaned over, lifting my lips to her, and she smiled and leaned over as well. Our mouths met in the middle of the aisle and we shared a brief kiss in the middle of class.

Sawyer, Randy, Will and I, got called into the principal's office halfway through first period. That actually caused more of a stir among the students than Sawyer and I kissing. I met eyes with a few faces as I left and was a little surprised with the sympathy I saw there. We were brought into the principal's office one-by-one and made to tell our version of the fight. While I'd been hoping that the school would just let it slide, it appeared that they weren't going to. They just weren't sure what happened. As I was the last one of our group to enter, I began to understand why they were so confused.

As I sat in the straight backed chair, I listened to the stern older woman before me as she gave me the conflicting details. As it turned out, there was a lot of debate over who had actually thrown the punch. Half of the witnesses claimed Josh did it, while the other half claimed I struck him. Sawyer stuck by my side, saying Josh was a bully and cornered me. Will stuck by Josh, saying I flipped out and started whaling on him, and Randy said he missed the first half, but tried to stop Josh from attacking me. The rest of the student body that had been interviewed was evenly split between the stories.

There were so many questions over the matter that the principal decided not to suspend either of us for the fight. She ended up giving Josh and me a week of detention instead, and ordered me more counseling, as well as a round of sessions for Josh. I'd been planning on continuing anyway, but it made me happy that Josh had to go now, too. Truly that was for the best. He obviously had issues with his brother's death, and would never be a better person if a professional didn't step in and help him. And I was positive Beth could help him. One small benefit of the dissolution of our friendship, I suppose.

Josh was entering the outer office as I was leaving it. Sawyer, having waited for me after her meeting, stood up and eyed us both nervously. I held Josh's eye and he held mine. Neither of us spoke and an odd tension built up in the waiting room. Finally, and surprisingly, Josh looked down and muttered, "Sorry."

My mouth dropped in shock until I understood. While Coach had let me go with only a few words the night of the dance, he had held Josh back and had a "conversation" with him. Knowing full well just how intense a conversation with Coach could be, I figured Josh had had the fear of God put in him, much more so than the principal, with an empty threat of suspension, ever could. Josh wouldn't mind getting a short vacation from campus for fighting, but getting ousted from the team next year—now *that* was enough to have him licking just about anyone's heels.

He was still glumly looking at the ground as I walked around him to Sawyer. I grabbed her hand and made for the door. Stopping halfway through the open doorframe, I turned to look back at him. He was still staring at the floor, his head bent down. For a moment, I remembered the happy, smiling kid that used to hang off Darren's shoulders, wanting to be just like his big brother. Seeing how little of that person was left saddened me.

"I'm sorry, Josh. I loved him too."

Josh lifted his head and looked back at me, tears in his eyes now. I swallowed at the sight, my own eyes watering. Josh only stared at me a moment, then nodded and made his way to the principal's office. Sawyer and I both exhaled together, squeezing each other's hands and preparing for the remainder of our day.

It went by smoother than I'd imagined it would. As I continued forcing myself to meet people's glances and acknowledge them with smiles or nods, they started feeling more comfortable around me. By Mr. Varner's class, some of the people around me felt comfortable enough to ask me if what they'd heard about the dance was true—if I'd really confessed that I remembered everything, if I'd really been sober and the rain had really caused the wreck. It made a knot form in my stomach and I had to fight the natural urge to shut down and not tell them anything, but with Sawyer squeezing my knee, I finally did confess the truth about the events of that night.

Mr. Varner snapped at the room on more than a few occasions, as whispers of questions and consolations swirled around me, but by the time class was over, the people in it looked at me differently.

It was much the same in the remainder of my classes. Most people just had no idea what to believe, and they'd taken my half-hearted denials, mixed with my silence, as an admission of guilt. It generally only took me explaining things once for people's questioning glances to turn sympathetic. And I found that the more I talked about it, the easier it was. Eventually, I didn't even tear up when people asked.

I was feeling a lot more comfortable in the school, and in all honesty, with myself, when I got to Astronomy. There was something healing in a handful of peers telling me that it was an accident, and that I wasn't to blame. There was also something soothing in those same students apologizing for thinking badly of me. It didn't make up for all the tiny tortures I'd endured, but it helped.

Don't get me wrong, not everyone instantly liked me again. As I walked through the halls or into the classrooms, there was still an occasional angry shake of the head and hard stare, but not everyone can be convinced of the truth. Some people will believe what they want to believe. Sometimes you have to, just to make sense of the world. I understood that, and didn't hold it against anyone who felt the need to make me the villain. I just wasn't going to agree with them anymore. That was my goal anyway.

As I walked through the Astronomy doors, my eyes automatically went to Josh. He kept his head down, not looking at me. I nodded my head, accepting the truth of our relationship, and made my way to my seat. I didn't know if Josh finally believed me, but I knew he'd finally leave me alone. I found what solace in that that I could, and silently wished him well as I watched him throughout class.

A few more people came up to me afterwards, and I made myself talk with them, being as open and honest as I could. One or two offered to walk me to my next class and I conceded, not sure if I wanted the company, but wanting to fit back in with people. They chatted about events in their lives, and I nodded and supplied a few "I'm listening" responses. My thoughts were more on Josh, though, as I watched him disappear to his next class.

My mind focused back onto the things I could feel good about in art class. Mrs. Solheim gave us back some of our pieces that she'd finally gotten around to grading over the break. Calling me Tom, and telling me, once again, how much talent she thought I had, she handed me back the charcoal drawing I'd done of Sawyer. She'd given me an A. I smiled as I smoothed out the paper image of the woman I knew so well, a woman who'd brought me back from the brink. My finger traced the curve of her cheek on the paper and I suddenly knew what I wanted to do with this piece that meant so much to me.

I tucked it in my backpack and got to work on the next image of the woman I loved.

Not too much later, I saw her again. Her black hair streamed behind her in the crisp breeze, her small frame wrapped in my letterman's jacket. Now I loved how my name across her back implied my claim on her. Underneath that jacket, I knew she was wearing her typical long-sleeved shirt, and I also knew that shirt was doing much more than just keeping her warm. Her thumb ring flashed in a sudden bright patch of sunlight and its triumphant shine matched the triumphant look on her face as she walked over to me. I smiled at seeing the happy glow in her eyes, wondering if I had anything to do with it.

She slung her arms around my neck when we finally met up in-between the buildings housing art and choir. She immediately leaned up to lightly press her lips to mine. My hands automatically curled around her waist and we held each other like we'd been apart all day, and not just for the last two classes.

"Why does it feel like forever since I've seen you?" she asked, echoing my thoughts again.

I grinned and shook my head. "Because it has been." She rolled her eyes, but laughed, the look of victory still on her face. I pulled back to examine her expression. "Something…going on?"

She grinned and removed one of her hands from my neck, showing me a note tucked inside her fingers. I grabbed it from her cool grasp and unfolded it with one hand while she watched me with a wry smile. As familiar handwriting popped out at me, I started and met her gaze again.

"Our note? The one Josh knew about?"

She nodded.

"What happened to it?"

She shrugged and hugged me tighter. "Your favorite 'ex' apparently stole it from my bag. I didn't notice then, but Sally told me that she heard Brittany bragging about it today." She gave me a wink and a sly smile. "So I made sure I got it back."

I shook my head at her, wondering how she'd accomplished that. "I love you," I muttered, before lowering my lips to hers again. She chuckled, but couldn't answer me since I wasn't exactly letting her speak. I didn't need her to say it back to me, anyway. I already knew exactly how much Sawyer loved me. She'd proven that to me on the highway.

Her fingers curled up to my hair as mine ran up her back, pulling her tighter. Behind her, I heard a series of disgruntled noises and I cracked my eyes open. I could just make out Brittany, standing several feet away from us, watching us kiss. I closed my eyes again, blocking her out. I couldn't help Brittany's petty jealousies…and I was fairly certain that was all it was for her. She had never shown me anything even close to resembling love, not even way back, when we'd been fooling around. It was one of the reasons that it had been so easy for me to discount the encounter. I was a toy to her, something she enjoyed playing with and didn't like to share, but she definitely wasn't above chucking me to the curb when it suited her purpose. That sort of game wasn't something I'd ever had any interest in playing, regardless of how attractive she was.

My hands tightened on Sawyer, reveling in someone who actually did care about me. As the noises from Brittany finally faded into silence, I remembered what I'd wanted to do earlier in art. I broke apart from our kiss and smiled down at Sawyer. Her mouth was still parted, her breath just slightly heavier and her eyes slightly glassy. It was an astoundingly attractive look, one that hinted at where our relationship could eventually go, and I swallowed at seeing it.

Blinking and stammering on vague, incoherent words, I reached behind me to my backpack. She released me when she understood what I was doing. Looking more put together, she watched me curiously. Grinning, I found the picture I'd drawn and handed it to her. She tucked our "note" in her pocket before taking my picture and unfolding it.

Her eyes widened as she looked over the intricate, charcoal version of her that I'd drawn. As she was speechless for so long, I started getting nervous that she didn't like it. Maybe she thought it was creepy or something. I started to anxiously shift my weight back and forth, waiting for some response from her.

Finally her eyes lifted from the paper; they were watery as she gazed at me. She shook her head and tried to speak, but couldn't. As I scrunched my brow, she finally swallowed and said, "You drew…me?"

I nodded and smiled, relaxing at the awe I heard in her voice. "I always draw you. I always have," I added in a whisper.

She looked back down to the paper, her finger tracing the same curve on her cheek that I had earlier. "You drew me…beautiful," she murmured quietly, clearly taken aback that I'd do such a thing.

My hand came up to her chin, lifting it so she'd look at me. "You *are* beautiful."

A tear dropped to her cheek and I brushed it off with my thumb. Her watery eyes flicked between mine as the chilly wind continued to blow her hair around her, lifting and releasing the ends in a continual wave of motion. "I love it. I love you, Lucas."

I smiled and bent down to kiss her again. By the time we broke apart, we were both late for our next appointments.

We parted ways in front of the purity club door. Sawyer playfully grabbed the edges of my jacket, pulling me to her for a quick kiss. I chuckled and turned it into a longer kiss. She sighed and looked at me a little dreamily as she pulled away. I shook my head as I watched her open the door and disappear into the packed classroom. Sometimes, it was still hard to believe that someone like her could love someone like me. But I could see now that that thought was more driven by self-hatred than anything else. Before the wreck, I'd never questioned the fact that someone as beautiful and amazing as Lillian had loved me; it had never even occurred to me back then that I wasn't worthy of her. No, all of my self-doubt was because of the crash, and my part in it. Self-loathing can do a number on your self-esteem and I was still working on that.

As I opened the door stenciled with the word "counselor" in bold, black letters, a smile crept to my face. I was working on that, and this was the person who'd help me.

Her smile was broad and beaming as she noticed me walking through her door. Her flaming hair was loose around her, large curls spilling around her shoulders, highlighting her crystal blue eyes. Those eyes glowed at me with genuine affection as I took my seat across from her. I sat with a peaceful smile on my face and marveled at how drastically my attitude about coming here had changed since the beginning. Aside from being with Sawyer, sitting down with Beth was one of the high points in my day.

"Good to see you, Lucas," She said warmly, her eyes crinkling around the corners, showing a lifetime of happy moments, one of which appeared to be me.

I beamed at her, relaxing back into my seat. "Good to see you too, Beth." Her smile widened at my casual use of her first name. I'd resisted speaking to her with any type of familiarity for a long time, but after my moment on the highway, I'd needed to let her in, to save myself.

Much like I had every day since I'd called her, I began telling her what was on my mind. She'd surprised me over winter break by showing up at my house every morning. She definitely wasn't under any obligation to do that, and it had seemed above and beyond anything a school grief counselor should have to do, but she hadn't listened to my halfhearted attempts to tell her it wasn't necessary. She'd simply told me it was, and goaded me to talk to her.

I hadn't been as relaxed and free speaking then as I was being now as I told her about my meeting with the principal and running into Josh throughout the day. Even after pouring out my soul the day of the highway incident, it had been a struggle to force myself to talk to her. After shutting down for so long, opening up was a gradual, painful process. Maybe that's what she'd meant when she said it was necessary to see me every day. Maybe she'd known that if she didn't strike while the iron was hot, I'd start closing up again. I didn't know. Like I'd told her once before, she was the one with all the diplomas, not me.

With delight on my face, I told her about giving the picture I'd drawn of Sawyer to her, and her reaction to me portraying her as beautifully as I saw her.

She smiled with one edge of her lip as she twisted a pencil in her hands. "Sometimes, we don't see ourselves as clearly as others do." I looked up at her and nodded, knowing she wasn't necessarily talking about Sawyer anymore. She smiled more at seeing me agree with her statement. Awhile ago, I would have disagreed with her. "I'm glad you'll be coming to see me for a bit longer, Lucas."

I nodded and looked down. I'd told her about my punishment for fighting with Josh, the additional counseling I'd been given, part of the school's new policy to try and rehabilitate students instead of just outright punishing them. As I considered how much being here had helped me, I thought maybe the school was on to something. I started to have a little hope for Josh. I hoped he'd open up to Beth easier than I had.

She continued as I thought about that. "Honestly, Lucas, I wish I had seen you earlier…the first day of school, if not immediately after the tragedy."

I looked up at her again, shifting my mind back to that horrid time. Mom had tried on a few occasions to get me to a counselor, but she might as well have stuck me in an empty room for all the good it had done me. I just hadn't been ready to talk to anyone. "I don't like talking about…stuff…to anyone."

She nodded her head, tapping her pencil on her desk a couple times. "I've noticed that." I chuckled and she added, "But you're doing so much better. You've come a long way in opening up, Lucas. That's very hard to do, especially to a complete stranger. You should be very proud of yourself."

Feeling embarrassed, I hung my head and shrugged. I wondered if she was proud of me for trying to escape life by living in a fantasy. I couldn't imagine she'd say that was healthy…or normal. I cringed, but asked her anyway. "Is what I did, creating a dream world with my friends, crazy?" I peeked up at her, cringing. "Am I nuts?"

She looked at me for a moment, tapping her pencil against her lip before answering. "Just you asking me that shows that you're not crazy." I found myself relaxing infinitesimally, and it surprised me. I hadn't realized I'd tensed waiting for her answer. I guess some part of me really had been worried that she'd confirm what I was secretly afraid of.

She smiled as she watched me sit back in my chair. "Lucas, you've been through something that most people can't even contemplate, don't even want to contemplate." She shook her head and I watched the red curls swish over her shoulders. I blankly let her words enter my head. "I think your mind dealt with it in the only way it could. It may not have been the healthiest option…but I'd say you're doing pretty well, considering."

I allowed myself a wry smile. "Considering, I almost tried to kill myself, to join my dream friends?" I was a little surprised at how casually I could talk about the biggest, well, second biggest, tragic event of my life. That was just a testament to how comfortable I'd become around Beth.

She smiled wryly in return. "But you didn't kill yourself, and you asked for help. You asked for my help. That's pretty huge, compared to how you were when you moodily slumped into my chair a few weeks ago. Don't you think?"

Her words echoed my earlier thoughts regarding my time spent here and I smiled at hearing our minds run in parallel. A soft laugh escaped me as I stared at my hands on my lap, remembering my moody first day. "Maybe…"

She sighed softly and I glanced up at her from the corner of my eye. "I can't imagine exactly what you've gone through, Lucas, but I can imagine your pain."

I lifted my head, another wry smile twisting my lips. "You can imagine the pain of murdering all of your friends?" I instantly regretted saying it, both because of how callous it sounded, and because a slice of pain went right through me at saying it. Things *were* better, but I wasn't like I was magically healed and the death of my friends didn't ever bother me anymore. It did. Healing doesn't happen overnight. It's painfully slow, and my friends' absence still shook me to my core. I hung my head again.

Beth took in my changed expression and placed a few fingers on my shoulder. I looked up and could tell tears were in my eyes. I blinked them away, not wanting to cry today. "You didn't murder them, Lucas. In your heart, you know that. It was an accident…a tragic accident."

I watched her face fill with sympathy for me. Feeling warm and safe in her spa-like oasis, I said something that I never would have uttered just a few weeks ago. "I don't think it was an accident."

She blinked and scrunched her forehead. I was certain she believed me when I said I'd been sober, and rain and speed had been my downfall that night. She also knew *I* was well aware of what had caused the crash, so I could almost see her mind trying to grasp what I meant by my statement. "Of course it was, Lucas. What else would it be?"

I looked down, not able to meet her eyes anymore. "It was carelessness, recklessness. It was me thinking that we were invincible and not…slowing down, to think about just how precious what I had been carrying was…" I peeked up at her, those tears in my eyes again. "It was me being stupid."

Her fingers clenched my shoulder sympathetically before pulling away. A soft, sad smile played across her lips. "Sort of the definition of 'accident', don't you think?"

I swallowed, shaking my head. "No…it feels…more like fate." I swallowed, not sure if she'd understand. I wasn't sure if I did either, it was just an overriding sense in me sometimes, like, no matter what I'd done differently that night…I'd still be here, in this office, mourning.

"You think you fated your friends to die?"

It sounded so silly when she said it, that I sighed and hung my head. "I don't know." I shrugged. "But, they *are* dead because of me."

Silence filled the room. Well, not exactly silence as she had some soothing, light jazz playing in the background, but Beth didn't respond to what I'd said. I let the silence between us stretch on for as long as I could stand, then I glanced up at her. She was watching me, a thoughtful expression on her freckled face. Finally, in a low voice, she spoke. "You can't accept forgiveness from others until you accept it from yourself, Lucas."

I swallowed back the ache that line gave me. It hit so close to home. Trying to shrug off the pain of self-hatred that always lingered around the edges of my being, I gave her a weak, wry smile. "That sounds straight out of a textbook."

She didn't give me the smile I expected in return. Instead, her look remained completely serious as she studied my expression. I could feel my eyes water again under that gaze, and I stopped trying to halt the feeling that I was having. I let my eyes fill and let the tears drop to my cheeks. Her face still showing no humor, her pale eyes watching my tears fall, she calmly said, "It's written in a textbook for a reason."

I could only nod as I silently cried. I supposed it was. I knew I had to let this go, this feeling of loathing I had for myself. I knew I needed to come to some sort of peaceful arrangement, if I ever wanted to move forward, and I knew my friends and Lillian would have wanted that for me. I knew Sawyer and my mom wanted that for me. And a tiny, tiny speck of me wanted that for me, too.

Finally, Beth's face relaxed and she sighed softly, bringing her hand back to my shoulder. "We'll get you there, Luc. I promise."

Chapter 23 – You Never Forget…Your First Time

"Getting there" took longer than I'd ever imagined it could. But I had as much help as one person could possibly ask for. Beth met with me daily, even after my ordered sessions were finished. I decided to forgo rejoining the purity club to continue meeting with her. I found our sessions infinitely helpful, and I figured Sawyer and I saw enough of each other that I could probably last the rest of the year without being in the club with her.

That wasn't to say I didn't participate in anything. Sawyer and Ms. Reynolds talked to Sally and convinced her to let me join social events for the club. I wasn't sure if, now that the school knew my story, it was suddenly socially acceptable for me to be a prim and proper Safe and Sound Club member, or if Sally just trusted me with Sawyer now, but after a brief talk with the principal, she had readily agreed to letting me go to games and dances and even a couple of choir concerts (I loved having the excuse to hear Sawyer sing, and she was wonderful at it), all to spread the joy of living life substance free.

As I got over the lunacy of one club trying to change teenage behavior, I started to see that the club *was* actually helping some people. As it grew in size, the club started putting on its own events—dances, fundraisers and bowling nights—all in an attempt to show kids how to have fun in a "clean" way. As Sawyer and I went to these events, I started to see people truly begin to come to life. Just like me, some of them had been hiding themselves away, maybe with drugs, alcohol or promiscuity instead of self-imposed isolation, but as they let that part of their lives go, they blossomed in a way that was inspiring to watch. It sort of made me proud to be a pseudo-member of such a life-altering group.

As winter started shifting into spring, the climate toward me thawed as well. A few assholes still chose to badmouth me, and Brittany still tried, in almost comical ways, to drive a wedge between Sawyer and I. At that point, her separating us was such an impossibility, that all her lame attempts at gossip mongering succeeded in doing was giving Sawyer and me something to giggle about during lunch. The majority of the student body, though, was open to the idea of taking me back, now that I was open to the idea of letting them.

Following the advice of Sawyer and Beth, I kept myself emotionally available to people; allowing them in, allowing them to talk to me and talking back to them in return. Most of them only needed to hear my story once, and then were content to let my past die and accept who I was now. Most people had just been confused by the swirl of rumors and my abject silence. They hadn't understood and had been afraid to ask.

Eventually, I formed a small circle of peers, friends even. Randy and Sally started becoming close in my life, hanging out with Sawyer and me often. Randy even tried out for baseball with me, and we both made the team. Eventually that team started feeling like a second family, the same as football had felt just a year ago, and I started being more involved in my teammates' lives. It wasn't the same as the tight group I'd had before, but it was enough to start bringing me back to life.

And Josh…well, after second semester started, and Sawyer and I came up with a schedule that got us four out of five classes together plus a free "study" period, I didn't see him much. The school wasn't big enough for me to never see him again, but without a class together, the contact we had was pretty minimal—brushing past each other in the hall, watching him fight with his girlfriend across campus, or occasionally spotting him talking with Will on the steps of the main building as Sawyer and I approached for first period.

He didn't speak much to me, but he didn't try and start anything either. It was almost like I'd become invisible to him. Almost. Sometimes, I'd catch him watching me from the other end of the hall or staring at me a little longer than was necessary as we passed by each other on the stairs.

I didn't know what he thought of me, if he still hated me, still blamed me. I'd thought about asking Beth what he'd said about me during their sessions, but decided against it. What she and I discussed was nothing I'd want her to talk about with anyone else, not that she would, and I had to believe that Josh felt the same.

It was nearly three months after our brief words to each other in the principal's office, when I was sure we'd never speak again, that we ran into each other in the first floor men's room. I was washing my hands when he walked in the door. I looked up in the mirror automatically and did a double take when I saw him standing in the open frame. His eyes locked with mine, and for a second, I was sure he was going to leave. No one else was in there, and I was pretty sure Josh didn't want to be alone with me.

Surprisingly, he didn't leave. He sniffed and looked down, then walked into the room, letting the door swing closed behind him. I stepped away from the sink, wiping my hands off on my jeans, and wondering what to say to him. He kept his head down and made like he was going to go to a stall to shut me out. But then he paused and looked back at me.

I swallowed and my face softened at the haggard look on his. The circles under his eyes were a deep, dark purplish-blue. His dark hair was shaggy and unkempt, as disheveled as his baggy clothes under his baggy letterman's jacket. He looked more tired than I'd ever seen him, and I couldn't help but think that no matter what struggles we'd gone through earlier in the year, I wanted to see him smiling and happy again. A tiny part of me even wanted him to start attacking me again. Even if his smile had been a vindictive one back then, it had at least been a smile.

"Are you…okay, Josh?" It occurred to me then, that even though Josh had a circle of friends, none of them were probably that invested in his happiness. Josh didn't exactly have a "Sawyer" to look after him.

He blinked, seemingly taken aback that I'd asked him that. He started to shake his head, like he was going to say he was fine, but then he sighed and seemed to slump. "No," he whispered. "I miss him."

I swallowed and nodded, walking over to stand in front of Josh. He looked up at me, blinking slowly, like he wanted to sleep, but hadn't been able to in a really long time. I completely understood that. "I do too…every day."

Josh nodded and looked at our feet. He was silent for long seconds and I started to think that maybe he'd said all he was going to say to me. I debated turning to leave, when he spoke again. "You swear you were sober…?"

I bit my lip and swallowed back the lump that suddenly seized my throat. Josh peeked up at me, just a hint of anger in his dark eyes as he waited for my answer, waited to see if I'd be truthful. I nodded and my voice was thick when it finally came out. "I swear, Josh. I swear on his grave. It was just a really horrible…accident."

Relief—and a small trickle of peace—coursed through me as that word passed my lips. It *had* been an accident and finally admitting that to someone made me feel a thousand times lighter. Josh cocked his head, gauging the sincerity in my voice. Finally, he swallowed and looked down again, but not before I saw the tears start to form. I let him keep his emotion hidden from me, let him keep his head down.

I put my hand on his shoulder, clenching it hard. "I'm so sorry, Josh. If I could do that night over…" I didn't finish that. It was pretty much implied that of course I'd do things differently. I just didn't know what.

What had happened wasn't something that I could have prevented without some foresight of what was going to happen. At the time I'd been doing what I could to be a responsible friend, driving my other drunken friends home. Maybe I could have slowed my speed, maybe I could have made sure my friends' seatbelts were safely buckled. But really, would that have changed the outcome? I felt another trickle of peace flow into me. I'd done what I could…the rest hadn't been up to me.

Josh looked up at my touch, his cheeks wet, and nodded solemnly. I wanted to hug him but didn't really want to stress this tenuous connection we were having. Wanting to help in some way, but not knowing how, I removed my hand and awkwardly put it back in my pocket. "I hear you got sent to Mrs. Ryans."

He nodded, his eyes guarded, and I continued with a shrug of my shoulders. "Yeah. I wasn't too thrilled to see her at first, either." Looking down, I added, "She really helped me though."

I bit my lip to stop myself from asking if she had helped him, if she was still helping him. I slyly peeked up at him, to read his face. He was staring away from me, gazing at the door. I wondered if he was debating leaving, but instead of moving, he spoke. "She has been helping, I guess. It's hard…but I'm starting to like talking to her."

I looked up and he met my gaze. Smiling, I nodded at him. "Good."

The silence stretched between us as we simply looked at each other. Thinking Sawyer was going to bust in there looking for me, I shifted to move. My adjustment broke our silent stare down and as my head twisted to the door, he spoke again.

"Do you still feel like killing yourself?" I hesitated and looked back at him, wondering if he knew about the highway. His eyes watered again as his face turned desolate. He shook his head and with a wavering voice asked, "Does that ever go away?"

Finally understanding that he was talking about his mental state more than mine, I turned back to him. "No, I don't want to die anymore." Pointedly holding his gaze, I calmly said, "It gets better. Day by day…it *does* get better."

He swallowed and nodded, his head hanging down again. Deciding it was warranted, I gave him a swift hug. "Call me if you need to, Josh." He mumbled something sounding like an agreement as he loosely hugged me back.

Feeling like Josh needed a minute alone to pull himself back together, I made my way to the door. As I was opening it, I heard him say, "I'm sorry for drugging you, Lucas."

I looked back at his sad, tired face, wondering if I'd ever again see that kid I used to know. I nodded at him and made my way out to the hallway, where Sawyer immediately grasped my hand and asked me if I was okay. I chuckled at her never ending concern and told her everything that had just happened.

Later with Beth, I repeated the encounter. She didn't seem surprised to hear it and I thought maybe Josh had told her already. It pleased me that he was opening up to her as well. Again, my hope for him soared. We talked more about Josh and then our conversation shifted to the topic it had started shifting to of late—Sawyer and I.

I talked openly to Beth about everything—past and present, and my virginal status was no exception. As the months of a comforting relationship with Sawyer went by, I started to feel something that surprised me a little. I started to feel like I wanted to move forward with her, beyond what I'd done with any girl. That was a pretty big step for me, considering the fact that I'd been holding out for a dead girl for a really long time now.

Expecting a typical "wait until you're married" response from the adult across from me, I was pretty surprised when she said she thought that was fine, as long as we were ready, emotionally and physically. She cautioned me to be safe with our bodies and our hearts. I found that much more helpful advice.

As it turned out, the physical aspect of safety wasn't an issue. Sawyer had confessed to me one night, during a frankly honest conversation, that her parents had put her on the pill after her suicide attempt, when the truth behind her reason for the attempt had come out. They'd assumed a "better safe than sorry" approach to the whole matter, and Sawyer hadn't felt the need to tell them it was an unnecessary precaution, since she wasn't planning on sleeping with anyone ever again after her one awful experience. Of course, once she'd met me, taking the pill had seemed wise to her, too, and she'd continued with it. It made me flush, thinking of how soon into our meeting that she'd been interested in me…like that.

She'd been responsible her first time; they'd used a condom. That turned out to be a good thing, since he'd turned out to be a two or three or six timing asshole. Since she was protected from pregnancy now, thanks to her overprotective parents, and both of our fairly inexperienced bodies were completely healthy, she'd told me that when we were ready to go there, she didn't want a condom barrier. She didn't want any barriers between us, physical or otherwise. The entire revelation made me oddly happy. I'd be the first man to be inside her, skin to skin. And hopefully the last. It wasn't exactly virginity, but it was enough to make me feel like I'd have a lifelong claim on her. Wow, I guess I was a little possessive.

That made our bodies pretty safe and sound, leaving just our hearts to consider. And as we spent more time together intimately, loving each other with tender kisses and caresses, I felt more at ease about the future of our hearts. She loved me…and I loved her. Now that I wasn't holding a part of myself away from her, the level of love I felt was nearly astonishing. It was something I'd convinced myself I would never feel again for a living person. And I wanted to show her how deeply I felt it, but I wanted to make sure I was ready for the right reasons. Well, to be honest, I held off partially because of nerves. But mainly, I held off because I wanted to make sure the moment had nothing to do with Lillian.

I hadn't dreamt of my friends since they'd said goodbye to me, and I felt relief *and* sadness from that. I knew it was all in my head, but then again, I'd known that all along. That didn't make the fantasy any less addicting, knowing it was fake. It had almost made it better, since I'd had some level of control, although never as much as I'd wanted. But still, a part of me wanted that fantasy back, if anything, just to say goodbye less painfully. It eluded me though and my dreams were constantly…forgettable.

As Sawyer and I got even closer to each other, I took this to be a good thing, like Lillian's absence was her way of saying, "Go ahead, live your life. I won't interfere." I wanted to tell Sawyer that. I wanted to tell her that I was finally ready to go through that final step with her, that I'd let my past with Lillian go. Days later, when we were in my room after baseball practice, I lazily ran my fingers through her hair and thought maybe I could finally tell her.

My mom had the night off from the diner and was having a nice dinner with Sheriff Whitney. Since their relationship had gone "public," they'd decided to tell his wife the truth. They had decided to do it together, and I'd supported their decision. A real relationship couldn't be continued on lies, from either party. From what I'd heard later from my mom, his wife hadn't been surprised by the announcement.

With a heavy sigh, she'd admitted that she'd known for a couple of years; her husband hadn't been that great at hiding the secret. She also admitted that she didn't mind. That seemed odd to me at first, until my mom explained it farther. His wife knew she was dying, and she wanted to leave her husband happy. Mom made him happy.

While living arrangements with his wife were going to stay the same, albeit in separate bedrooms, so the sheriff could care for her until she passed, his relationship with Mom was now out for everyone to see, and date nights were a more frequent thing. My mom was happier than I'd ever seen her, and I let my misgivings about the nature of their relationship go. If all parties were okay with it, who was I to criticize it?

So Mom was out with her boyfriend for the night, and Sawyer's parents weren't expecting her back for another couple of hours, since they were pretty comfortable with me at this point and allowed Sawyer much longer "visits." We were alone…completely alone. No parents…no ghosts. No one but the two of us were in my room, and in my head.

As we kissed and wrapped our arms and legs around each other, I felt like it was the perfect time to tell her that I wanted to be with her, that I was ready to be with her. I just didn't know how to bring it up. But, as she so often did when we were together, Sawyer spoke my thoughts for me.

Her hand came up and the backs of her fingers ran over my cheek as she lovingly gazed up at me. I leaned down to kiss her, but her voice stopped me. "I feel like we've gotten really close, Lucas. And if you're ready to move forward…so am I." I pulled back and gazed at her suddenly serious expression. Her eyes flicked between mine as she continued, "I don't want to rush you, if it's still too soon after…" She shrugged and bit her lip. "I just wanted you to know…that if you were ready…I wouldn't say no." Her hand cupped my cheek as her eyes looked over my face. "I love you," she whispered.

I swallowed back the almost overwhelming emotion at hearing her simple declaration. It passed so easily from her lips, yet carried such weight with it. "I love you too, Sawyer." My fingers running through her hair stopped at her jaw and my thumb brushed her tender skin. I thought about her words, about everything we'd been through this year, about everything we'd been through in our short lives. And, as I traced the perfect heart-shaped arch of her upper lip with my thumb, I thought about Lil…about everything I'd lost with her, because we'd waited for so long. "I am ready, Sawyer. I'm ready…right now."

I leaned in to kiss her, but she pulled away from me. She eyed me warily. "Are you…sure?"

I smiled and my hand came up to tenderly stroke across her brow, following a long piece of hair at the crown all the way down to her shoulder. "I couldn't be surer." I followed where the long lock hooked over her shirt, lightly grazing the fabric with the back of my knuckle. "If this past year has taught me anything…it's don't put off the important things." My eyes lifted from where they'd been watching my fingers trace the swirl of her hair. "I waited so long with Lil…I never even got the chance to tell her I loved her, much less…"

I swallowed back that thought and started on a different one. "You and I have held off until I was sure I could…be with someone else." My eyes searched hers intently. "I *can*, and I don't want to wait anymore. I don't want to hold back being with someone I love…and I love you, Sawyer. With everything inside of me, I love you and I want to show you." I looked down and felt the heat in my body, the desire in my voice. "I want to make love to you…"

I raised my eyes to hers. They misted as she gazed up at me and then her hands tangled in my hair and pulled me to her. Her lips met mine and I shifted my body, so I was lying more directly on top of her. One of her hands trailed down my back as I pressed my body into hers. She gasped at the feel of me and hitched her leg around mine, drawing us tighter. I deepened the kiss.

Her hands tugged at my shirt and I helped her lift the fabric over my head. Her eyes drifted down my chest as her fingernails lightly dragged down my muscles. I hissed in a soft breath while hers caught. Our eyes met again and my body heated even more at the desire I saw on her face. Our lips met as her hands reattached themselves to my wavy mess of hair. My hand slid up her shirt as our mouths tasted, felt, caressed each other's. I felt her breasts through the light fabric of her bra, and a quiver went through my body. She moaned in my mouth when I ran my thumbs over the sensitive peaks. Needing more of her bare skin, I tore the shirt off of her and paused to stare down at the black see-through bra that was the same dark shade as her hair. I stopped breathing.

"Do you like it?"

I managed to drag my eyes up to her face, and her lips twisted in a soft smile.

"The underwear matches," she whispered.

I closed my eyes as a shudder went through me and a throb pulsed through my lower body. "Yeah," I whispered. "I like it." My fingers ran behind her back as my lips traveled along her jaw to her ear. Gently tugging on a lobe, I muttered, "I almost hate to take it off…"

She whimpered and arched her back, and my hand bunched the fabric and unsnapped the hinge. Smoothly, I pulled it off her shoulders and gazed down at her undeniable beauty, unadorned and unhampered by seductive fabric. She was perfect. "You're beautiful," I murmured as my head lowered to taste that tempting skin. She was panting and rubbing her legs up mine when I finally switched to the other one.

I trailed soft kisses down her abdomen. My hands lightly ran down her sides, tickling her, and she laughed softly and then groaned. I flicked my tongue in her belly button and closed my eyes at the sound she made. It went straight to my already hard body and I knew I needed her to touch me soon. I drew a line with my nose to her waistband and kissed the button on her jeans before I unhooked it.

She helped me unzip and remove them. I bit my lip when I saw the aforementioned matching see-through underwear and had to look away from the overly erotic sight before I lost it. The second we had successfully pulled her jeans off of her, her hands came up to my jeans. I was so ready for her, that the feeling of the tips of her fingers brushing against me through the denim fabric made me suck in a quick breath and mutter her name.

She rolled me to my back as she unzipped them and slid them down. I lifted my hips so she could get them off, and she kissed me, through the fabric of my boxer-briefs. I gasped and stilled my hips to keep myself from finishing this before we even started. Not noticing what that nearly did to me, she pulled my jeans all the way off.

Not wanting to completely lose it if she did that again, I slipped my boxers off while she was preoccupied with dropping my jeans to the floor. When she swiveled back, her eyes widened as she took in the sight of me naked. I flushed as her eyes stayed focused on my lower half. Nerves suddenly tightened my stomach at what we were going to do, what I was finally going to do. Maybe Darren was right, maybe I'd built sex up too much in my head. Now the expectation of it was sort of squashing me.

"I'm nervous," I whispered.

Her eyes immediately flew to my face. "Why? It's just me." She smiled encouragingly, like those words would help me.

I swallowed and shook my head, sitting up on an elbow beside her. "Exactly….it's you." I sighed and ran a hand down her arm, my eyes tracking the movement. "I don't want to disappoint you," I whispered.

Her hand moved under my chin, lifting me and making me look at her. "You…could never disappoint me, Lucas. Never." I started to protest, but she quickly leaned over and kissed me, cutting off my words. "I'm not feeling overly confident about myself either, you know. I mean, the last guy I was with rated me a three." I shook my head but she quickly cut me off again. "But I've always felt comfortable being with you, and I *know* this will be perfect…because it's you and me. That's all that matters, that's all that's ever mattered…you and me."

I sighed and let her deepen the kiss; she drew me into her mouth, into her passion as we lay side-by-side. I wanted to believe her. I wanted to believe I wouldn't mess this up. Possibly still feeling my tension, she ran her lips to my ear and huskily whispered, "Just tell me what you need…and I'll do it."

The answer slipped out of my mouth without any conscious thought. "I just want you to touch me," I whispered.

She groaned at my words and slipped her hands down my sides, running them along my hips. I started to move on top of her when she slipped her hands under her own underwear and slid them off. I paused, taking in the entire effect of this beautiful, naked woman lying on my bed…for me.

My breath spiked and a sharp ache went straight through me. With my eyes never leaving her sensuous body, I watched the way she slid her hands over herself, along her curves, over her hip bones, across her stomach. I again began to move over her, needing to be with her, and was again distracted by her hand, dipping down to touch my inner thigh.

My breath increased as I waited for her to feel me. I wasn't sure how much anticipation I could take. Just when I was sure I was as hard as it was humanly possible to get, her fingers touched me and I stiffened even more. I felt her lips press against mine at the same time that her thumb caressed me. I tried not to, but a deep groan followed by a quick inhale through my teeth, escaped my lips.

I automatically deepened the kiss, matching her intensity and breath as her hand ran down the length of me. I nearly whimpered at the electricity coursing through my body. Hearing gentle words of encouragement, I moved my hips against her hand. I sucked on her bottom lip as she squeezed me harder. I loved the feeling of her fingers around me, and imagined that we were already joined together.

I relaxed into the rhythm of her hand and all of my nerves vanished with the rightness of the movement. Our lips never stopping, our breath only increasing, Sawyer took her free hand and with a gentle prodding, urged me to finally move myself directly on top of her.

Still gently moving into her hand held in-between us, I felt a wonderful tension building and knew I was getting dangerously close. I panicked for a moment, suddenly worried that I'd lose it before we really started. But it was approaching fast, closer and closer with every second, and eventually I stopped worrying about it. I heard Sawyer's name pass my lips with a "more" and "yes" followed close behind. My forehead rocked against hers, my fast pants matched hers, and my hands dug into her shoulders.

Just as I felt my stomach clench with the start of my release, her hand let go of me and her other hand stilled my hips. The feeling immediately faded from me and a disappointed whimper escaped my lips before I could stop it.

Her mouth came to mine, kissing me softly, bringing me down a little with soothing touches and soft words. Her gentle kisses traveled to my ear, where she whispered, "It's okay, Lucas. This will be better…I promise."

With that, she adjusted her legs and guided me to her. Her warmth called to me, and I ached with the need to push myself deep inside of her. I resisted, though, and lifted my head to gaze at the pale, gray eyes looking back at me so lovingly.

"This means everything to me, Sawyer. You mean everything. I love you."

Her eyes misted over as her hand urged me to begin. I gasped as I slid in. "I love you too, Luc," she whispered, as she removed her hand and pulled my hips towards her, sinking me all of the way inside of her with a deep moan.

I was overwhelmed as she took me in, inch-by-inch, until our hips rested flush together. She conformed to me like she was made…just for me. I couldn't do anything. I couldn't breathe, couldn't move. All I could do was lie there and try to absorb the fact that I was within her—we were one.

"Move in me, Lucas."

Her sweet voice awoke me from my over-stimulated state and I inhaled a deep, steadying breath. Slowly, I moved my hips back and then equally slowly, forward again. I would never, no matter how many more times in my life that I do this, forget that first push. It was electric. It was earth shattering. It was exquisite pleasure, made all the more so because I was experiencing it with her.

It started at the very tip of me and shot all the way back through my body in shuddering waves. I cried out with the ecstasy of it and dropped my head to her shoulder. Her hands came up to cradle me, and our hips started a slow, easy rhythm—neither one of us wanting to rush this moment.

I sort of felt like I should be doing something more for her—touching her, kissing her or whispering words of undying love, but I found that all I could do was keep my head buried in her shoulder, making whimpering noises as explosive new feelings and sensations rocketed through me. Even though I knew this wasn't her first time, like it was mine, there were enough moans and general sounds of approval passing her lips that I believed that, whatever I was doing, it was enough for her.

Of their own accord, our hips started rocking together faster and my whimpering changed to some sort of uncontrollable groaning. I felt that unbearably wonderful tension building in me again, but stronger than I'd ever felt it before. The need to relieve that wonderful pressure was so strong that I grabbed her hips and started moving more aggressively. I gasped at the sensation and muttered incoherent words of "more" and "harder." It was working; the buildup was coming.

Her murmurs of pleasure turned into outright cries of ecstasy. As I panted with pure need, she threw her head back and cried out my name. I sat up slightly to watch her, her black hair spread out over my white pillows, her chest heaving with her exertion, her pale eyes closed. It was the most beautiful thing I'd ever seen. And then I felt it—I felt her squeezing me in the most intense and erotic way. I'm pretty sure an, "Oh my God, Sawyer," fell from my lips before my stomach clenched and I started releasing inside her with an intenseness I'd never felt before.

She pulled my head tight to her neck as our hips slowed to gentle rocking. I tenderly kissed her neck, her cheek, her lips, and then I carefully removed myself from her. Gently, I scooped my arms underneath her, rolling onto my back and bringing her with me. She laid her head on my chest as our hearts slowed in time with our breaths. "God, Lucas…I felt you."

I kissed the top of her head and squeezed her tight. "I felt you, too." I pulled back to look at her; her gray eyes danced with happiness. "I love you so much, Sawyer. That was…amazing."

I smiled and she laughed and then softly kissed me. "I know. I told you that you wouldn't disappoint." I chuckled and she ran a finger down my cheek. "I love you, too, Lucas…so much." She laid her head back down on my chest, snuggling her legs up close to mine. As a shiver went through us, I brought a blanket around our bare bodies and she burrowed even closer to me. Closing my eyes, I let out a long exhale, reveling in the stillness that I felt.

"Are you okay?" she whispered, breaking our silence.

She looked back up at me, concern in her eyes. I knew what she meant by that question. She wasn't asking if I was physically all right—I was—she was checking on my mental state, just like she always did. I'd just done something with her that I'd always assumed I'd do with Lillian first. She wanted to make sure I was okay with my decision, after the fact. I looked away, looking inside myself. Was I okay? Searching the bits and pieces of my heart and head, all I could find in me was happiness. Happiness, and a calm depth of peace that I'd thought was lost forever to me.

I turned back to her and kissed her forehead. "Yeah, I'm great."

She sighed happily, placing light kisses along my chest. I smiled wider with each pass of her lips over my skin. I felt like I could stay there, naked in my bed with her, for days. I hated that we'd eventually have to separate. She lifted her body up and kissed my jaw before propping her elbows on top of my chest and settling her head into her hands.

As she dropped one of her hands to lightly stroke my cheek, the scar on her other wrist was exposed. My eyes locked onto it, hating what she'd done to herself, remembering what I'd nearly done to myself.

She noticed my gaze and spoke softly, "Did you know…that I didn't fail in killing myself?" My eyes went back to hers, surprised and terrified. Her eyes flicked between mine as her hand on my cheek twisted, so her knuckles brushed my skin. Her eyes went to the scar I knew was visible on the wrist I couldn't see. "I succeeded at my attempt. I died at the hospital."

My hand came up from her hip to grab the fingers caressing my face. I kissed the knuckles, holding them to my lips as I swallowed the horrid knot in my stomach. I couldn't imagine her gone. A soft smile lit her lips as her hand clenched mine, her beautiful gray eyes on our fingers. "For a full minute, I was dead. But somehow, somehow they brought me back." Her eyes shifted back to mine and she gave me a pointed look. "And there is nothing quite like death, to make you reevaluate your life. I think you get that."

I pulled her hand away from my lips and twisted it around so I could see her scar. I grabbed her other wrist and brought it around to where I could see both of them in my vision, together. Her hands tensed, and she seemed a little reluctant to let me examine them so closely, but of course, she did. We had no secrets anymore. I placed light kisses along each one, feeling the difference in the texture of her skin, where she'd tried to sever herself from this world. I was so grateful she hadn't been allowed to give up.

"I'm glad you came back," I whispered.

Her hands twisted in mine to reach up and grab my cheeks. Her eyes glassed over with moisture while she looked over my face, and her features took on that expression that was so beyond her years. I instantly remembered every wise word I'd ever heard her say to me. I understood so much better now how she'd come to earn that wisdom.

She leaned down, placing a light kiss on my lips. "I'm glad you came back, too."

Chapter 24 – Graduation

Spring started stretching out into longer, warmer and sunnier days, a hint at the promise of summer approaching. It energized the student body, creating havoc for the teachers, who had the difficult job of trying to wrangle all that energy. I felt both an eagerness and a resistance for summer to arrive.

I felt eager to get away from the confines of assignments, tests and homework, and to relax for a few months before starting college. Sawyer and I had applied together to different colleges and universities. We both received acceptance to Oregon State, so we'd decided to enroll there. Choosing that school was a no brainer for me; I was going wherever Sawyer went. We weren't doing the long distance relationship thing, because I wasn't letting her get more than a few yards from me, a mile at the most.

Sawyer's parents had surprised her by admitting that they'd invested in an education fund since she was a baby. Even though times had been hard for their family when they'd left everything and moved, they hadn't touched the fund, not wanting to steal Sawyer's chance at a promising future. As they had both gotten jobs in the meantime and were doing quite well now, things were really starting to look better for the Smith family.

Being a struggling single mom, my mom hadn't been able to plan for my education quite like that, but Coach had some influence with the coach at Oregon State—he was his brother-in-law or something—and I was allowed to try out for the football team. Even though I hadn't played at all this year, I did well enough that I was offered a partial scholarship and a position on the team. I'd be second or maybe even third string, but I thought that wasn't too shabby for a freshman who'd taken some much needed time off from the game.

It made Sawyer roll her eyes that she was seriously going to be dating a college football jock. I laughed as I told her that she already had the prerequisite boyfriend's letterman's jacket. Of course, hers was a high school one. I jokingly told her I'd get her an Oregon State one, with my name in garishly large letters across the back.

She'd started tickling me then, and I'd retaliated by playfully tackling her. One thing led to another, and by the end of our play fight, we had collapsed in my bed, naked and breathless, hearts racing and bodies spent…and deliriously happy. She'd finally conceded that dating a college quarterback might not be so bad, even if he was only second string.

Those were all the things I was looking forward to. What had my stomach twisted into painful knots, was the upcoming anniversary of my friends' deaths. I felt it approaching me as the school year started closing. Their deaths had happened not long after school had ended the year before. Because of the differences in days off and a couple of school closures in January, the anniversary was going to fall exactly on graduation night. It sort of felt symbolic and appropriate…and it sort of sucked.

The circle of close friends that I'd managed to surround myself with by the end of the year were all understanding and supportive of what the upcoming day meant for me. Randy and Sally, who had started dating after going to a Safe and

Sound Club dance together, had been especially sympathetic. In a way, it was just as hard for them, my friends weren't only *my* friends, after all, but even so, I don't think they fully understood my apprehension.

It had been months since I'd seen any sort of vision of my friends. The dreams had stopped once my friends had painfully said goodbye to me the night of the dance, but I'd continued to have vivid memories of them around places that we'd been together: Darren and I at the river, Sammy and I playing video games while Darren napped on my couch, and Lillian. There were so many memories of her, that for a while, they'd nearly assaulted me at every turn.

Sawyer helped me through the painful ones, and I struggled through the happy ones. A part of me was having a hard time leaving this town for that very reason. The memories, although sometimes painful, were all I had left of them. When I changed towns, there'd be nothing to remind me of them. I'd lose that, too. But…I supposed that was just a part of letting go.

And I wouldn't have to give up *every* reminder. Surprisingly enough, Josh *had* called me. He'd been a crying, blubbery mess, and I'd rushed over to his house to check on him. I'd actually driven my mom's car over there, which was saying a lot about how worried I was for him. Driving was still something that made me edgy, and I generally avoided being behind the wheel.

But Josh had needed me, and I'd dropped everything to help him. Being in his house again had hurt, and I had a sudden appreciation of just how hard it was for Josh. Everything in there was the same—every picture frame, every childhood keepsake, and every accolade Darren had ever won. They were all in the same spot they'd been in while Darren was alive. And his room, right across from Josh's, was exactly the same, nearly a shrine of his life. It even still smelled like Darren when I entered the room and found Josh sobbing on the floor.

We'd talked for hours. It had been the most he'd said to me since Darren had died. He confessed how much he'd hated me, simply because he'd needed someone to hate. It hurt too much to miss Darren with no one but fate to blame. He hadn't understood that at the time, truly believing that I'd been careless and gotten behind the wheel drunk with friends who'd been reluctant to join me.

Apparently, Brittany had been very convincing when he'd talked to her at his brother's funeral. It inflamed me that she'd taken that painful moment to twist Josh against me. She really was a manipulative, vindictive little bitch. He'd told me that he'd heard about the sheriff and my mom while listening to some waitresses gossiping at the diner. After Brittany's story of witnessing me drinking at the party, he'd figured my connection with the sheriff had let me get away with killing them all.

I assured him that it hadn't happened that way. He said he knew that now. Mrs. Ryans was helping him see that he'd been transferring his grief into anger and using the swirling gossip to fuel it. But it was all just a distraction, so he wouldn't have to deal. Now that he had to deal, he was struggling with it.

I told him that I struggled too, but we could lean on each other. He'd agreed, and we'd started meeting up after that. It brought me comfort that I could possibly mend the rift with Darren's family. His parents were still distant from me, neither condemning nor supporting, but I felt like I could reconnect with his little brother, and that brightened my spirits considerably.

Mom was equally eager and resistant to see me go off to school. A part of her didn't want to let her baby out of her sight, especially with the tumultuous year that I'd had. I think it was only the fact that I was leaving with Sawyer that made her okay with it. Those two had bonded in a way that almost overshadowed how my mom had bonded with Lillian. Sawyer saved my life. Sawyer was a godsend to my mom. And to me, too.

But Mom was also nearly giddy for me to leave. That fact was mainly because she was preparing to move in with her boyfriend. A few weeks ago, his wife's health had taken a turn for the worst. Sheriff Whitney had stayed with her at the hospital, right up until the very end, offering the friendly comfort and companionship that a lifetime of marriage had afforded them. It was bittersweet for me, and maybe for Mom too. She'd finally get to have the relationship she'd wanted with him for years, but at a heavy price.

The sheriff had been understandably sad after his wife's passing, plagued with guilt and remorse and an underlying joy that he could move forward with my mom now, or so he confessed to me one night as we sat together on my couch, watching a baseball game. During that conversation, he confessed that he'd decided to not charge me with anything that fateful night, partly because of my mom; he didn't want her hating him. Then he'd turned on his cushion and given me a hard, steely look.

"But more than that, Lucas…I didn't want to punish you farther." He looked away from me and his voice softened. "When I told you at the hospital that they were gone…when you completely lost it…that's when I decided to not charge you with anything."

My mouth had dropped open, and I'd tried to respond with something coherent, but couldn't. He looked back at my floundering face and then nodded, a small smile on his lips. "So, don't blame your mom for that. It was me." He sighed heavily and dropped his head. "There was nothing I could legally do that would punish you any more viciously than how you'd already been punished." He looked up and I swallowed and nodded. His brow furrowed. "I'm sorry if that decision caused you more problems. I understand that some people were upset that you didn't get in trouble?"

I hung my head. "Yeah…some."

His hand came up to my shoulder and I looked back at him, at this stern but caring man who would probably be my stepfather one day. "I am sorry for that, Lucas. I was trying to make things better for you. I guess I didn't."

I stared at him for several seconds before answering. "You did help. I don't think I could have dealt with anything…more than what I had to. So…thank you."

He nodded, his eyes just slightly wetter than usual. With a chuckle, he slung his arm over my shoulder and pulled me into a quick side hug. My mom came across us like that, and I thought she was going to start bawling right on the spot. She had desperately wanted her boys to be friends and couldn't be more thrilled at seeing it start to happen.

And it was, in a way. Being around the sheriff still brought that horrid accident to my mind, but the longer I spent with him, the more new memories started forming over those painful ones—mom snuggling with him on the couch, the sheriff and I tossing a ball in the backyard, laughing together over the antics of the local town crazy, who wandered around main street buck-naked. I would never forget my friends, or that night, but I was beginning to believe that we could be a family together, a happy one even.

So with excitement and trepidation, I got ready to graduate from this small school of mine. Walking down the halls on my last official day there, I couldn't help the tears that sprang to my eyes. I thankfully didn't start crying as I went about my last day, but it did affect me. I was tied to this school in a more emotional way than I'd realized on my first day back from the crash. This school was such a big part of the friendships and loves that I'd formed. A part of me struggled with letting that go.

"You all right?" Sawyer asked, as she reached down and clasped my hand with hers, letting our fingers weave together, as she preferred. Her hair was pulled into adorably cute pigtails, the same way she'd had it styled on our first day together.

I smiled at her question as we walked to the cafeteria on our way to have lunch with Randy and Sally, who were giving each other light pecks of affection as they walked in front of us. I watched the large linebacker and the plump, frizzy-haired girl who'd stolen his heart, and my smile widened. Life could certainly surprise you sometimes. I'd never have pictured those two together at the beginning of the year. Looking down at the gray-eyed angel gazing up at me with open adoration reconfirmed those thoughts. I'd never have believed on that first day that I could feel the way I did when I looked at her, when I made love to her. I'd never have imagined that feelings that strong were even possible outside of sappy romance novels.

Leaning down to brush her lips with mine, I smiled against her mouth. "I'm wonderful." My free hand reached up to stroke one of the long tails of her hair and I had a brief "school girl" fantasy flash through my head as I pulled away. My smile widened. She looked doubtful, though, as she searched my eyes, and I shook my head at her boundless concern.

My eyes flicked over the loud, boisterous cafeteria as we entered it. Some of the students looked up when I entered, some smiled and shot me a wave. Some looked at me blankly for a moment before returning to their conversations. Josh met my gaze while I waited in line with Sawyer, deciding to splurge on our last day with some hot food that I'd heard was nearly edible and vaguely resembled pizza. Josh gave me a polite nod before he went back to what looked like an argument with the girlfriend he always seemed to be in a tiff with.

Some of the students snacking on their midday meals had spilled out into the warm air of the sunny, near-summer day, and we decided to join them, picking a vacant spot under a shady tree. Even though Sawyer and I were dressed in typical summer garb, shorts and light t-shirts, her shirt was still long-sleeved. She still played with those sleeves on occasion, stretching out the fabric with her habit. I knew now why she dressed that way, and as we held hands while sitting in the grass, my thumb came up to sweep the scar at her wrist. She didn't flinch anymore when I did that, completely comfortable now with me exploring her body. Besides, I think she understood that I did that as a silent thanks to the heavens for keeping her here…for me.

My eyes drifted over the familiar buildings and memories of my friends assaulted me. I drew them to me, absorbing them, never wanting to forget a moment that I'd spent here with them. I felt a chin rest on my shoulder and I pulled out of my thoughts to gaze down at Sawyer sitting close by my side.

"You sure you're okay? You seem a little…down." She kissed my shoulder and then rested her cheek upon it.

I kissed her forehead and allowed myself a sad smile. "I guess I'm just…reminiscing."

She lifted her head and held my gaze. "About Lillian." She said it calmly, but I knew enough about her to know that a trace of sadness was there, buried deep under the surface. She knew that what she and I had went *way* beyond what Lil and I had ever shared together, but she also knew that Lil would never leave my heart. Unlike an ex that I had simply drifted apart from, Lillian had died in the middle of our love affair. And a part of me, a miniscule part of me, would always be in love with her.

I kissed her head again and shook mine. "No, not just Lil." My eyes swept over the campus again. "All of them. I feel like once I leave here…I'm leaving them all behind, for good."

Her hand came up to touch my cheek and I looked back at her. I blinked when I realized my vision was watery and I couldn't see her clearly. Great. Guess I *was* going to start crying today. She brushed one tear that had managed to escape away before our lunch mates saw it. Her gaze softened as she watched the emotions sliding across my face.

She nodded and looked thoughtful for a moment. "Do you want to talk about it?" Her eyes swept over the campus before returning to mine. "It will help you to remember, if you say it out loud."

Smiling, I nodded. I looked down, gathering myself, and then I started telling her about every moment I remembered with them. I was a little surprised at how easy it was to talk about them now, but months of counseling had taught me to open up, and nobody on this earth made me more comfortable than Sawyer, so opening up to her was particularly easy, especially now that we were so close.

Some of the memories I had were hard, and my eyes watered again, but, luckily, no more tears fell. Some memories were humorous and we shared some good laughs. Sawyer held my hand and listened with rapt attention while I told her stories about people she'd never gotten the chance to meet. It made me a little sad that she never had; she would have loved my friends. But then…if she had met them, *our* relationship would have been completely different.

Randy and Sally interjected with some stories of their own, and I listened intently to their tales of my friends. Hearing about them through other people's eyes was healing. Eventually, a small circle formed around us with more people sharing their recollections. More tears sprang to my eyes as I listened to others share their memories. It lifted my heart at hearing how deeply my friends were missed, and not just by me. It lifted my heart that they would never be forgotten.

As the small circle, that was starting to feel like a group therapy session, widened and the stories grew more joyous, I noticed Josh on the outskirts, listening. I motioned to him with my finger, but he shook his head and stayed where he was, yards away from the happy remembrances, but still absorbing them.

I understood. Even in the midst of all the warmth I felt from the group, a part of me felt alone and sad. A part of me wanted to pull away and retreat into my shell, but I knew that wouldn't do me any good, so I stayed. I stayed, listened, and even contributed stories of my own. By the time people started heading off to class and it was just Sawyer and me, enjoying our free period in the sun, I felt like the memories were molded and encased in plaster—never to escape my head.

That evening, Sawyer came to my house, all decked out in a beautiful lavender dress. Her super black hair had the front layers pulled back into a simple clip, exposing her long elegant neck. I told her that she looked amazing and pressed that silky material to my body. My fingers easily slid along her contours and my head rewound itself to our last encounter—the sounds she'd made when my lips had traveled over that smooth skin, the rapid pulse of her heart as my tongue had swept tiny circles along the artery of that slim neck.

Her eyes smoldered as they met mine and I thought maybe my steamy thoughts were apparent on my face. Either that, or she liked the black slacks and the crisp, dark blue shirt that I was wearing, complete with a tie this time. Maybe she was having steamy thoughts of her own. I hoped her thoughts were in line with mine again. Her fingers slid down my tie, trailing down my chest, as she looked over my more-orderly-than-usual hair. She bit her lip and returned her attention to my hazel eyes, eyes that I imagined had to be smoldering right back at her. "You look great," she whispered.

I smiled and pulled her even tighter, wishing my mom wasn't in the house getting ready for the graduation ceremony, wishing we had more time before we had to leave for the ceremony…wishing I could rip her clothes off right here. Well, maybe tonight…afterwards? Now that we were having sex on a regular basis, I found myself wanting it all the time. Luckily, Sawyer had an appetite that matched my own. We were well on our way to rivaling Darren and Sammy's weekly average.

Her eyes dragged over my body and I felt the heat of that stare even through my clothes. My body started reacting to her, to the curves of her body, emphasized in that satin material, to her fingers exploring my chest muscles, and to her eyes mentally undressing me. Just as I was about to pull the telltale sign of my desire away from her, she pressed her hips into mine.

She reached up to kiss me, a playful smile on her lips and lust clear in her eyes. "I wish we had more time," she whispered as we kissed fiercely, her words again matching my thoughts as we stood clenched together just a few feet from the front door. She hadn't made it very far before our hormones had taken over.

I started to back her into the door, not much caring anymore that my mom was in her bedroom. She gasped as I pressed against her. My lips traveled down to her neck, back to that artery, where her heart was racing again. "You are driving me crazy…I want you." An erotic noise passed her lips and her hands ran down my backside, pulling my hips and grinding me into her. I started to run through places in my head where we could go and my mom wouldn't interrupt us.

"Lucas…is that Sawyer? Are you guys ready?"

"God, yes…" I heard myself mutter. Sawyer started laughing and I tore myself away from her body, laughing as well. As we stepped away from each other, I tossed an answer to my mom's creepily well-timed question over my shoulder. "Yes, Mom, Sawyer's here."

Shaking my head, I twisted back to face her. She was still braced against the door, still laughing, her cheeks flushed from embarrassment and desire. My body twitched and I sighed, knowing I had to wait for that wonderful connection. My smile turned into a wry one. "When are we leaving for college again?"

She giggled more and reached out for my hand. I grabbed it, and together we headed over to the couch so my body could calm down a bit before my mom stepped into the room. I looked over at her as we sat. "Needless to say…I really like your dress."

She rolled her eyes and laughed again. "I should have remembered that fancy dresses are your Achilles' heel."

I smirked at her comment. My gaze went to the space above the television set. The wall there had been empty for a long time, but Mom had slowly started putting up pictures of Sawyer and me. Amongst the random everyday shots, was the picture that had been taken of us at the winter dance. In it, Sawyer was gazing up at me and I was gazing right back down at her. Even from the profile of our faces, the look of love passing between us was unmistakable. The photographer had been right when he'd assured me that it was perfect.

Right beside that picture, was one that had been taken a few weeks ago at Senior Prom. Sawyer's mom had gone behind her dad's back and splurged on a magnificently fitted, long-sleeved dress. It had been low cut with a high slit up one leg. In a midnight-black shade that beautifully matched Sawyer's hair, the tight gown had emphasized every curve of her body. My body had really liked that. We'd barely made it through half of that dance before our overly aroused bodies had needed a change of locale. Sawyer was right…I did have a thing for her in sexy dresses.

We were both chuckling about it when my mom finally joined us in the living room. She was wearing a summery dress with large flowers printed on it. She had left her hair down, curling it into large waves that nearly hid the gray streaks. With a beaming smile on her face as she watched the two of us holding hands on the couch, she looked half her age. I smiled at her youthful enthusiasm for the potentially boring event.

She crossed over in front of the couch and grabbed a smooth strand of Sawyer's hair. Her eyes watered as she examined my girlfriend. It made me chuckle that she was nearly crying already; she'd be bawling long before I was actually handed my diploma.

Her hand trailed down the satin covering Sawyer's arm, down to her wrists.

She grabbed Sawyer's fingers and squeezed for a second while Sawyer smiled up at her. "Sawyer, honey, you're so beautiful. That dress is lovely." Mom turned to look at me. "Isn't she lovely, Lucas?"

I tried to hide a grimace, but Sawyer saw it and giggled. We both knew what I "thought" of her dress. "Yes, Mom, she's beautiful." I whispered that last part directly at Sawyer, and her cheeks flushed to a blush more perfect than any brand name makeup could hope to mimic.

Mom patted my shoulder. "You're very handsome as well, Lucas. I swear, you look more like your father every day." I looked up at her when she said that. We didn't often speak of my dad. Honestly, we didn't ever speak of him. Mom's smile was a sad one, and I wasn't sure if I wanted to look more like my father every day. Her melancholy almost instantly shifted back to radiance. "Neil will be here in a minute, and then we'll go."

She took a seat in the chair next to the couch and demurely crossed her ankles, her face dreamy at the mention of her boyfriend. Looking down, she worried her lip. "Um, I won't be back after the ceremony, Lucas." She peeked up at me, and I swear she was blushing. Finally, she raised her chin and gave me a level gaze. "I'm going to stay overnight with Neil."

I had no idea what to say to that. On the one hand, I had accepted their relationship, and I was thrilled that she was happy. On the other…my mom had pretty much just told me she was having sex tonight. My stomach twisted a little bit as I flatly said, "All right."

She grinned like a school girl, and Sawyer chuckled beside me. Mom shifted her focus to her. "Are your parents coming tonight, dear? I'd love to chat with your mom again."

Sawyer nodded. "Yeah, they're meeting me there. A bunch of us senior girls are having a sleepover at Sally's house afterwards, so I'm taking my own car." I watched her blankly, not realizing that she'd made plans without me. Her hand subtly squeezed mine, but she didn't turn to look at me. I wondered over her move; it was obviously supposed to convey something to me. Then it hit me so hard I actually groaned, quickly shifting it to a cough when my mom looked at me oddly.

Sawyer had just lied. She had no intention of going over to Sally's tonight. She was staying overnight…with me. Maybe she'd originally planned on staying most of the night with me and then heading out to Sally's before morning, but my mom had just handed her an overnight pass. Mom wasn't coming home tonight…and Sawyer wasn't leaving me. My slacks got a little uncomfortable as I thought about that. I squeezed her hand back much harder than she'd squeezed mine.

I could not concentrate on any of the conversations we had after that, while we waited for Neil to show up. I was ready for the dressed portion of the evening to be over with. Although, I'd have to tell Sawyer at some point to not change out of that dress after the ceremony…

Sheriff Whitney, uh, Neil, pulled into a parking space right beside the space I'd parked Sawyer's car in. Even though the drive to the high school was a fairly short one from my house, I exhaled with relief when I turned the key off. I generally let

Sawyer drive us everywhere, but tonight had seemed like the kind of occasion where I should be more of a gentleman and drive her. Especially with her looking so nice in that silky dress.

Her hand came out to my knee as I watched Neil get out of his car and walk over to my mom's door, escorting her from her car just like I wanted to escort Sawyer. Maybe he felt the evening called for a little chivalry, or maybe that was just a remnant of his generation. That's probably just the way things were done back in the day…he was quite a bit older than my mom. But if that didn't bother her, I suppose I shouldn't let it bother me.

I looked back at Sawyer as she squeezed my knee. Her face had a warm smile on it; mine matched as I gazed at her. "You did great, Luc."

I knew she was talking about my driving, and I felt my cheeks flush with heat, both at her encouragement and at the fact that she felt like she needed to encourage me. Eventually I would get past this obstacle and feel more at ease behind the wheel again. It was just going to take a lot longer than I'd anticipated. At least I didn't get panic attacks at just the thought of getting behind the wheel anymore. That was something.

I nodded at her and opened my door. She waited in her seat, knowing I wanted to be all grownup-like for her, and watched me walk around the car. I swung open her door and swiftly swept her into my arms for a quick kiss, surprising her and making her let out a short squeak. An unhappy grunt behind me got my attention, and I twisted to look over my shoulder. I immediately met gazes with Sawyer's intimidating father. It would seem they'd also just arrived. He'd gradually accepted that our purely platonic friendship had shifted to something much deeper after that day on the highway, and while Sawyer assured me that he did indeed like me, he generally did not like seeing me with my hands and mouth all over his baby girl.

I instantly stepped away from her, not wanting to get her into any unnecessary trouble that might prevent her from spending the night with me, or with Sally, as her parents believed. They might have accepted our relationship, but they weren't about to condone us having sex. Even if Sawyer and I were both eighteen now, and technically adults, they were still parents and, much like my mom, they were most likely pretending that the two of us had decided to hold off on the physical stuff until we were away at college, if not married. I wasn't about to let it slip to any of them that that was most definitely *not* the case.

Sawyer calmly walked up to her dad and slung her slim arms around his massive neck, giving him a light kiss on the cheek. You could see the big man practically melt as he hugged her back. Her mom broke off from chatting with Neil and my mom, and gave her daughter a warm hug when her father let go. Then her mom hugged me and told us she was proud. Sawyer's dad merely nodded and grunted at me again.

Walking hand in hand, Sawyer and I parted ways with our parents and headed to the back of the gym where the rest of the seniors were waiting. There were about eighty of us in this small school, and most were having conversations with friends in groups of five or six. Everyone was dressed semi-formally, most already wearing their graduation robes slung open over their shoulders.

Sawyer and I were handed ours by Sally, who immediately started chatting with Sawyer about her party. I had no idea if Sally was aware that Sawyer wasn't really coming over or not. From the sound of it, Sawyer hadn't told her yet. As I tuned out their girl talk, I took a look around at the assembled students lounging about in the choir room, waiting for their five seconds of acknowledgement for four years of hard work.

It was a sea of blue before me. Blue robes and blue square hats with blue and white tassels hanging off the top. The room screamed school spirit and buzzed with the excited energy of people ready to leave that spirit behind. I looked over the students I'd become close with over the last couple months and gave them brief smiles when our eyes met. Randy waved at me, and I waved back. He was talking with some of the senior football players, Will included.

Will rolled his eyes at me when mine met his, but he made no move to antagonize me. While we had never warmed to each other, the level of teasing had died down once I'd started standing up to him. I narrowed it down to "little man on campus" syndrome. For a long time I'd had everything he'd wanted—a successful position as quarterback on the team and Lillian firmly by my side, completely head over heels in love with me. Seeing me fall from that height had been too tempting of a target to stroke his ego with. I hoped severing our friendship was worth it to him. It wasn't for me.

My eyes passed over several teachers in the room, Ms. Reynolds and Mr. Varner among them. Oddly enough, they were talking closely together. As I watched, his hand brushed against her thigh suggestively. I grimaced at the thought of her dating that jerk. After everything she'd done for me this year, I felt a little protective of her; I would hate for her to end up with an asshole. As she brushed his fingers away, a wry smile touched my lips. Maybe she was well aware of his nature and could see past the face that drove the high school girls to distraction. Good. I'd rather see her with a man who *looked* like a troll, than with a man who actually *was* one.

With irritation on his face, Mr. Varner's eyes slid over to mine. They narrowed when they took me in. I knew I'd been staring at him with an expression that probably looked smug, and I didn't change that expression any as I continued to stare at him. The guy was a jerk and deserved to be shot down. He broke our eye contact, walking away from Ms. Reynolds.

Her perky, pixie cut hair turned to look over at me and her beautiful smile widened. Now that I knew the bloodline, I thought I could see the resemblance to Sawyer in the shape of her eyes and the color of her brown hair, hair that more matched Sawyer's mom's, since Sawyer dyed hers. The body was also a pretty close match as the skirt Ms. Reynolds was wearing clung to her thighs and the flowery blouse plunged deep to show her cleavage. After a brief smile and nod to her, I turned to take in the other students, needing all references to Sawyer's body out of my head.

As I started to space out, staring at the sea of blue and white, I suddenly clearly saw Darren, Sammy and Lil, all in their gowns, talking with each other with mile-wide grins. I hadn't envisioned them like that in weeks, and I smiled, welcoming it, especially today. Darren looked over at me and waved with a playful glint in his dark eyes. His dark hair, in typical disarray, emphasized his devilishness. I grinned as I imagined that Darren would have had some prank planned for his brief moment of fame. Knowing Darren, he'd have gone up on stage only wearing boxers under that robe, and he'd have taken that moment to flash the crowd to thunderous applause from the student body.

My gaze shifted to the imagined version of Sammy holding Darren's hand. She'd of thought that was hilarious and would have been hollering the loudest of anyone for him. His antics never really made her angry. Irritated sometimes, sure, but never angry. She very rarely had anything but a happy grin on her face and my vision of her right now was no different. She turned her auburn head to say something to Lillian standing next to her and my gaze shifted as well.

A twang went through me. That probably wouldn't ever stop when I pictured her, but the ache was a dull one as she met my gaze and smiled at me. A sad smile was on my face as I imagined that if last year hadn't happened, last year to this exact date, I'd be standing over there with them, laughing about all the trouble we'd caused in our last year and planning to go out with a bang before we separated for college. I swallowed and my hands clenched involuntarily.

"Hey." A soft voice beside me broke my vision, and I blinked several times before looking down at Sawyer beside me. I knew my eyes were wet as she looked up at me. "You okay?" She lightly shook our joined hands and I relaxed my death grip on her.

I nodded, but then stopped and shook my head. With a slight lift of my lip, I shrugged. "It was today." She nodded and leaned against me, understanding what I meant. The accident had happened today. I swallowed and continued, "I would never have imagined a year ago, that I'd be graduating today without them…"

My voice trailed off as my throat closed up. Sawyer's eyes watered and she nodded again. "They'd be so proud of you, Luc."

I closed my eyes at that and nodded. Yes, they would. They'd be thrilled that I'd survived this year, survived the torment, whispers, and the self-inflicted pain. They'd be proud that I was moving forward. They'd be joyous that I had a potentially great life ahead of me, with a pretty amazing girl beside me, and even though I wished with every speck of life inside my body that they'd survived, too, I was proud of them. Proud that I'd known them, proud that I'd loved them, and proud that they'd loved me too. Proud that we'd had the kind of friendship together that some people went their entire lives without experiencing. And I'd hold that to me…forever.

Eventually Mr. Varner and Ms. Reynolds organized us into a few long alphabetized lines. Being the only 'W' in my class, I was in the back of the last line. Sawyer looked back at me from farther up our line and smiled brilliantly, the tassel on her hat swishing as she turned her head. She mouthed "I love you," and twisted back around before I could say anything back. I smiled as I watched her talk to Sally, who was standing in the line right next to her.

Ms. Reynolds came down each line, congratulating the seniors. She stopped in front of Sawyer and gave her a few words, her eyes glistening as she beamed at her relative. They shared a swift hug and then Ms. Reynolds continued down the line to me. She shook her head as she stood in front of me, and I knew she had a ton of things she wanted to say to me. I could imagine them: You've come a long way, I'm glad the Safe and Sound Club was a help to you, I'm sorry I ever doubted your innocence, I'm here if you need me. All she ended up saying was, "I'm proud of you, Lucas." I grinned as I watched her move back up to the front of the line. That was enough.

She opened up the door and headed out to the gym. With a look of utter boredom on his model face, Mr. Varner told the assembled kids that it was time to get this over with. He flung his hand towards the open door Ms. Reynolds had just walked through. When the first girl in line, Abby Adams, didn't move fast enough, he started making a "get a move on" gesture with his hand, continually spinning it in a circle while the line eventually trudged forward.

Mr. Varner was either irritated that he'd been put on senior duty or irritated that Ms. Reynolds had shot him down. I was hoping it was the latter, but really, just his being irritated was fine with me. He had a hopelessly exasperated look on his face by the time I got to him, and I gave him a brief smile. He glared and put a hand on my shoulder, holding me back from the rest of the group.

His eyes searched my face. "You sober? I don't need you up there slowing things down."

I rolled my eyes and jerked away from his touch. Here was one person who was going to think the worst of me no matter what. I tried not to take that personally when I thought over his sour mood all year. He just didn't care much for kids, it wasn't necessarily about me, although I was pretty sure he disliked me more than the rest. I seriously had no idea how I'd managed to get an A out of his class.

I raised my chin as I held his gaze. "I don't drink." My eyes flicked over to the now empty doorframe and then back to him. "And I have no intention of holding up your…plans, Jonathan." I couldn't help my impish grin; I was pretty sure his "plans" weren't the ones he wanted.

He narrowed his eyes even more and shoved my back to get me walking again. "You're already holding up my plans," I heard him mutter as I stepped out onto the lacquered floor of the gym. Once again, I thought Mr. Varner had chosen the wrong path in life.

I blinked as I stepped out into the comparatively brighter room and paused a second to take in the sea of faces in the bleachers. Several younger members of the student body were here, saying goodbye to their older friends, and I recognized several parents of the kids in my class. As I stood alone by the choir room door, several heads in the bleachers turned to look at me. I was suddenly reminded of the packed gym laughing at me as I stumbled around like an idiot, doped out of my head. I was pretty sure this crowd wouldn't start laughing, jeering or throwing rotten tomatoes at me, but the scrutiny was making my cheeks heat.

I hurried to the last row of folding chairs set up before a makeshift stage in the center of the gym floor. The kids in my row were almost all seated by the time I scurried over to them. I sat down on the edge and looked over my row of blue-clad peers to find Sawyer, who was leaning forward in her seat and looking back at me.

Her head was cocked and her brow furrowed; she was obviously wondering why I'd been late. I smiled at how much she worried over me and shook my head at her, wanting her to enjoy her moment, her accomplishments. I wanted her, for once, to put my heart aside, if only for a few moments.

I settled back in my seat while the robed students in front of me shifted, preparing for at least an hour of tedium. I looked behind me at the students and parents watching their loved ones, looking for my mom. I found her right away. She was sitting almost directly behind me in the center of the bottom section of bleachers. She was sitting in-between Sawyer's mom and Neil, but she wasn't looking my way, she was bent down in conversation with someone sitting in front of her.

My eyes widened when I realized who she was talking too. I don't think I could have been more surprised. She was talking to Josh. I wasn't sure what startled me more, the fact that she was actually having what looked like a serious conversation with him, a hand supportively on his shoulder, or the fact that he'd actually come to the ceremony. He had no real reason to be here. I mean, he had a few friends in the class, but he was probably going to see them at some after party anyway. Why sit through the pomp and circumstance if you didn't have to?

They finished their conversation and my mom leaned down to give him a swift hug. I remembered then that my mom didn't know all of the things Josh had said and done to me over the year. All she knew was that he was Darren's little brother, and that he was probably as broken up over the loss as I was. I was instantly glad that I'd never told her about any of his torments. He might have been an ass to me, but he deserved my mother's kindness. Even if he had implied that she was a whore.

Josh, looking a little uncomfortable, loosely returned her hug and then nodded politely at Neil before twisting around to face front again. The principal started the ceremony, and the room quieted down as people turned to listen. I ignored it and kept my gaze on Josh. He stared right back at me, his face blank. Finally, one edge of his lip lifted to a smile. I smiled at seeing it, figuring that was the best I was going to get. It was something, though, and much better than him flinging a rock at me.

I twisted around to listen to the monotonous tones of the principal as she went about her prepackaged speech. I spaced out as her level voice lulled me into a semi-conscious state. I thought about the year and everything that had happened. I thought about the people I loved now and the people I'd loved then. I thought about my friends and how they should be here for this.

Ms. Reynolds had confessed that the school had agonized over what to do for them. Some members of the faculty had wanted to have a memorial during the ceremony, showing slides of them and having some students give speeches. My stomach had twisted at the thought of having to sit through that. I wasn't sure if I could, even after all this time.

Some other teachers had wanted to only do a symbolic memorial, saving empty seats and acknowledging their names in the correct places among the other students; pointing them out, but not dwelling on the tragedy. I thought that would have been a really decent thing to do.

But a few of the more vocal teachers, and I'm assuming Mr. Varner was among them, had raised quite a ruckus over the whole thing, insisting that there had been memorials over the summer and the students had had the entire year with a grief counselor on staff to deal with their pain. They felt that graduation should only celebrate the accomplishments of the living, and the dead shouldn't be brought up during such a joyous time.

I had been really offended by that, especially since I was pretty sure that the teachers complaining had just wanted to speed up the ordeal so their summers could start already. Unfortunately, the principal had agreed with the louder faculty members and nothing was being done. On the anniversary of my friends' tragic deaths, nothing was being done to honor them. The longer I sat in my hard backed chair, the longer that thought didn't sit well with me.

They were people, people I loved dearly. Not "events" that could be tossed aside because bringing them up might make some people uncomfortable. I knew it would be hard for me to hear their names and be reminded of their absence, but it was their right. They'd struggled through years of learning. They'd all been decent, if not good students. They'd all participated in extracurricular activities and had been active members of the community. They'd all been loved. They would have graduated, with honors, if their lives had continued normally. Well, Darren would have just squeaked by, but I'm positive he would have graduated.

They deserved better than being swept under the rug. They deserved their recognition.

Chapter 25 – A Time to Say Goodbye

After the hour of long speeches and "make your life mean something" well wishes finally passed, the first rows of students stood to make their way to the stage. They were antsy as they waited in line while the principal addressed them one at a time. A spattering of applause came after each name as the student grabbed their coiled piece of paper.

Occasionally one student's name would inspire greater applause than another. That was usually due to a small prank that the student was pulling, although no one tried anything as dramatic as flashing the crowd, like Darren would have. Sometimes it was because that student was perceived as popular, like the thunderous noises Brittany received. But I knew better than anyone that popularity didn't have anything to do with worthiness, and I was content with the fact that I would probably only receive a near silent, polite form of clapping.

Finally, my row stood to a burst of applause and we made our way to the waiting area; I think the noisy reaction had more to do with the fact that we were the last row than with the student's name currently being called. Sawyer looked back at me when her name was the next to be called and gave me a dazzling smile. I smiled back, happy that after all was said and done, I'd still have her. That warmth was going to stay with me for several years to come, maybe forever.

Her name was finally called and I brought my fingers to my mouth to let out an ear-splitting whistle for her. Her applause was decently loud anyway—she had done a much better job of integrating herself this year than I had—but I liked doing my part to help her feel wanted. It was the least I could do.

She giggled as she took her diploma and shook the principal's hand. Her cheeks were flushed from the slight embarrassment of everyone's eyes on her, and she was gorgeous to me as she headed down the stairs on the other side of the gym. She kept her eyes on me as she walked back to her seat, a wry smile on her lips. She was well aware that I'd created the ruckus. I chuckled as I watched her sit down.

By then, I was next in line, and the last to go up. A silence hit the room the second before my name was called. I felt the heat of every set of eyes on me and raised my chin, determined to make it through this. Some people still thought poorly of me, and most couldn't help but think of the tragedy when they looked at me, but I didn't need to let my sorrowful past define me. As Sawyer had told me once, we can choose who we want to be.

"Lucas Michael West," the principal flatly intoned.

The applause started off just as light as I'd imagined it would be, but by the time I made it to the center of the stage, it was significantly louder. Not anywhere near the level of Brittany's saunter across the stage, but elevated nonetheless. A smile crept up to the corner of my lip as I let the acceptance I'd been so sure I'd never get wash over me. I let my own acceptance wash over me as well. What was that Beth had told me? *You can't accept forgiveness from others until you forgive yourself.* My smile widened as I let myself bask in that forgiveness. I felt better than I'd felt in a while.

I firmly grabbed the principal's hand and shook it, taking my diploma with my other hand. She gave me a tight lipped smile and a brief nod of her head. Her handshake was crisp, brief and to the point—you've graduated, great, next please. After we separated, she started turning back to the microphone, obviously assuming that I'd continue down the stage and make my way to my seat without her direction. I didn't intend to do that yet though.

Fighting a sudden nervous knot in my stomach, I stepped in front of her, directly in front of the microphone. Looking startled at my bold maneuver, she stopped and stared at me instead of pulling me back. I took her moment of hesitation to look out at the crowd of shocked faces.

Quiet instantly fell on the gym as people wondered what the heck I was doing. I cleared the frog out of my throat and started the speech I'd only just thought of while sitting and waiting for my turn.

"My name is Lucas West," I paused, my cheeks going a bit red as I realized that even if they hadn't already known that, which I was sure most of them had, the principal had just announced it over the microphone. "But, you all already know that." My eyes drifted over the crowd, spotting my mother, looking proud, but confused. "I know you all want to get on with your evening…but I can't let this night go by without acknowledging…the three people who should be standing up here with me tonight."

From somewhere in the pin-droppingly silent gym, I imagined that I heard Mr. Varner sigh. I swallowed and glanced at the principal. She looked torn between jerking me away from the microphone and letting me finish, since I obviously had the attention of everyone out there. I tried to ignore that fact as I continued on with what I had to do. My eyes went back to the assemblage before me. I sought out Sawyer and held her gaze, pulling strength from her approving eyes.

"Darren McCord…Samantha Carter…and…Lillian Tate." My voice cracked on Lil's name, but I ignored it. My eyes flicked over the crowd, resting on people I knew and people I didn't know. "They died one year ago tonight and deserve some recognition. I ask that we all take a moment of silence, for the three lives that were lost. They may be gone…" my eyes shifted to rest on Josh's, his face white, his cheeks wet, "…but they are not forgotten."

I lowered my head and felt a rustling of several bodies doing the same. A thick silence permeated the room and all I could think about was *that* night. I tried to focus more on the earlier part of the evening—laughing with Sammy, clowning around with Darren, kissing Lillian. Up until the end, it had been an amazing night for all three of us. It brought me some odd sort of peace that their last night on earth had been a good one.

When my memories had run their course, my head lifted. I gazed out over the crowd again. Some heads were still down in reflection, some already in tears. Some were staring at me with a hardened expression, maybe wishing I hadn't brought this up here, maybe still believing the gossip that swirled around the town. When I felt the principal take a step towards me, I continued before she could stop me.

"I know a lot of assumptions about me…and that night, have been going around this town, and I know I haven't done much to dissuade those rumors…" I watched every head lift to regard me. As my voice through the microphone died out, complete silence fell over the room again. "Maybe my silence even helped to make the rumors seem true."

Locking eyes with Sawyer, I swallowed and continued, "I hope you can all understand that…that I've been going through some stuff." Sawyer gave me a warm smile and I started talking like I did when I was alone with my counselor, not conscious of the eyes on me, just feeling the need to release this burden from my shoulders.

"I remember everything about the accident." I shook my head as I kept my eyes on Sawyer's glistening ones. "I've always remembered everything." I heard a buzzing noise start around the gym as people absorbed that, and my eyes went back to the crowd. A lot of the students weren't surprised by this since I had been speaking to them more often of late, but some of the adults in the audience seemed genuinely shocked, and a few seemed angered.

I closed my eyes and sighed, wishing I didn't have to do this. Wishing my friends were sitting in their seats, laughing at me making a spectacle of myself. But wishing changes nothing and this was my reality, a reality I needed to share tonight. "Darren, Lil and Sammy were drinking…Darren was very drunk. I'd been drinking soda, so I took the keys from him." I looked out at the crowd. Silence had hit the gym again upon my words, and I found an odd sort of strength from it. I'd been worried that some disbeliever would stand up and start verbally abusing me at that point, but everyone was quiet, listening.

"The wreck wasn't caused because I'd been…messed up." I closed my eyes. "It was that freak rainstorm. We hit it on the way home and Darren's car started hydroplaning on the road." I paused, feeling the slice of pain that always hit me when I thought about that moment. I reopened my eyes and searched the audience until I connected with my mother. I focused on the love I felt pouring from her and in a much quieter voice, continued. "I made a mistake. I was driving too fast and all I wanted was to stop…so I slammed on the brakes. I completely lost control of the car and we were right at that sharp corner. I couldn't do anything to stop us, and we hit the rail hard…and went over." I kept my eyes on my mom's. There were tears streaming down her cheeks. My voice cracked when I started talking again. "I made a mistake…and they all died because of it."

I looked back over the crowd and saw several faces with unshed tears and several more with wet cheeks. I was a little startled to realize that mine were wet as well. "They were my best friends, and I miss them every day, and I know several of you feel the same way." I let my eyes drift back down to the seniors before me. "They would have loved to be here, graduating with us today."

I swallowed noisily. "I would give *anything* to be able to go back to that night a year ago, knowing what I know today, and change everything that happened. I'd leave earlier, or drive slower, or make us all walk home, even." I sighed, knowing that once again, wishing did nothing. "No…I'd convince them all not to go in the first place. I'd convince them to stay at my place and stay safe. I know I can't go back and change anything, but I'd give anything to have my friends…*our* friends…back."

I sniffed and searched the thoughtful eyes of the students in front of me, most of them welling with tears. I stopped when my eyes came upon Sawyer's again.

Hers were as wet as mine as she nodded her encouragement. "I've thought of joining them so many times. I thought everyone's life would be better if I'd never survived, if I was dead as well. And I wanted to die. I tried to…die with them." I looked back at my mom. Her face was pale white as her mind went back to that awful day by the highway when I'd been set on taking my own life.

I swallowed and spoke directly at her. "I wanted to make everyone's life easier. I wanted my torture to end." I paused as I watched her start to sob quietly in the stands. Neil put a comforting hand across her shoulders and pulled her to his side. Sawyer's parents, their faces as wet and distraught as my mom's, patted her back in sympathy. My eyes drifted from her down to Josh. He was staring at me wide-eyed with his mouth open. He hadn't known that I'd gone from wanting to die to trying to make it happen. With a small voice I spoke to him. "But I can't change the past and I have to live with what I've done. And I will."

Peeling my eyes away from Josh's stricken face and my mom's pain, I inhaled a deep, cleansing breath and swept the room again. "If some of you still choose to believe the lies, and still choose to hate me…I won't hold that against you." I set my jaw and raised my chin. "But, I won't be joining you in hating me anymore. I made a mistake, a mistake that anyone could have made." My voice and face softened and I looked down and shook my head. "I've taken my penance, and now…I'm moving forward. Now, I'll do what Darren, Sammy and Lillian would have wanted me to do." I looked back up, my eyes automatically going to Sawyer's beaming face. "Now, I'll live."

I stepped away from the podium and blinked a few times while I looked around. There was no stoic clapping like you'd expect after a speech like that, just a few sniffles and a few muttered words, and a sea of appraising, thoughtful faces. I wasn't sure if my speech had changed anyone's feelings about me—those who still believed the worst, after all this time, would probably always believe the worst—but I'd needed to do it, and as I stepped down to rejoin my classmates, I felt a calm peace flowing through me that I had.

The principal quickly wrapped up the evening and then the entire gym erupted in celebration. I joined in. I'd done it. I'd made it through the year in more-or-less one piece. As the crowd of graduated students began to disperse, I found Sawyer and lifted her about a foot in the air. She squealed and hugged me tight, whispering how proud of me she was for my speech. I set her down and grabbed her face, giving her a long, slow kiss that didn't end until some of the students around us started clapping our backs to congratulate us.

Many more people than I would have expected gave me approving words for my tribute to our lost classmates. Ms. Reynolds came up to me with tears on her cheeks, telling me my speech was beautiful. Mrs. Solheim approached me a minute later, making Sawyer laugh when she called me Tom. At hearing Sawyers' voice, she turned to acknowledge her and blinked, like she was staring at something that couldn't be real. Sawyer looked at her oddly, but I understood my flighty teacher's reaction. Mrs. Solheim probably thought she was seeing art come to life right in front of her face. I'd drawn, painted and sculpted various versions of Sawyer all year, and even though Mrs. Solheim talked to Sawyer at the beginning of the school year, when

Sawyer had been collecting homework assignments for me, I don't think she'd realized that my subject was an actual person until this very second.

As I watched my odd teacher recover herself and turn to float among the seniors, a hand clapped my back. I twisted to see Coach standing behind me. I blinked and shook my head, like *I* was seeing something that couldn't be real. Coach had actual tears in his eyes. With pride clear on his face, he grabbed my shoulder and drew me in for a swift hug. That startled me too.

Quickly letting go, he crossed his arms over his chest and leaned back, appraising me. "That was nice, Luc…what you did." He shook his head and gruffly said, "Stupid principal should have done it." I smiled at that and nodded my agreement. He sniffed again, his eyes getting even mistier. Extending his hand to me, he spoke in a heartfelt voice, "You're a good man, Lucas. It's been an honor knowing you."

My eyes misted as well as I grabbed his hand and shook it. "You too, Coach." I heard Sawyer sniffle and I put my arm around her waist as Coach and I released each other. She laid her head on my shoulder as I smiled at the much softer looking Coach in front of me. For once, we felt more like equals than a teacher and a student. I suppose that was a natural feeling to have after graduating. He clasped my shoulder again and turned like he was leaving.

"Coach?" I said, as he twisted. He looked back at me with raised eyebrows and I again saw the resemblance to me that Darren used to tease me constantly about. One day I'd have to ask Mom if we were related. Maybe distant cousins or something? "Thank you, for your help with college."

He smirked and shook his head. "That was all you, Lucas." Abruptly his face got that stern "coach" look that he could do so well. "But don't make me look bad in front of my sister's husband."

I smiled and shook my head as he walked off.

Several students came up to Sawyer and me after that, offering congratulations and appreciations for my speech. Even Will approached me and grudgingly told me that my moment of silence was a nice thing to do. Of course, then he tried to make me fall as Sawyer and I headed for the bleachers to rejoin our parents. It wasn't as if Will had instantly grown up since being handed an honorific piece of paper.

Shaking my head at his weak attempt, I clasped Sawyer's hand, and we headed over to where her parents were talking with my mom and Neil. Sawyer's mom had wet cheeks, and her face beamed when she glanced at me. I suddenly got the feeling that she'd finally seen me as a potential husband for her daughter tonight, and she approved. I couldn't help but smile at that thought.

Just as we took the first step to climb up to them, Josh stepped down to stand in front of me. His face was tired and blank, but his dark eyes looked like they'd been wrung out a couple times. I motioned for Sawyer to go ahead, telling her I'd be there in a minute. She nodded and squeezed my hand before letting go.

Josh's eyes watched her leave before slowly turning back to me. I swallowed, waiting for him to speak. After another couple seconds of silence, he finally did. "That was really nice…what you did for Darren, for all of them. Thank you."

I felt my eyes watering and didn't know what to say in return. I found myself nodding and saying, "They deserved some recognition…especially today." My voice was soft and a touch hoarse.

Josh's eyes watered as well and he clapped me on the shoulder before twisting to walk past me on the stairs. I turned to watch him leave, mentally wishing him a happier year next year. Once on the gym floor, he turned to look back at me. His eyes studied mine for a moment before he nodded and quietly said, "I believe you, Lucas. Good luck next year."

Those damn tears in my eyes trailed down my cheeks as I nodded and told him my well wishes for him. He returned my gesture, then turned and disappeared into the sea of robed students milling about the gym floor.

After congratulatory hugs from Sawyer's mom and, surprisingly, her dad as well, I was engulfed by my mother, who sobbed and told me repeatedly that she loved me and was very proud of me. I tried to pull away from her near hysterics, but then I stopped and let the slight woman cry on my shoulder as long as she needed to. I'd done something to her when I'd tried to end my life, and this was her way of healing. I wouldn't deny her that.

When she was finally more put together, Neil gave me a swift hug and a handshake, and took Mom's hand, leading her from the gym, back to his home where they were probably going to make love all evening. I closed my eyes and shook my head to block out that thought. I said goodbye to Sawyer's parents, who had a word with Sally before leaving the gym and heading home alone. By the look on their faces as they waved at the door, Sally had convinced them that Sawyer was indeed going to her party.

I gave her a sly smile as I realized why she hadn't broken the news to her friend yet. She gave me a wry smile back, her adorable dimple smiling at me too. "Sally is an awful liar. Now that she's convinced my parents that I'm really going to be at her house all night, I'm pretty much free until morning." Giving me a quick kiss she added, "I'm going to go tell her what's really up."

I smiled as she pulled away, but then frowned. "Do your parents still not trust you?"

She laughed and stepped back into me, her arms going around my neck as she leaned up for a kiss. "They trust me fine. But you? They're pretty sure you would use any opportunity to get into my pants." She laughed again, and I laughed with her.

My hands ran around her waist, imagining that dress again. "It's not getting into your *pants* that's interesting me right now." I cupped her backside through her robe and she giggled. Leaning in close I added, "You are going to keep that dress on for a while longer…right?"

She gave me another light kiss before disentangling us. "Oh yes, Luc. I wasn't about to change something that makes your eyes look like that."

She walked away then, to go talk to Sally, and I furrowed my brow. "Like what?" I called across the gym to her. She turned her head and laughed, but didn't answer me. I grinned as I watched my beautiful girl walk over to her friend to break the news.

Sorry, Sally, tonight my angel is staying with me. I loved that thought.

Walking hand in hand with Sawyer to the parking lot, I started gearing myself up for the drive back home. I knew I could do it, but I still had to give myself a mental pep talk. I waved at various groups of people that we walked past, a little amazed at how different things were now, than at the beginning of the year. I'd made it, though. As hard as it had been, it was over now. I clenched Sawyer's hand as we reached the first parked cars.

"Lucas?"

A voice calling to me got Sawyer's and my attention, and we stopped walking and turned to look behind us. I smiled brightly at seeing Beth trotting over to greet us. Her red curls bounced around her shoulders as the wide smile on her face matched mine. "Good, you're still here."

"Hi, Beth," I said, releasing Sawyer's hand so I could give her a warm hug.

She returned it, her hands coming down to my arms as we pulled apart. Pride showed in her pale eyes as she looked over my face. "That was amazing, Lucas, just…amazing." I blushed and looked down. It wasn't that incredible. She laughed, and I looked back up at her. "No, I'm not exaggerating. Considering where you started this year, *that*," she indicated behind her, "was amazing."

Embarrassment over her praise washed through me, but then a feeling of seriousness replaced it. "Thank you…for not giving up on me." I raised one lip wryly. "Or having me committed."

She laughed again and shook her head. "I would never have done either of those things, Lucas." She patted my arm, looking over to Sawyer before turning back to me. "You call me if you need…anything, okay?" I nodded and gave her another swift hug. In my ear she whispered, "I told you we'd get you there, Luc."

I bit my lip and nodded again as we separated a final time. I grabbed Sawyer's hand and turned with her to leave. As we did, Beth knowingly said, "Have a good night, you two." Sawyer giggled and I turned my head to look back at Beth, giving her a quick grin. I could still hear her light laughter when we reached Sawyer's car.

It felt like just moments later that Sawyer and I were standing alone in my bedroom. The room was subtly lit by the half-moon hanging thousands of miles above us and the intimacy of its pale light wrapped around us. We stood by the side of my bed and simply gazed at each other. My heart warmed at the sight of her silver-in-the-moonlight eyes drinking me in. I sighed and lowered my head to hers, giving her a soft kiss, filling it with every ounce of love that I felt for her.

"I love you," I whispered between our kiss, feeling the need to verbalize what I felt for her too.

She sighed with a sound that matched mine. Her hands came up to my face, one stopping at my cheek, the other tangling in my hair. The move brought her body closer to mine and her breasts pressed against my chest.

"I love you too," she whispered.

My hands came up to rest on her hips, our lips moving more intently now. As my hands circled her backside, she made a soft noise and stepped into me, her hips resting against mine. I was ready for her and I heard an, "Oh, Lucas," fall from her lips before my tongue stole all speech from her.

My fingers lightly traveled up her trembling body to her neck, threading through some long, silky strands of her hair before finding the zipper of that fabulous dress. I groaned as I pulled the zipper down, anxious to see what was underneath but sorry to see that thin, clingy material leave her curves. I pulled back, my breath coming harder through my parted lips. Hers was, as well.

Pulling the now gray-looking dress down her shoulders, I exposed her creamy skin inch-by-inch. She gasped when her shoulders were free. I gasped when her breasts were free. Following that silky fabric down the contours of her body, I shoved it to a point just past her hips, and then dropped it. It fell to her feet in a loose pile, and I took a second to admire the scantily clad beauty before me.

Her bra and underwear were a startling white. They had to be, for they seemed to glow in the pale light of the moon. They were lacey and provocative, barely containing her curves, her body nearly spilling out of the partial cups. My head bent to automatically taste the tender skin above her breast while my fingers wrapped around to unveil them. Her fingers loosened my tie and started making short work of the buttons on my shirt as I unclasped her bra.

She pulled me over to my bed, stepping out of her shoes and the pile of her dress. I kicked off my shoes as I followed her, my head still bent, my mouth moving over her exposed chest. She pulled off my tie and shirt when the backs of her legs hit the bed. She started in on my slacks when I moved over to the other breast.

I was barely conscious of my pants sliding down my legs, my whole being focused on feeling her body. It wasn't until her hand wrapped around me that I became aware of my body again. I found my way back to her mouth. Our kisses were more passionate now, as our fingers and palms explored the other.

Our breaths nearly as frantic as our mouths, she pulled my neck, urging me to lie down with her. I did, pausing only momentarily to slip off my socks and underwear. She watched me with hungry eyes until I joined her again. I lay on top of her, pressing my aching body against her underwear. I could feel how ready she was for me, too, and I swore under my breath. She ground her hips against me and a low swear passed from her lips as well.

I trailed my mouth and tongue down her body, wanting to know what every part of her tasted like. Every section was different: the trace amount of flowery perfume along her neck, the barest hint of sweat between her breasts, the faint amount of lavender body wash around her belly button. My fingers looped around her underwear and tugged them down. As I watched them slide down her thighs, the only thought in my head was—I needed to taste her everywhere.

I let my hands travel back up her thighs, kissing along the inside. I heard her breath hitch in anticipation. It made me throb. I stared at the spot I wanted to be more than anything. She squirmed in my hands. I knew she wanted me to be inside her too. And I would be…in a minute.

Just as I was bringing my tongue down to taste that delicate skin, her hands pushed back on my shoulders. My breath was heavy and my eyes felt hooded as I snapped them up to hers; hers were heavy with desire too as she looked down on me, but I could also see a hint of uncertainty.

Sawyer and I were completely comfortable with each other, but this…? For her, this was probably more intimate than everything we'd already done. For me too, I suppose. If our positions were reversed, I'd probably be feeling a little self-conscious about myself, regardless of how comfortable I was with her. Even boundless love didn't always overcome insecurity. I understood that. Truth be told, I was a little nervous about this too, as I'd never done it either, but I wanted us to experience everything together, even if it kind of scared us.

She apparently felt the same. After staring down at me for just a moment, she bit her lip, and then reached over to cup my cheek; her thumb ring, the only adornment on her body, was cool on my warm skin. She drew me to her, opening herself to me, welcoming me as she always did. I didn't hesitate. I dropped my mouth and ran my tongue up her. I heard the noise I made, but it was instantly drowned out by the loud cry from her. The taste…was indescribable.

"Lucas…that feels so…" She started panting and moaning in a pattern I knew well and I ached with the thought of satisfying her this way. Just when I started to wonder if I could, her need-filled voice rang in my ears. "Oh God, oh God, Lucas…"

She didn't have time to say anything else. I moaned as I felt and heard her release. I was so in tune with her body, it was almost like I *was* her and I'd just come as well, even though my throbbing body assured me that I hadn't.

I pulled away, breathless and aching. She reached down for my face and pulled me to her mouth. Needing her so bad I could barely take it anymore, I slid into her and cried out in her mouth when our hips rested together.

We stayed connected, without moving, until my body calmed down a bit. Then we slowly began to move. We both exhaled in relief. It was the most intensely profound connection I'd ever had, emotionally or physically, with another human being. Our movements stayed slow as we each experienced the other in the silvery near-dark of my bedroom. I whispered in her ear how much I loved her and she murmured that she loved me in return.

We were in complete unison, feeling like we'd done this for years instead of months. Eventually our joint need drove us to move faster, until I felt all of my other senses dulling as my body focused on one outcome. I heard myself moaning and heard her begging for me to finish with her. I didn't need to be told twice; I started to crest, murmuring her name as I fell over the edge. She clutched me tight and to my surprise, she cried out again, her body tightening around me as she climaxed a second time.

We slowed our movements and I carefully started to remove myself from her. Her fingers went to my hips, stilling me. "No…please, stay, just for a little bit."

I left myself inside of her, and let the rest of me carefully sag on top of her. "As long as you want, Sawyer," I murmured breathlessly.

Her hands came up my back, tracing light patterns into my skin as her legs wrapped around me, trying to pull me even closer. It was impossible. We couldn't get any closer. She brought her hands up to hold my head as I lay across her, my breath still fast, my heart still racing. Her fingers tugged through my hair, stroking repeatedly, and my body slowly started calming down. She kissed my head as I buried it in her neck. When I felt wetness on my cheek, I pulled back, confused. Looking up at her face, I noticed that she was crying.

I immediately pulled out of her and adjusted some of my body weight off of her. "I'm sorry, am I hurting you?" I whispered, wiping tears off her cheeks.

She looked up at the ceiling, shaking her head while cringing in embarrassment. Swallowing, she swiped her fingers under her eyes. "No, no of course not."

Still confused, I swept my hands over her face. I didn't want her to feel anything but happy, like me. Seeing my expression, she sighed and rolled her eyes, a slight laugh escaping her. "Sorry, I'm totally being a girl right now."

"Sawyer?"

She brought her hands to my cheeks, soothing my fears with a warm smile. "I'm sorry. It's just…with everything we've both gone through…" She searched my face, new tears moistening her eyes. "This is overwhelming, what I feel for you…and sometimes…" Her voice warbled, but she swallowed and steadied herself. With a clearer voice she said, "Sometimes, I can't believe we made it here…together."

I sighed and rested my head on hers. "I know exactly what you mean," I whispered, rocking my head against hers and kissing her tenderly for a few minutes. This could be just as overwhelming for me sometimes.

When I pulled away, she bit her lip. "I have a confession." I cocked an eyebrow at her. She grinned devilishly before answering me. "While that was…amazing, Lucas, sex really wasn't why I wanted to stay with you tonight."

I shifted to her side. She twisted to face me, her legs entangling with mine. "No?" I said distractedly, as I ran my fingers through her hair.

She bit her lip again, her eyes darting down to my chest, before lifting to meet mine again. "No." Her hand came up to cup my cheek, stroking soft circles into my skin. "I wanted to make sure you were okay tonight…in case it was difficult for you. In case you had a dream."

I stopped stroking her hair as I started to understand what she meant. She'd planned on staying with me tonight because it was the one year anniversary of my friends' deaths. She was worried I'd have a nightmare and wake up screaming…alone. And she didn't want me to be alone; she never wanted me to be alone. I sighed and shook my head, amazed at her compassion. I leaned in to kiss her.

"I'll be fine, Sawyer." Resting my head against hers, I whispered, "But I *am* glad you're here." I hadn't dreamt of them in so long, that I was pretty sure I wouldn't tonight. But…you never know.

I pulled her tight to me, reveling in the lemony scent of her hair as my face buried into her shoulder. Her arms came up to rub random patterns into my back and I felt exhaustion start to take me over. I whispered how much I loved her, and then gave into it.

I gradually became aware that I was back at school. I was in the first floor hallway of the main building. I looked around the empty space, and all I saw was locker upon locker. Some were closed, some were open, papers and books spilling out of them to the floor. Posters taped to the wall were torn and battered. A poster from the Safe and Sound Club, wishing all of the kids a "safe" summer, was ripped in two. The loose pieces hung around the archway leading outside like paper curtains.

The floor of the hall was littered with stray pieces of paper, streamers, tassels from graduation caps and scores of commencement ceremony pamphlets. It was like the entire student body had ripped out of there after graduation, littering and messing up the place in their joy of school being over, if only for the summer, for those not leaving these halls for good. The janitors were gonna be pissed.

Laughter from the opposite end of the hall got my attention, and I turned to look. A wide smile broke out on my face as I watched Darren, Sammy and Lillian materialize and start to walk towards me. They were all wearing their caps and gowns. Sammy and Lillian clutched scrolled diplomas tightly in their hands. Darren, walking between the girls, was tightly holding their free hands as they all three looked at each other with bright, smiling faces.

As one, they turned their heads to stare at me. Every face was calm and peaceful. Every set of eyes was warm and loving. Mine misted over at seeing them again. It had been months. Darren nodded at me, a warm grin on his face, his dark eyes glowing with the life I knew they didn't really have anymore. His dark hair stuck out every which way, as untamable as himself.

On his right, Sammy beamed with a bright smile. Her auburn hair seemed to find every ray of light in the room and glowed like an autumn sunset. Her golden eyes regarded mine with a slight hint of moisture, and she nodded as well. After acknowledging her greeting, my eyes shifted to Darren's left, to the first love of my life.

Lillian gleamed as golden as the sun. Her pale hair was nearly painful to look at, and her eyes were a bright blue, as perfect as a cloudless spring day. Her smile was brilliant as she gazed at me. My breath caught at seeing it. Even long-deceased, her beauty still tore my heart.

"Hello, Lucas." Her voice, so long gone from my ears, closed up my throat and I shut my eyes, absorbing that sound forever.

After long seconds, I reopened them. They had all stepped closer to me during my silence and were standing in a small circle around me. Each one reached out to touch a part of me; Sammy, on the side of me, touched a shoulder, Darren, on the other side of me, touched my other shoulder, and Lillian, directly in front of me, reached up to touch my chest. I inhaled at the warmth and peace in their physical contact. Much like before, they felt completely real.

I smiled at each one in turn, my eyes lingering on Lillian last. "I never thought I'd see you again," I said, when I could finally speak.

Lillian's eyes watered and a slight frown marred her features. "We never meant to push you over the edge, Lucas." She shook her head, her pale hair under her graduation cap brushing over her shoulders. "We only wanted to help."

I felt Darren's hand on my shoulder tighten and I twisted to look at him. "Yeah, we're sorry about being…harsh."

I shook my head at them all. "It's not your fault. What I almost did…that wasn't your fault."

Lillian's hand came up to my cheek, drawing my eyes back to her. "It wasn't your fault either, Luc." I knew what she meant. I knew she was now referring to the accident that had claimed them. I swallowed and felt the tears rise in my eyes. "It was just an accident, Lucas. That's all."

I swallowed again, my throat feeling raw and dry. "I know," I whispered. "I know."

Lillian smiled brilliantly again and I felt my heart fill at seeing the joy on her face. Her hand patted my chest, smoothing out the plain t-shirt I was wearing. "You seem better." She shook her head again. "You don't know how much peace that gives us."

I looked over all of them again, clearly seeing that peace in their features. It was like looking at a mirror image of my soul, which I suppose every meeting with my dream friends had been—a representation of some part of my subconscious that had needed to work things out so I could eventually heal.

"I think I understand your peace perfectly." My eyes rested on hers again. "I feel it too."

Almost as if on cue, Lillian and Sammy turned to look at Darren and then took several steps away from me. They leaned back against the lockers and turned to talk to each other, tuning Darren and I out. Their clothes changed to basic jeans and t-shirts and, for a moment, they looked exactly like I'd expect them to look if I ran into them between classes. The sight made me smile.

Darren bumped his fist into my shoulder and I twisted to look at him. He was in regular clothes now too, and had a devilish grin on his face. I grinned at seeing it. Looking over his shoulder at Lil, he quickly turned back to me and lowered his voice.

"Hey, good job on the…you know." He raised his eyebrows suggestively, and I flushed, knowing he meant the end of my virginal status that had been an ongoing joke between us.

"Gee, thanks," I muttered.

He laughed and then a more serious expression took over his face. "You're a man now." He barely got through saying it, before breaking out into more laughter.

"Oh, God," I sighed and shook my head, watching an oblivious Lil over his shoulder. I supposed she knew, since they all knew what was in my head, but I oddly didn't feel as guilty about that as I would have. I guess I really had moved on. I shifted my focus back to a still laughing Darren. A chuckle finally escaped me as I memorized his gleeful face. "Are you done?"

He clapped my shoulder. "Yeah, I guess so."

As the laughter died between us, his face got serious for real. "She's good for you, you know."

I smiled over at him, knowing exactly who he was talking about. "Yeah, I know." I thought of my physical body, bare, and securely wrapped in Sawyer's warm embrace and sighed contently. "I know."

He glanced over his shoulder at Sammy, who looked over and smiled the soft smile that she reserved only for him. He looked back at me, pure contentment on his face. "Don't ever forget it."

I shook my head. "I never could."

He smiled and nodded, then looked down for a moment. When he looked back up, his eyes were moist. "You were my best friend, Lucas." His eyes glistened more. I felt mine glistening in response. "You were my brother." His hand came up to my shoulder. "I love you, Lucas."

I sniffed and nodded. "I love you, too, Darren. You were my family."

I gave him a firm hug, clapping him on the back as he clapped me. Pulling apart, he jokingly slugged my shoulder, and I laughed. Smiling and stepping back he said, "Thank you…for being there for Josh. I know he can be a dick, but he needs you."

I nodded at him and smiled as I watched him walk over to Lil and pick her up in a warm, friendly hug. As I watched Lil giggle and struggle to get away, Sammy was suddenly standing directly in front of me.

"Lucas!" She exuberantly encased me in a hug. Laughing at her display, I clenched her back just as warmly. She pulled back, her golden eyes taking me in just as surely as I was taking her in. "You are still the best," she beamed.

"And so are you, Sammy." I shook my head, regarding my beautiful sister, by friendship if not by blood. "I don't know if I ever told you, but you were the sunshine in my day. You made everyone around you happier, just be being there." I let out a soft sigh. "You have no idea how much I miss that."

She grinned and tilted her head. "Right back at you, Lucas."

I shook my head at her comment and looked over her shoulder to Darren, talking with Lil. Sammy turned and followed my gaze. "Be good to him," I said. "He needs you."

She smiled at my words and turned back to me. "I know…I need him too." She leaned forward and gave me a soft kiss on the cheek. "I love you, Lucas."

I swallowed back the emotion in my throat and gave her a swift hug. "I love you too, Sammy."

She turned from my grasp and walked across the hall to Darren. He gave her a dazzling smile as he slung his arms around her waist and drew her into him. He bent down to kiss her and I smiled at seeing the love that they had shared so easily in life. I hoped that, wherever they had gone, that love had followed them there.

As I watched their tenderness, I felt a warm hand slip into mine. "They always were good together."

I looked down at Lillian's golden head as she stood by my side, also watching Darren and Sammy. She looked up at me when she felt my eyes on her; a slight smile was on her lips. "So were we," I whispered.

She smiled wider and rested her head on my shoulder. "You're lucky to have her, to have someone who loves you that much." She looked up at me after she said that, moisture in her eyes as well as adoration.

I swallowed at the remembered look of love on her face, but a slight smile came to my lips at the remembered look of love on Sawyer's face. "I know." My smile shifted to a frown as I turned my back on Darren and Sammy to focus solely on Lil. Gently grabbing her arms, I looked down on her and searched her eyes. "I loved you, Lillian, I *always* loved you." I shifted my gaze to stare at the ground and shook my head. "I wish I'd told you that while you were alive."

Her hand came up to my chin, lifting my head so I met her eye again. "I always knew how you felt, Lucas." A brilliant smile lit her entire face. "And I always loved you too."

I sighed as I absorbed her beauty, on the inside as well as the outside. As her arms went around my waist, mine went around her shoulders, drawing her in tight. Into her hair, I told her, "You will always be my first true love and I'll never forget you or stop loving you." I kissed her head before laying my cheek on it. "Some things never stop."

She shifted underneath me and I lifted my head to let her look up at me. Her eyes were moist again. "I feel the same, Luc. I've always felt the same." She leaned up and gave me a soft kiss, and I closed my eyes, memorizing it. When she pulled away, she whispered, "You and I will be eternally connected but…I want you to have a good life, Lucas." I opened my eyes. A smile was on her lips even as a tear rolled down her cheek. "I want you to live and be happy…you and Sawyer both."

I brushed the tear away with my thumb. "I wish you'd known her. You would have really liked her."

She nodded, her smile widening. "Yeah, I wish I'd known her too." She laughed softly and my core brightened at hearing the sound; I'd never forget that sound. "Of course, if *I'd* known her…you wouldn't." She gave me a twisted smile and shook her head as she added, "At least, not like you do now."

I averted my eyes, feeling that guilt that I hadn't felt earlier starting to creep up on me. Being okay while talking about sex with Darren was one thing, standing right in front of Lil while she referenced it, quite another. "Lil…"

Her hand came back up to my chin, making me stare at her again. "Don't, Luc. It was meant to be. I wanted you with her, from nearly the beginning." She gave me a pointed glance. "There's a reason you and I could never…go there. We weren't supposed to. It was always supposed to be you and Sawyer. You're both alive and in love, and I don't begrudge you for either of those things."

I sighed as I looked over her clear, untroubled blue eyes. "You're right…you always were right."

She smiled and laughed again. "I know." She bit her lip and tilted her head to the side. "I'll miss you."

My arms around her shoulders tightened as I pressed her to me, nearly squeezing the non-existent life from her. "I'll miss you too."

We held each other for long moments, while I memorized everything that I could about her: the peachy smell of her body wash, the way her pale hair caught the lights, the feel of her slender, curvy body against mine, the way her fingers felt as she lightly rubbed them along my back. I inhaled deep, tucking it all away to the corner of my brain that would always belong to her.

My eyes were wet as we pulled apart. I raised a corner of my lip, feeling the end of this goodbye approaching, not that I'd say that word to any of them. Our arms simultaneously slipped from each other's bodies down to our hands. Our fingers laced together as we leaned into the other, heads pressed together. "Until we meet again, then?" she said quietly, feeling the approaching goodbye as well.

I smiled and nodded against her head. "Yes…whenever that may be."

"I hope it's a lifetime from now, Lucas." She leaned up to brush our lips together. I reveled in the warmth of her kiss, feeling both the love and friendship behind it. She met my eye when she pulled away. "We'll be waiting for you."

As our bodies pulled apart, our fingers finally separating, Darren and Sammy stepped up to Lillian and each took one of her hands. She looked at each in turn and then the three of them turned to smile at me. I looked at each friend, at each loved one, and slowly exhaled.

"You will always be a part of me…all of you." My eyes watered uncontrollably, and the tears finally did make it down my cheeks, but my smile was exultant and the overriding emotion I felt was joy—joy that I'd known them, joy that I'd loved them and joy that, in my own way, I'd always be connected to them.

They all beamed at me, all with tears either in their eyes or in Sammy's case, dripping off her chin. Darren sniffed and reached out to clap my shoulder. "Just don't let that part…be all of who you are. Stay in the real world, Lucas, you belong there." He nodded at me, clutching my shoulder before releasing it.

I nodded back at him and then at each of them. "I know. I will. But I'm keeping you all with me," I patted my chest, "here…always." As more tears dripped off my cheeks, I slowly shook my head. "I'm a better person for knowing each of you. Thank you for the friendship you gave me. I'll never forget it."

We each hugged again, longer this time than before, and then Darren grabbed each girl's hand and started leading them down the hall, to the main doors highlighted in that slightly twisting paper curtain. I stayed standing in the same spot, a huge smile on my tearstained face, as, in my watery vision, I watched Darren sling his arms around Sammy and Lillian's shoulders and pull them in tight. He kicked at some of the papers and streamers on the floor, launching some up to land on the girls.

They all three laughed, the sound nearly breaking my heart with the joy it gave me.

As they reached the door, they started to fade into a sort of transparency. When I could just barely make out their hazy appearance, Lil turned her head to me. Over Darren's shoulder she smiled warmly, winked, and then nodded. I returned her warm gestures. Just as they finally vaporized into the stale air of that hallway, a hallway that we'd walked countless times in life, a warm hand grabbed mine.

I looked down on a black-haired angel with the most beautiful shade of gray eyes. Sawyer looked up at me with clear love and devotion on her face. I smiled at her and felt the familiar, calming comfort that she always gave to me. She squeezed my hand tight and leaned into my side. Wiping my tears dry with her fingers, she whispered, "Come on, Lucas…it's time to wake up now."

I nodded, sighing contently, and then, for the first time since the accident that had taken my beloved friends from me…I completely woke up.

The End

S.C. Stephens is an independent author and publisher who enjoys spending every free moment she has writing stories that are packed with emotion and heavy on romance. She wrote Thoughtless, her first attempt at a full length novel, in 2009. Since then she has written several other novels, and plans to have them all released as ebooks in the near future.

The Thoughtless Series:
Thoughtless
Effortless

Collision Course

The Conversion Trilogy:
Conversion
Bloodlines
'Til Death

Conversion: The Next Generation

It's All Relative

Not a Chance

You can contact S.C. Stephens at:
ThoughtlessRomantic@gmail.com

16261271R00177

Made in the USA
Lexington, KY
14 July 2012